All Through the Night

All Through the Night

SUZANNE FORSTER

THEA DEVINE

LORI FOSTER

SHANNON MCKENNA

KENSINGTON PUBLISHING CORP.
http://www.kensingtonbooks.com

BRAVA books are published by

Kensington Publishing Corp.
850 Third Avenue
New York, NY 10022

All Kensington titles, imprints and distributed lines are available at special quantity discounts for bulk purchases for sales promotion, premiums, fund-raising, educational or institutional use.

Special book excerpts or customized printings can also be created to fit specific needs. For details, write or phone the office of the Kensington Special Sales Manager: Kensington Publishing Corp., 850 Third Avenue, New York, NY 10022. Attn. Special Sales Department. Phone: 1-800-221-2647.

ISBN: 1-57566-869-6

First Kensington Trade Paperback Printing: October 2001
10 9 8 7 6 5 4 3 2 1

Printed in the United States of America

Contents

STRANGER IN HER BED

Suzanne Forster

Prologue

"Admit it, Kerry. You'd *love* to have your toes sucked."

"Admit I'd love wha—? I don't remember saying I'd love that—them—sucked. My toes, I mean."

"Just for the sake of discussion, let's say you would. How do you think it would feel?"

Kerry Houston took a quick, furtive sip of her wine. They'd been building toward a moment like this all evening, and it had been all she could do to fight the seductive pull of his voice, especially when it dropped to those sexy lower registers and got all fuzzy and intimate. He'd been given unfair advantage, she decided. He'd been blessed with an instrument that could give a woman the shivering fits and send her running in search of her vibrator.

Only Kerry didn't have a vibrator.

She shifted in the chair, tugging at her silk kimono. Her town house was drafty and normally she went to bed in three sets of flannel. But before they started this little adventure of his, he'd casually suggested a dark candlelit room, loose, comfortable clothing and a glass of wine to relax her. Now she knew why.

How would it feel? Wet, warm, slippery, strange . . .

"Squishy?" she ventured.

"Squishy . . . works." He didn't sound too sure. "Would your toes prefer a man or a woman?"

"They'd prefer a podiatrist."

Kerry got no reaction to her diversionary tactics. No reaction at all. This guy was hard to fluster, and even harder to sidetrack. He seemed as bent on finding her soft spots—literally—as a grand master chess player was on winning a tournament, but a grand master didn't have this guy's focus.

"And would you like this fantasy man to remove your shoes and stockings?" he asked. "Perhaps massage your feet and individually stimulate each toe? Using a decadent chocolate ganache syrup, of course."

"Did we ever establish that I *wanted* my toes sucked?"

"Shhhhh . . . can you hear that, Kerry? Can you hear how hard your heart is beating?"

All she could hear was a faint beeping noise that sounded like her cordless phone when it was low on batteries.

"Did you answer my question?" she persisted.

"If not your toes, then something else? Fingers, earlobes, elbows, kneecaps, pipkin?"

"Pipkin? Isn't that an apple?"

"Kerry," he admonished gently, "the more open and receptive you are, the better this will be. Breathe and let yourself go; imagine that you're floating on a warm water bed and that your every whim and caprice is being indulged. Anything you wish is yours. Whatever you secretly desire in life has already imprinted itself on you. All you have to do is recognize its existence."

He hesitated, letting her float, letting her float . . .

"It's true, Kerry. Pleasure beyond anything you can imagine awaits you. Beyond *anything*, if you're willing. . . ."

Kerry's eyelids were starting to flutter, among other things. The effect he had on her was strangely hypnotic. It was like listening to the music of a dark melodic river. Soothing, and yet there was a single grain of sand in it that gently abraded her senses. It kept her mesmerized. And more importantly, he was right. She ought to at least try to answer his questions. That *was* the point of this exercise.

"I've never thought of my toes as erogenous zones," she

said, absently aware of the soft beeping. It seemed to keep pace with her heart, her breathing.

"Well, then, we'll have to find some that are."

"Zones? Erogenous? I don't think I have any."

"Sure you do. The body is one big zone, a veritable playground. There's the back of the knees, the insides of the wrists, the breasts, and of course, the lips, both sets. Are your lips very sensitive?"

Both sets? Kerry's eyes sprang open to a dark, candlelit room. Her stomach was falling through a hole in the earth to New Zealand. "Maybe we should stick to the toes? I think I can feel something tingling." And for sure it wasn't her toes.

"Tingling?" He laughed, and the sound was low-down, steamy sex personified.

"Tingling is good," he said. "Just imagine how it would feel to have the soles of your feet massaged with warm, scented lotion and some nice sharp knuckles, gently working out the knots along the ball. Would you like that?"

She was weakening. *Of course she would.* Was he crazy?

"Feel the deep pressure on your arch and the firm palms of my hand, working both sides of your foot, kneading, pleating with my thumbs. How do you like to be touched? In your fantasies, how does it happen—lightly, firmly?"

"I don't think I have fantasies."

"Of course, you do. Everyone has erogenous zones *and* fantasies. Let your mind run free, Kerry . . . Visualize a man who becomes aroused at the mere sight of you, magnificently aroused. And say this man is naked so he can't hide his burgeoning desire. Maybe he's a servant and you're a princess."

Kerry rather liked the aroused-at-the-mere-sight-of-her part, but she wasn't sure what one did with a naked serving man when he wasn't serving.

"Hmm, not much reaction there," he said. "Is your finger properly positioned, Kerry?"

She blushed and nodded, hoping he couldn't see her.

"Was that a yes?" he prompted.

"Oh, sorry, yes. It was a yes. My finger is . . . you know."

"I do know. Relax now, Kerry, breathe . . . see yourself flying across a field in a sheer white nightgown . . . you're being chased down by a highwayman on a horse, who drops to the ground when he reaches you, rips open his breeches and passionately takes you against a huge tree."

Oh . . . my . . . oh . . . a ravishment fantasy.

"Anything?" he asked.

"Nope," was all she could manage. If she'd said more, something would have leaped out of her mouth, probably her heart.

"Then how about this one; how about a man who's tall, dark and sexier than sin, and he's right behind you, whispering naughty things in your ear while you're waiting in line at the bank."

Kerry was about to protest when it became apparent that the beeping sounds were not her cordless telephone. They rang out like chimes, and they were keeping time with her heart. Her wild heart.

Did she want someone to whisper naughty things in her ear?

"Well, of course, that depends on the man," she said, feigning aplomb. But naturally, it didn't work. Nothing worked. The chimes had become a chorus and were in danger of being drowned out by buzzing and pinging noises. What in the world was going on?

"I think we've touched a nerve," he said softly.

His irony seemed to generate more sound and fury. Whoops and flashes of light made it look like there was a pinball machine in the room.

"What does this noise mean?" she asked.

"It means you do have fantasies, Kerry. Hot ones. That finger glove you're wearing is registering your vital signs and giving you feedback."

The translucent sheath on her index finger was wired into her computer, much like her mouse and audio speakers were, but Kerry had forgotten all about it until he asked. Apparently it was measuring more than her heart rate. Good thing it couldn't read her mind. The machine would go up in smoke.

"Fortunately, I can take care of that," he said.

"What?" She sat straight up in the chair. "What are you going to take care of?"

"I'm going to take care of you, Kerry. I'm going to devise the perfect fantasy for you. The one you've been waiting for, the one you don't want anyone to know about. Your deepest secret, your deepest need, your deepest desire. I'm going to give them all to you."

The game began to wail like a police siren.

Kerry made an instant executive decision. "Go to sleep," she said, pulling off the finger glove and tossing it onto her desk.

"Kerry, you understand what happens when you voice that command. The game will be over."

"Yes, I have to . . . please, that's it for tonight."

"Are you sure?"

"*Go to sleep.*" Kerry repeated the command firmly, knowing he wouldn't obey otherwise. As a backup she positioned the mouse and aimed the arrow at an icon in the upper corner of her computer screen. It had the image of a man snoozing, a vapor trail of Zzzzzzzzs above him and one word below him, SLEEP.

She clicked the mouse and fell back against the chair, watching the computer screen go dark. "Whew," she whistled softly. "Now that was *some* video game! Maybe I shouldn't have set the Sensuality Level so high."

She'd been a game tester for Genesis Software for a few months now, but this was by far the best idea they'd ever sent her for their new adult line. It was an interactive voice recognition game, and it felt like the game guide, otherwise known as Mr. Quick-Where's-My-Vibrator, was right there in the room with her.

She grabbed her legal pad and began jotting notes.

I love this game! It's like foreplay only more convenient. You can stop whenever you want to and throw in a load of wash.

Her next tip was crucial.

There's just one thing missing. Your game guide needs a face to go with that voice. Maybe a body, too. Oh, my, yes! Let's give our customers the full experience.

When Kerry was done making notes, she fell back in the chair and actually giggled. She hadn't done that in a long time. There had been nothing resembling whimsy in her life for some time now. But, crazy as it seemed, she couldn't shake the feeling that there was a new man on the horizon, and that something was about to happen. It felt like the heavens had opened and dropped him into her lap. Of course, that was ridiculous, she told herself. What the heavens had dropped was a compact disk.

She picked up the silky finger glove and felt a sharp little quiver of anticipation at the mere thought of slipping it on. Or was it foreboding? Whatever it was, she dropped the sheath like a hot potato.

"For heaven's sake, girl, get a grip. It's a game. It's *only* a game."

Chapter One

Kerry stared at the front door of her house as if it had the power to reach out and grab her. She was bundled up like a linebacker, both for the winter weather and for defensive purposes. She had a mission to accomplish out there in the cold, cold world, but she hadn't gotten any further than this impasse with her door. No surprise there. She hadn't been out of her house in days, maybe weeks.

"The only thing to fear is fear itself," she intoned, wishing she knew who'd come up with *that* line. Obviously not someone who lived in her neighborhood.

She yanked her fur trapper hat down tight, snapped the earflaps under her chin and checked her parka pockets. The pepper spray and police whistle were there, but she wasn't sure what good they would do her. You needed an armed tank for this neighborhood. Just the thought of venturing out made her so nervous she'd seen a psychologist recently, and the woman had told her it was no surprise she was a little paranoid. She had reason.

Kerry lived in an area that had once been the pride of south Philly, but lately the neighborhood had been under siege. A pack of young thugs had moved into the "hood" and claimed it as theirs. Kerry herself had been mugged twice, and the attacks had left her feeling terribly vulnerable.

She should have moved months ago, when the area started going downhill, but her quaint red-brick town house had been left to her by her grandparents, whom she'd adored. They'd taken her in and raised her when it became clear that her single mom—their only daughter, Paula—wasn't financially or emotionally able to take care of a child. Freed of that burden, Paula had gone off in search of herself, and Kerry had rarely seen her mother after that. Her grandparents were the only real family she knew.

A loud rap on the door startled her out of her reflections.

"Kerry, it's Malcolm! Are you in there?"

Kerry struggled to calm her drumming heart. Malcolm lived in the studio above the garage in the back. He was her new tenant, and a sweet guy for the most part, but his mind was a Nintendo game. He actually thought that cell phones and Palm Pilots were part of a government plot to spy on the citizenry. The way he scrutinized Kerry's computer equipment, she assumed that was suspect, too. She had him pegged for a conspiracy theorist and maybe a technophobe. Of course, she hadn't figured that out until *after* she'd rented him the room.

"Hold on, Malcolm," she called out. "It may take me a minute."

The floor seemed to roll beneath Kerry's feet as she started for the door. Her face was flushed, and the way her pulse was skittering, she wasn't at all certain she was going to get there. A little paranoid? She couldn't seem to walk. *Or* talk. It felt like something was caught in her throat—probably her heart. And by the time she did get to the door, her palms were so slippery she couldn't get traction on the knob.

She lived on a side street, but traffic noise roared in her ears as she opened the door a crack.

"Are you okay, Kerry?"

Malcolm's brow was furrowed with concern. He was

wearing his navy pea coat and knit cap, as always, and his luxurious beard reminded her of the fisherman's in the Gorton's ad. He had the guy's great baritone voice, too, except that Malcolm appeared to be at least twenty years younger. His eyes were a surreal delft blue, and there wasn't a line on his face, despite hair as snowy as the deep drifts outside.

"I'm fine," she said, but her shaky voice didn't seem to fool him. It probably wouldn't have fooled anyone.

"Here, I brought this for you."

Her tenant made a quick, awkward presentation of a can of soup. Chicken noodle, Kerry realized by the label. She could remember her grandmother fixing that for lunch on rainy days, along with grilled cheese sandwiches.

"Soup, Malcolm?" Kerry didn't know quite what to say.

"Sometimes I wonder if you get enough to eat," he confessed.

Touched, she opened the door enough for him to step inside. "Thank you," she said as she took the can.

Malcolm had brought little offerings on other occasions, and Kerry hadn't had the heart to tell him not to. She sensed that he wanted to help, and Lord knew, she could use some. Today, however, his other arm was tucked behind his back, making her wonder if he had another surprise in store.

She didn't ask. He seemed preoccupied.

"Santa just mugged someone," he said.

"Oh, Malcolm"—Kerry shook her head—"stop that now."

"No, it's true, one of the nuns from Our Lady of Perpetual Weeping. He knocked her down and took her fanny pack."

Kerry might have laughed if Malcolm hadn't seemed so perfectly serious. She didn't know what Santa he was talking about, unless it was one of the Salvation Army volunteers on the corner down the block. None of them had ever gone haywire that she knew of, but anything was possible.

"Might as well live in Bosnia," Malcolm muttered.

"No kidding," Kerry agreed. If anyone knew how bad it was, she did. The second time she'd been mugged a crowd had collected to watch as if it were a sporting match, and no one had lifted a finger to help her. She'd implored them to call the police, but they'd done nothing except scurry away. That's when the fear had set in. She'd recognized one of them as her own next-door neighbor!

"Kerry, why do you stay?" Malcolm asked.

Kerry didn't have a ready answer, except that she loved the place. The town house had a storybook charm about it that had always made her feel safe and secure, at least while she was inside. The breakfast nook walls were hung with sayings done in her grandmother's hand-stitched embroidery, as was the upholstery in the living room and the cushions on the window seat.

Nothing had been safe from Gramma Laura's needle except Grandpa Dan's buttery-soft, old leather rocker. No one was allowed to touch that chair, even to drape a doily over the headrest, which her grandmother had tried on a few occasions. It was where he'd rocked Kerry endlessly, telling her stories about how wishes always came true if you wished hard enough. And Kerry had probably believed him once, impressionable child that she was.

This was how she kept her grandparents' memories alive, she realized, by staying. But she couldn't tell Malcolm that.

"I'll have noodle soup for lunch today," she assured him. It was the kindest way she could think of to get him to leave. And she did need him to leave. He meant well, but he could get spookier than she was, if that was possible.

"Oh, sure, good," he said, seeming to get her drift.

He turned toward the door, and Kerry saw the bouquet of tulips he'd been hiding behind his back. They were bright spring colors, pink and deep rose reds, sunny yellows and oranges. It wasn't a bouquet, it was a rainbow.

"Tulips, Malcolm? Where did you find tulips in the middle of winter?"

Apparently her tenant had forgotten all about the flowers because his shoulders lifted in surprise. "The tulip store?"

Kerry did laugh at that, and when Malcolm turned around, his blue eyes were twinkling like stars. She accepted the flowers and thanked him warmly, but for the first time since Kerry had rented him the room, she wondered about her new tenant. For a fleeting moment, she wondered if it was possible that Malcolm was hiding something other than a bouquet of tulips.

She didn't ask.

Kerry's cordless phone had become the enemy. It sat on the enormous tower of mail-order catalogs that she'd been collecting since she started working out of her house, and it had begun to ring shortly after Malcolm left. She could have broken a Guinness record with the tower, she imagined. Kerry Houston, Catalog Queen. But that was beside the point.

Her ringing phone was the point. She knew exactly who was calling, which was why she hadn't answered. She'd finally had the sense to turn down the volume, but that hadn't turned off the emotion churning inside her.

One look at the Caller ID number had told her it was starting all over again. The Genesis Software people would not give up! Genesis was the company she'd left three months ago, under the most embarrassing of circumstances, but their human resources person kept calling and insisting that she come back. He'd offered her everything under the sun, including more money, big money. She'd actually bundled up today with the thought of going over there to negotiate a new employment contract, that's how much damn money it was.

The man had tempted her, and she'd almost succumbed. But in point of fact, there wasn't a salary big enough to pay for the humiliation she'd been through at Genesis. Even if she could get out her front door, she would never go back there.

She peeled off her hat and the parka, along with several layers of clothing, and piled it all in the leather rocker that sat next to the catalog tower. The weather wasn't the only reason she'd bundled up. The bulk was meant to make a very average, five-feet four-inch woman look less vulnerable. If the local toughs thought she was an undersized hockey player, all the better.

She picked up the phone and dialed the software company's number with purpose and resolve. She didn't know the man who'd been calling as anything other than Phil in Human Resources, but she was ready for him when he came on the line. She didn't even bother to introduce herself. He had to know her voice by now.

"I want you to stop calling me, Phil. I'm not coming back and I never will."

"I've never called you Phil . . . and did you intend that to rhyme?"

Kerry smiled despite herself. Lucky for him that she had smiled or he might have gotten another verbal one-two. It also worked in his favor that he had a great voice. He was no Mr. Quick-Where's-My-Vibrator, but his conversational tones were low and masculine and sort of steamy, like a pot on simmer. That might even be the reason she'd allowed him to call as often as he had. Yes, she rather liked Phil's voice. It shivered up a person's neck like warm air currents. Nevertheless, she had to be firm with him now.

"I'm quite serious," she told him. "I have no desire to work in design anymore. I'm perfectly happy as a game tester, and if you call me again, I'll be forced to report it as harassment."

"Hey, hey, no one's harassing anyone here. If you don't want me to call again, I won't. But could you answer one question? Why are you so adamant? Do you feel as if you were treated unfairly here? Was anyone unprofessional or improper?"

She was treated like yesterday's news, trashed by the boss himself, but it was a highly personal situation and she wasn't going to discuss it with a veritable stranger.

"There's improper and there's improper, Phil. One's about wearing hoop earrings and a leather micro-mini to church. The other's about acting boorishly without a thought to the pain you cause others. I'll let you figure out which is which."

With that, and an icy-bright best wishes for the holidays, she pressed the OFF button and considered herself well rid of the pest and his simmering pot of a voice.

Joe Gamble's telephone headset was calibrated to pick up noises as faint as normal respiration. People breathed and he could hear them. Unfortunately. Because right now he had a dial tone trying to buzz-saw a hole through his head. Kerry Houston had just cut him off at the kneecaps, and he was probably lucky it wasn't higher. She hadn't let him get in one more word, much less the last one.

Damn, it annoyed him when that happened.

It annoyed Phil, too. Technically Philip was his middle name, but since she refused to talk to Joe Gamble, and most everyone else at Genesis, he'd had to resort to the subterfuge. He snapped off the headset and draped it over his halogen arc lamp. Apparently there were still a few people who could not be bought, and she was one of them. He admired her for that, but how was he going to get her back if not with filthy lucre?

The game he'd been uploading suddenly flashed onto his computer screen, distracting him. An array of multiple-choice questions appeared against a background of pink cupids, pouty red lip imprints and silhouetted females of the supermodel variety. It was pretty garish, plus the music playing through the speakers sounded suspiciously like the "Love Boat" theme.

"Preferred breast size?" Joe read aloud.

It wasn't the first question that came up, but it was the first one to catch his eye. A set of multiple-choice answers followed: (a) plums, (b) peaches, (c) Texas grapefruit or (d) honeydew.

"What?" Joe remarked dryly, "no seedless watermelon?" He clicked on the FEEDBACK icon, and then RECORD. "The fruit references aren't going to fly," he said, leaving a message for the game's architects. "I don't want to ruin the fun, but is it possible for you pervs in design to think in terms of small, average, full . . . something like that?"

Joe was evaluating a Genesis product in the design stages with a working title of "Build Her and She Will Come." The idea of the game was to let men visualize and create their ideal mate from head to toe, including her physical characteristics, but globular fruit was certain to offend a key demographic who might buy it for their brothers or male friends, namely women. And the title was certain to offend everyone.

He clicked on "Peaches," just for evaluation purposes, of course. Honeydew was excessive, plums were vaguely pre-pubescent and grapefruit had never been a big favorite. Made his teeth hurt.

An animated cupid thanked him for his answer, and then pointed his little pink arrow to the next question: "Preferred leg length?"

This one had a flower theme. The design team was having way too much fun, Joe thought, as he read the choices under his breath. "(a) Long-stemmed American Beauties, (b) daffodils, (c) daisies or (d) Christmas cacti."

Joe figured the last one must either be a nod to the season or a woman who didn't shave her legs. He clicked the first one. Okay, so he liked long stems. That didn't make him a pervert, too, did it?

On the right side of the screen was a computer matrix outline of a woman, who was materializing as he made his choices. The woman didn't concern him as much as the cupid, flying around her in a presentational way, pointing to each body part that appeared.

"Fellas? Lose the fruit, the flowers *and* cupid."

Joe scrolled back to the questions he'd skipped over and settled in to finish the game. By now he was curious what this arrangement of X-rated body parts was going to look like when it was finished. Maybe that was a plus. Once you got the woman started, you *had* to finish her.

Oops, he thought with a faint smile. *Better not go there, either.* The game was booby-trapped with double entendres.

Joe's office was also his own personal think tank and where he did most of his creative work when he wasn't traveling on business. The walls were lined with traditional cherry bookcases that groaned with the weight of his varied interests and his research, and he worked at a desk, like everyone else. But most everything in his office was computerized, digitalized and automated. He could open the skylight and look up at the starry sky by speaking to it—the skylight, not the sky. He didn't have a lock on Mother Nature yet, but technology, that he took to its limits . . . because he could.

By the time he'd finished the questions, he was glued to the screen, but not because the game was that good. It was the challenge of making it better that absorbed him. Probably more than it should, considering the state of his personal affairs. What affairs? to be exact. His office overlooked a green belt, planted with Japanese cedars, and there was the equivalent of a winter wonderland right outside his window, but he rarely took the time to look at it, much less experience it. There didn't seem to be any way to unglue himself from whatever the current project was.

A wall panel opened behind him, revealing an office-sized refrigerator and microwave. Joe glanced at his watch, only mildly interested in the lunch reminder. He'd programmed the panel to open at twelve-thirty because he had a bad habit of forgetting to eat.

It was curiosity more than hunger that made him open the refrigerator today. The pizza caught his eye, but he picked up the container of East Indian tandoori instead and popped it in the microwave. It was spicy as hell, which almost let him overlook the fact that it was low-fat and "good for him," according to his assistant.

Moments later he walked to the window with his steaming food, still in its microwaveable container. But it was the wonderland outside that had finally caught his attention. For some reason he was reminded of the Godzilla-like snowmen he'd made when he was a kid growing up on the family farm. He'd even gone on great treks into the woods to find a tree on Christmas Eve because his parents were too poor to afford one. What had happened to that kid?

To say that Joe Gamble worked too much was an understatement. He could have taken an Olympic gold in working. He just wasn't sure why. His married friends had suggested that he was avoiding something, which was a nice way of saying he was a commitment phobe, but how could he be when there'd been no relationships to be phobic about? He'd been married once, almost on a dare, while he was in college. It was a crazy, impulsive thing that happened mostly because her wealthy parents were determined to split them up, and it only lasted a year before his bride decided her doting father was right. Joe didn't have enough money to make her happy. That experience had left him gun-shy, especially now that he did have money, pots of it.

He'd dated over the years, but none of the relationships would have been considered long term. No smart woman wanted to play second fiddle to a man's creative obsessions, and, sadly, the women he'd met had never challenged or absorbed him the way a new idea did. Work had always been enough, but that was changing now. Something was missing. He was restless and unfulfilled, and stranger yet, the only thing that seemed to intrigue him at the moment *was* a woman. Kerry Houston had sparked his interest like nothing else had in a long time, and he had a hunch it was because she was as good at this idea stuff as he was. Maybe better.

A heaping forkful of tandoori got him some rice, raisins and a savory chunk of chicken and sauce. He ate slowly, reflecting.

He'd debated the wisdom of telling Kerry who he really was, but he'd learned over the years that his presence had an inhibiting effect on even the best and the brightest. It was one of the reasons he'd stopped sitting in on the various creative teams' brainstorming sessions and started videotaping them instead, with the members' knowledge, of course. That was how he'd first discovered Kerry Houston, watching her interact on tape as a new designer on one of the teams. He'd immediately given a bonus to the human resources person who hired her, a guy whose name wasn't Phil.

Kerry was inspired, and watching her had inspired him. He loved the way she brainstormed. She was quietly intent at first, offering feedback only when she had something cogent to say. But it soon became apparent that she absorbed the collective energy like a sponge, because when she pitched an idea, she was as quick and kinetic as lightning.

Those eyes were like bolts from the sky. And, God, that attracted him. He would never have described her as a hot number. You couldn't even call her sexy in the way men normally thought of those things. But that *fire*.

At some point an idea would drive her right out of her conference chair, and every head would swing her way, riveted. They might be a little envious of her passion, but they couldn't take their eyes off her. Her color was high and her voice took on heat as she raced to get the flow of thoughts out as swiftly as they came to her. Even her body showed signs of arousal when she got that excited . . . and so had Joe showed some signs, although that had nothing to do with why he was trying to get her back. She was his best person. She kicked butt.

Joe finished off the tandoori and left the container on his desk as he went back to his chair. He'd actually had hopes that Kerry would revitalize his entire design division, and then one day she was gone. She excused herself from a strategy session to take a potty break and never came back. She'd never explained her exit, either, although he'd learned later what happened, and he'd blamed himself. He'd had his people track her down, offering career amnesty, and making increasingly generous offers to get her back, but she'd said no to everything, including him.

He rarely attended company functions, and he'd only met her in person one time. It was a few months after she'd started, and there'd been a meeting in which he'd congratulated her on something. He couldn't even remember what it was now, he'd been so intrigued with the idea of meeting her face to face. He'd expected to see sparks fly when they shook hands. Instead it was an internal reaction, and the sparks were icy hot. His gut would probably never be the same. Most guys would have known that this was the beginning of something incredible. Joe knew it was the end. He had no idea if Kerry felt the same way, but he made a strategic decision to back off the very next day. She was much too valuable to mess with, in any sense of the word.

Joe came out of his preoccupation with Kerry Houston to the frustrating awareness that he'd recreated her on the screen in front of him. The gaze wasn't fiery enough, but it was none other behind the impish smile. Apparently she was determined to annoy him in every possible way. She wasn't even that cute, with her mousy brown hair and the mole near her lip that matched her intensely dark eyes. He'd been going for Cindy Crawford, anyway.

Still, he continued to stare at the image until his body reminded him of the power a woman could have over a man, even when all the poor sucker had was a cartoon characterization of her. There was a tug of anticipation deep in his groin, and various muscles were yanking at the bit. He couldn't tell if he was angry or aroused, but one was as good as the other for his purposes.

Something had to be done about this Houston woman.

Chapter Two

"Stuck in your house with no one but a computer-generated hunk in a voice-recognition game for company? *Great*," Kerry murmured as she hovered at her front window, looking out at the snow-covered bowers of Lover's Park across the street.

She couldn't actually see the four stone paths that radiated like spokes from the park's circular courtyard, but she knew they were there, dozing under the soft white blanket. Also heaped in graceful drifts was the statue the park was named for, a marble replica of a man and woman in a longing embrace. Her grandfather had told her the story of the couple who inspired the statue, and Kerry had been touched by its poignancy. But she couldn't concentrate on anything except her own misery this morning.

"Kerry, come back and play. It's lonely in here without you."

Startled, Kerry turned and saw that her computer monitor was on. It glowed brightly from the maple secretary that was tucked in the far corner of the room.

"Hey, I thought I turned you off!" she exclaimed.

The image of a man's face smiled from the screen, and his sonorous voice reached out as if to touch her. "Are you sure it's me you want to turn off?"

He was dead right about that. Moments ago she'd abandoned him—and the game she was *supposed* to be testing for Genesis. It was possible she hadn't turned off the computer in her rush, but who could blame her. She was being seduced by the dark side! His voice was bad enough. Now she had his face to contend with, too.

George, the game's creator at Genesis, had responded immediately to her feedback about a male face to go with the voice. Maybe he'd already been working on the problem because in record time he'd come up with a breathtaking simulation of Jean Valjean, the lead character in *Les Miserables*. How had George known she loved *Les Mis?*

The new and improved version of "Discover the Secret, Sensual You!" was waiting in her E-mail queue this morning when she woke up. And so was Valjean's wounded, penetrating gaze, his strong features and sensual mouth. The main difference was his shoulder-length waves. This man's hair was shorter, olive-black and cut adorably close to his head, a lush, curly crew.

Of course, she would *never* have called it adorable to his face. Valjean was just such a guy's guy, male through and through.

Kerry's mistake had been to download the game immediately, and nothing had been quite the same since. Whoever had coined the phrase "love at first sight" couldn't have been thinking about a video game. Was it possible to be infatuated with a nonperson, with dots on a screen?

And could she *be* more desperate?

Kerry reached down and yanked up her wool slipper socks. The elastic was going and they kept slipping down. So very attractive it was, too.

"Did I say something to offend you?" the screen image asked.

She insisted on thinking of his face as an image to remind herself that he wasn't a man. He was hundreds of pixels. Too bad she hadn't been smarter about his name.

"No, you didn't, Jean. I'm fine." He'd introduced himself as a guide and given her a set of verbal directions, which included assigning him a name. He'd encouraged her to pick one with personal meaning, and she'd impulsively said Jean, and then she couldn't figure out how to delete it. How she wished she'd said Biff or Game Guy.

"Because if I did," he said, "just repeat the offensive parts, and then say 'Down, boy'." His smile hinted at irony. "I'm self-editing."

I wish I were!, Kerry thought. If only she could edit some of the lurid fantasies dancing through her brain. He had her thinking about handsome strangers whispering erotic things in her ear at the bank, about plundering highwaymen and huge trees! She could only imagine what her heart rate must be now, after a night of moist dreams about aroused slave boys. But then that was the point of the game, she supposed, to encourage fantasies. She could give it an A+ on that score.

"Are you coming back, Kerry?" he asked. "We can't continue if you won't sit down and play. There's nothing to be afraid of, unless there's something you don't want to know . . . about yourself."

"And what would that be?" she challenged. "Since you seem to know so much about me."

"It's difficult to say, since you refuse to wear the finger glove. But I'm sure we'll find something."

"Are you laughing?" Kerry walked over and peered at the screen. She thought she'd heard suspiciously muffled sounds, but she didn't detect anything in his expression. *"Jean?"*

"Mais, non," he assured her. "How could I possibly take pleasure in your difficulties? That's not what I'm here for."

"And what *are* you here for, pray tell?"

"To free you from prudish notions and blocks to your sensuality."

Now it was all she could do not to laugh. "And you think quizzing me about my erogenous zones and suggesting smutty talk in financial institutions will do that?"

"It's a start."

There wasn't a hint of sarcasm in his voice, which was

more than she could say for hers. "I can hardly wait to see where we go from here."

"Excellent, let's be on our way," he said.

But, of course, he'd taken her literally.

Suddenly the computer screen was awash in color, and music swelled through the speakers. There were clouds, blue sky and a rainbow arch with dazzling colors that changed continuously. A silver bird soared from the bottom of the screen toward the top, dipped and soared again. Kerry recognized the music as "Somewhere Over the Rainbow," and it struck her that all the fanfare was incredibly corny, and yet, she was quite captured by it.

Instead of a brick road, a sparkling staircase materialized, and a woman ascended it. Near the top she became a bird and ribboned through the clouds before soaring off to somewhere unseen.

"What's happening? Jean? Where are we going?"

"On a tour."

"Of what?"

"Of you, a grand tour of Kerry. I'll be your guide, but you're the landscape *and* the traveler, so you choose the itinerary. Where would you like to start?"

"How about my brain? I must be crazy for agreeing to this."

"How about your skin?" he asked, ignoring her comment. "Did you know that there are over a hundred receptors in the fingertips alone? The skin is our most sensitive organ. Of course, you have membranes that are richer in nerve endings, but we'll get to those later. Why don't we start at your toes and work our way up."

"Oh, please, not my toes."

The irony in his expression told her that he was coming to understand some things. Maybe he was programmed to know when he was dealing with a sexually repressed woman who was afraid of her own front door, and *that* was on a good day.

"Let's take a deep breath and start over, Kerry. Are you

comfortable? Wearing loose clothing? Do you have a soothing cup of tea or a glass of wine?"

Do I take antipsychotic medication?

"Can't get much looser than this charming sweatshirt dress." She lifted her cup of Quiet Woman herbal tea and saluted him. She decided not to mention the L-tyrosine, an amino acid she'd found in a nutritional supplements catalog that was supposed to be an anxiety-buster. Couldn't have proved it by her, anyway.

"It's okay," she told him, "I'm ready. Lead on, fearless guide. Take me where you will, but be gentle. I bruise easily."

She actually wasn't kidding, and maybe he could hear the sigh of resignation in her voice. She had ducked and dodged and avoided this adventure as long as she could, primarily because it had become personal. It wasn't about testing the game anymore, although she certainly needed the job, and the money. It was about self-discovery and why that seemed to frighten her so. *Was* there something about Kerry Houston that she didn't want to know?

"Kerry, if I'm to be your guide, there are two conditions. First, you will have to entrust yourself to me for this journey," he told her. "And while we're on the subject, how do you feel about that?"

"Entrusting myself to you?"

"Yes, does that make you feel warm or cold?"

Warm or cold? What an odd question. Still, all those receptors he was talking about on the surface of her skin were registering a chill in the air, but the blood flowing through her veins felt hot.

"A little of both. I think I want to shiver."

"Exactly. That's how it's supposed to feel when fear and excitement go head to head. Don't fight those feelings; they're completely natural and the perfect alchemy in which to create . . . something combustible."

Oh, good, she was going to explode. At least she'd be warm.

"I think you're ready for the tour," he said, "but let's try a little experiment first, if you're willing. I sense some romantic pain in your past, and I think that might be getting in your way."

He had to be kidding. *Some* romantic pain? She was riddled with it. She didn't know where to start. All her life she had seemed to invite men who were users and takers. They took advantage, took her for granted, took her for a ride, took her for everything she was worth, emotionally speaking. She was Velcro for the jerks of the world. It was so bad, she'd sworn off the opposite sex three years ago, at just twenty-five. The only exception had been a certain CEO of Genesis Software, and he'd been the biggest jerk of all.

"Is it anything you could talk about?"

"I could talk forever. Got a minute?"

"Let's go for the most painful or the most recent, whichever is shorter."

Maybe he *was* sarcastic? That was probably not a bad thing. She wasn't sure she could relate to a man who wasn't at least minimally sarcastic, not given her affinity for meanies.

"That's easy, they're one and the same," she said. "Picture this, a brand-new software designer for a major company—that would be me—being blown off by the guy who runs the place—that would be him. He flirted with me, at least I think he was flirting, and then he subjected me to the worst kind of public ridicule and humiliation. It was awful."

She shuddered.

"Tell me about the public ridicule part."

So she did. She told him how Joe Gamble had surprised everyone at Genesis by showing up at a company picnic. But it was Kerry who got the biggest surprise because she had no idea who he was when he joined her at a bathtub filled with iced beer and congratulated her on Women-Wealth, her idea for encouraging women to storm Wall Street with a game that simulated trading real stocks. Gamble was notoriously reclusive, and all Kerry, and most of the other employees at Genesis, had ever seen of him was a ten-year-old snapshot in the company newsletter.

He arrived at the picnic fresh from a climbing expedition in the Italian Alps and he was still heavily bearded. Plus, he was wearing sunglasses. How was she supposed to know that the guy who flirted with her and gave her a card with only his E-mail address on it—gamesman@genesis.com—was the president?

She'd sent him an E-mail that night, and maybe it was a little suggestive. She'd said, "Let the games begin, but beware, I've been known to play dirty. Naked at dawn, weapons drawn? Let's see how big *your* gun is."

Okay, it was a lot suggestive. She'd probably had a beer too many at the picnic, but did he have to make such a big deal of it? By the time Kerry found out about her mistake, everybody in the design division was whispering, and Gamble's assistant, a snippy little thing with Altoids breath and bright blue eyes, courtesy of her tinted contacts, had confronted Kerry about her "tacky and inappropriate" behavior.

She'd actually used the words "appallingly lewd" and warned that a sexual harassment suit was in the offing, and before it was over Kerry had been told to fold her tent and leave Genesis. The assistant's parting remark was that Gamble had sent her to deal with Kerry rather than do it himself to avoid "embarrassing" either of them further.

Chicken, coward, yellow running dog.

"I walked out that afternoon," Kerry said, still smarting from the fiery sting of rejection, "and I haven't been back since."

She hadn't told the whole story, but it was as much as she was willing to say. She'd left that afternoon, but she didn't officially quit until the next day, and it wasn't totally because of Joe Gamble's cadlike behavior. The next morning as she was leaving for work, she collapsed on her doorstep, gasping for air, and that was as far as she got. She'd been dealing with anxiety symptoms because of the muggings, but nothing to compare with these. She'd barely left her house since.

She couldn't blame that on Joe. It was her neighborhood.

Kerry finished her story with a shrug of indifference, but she was sad inside, and even though her "fearless guide" couldn't see it, he could probably hear it. Maybe it was in how she phrased things, her syntax, but he seemed to be able to detect her moods. He was good, and so was the game.

"That was your most recent?" he asked.

"Romantic fiasco? Yes, and my quickest. So now you know why I'm wary of men."

"I know why you're wary of that man. He's not worthy of your pain. He's not worthy of anything. Kerry, save your tears for someone who knows what they cost, someone who will treasure them—and you—because he knows how deep your feelings cut. Don't waste another drop on him."

"Jean?" Kerry sat up to look at him.

He'd spoken with so much conviction—or was it passion—that he'd brought her up out of the chair. She studied his features, surprised at the furrows in his brow, the tension in his mouth. He could have been scowling, but he wasn't angry. She could almost believe that he cared.

"Do you actually feel things, Jean?" she said. "I mean human feelings?"

"I'm not sure. Can a man feel things without a body?"

"I don't know," she said, "but a woman can *not* feel things with a body. I haven't felt much of anything but fear in quite some time now."

"Which is why I'm here, to help you throw open the doors and windows and feel whatever you want to feel, the entire rainbow."

She smiled and so did he. Was that coincidence or could he see her?

"How do you feel about riddles?" he asked her.

"Pretty much the same way I feel about men . . . but go ahead, if you must."

"I must," he said with a tone of wry forebearance. "Remember the fantasy I promised you, the one that could anticipate your every need, wish and desire? I'm going to need a little more information."

Kerry bent over and hitched up her socks, which made it that much more convenient to get up from the desk and walk over to the window. A fluttery chill passed over her, like curtains caught in an updraft. Maybe she should put on another sweatshirt.

Who said she wanted all those things anticipated?

Several moments passed, and the chilliness felt less and less like a draft. It was her skin. She was a porcupine inside out. The quills pricked her. So far, she wasn't too crazy about this rainbow of his.

Abruptly, she said, "What's the riddle?"

"Are you sure?"

"It's just a riddle isn't it?"

"Kerry . . . is something wrong?"

The way he said her name brought her gaze to the screen, to him. Something inside her lifted and spilled over as softly as sand in an hourglass. It turned on its head, and took her with it. Not that it was a bad feeling. Oh, no, no, no, she would have traveled the world over for that feeling. It was wonderful, as light as a handspring. But that was the good part. His voice did everything else sand could do, too—sift, drift, swirl—and suck you down into its depths.

They should offer medical coverage with this game, Kerry thought. It was dangerous.

"Riddles can be pretty annoying," she said.

"You'll like this one," he assured her. "All you have to do is describe two things you would do with a strawberry that have nothing to do with eating it."

"A strawberry?" Not the kind of puzzle she expected.

"Well, they don't make good doorstops. I dropped an entire

box of them once. Didn't find the one hiding behind the door until it was too late. Strawberry puree."

The small room was silent except for the soft music coming from the speakers. But outside, the neighborhood hooligans were at it again. There were shouts, cars backfiring. Kerry blocked the sounds from her mind.

"What would anyone do with a strawberry besides eat it? I suppose you could drop it in a flute of champagne."

He lifted an eyebrow. "I was hoping for something a little more imaginative."

"Sorry, I can't think of a thing."

"I can tell you what *I'd* do with it."

"Down, boy," Kerry murmured. His voice had a sexy edge that warned her not to go there, but the remark hung in midair like a helium-filled balloon, daring her to let go of the string.

"Okay, what would you do? Make puree and massage my toes?"

"No, but that's not bad. Actually, if I had a *very* ripe strawberry, I think perhaps I would crush it in my hand, let the juice run down my fingers and pool in my palm. When it was warm, I'd drizzle it over a very tender part of the body and delicately *lick* it off."

"Lick it off," she echoed faintly. "But that would be eating . . . wouldn't it?"

"You're right. Shall we go for number two?"

"No!" She was too far away to turn the machine off. Computers ought to come with remotes, dammit.

"Too bold?" he asked.

"No, no, it was fine. I always gasp as if I'd just finished a marathon."

"Kerry . . . maybe you should come back here and sit down?"

She almost gasped again. "How did you know I got up?"

"The volume of your voice went down. You're either talking very softly or you've moved away. Come on back. I won't bite . . . I won't even lick."

"Gee, darn," she said under her breath.

He laughed, and finally, she did too. She gave herself another moment and then went back, but only as far as the old leather rocker.

"We could go on with the tour," he said, "if you're ready."

"Ready as I'll ever be." What a beautiful thing cynicism was. Those sharp-edged scissors kept everyone away except him. But that was only because he wasn't real, right?

She went back to her desk and sat down, although she would love to have stretched out in the rocker. A little distance would have felt safer, she was sure.

"I'd like you to relax and think about something for a minute," he said. "Think about your sense of touch. What does it mean to you?"

She closed her eyes and dropped back in the chair. "Everything. I love to touch. I love the feel of things. It's very sensual, touch."

"And being touched? How do you prefer that?"

"It depends on who's touching me."

"Who would you like to touch you?"

"Your voice." She barely had the words out of her mouth before her own voice dropped to a whisper. "I'd like it all over me like a big warm blanket."

The husky catch in her throat surprised her. And him, as well. When she opened her eyes, he was staring at her, and he seemed as perplexed as he was intrigued.

"I don't seem to be programmed to respond to that," he said.

Had she actually shocked him? Good, she didn't want to be the only one.

Brightly she asked, "Too bold?"

"I don't seem to be programmed to answer that, either."

Kerry tilted an eyebrow. "Well, you must know that your voice is amazingly sexy. I probably shouldn't be saying this, but I have another name for you, besides Jean, I mean."

"And what is that?"

"It's Mr. Quick-Where's-My-Vibrator."

Was he blushing? Oh, this was fun. His handsome face was now frozen in a perplexed expression, and it appeared that she'd jammed the program. Little Kerry Houston, who'd run from her workplace rather than confront her big bad boss when he had her fired, and who hid from the outside world like a hermit, had just beaten the system! At least she could fluster someone, even if it was only a virtual hunk.

"Let's take a deep breath and start over, Kerry. Are you comfortable?"

Now he was repeating himself!

"I'm just dandy," she said. "How are you?"

He didn't seem to hear her. "Remember the fantasy I promised you, Kerry, the one that could anticipate your every need, wish and desire? I'm going to need a little more information."

Poor Jean. She'd blown his fuses. "I'm not a woman without fantasies, you know. Listen, I have fantasies. I have a few fantasies that might shock you."

He appeared to blink and wake up at that point. "Could you name one?" he asked.

"And I love to touch things, too," she announced. "Do you know what I really love to touch? Buns, behinds, tushies, cheeks. Not that I go around doing that, but they look so firm and springy."

"Kerry—"

"And my favorite article of men's clothing? I know you didn't ask, but in case you're curious, it's a belt. Belts are long and leathery and they buckle in the sexiest way. They're well-placed on a man's body, *if* you know what I mean."

"Kerry—"

"Do you know what I mean, Jean? The place I'm thinking of that belts are close to? Do you have a pet name for yours? I like package, myself."

"Kerry!"

"Yes?"

"I told you that there are two conditions to this journey."

"Yes, I remember, that I entrust myself to you, and . . . hmm—"

"I didn't tell you the second one."

"Oh . . . right."

"The second condition is that you don't bluff. You can't win this game that way. You can't win this game without being willing to lose it, to give everything away. Do you understand me, Kerry? You have to be willing to give everything away."

On some level, Kerry understood exactly what he meant, and now he *was* talking fantasy. She had worked too hard to make herself safe behind these walls. She couldn't give an inch, and he wanted *everything*? Dear God.

Chapter Three

"Mmmmmmmmm . . ."

"Now there's an interesting sound. You okay, Kerry?"

"Mmm . . . mmm . . . mmm . . . *mmmmmmmmmm* . . ."

"I guess that was a yes?"

Kerry sighed deeply and felt a ripple of pleasure spiraling toward her toes. She was draped in her chair with her feet up on the desk, and the desire to stretch was so irresistible she made no attempt to fight it. She didn't even worry how it might look as she arched her back and slowly swiveled her hips, moving her shoulders in a languid counter rhythm. Another moan slipped out, another contented sigh, another kitten purr of pleasure.

This guy was some tour guide.

He'd suggested a relaxation exercise before they began, and boy, had it worked. She was as flushed and rosy as if she'd just come out of a steam bath, and there wasn't a part of her that wasn't humming.

She'd been uneasy about the exercise, especially when he told her that it involved hypnosis and that he would be putting her in a light trance. But finally she'd agreed to do it. This *was* just a game. What could he do to her, after all, besides talk? But, oh, baby, could he talk. The way other men plied you with fine chocolates and kissed your fingertips, that was how he could talk. Astaire danced like he could talk. Sinatra sang. Jean's voice was steamy stolen kisses in the backseat of an old Chevy. It was fantasy phone sex.

"Kerry . . . are you still with me?"

"I wish," she murmured. It hardly mattered what the man said—it was all sweet seduction.

"You wish?"

"This must be what puff clouds feel like," she said, releasing another languid sigh. "A little breeze, and I would be on my way, floating, floating . . . just floating."

"What do you wish for, Kerry?"

"I could just float all day . . . did I mention I felt like a puff cloud?"

"Kerry, stay with me, girl."

With you? I am so with you, Jean.

"You said something about a wish."

What did she wish for? So many things . . .

No, just one. One little thing.

"Care to share?" he asked.

"Well, I wish I could move." She lifted her arm and it flopped back down. "I'm as limp as linguine. That hypnosis was amazing."

"It only works with a willing subject."

She smiled through drooping lids. "I didn't know I was that willing. This is a little bit of heaven, this weightless sensation. And I'm *so* warm. I've never been so warm."

"You released some tension, and now you're glowing. Technically, it's just blood, rushing to the surface."

"Glowing, yes, that's exactly what it feels like."

When he'd suggested hypnosis, she'd immediately thought of some guy on a stage, making people bark. But the sounds of a babbling brook and chirping birds had overridden her concerns, and the screen was transformed with kaleidoscopic images of slowly swirling pink clouds, sifting sands and dark green oceans.

She found it impossible not to watch.

It was like a peek at infinity.

Her lids were already heavy when Jean's voice entered

the mix and he suggested she rest her head. She was gone before her eyes closed, but it had seemed as if he were right there, whispering strange, yet deliciously soothing things in her ear and putting her in a trance with his warm breath. His voice ebbed and flowed like a drug in her bloodstream, and even though she couldn't recall exactly what he'd said or what she'd done, she was quite certain she'd followed his suggestions without question. That was what you did when you were hypnotized.

When she came to she was slumped in her chair like a rag doll and sighing out sounds of satisfaction. She was so mellow her sweater socks were down around her ankles and she didn't even care. But what really fascinated her were the contradictions. Her body felt heavy and light at the same time, relaxed, yet deliciously aroused. Nerve endings twinkled like strings of Christmas lights, but her muscles were as fluid as the music coming from the speakers.

She'd heard about things like full-body orgasms, but she didn't think they were possible, especially if you had yet to have one of the garden variety type. The one smart thing she'd done with the string of losers in her life was to *not* sleep with them. She may have been used, but not in that way. Some protective instinct had kept her from surrendering body and soul to these men, despite their bad boy charm—or maybe because of it.

Her first boyfriend in college was the closest thing she'd ever had to a grand passion. She'd loved him and wanted to give herself to him, perhaps too soon and for the wrong reason. She'd hoped it would bring them closer, but her own desperation should have warned her what would happen. Brad Styles repaid her trust by having sex with one of Kerry's girlfriends the night after he'd taken Kerry's virginity. It was devastating. Most nineteen-year-old coeds would have been able to put it behind them, but for her it was a life sentence because it validated her belief that no man would ever really love her.

Her father hadn't. He'd deserted his family when Kerry

was a toddler, and her mother's bitterness had prepared Kerry to expect the worst from men. Even after Paula was gone, Kerry could hear her mother's warnings, but she didn't want to believe them. She'd had hope and her whole life ahead of her. Without realizing it, Kerry had desperately wanted Brad to prove her mother wrong—and to prove to Kerry that she was worth loving.

After that it was users and losers, men who confirmed what her mother had told her. She might not have consciously known it, but Kerry was afraid to take another risk on a good guy and have her heart broken again. It was easier to lock herself off, and when she did become involved, it was with men who acted exactly the way she expected—and believed she deserved.

With a romantic past like hers, Kerry hadn't spent a lot of time thinking about orgasmic experiences of any kind. But something had happened here today, something incredible. It felt like someone had switched bodies on her. She tried to bring back a detail or two of the experience, but the only thing she could remember were the feelings. Such wildness.

"*Zhhaa—?*" She was trying to say his name, but her voice cracked, and she couldn't clear away the raspiness. Where was her tea? One eye blinked open, and she spotted the cup of Quiet Woman on her desk. Nope. Too far.

"Yes, Kerry?"

"Did anything unusual happen while I was under?"

"Other than the noises?"

Ah, yes, the noises. Kerry could feel one building in her throat now. She tried to stop it, but her eyelids fluttered, and she flushed even warmer, if that was possible.

"Mmmmmmmmmmmmmmmm . . . oh, my . . . oh . . ."

"Kerry?" The noise *he* made was husky with disbelief. "Does that feel as good as it sounds?"

"Better," she whispered, "oh, much better. It feels like I want to take my clothes off. I swear it does. Isn't that amazing?"

She laughed and flopped her arms wide. "I'm the original abominable snow woman."

"Original, maybe. Abominable, never."

"Ohhhhhhhhhh, Jean, that is sooo sweet. You're just an old sweetie pie, that's what you are. And I'm just so warm and breathless. You wouldn't mind, would you?"

"Wouldn't mind?"

"If I took something off?" He'd told her not to bluff, but she wasn't bluffing now. She was glowing, alive, and not the tiniest bit afraid.

"I don't think—"

"Oh, right, I'll bet you're not programmed to answer that, are you?" She sighed. "Oh, well, it'll be okay. You can't see me anyway . . . can you?"

He took too long to answer so she hiked up her heavy fleece dress and purposely flashed some leg as she peeled off one sweater sock. It was the blind man test. If she did something startling right in front of him and got no response, he probably couldn't see her. *Or* he was a very smart man.

"Jean?"

Nothing. Maybe one sock wasn't startling enough. She pulled off the other one and dangled the pair in front of the screen, wondering how he'd managed to turn her drafty old town house into a sauna—and her into an exhibitionist.

Not a twitch from the man. She had to bend forward to get a closer look at the screen, but she couldn't detect any signs of life at all, even simulated ones. At the very least his eyes should be dilating. Maybe the computer *was* frozen.

"That didn't bother you, did it?" she asked. "By any chance?"

"Bother me? What was it that should have bothered me?"

"Uh . . . nothing." At least she knew he was there, but she still had no idea whether he could see her or not. He might have been probing for information. This was becoming a challenge.

"Excuse me, then," she said, "while I finish with this activity that *isn't* bothering you."

His sexy mouth hinted at a smile. "Don't mind me."

A definite challenge. Her mind was generating enough watts of suspicion to light up the neighborhood, but she could not crack this guy's code. Unfortunately, she was *really* glowing now. Some might have called it perspiring.

Off with the dress, Alice.

Years of use had made the crew neck of her dress loose enough to slip off her shoulder. From there she got her arm out—and realized she was dealing with a straitjacket, not a dress. Graceful it wasn't, but she knew better than to stand up and pull the bulky thing over her head. It was ankle length, and she would be too wobbly. Not to mention *exposed.* She could just imagine getting stuck, her arms and head inside, the rest of her outside.

She liberated the other arm and inched the dress down to her behind. It took a near back flip to get it to her ankles. Kicking her feet free was another high point, but it brought more blood rushing to the surface. Her color had to be approaching magenta by now. As she wiped the dampness from her brow, she realized the thermal underwear had to go too, but, then, oops, she would have nothing left but a pair of high-cut bikinis and a tank top.

"Pretty damn sexy," she murmured, when she was finally down to the essentials. She'd never thought of herself in those terms before, but then she'd never undressed for a man in quite this way before. Actually, she'd never undressed for a man in any way, but her guide didn't need to know that.

She straightened her tank top and felt a *zing zing* of electricity run through her. There were a couple parts of her that were still humming—and quite urgently aroused. Her breasts were taut and budded. They didn't seem to care whether the rest of her was glowing or not. They'd just come in from the cold.

"Would you look at that," she whispered in disbelief.

"Look at what?"

"The twins. I look like Cindy Crawford without a bra."

He made a throat-clearing sound, and she glanced up, startled. "Oh, sorry. It's just that I'm so warm and they're so . . . perky."

He seemed to be staring at her, and there was a pensive quality to his expression.

"Jean? You're awfully quiet. Is everything okay?"

"Yes, everything is fine."

"You sound a little tense. Is it me? Am I doing things you're not programmed to respond to?"

"I wouldn't put it exactly that way, but there are times when someone like me . . . when someone like me . . . wishes . . ."

Oh, don't stop now.

She was so caught up with the words she couldn't breathe. But his sea-deep eyes were beautiful. They seemed to be imbued with the ocean's hypnotic power.

Wishes what?

It sounded as if he'd cleared his throat again, and that possibility astounded her. Why would a computer simulation be hoarse?

"Jean? You were saying?"

"There are times when someone like me wishes he were real, Kerry. This is one of those times."

"Oh, me too, Jean. I wish you were real. I really do."

Her voice betrayed her, too. It was so raspy she could hardly get the words out. She grabbed for the tea to clear her throat, but she didn't have a firm grip on the handle, and some of it slopped on the keyboard.

"Oh, God," she whispered, staring at the poof of smoke. There was a hot sizzling sound, a shower of sparks, and the computer screen went dark.

Kerry jumped up from the chair and flipped the keyboard upside down to drain the spilled tea. She had a sinking feeling it was too late, the damage had been done, and she had no idea how to fix it. She'd never been into the nuts and bolts hardware. She was an idea person. Or she used to be.

"Jean? Are you there? Are you there? Oh, no, please tell me I didn't short out the keyboard!"

Not only wasn't he there, but the computer didn't seem to be there, either. Kerry did everything she could think of to get it restarted, but it was like trying to resurrect the dead, and she wasn't likely to get any help. It was late afternoon and one look outside told her she wouldn't get a repairman today. It had been snowing again, heavily, and the road was heaped with white.

Distraught, she picked up the game box and was gripped with the crazy need to apologize to it. It almost felt as if she'd killed someone. Of course, that wasn't true. It was a game, and he was the guide. He would be in every single copy that Genesis put out, wouldn't he? All she had to do was get her computer fixed and ask them to E-mail her a new copy of "Discover the Secret, Sensual You!"

It would be Jean in there, wouldn't it?

Somehow she didn't think so.

Chapter Four

"Kerry, come back and play. It's lonely in here without you."

Kerry heard the distant plea through a smothering veil of sleep. She was in deep slumber and might not have awakened at all if the hauntingly familiar voice hadn't coaxed her repeatedly.

"Kerry, come back and play—"

"Play?" she breathed into her pillow.

"Kerry—it's me."

She rolled over heavily and laid there in the darkness, vaguely aware that someone was about, and that she was too groggy even to open her eyes. The pale glow permeating her eyelids made her wonder if she'd left the television on in the living room. But she never used the television. She was always on her computer.

"Kerry, it's lonely—"

Her computer? She forced open her eyes to an aura of flickering blue light. It *was* her computer. The monitor was on. How could that be?

"Kerry—"

"Who's there?" Suddenly the voice was perilously close, a male voice.

"It's me," he said. "I'm here with you."

"With me?" Kerry could see nothing except the pulsing light, but her heart exploded with adrenaline. She dug her heels into the mattress and reared up, shoving herself back against the headboard.

"Who is it? Who's there?" She clutched the comforter to her body like a shield, unable to do more than whisper. What was going on? Who was there? Her eyes strained to make sense of things, but all she could see was a dark form silhouetted in the doorway.

The voice wasn't coming from the living room.

It wasn't coming from her computer.

There was a man standing right there in her bedroom—a tall, silent man, haloed by spikes of blue light. If this was a bad dream, it was a very, very bad one.

"Who are you? What are you doing in my house?"

"I'm sorry if I frightened you," he said.

His voice. She knew that voice.

"Tell me who you are."

"You know who I am."

"Tell me who you are!"

"I'm your guide, Kerry. It's Jean."

She couldn't see him well enough to distinguish his features, but she did know that voice. She'd been mesmerized by it. Hypnotized.

"Jean from the video game?"

"I've come, Kerry. I'm here. You can see me, can't you?"

She didn't know whether to be incredulous or horrified. The chill she felt cut to her bones. Either someone was playing a very cruel joke, or she had lost her mind.

"You *can't* be here. You're not real. You're pixels, hundreds of them."

"Not anymore. And it's all because of you."

Kerry didn't know what to do. Terror gripped her as she tried to reason things through. This had happened to her before when she tried to escape her problems with sleep. She dropped fast, deep, and dreamed profusely. Wild flights of hope and freedom. Often she dreamed that she was free of the fears and could walk out her front door. This was one

of those. It was wish fulfillment, Freudian wish fulfillment.
Either that or she'd taken too much L-tyrosine.

"You're not really here," she told him. "You're some figment of my loneliness and frustration, and I'd like you to
go."

"I'm not a figment, Kerry, feel me, pinch me. I'm real."

"No! Stay there!" She threw up her hands, but he was in
the room, at the foot of her bed, before she could stop him.

"No further," she told him. "*Please,* I believe you."

Her grandmother's antique lamp sat next to her bed. She
stretched over and tried to turn it on, but the key was loose
and the lamp wouldn't light. Frantically she twisted it
again. Maybe she'd shorted out the whole house. But, then,
how could the computer be working?

She kept one eye on the man at the foot of her bed as she
felt for a weapon. Her vision had adjusted to the dark, but
he was still too brightly haloed with light.

Damn. No electricity meant her curling iron was useless
too. She kept it on her nightstand, plugged and ready. Guns
frightened her, and the iron got hot enough to sizzle water
in less than thirty seconds. She had the scars to prove it.
There was a brick stashed under the bed and a baseball bat
behind the door, in case of break-ins, but that had never
been a problem before this. Her doors and windows were
triple locked, and she had an alarm system.

"How did you get in here?" she asked.

"I have no idea. I'm here, that's all I know. Touch me, see
for yourself."

Kerry's heart leaped as he held out a hand to her. How
could he be here in her bedroom when just this afternoon
he'd been the sexy heartthrob on her computer screen,
watching her undress? Oh, God!

"You can't be real," she protested. "Because if you're
real, then I should be screaming, right? Or calling the police—"

There was a phone on her night table too. She lunged for
it, but he was there before she could punch a single number.

The receiver fell to the floor as he caught her wrist. His grip was powerful enough to push her back on the bed and hold her there. Not painful, but firm.

"Don't do that, Kerry. *Hear me out, please.* I am real, but not in the way that you think. I'm only here because you wished that I would be."

"I didn't wish anything of the kind!"

"Yes, you did, just before you spilled your tea."

She shook her head in confusion. She had no idea what he was talking about, and the sheer strength of his hold was terrifying. She might have been able to see him if it weren't for that damn blue light. He was close enough. Lord, was he close.

"Try to remember," he urged. "It's important. You said something like, 'Me too, Jean. I wish you were real.' Do you remember that?"

Someone was crazy, and it wasn't her. Whoever this guy was, he must have been watching her through the window today. He was a Peeping Tom who spotted her undressing and overheard her conversation with the video game.

"There's five hundred dollars in my bunny slippers in the closet," she told him. "Take it and go. I won't call the police. I won't scream. I won't do anything. Please, just take the money."

He released her arm and fell silent, as though he didn't know what she was talking about. *As though he wasn't programmed to respond.* She wanted to throw up her hands. What kind of crazy nightmare was this?

"I don't want your money," he said.

She chanced another look at him and thought she could make out the enigmatic features that had graced her computer screen—the same sea-deep eyes and sexy black hair, shorn close but curly. The same strong, handsome, haunted face. Fine details were lost in shadows, but this had to be him. She couldn't be having a dream this elaborate, could she?

Was it him, Jean, living, breathing, above her?

The comforter had slipped away, exposing her tank top. She took advantage of his retreat and yanked the blanket back, tucking it around her. She'd worn her underwear to bed? That was something she never did. It was much too cold, among other things.

Calming her voice was an effort. "Well then," she said, "if you don't want money, what *do* you want?"

"Actually, it's not that easy to explain."

"Please! *Try.*"

"All right, but I don't want you to take this wrong, okay?"

He retreated farther, walking to the other side of the room, possibly to think about what he was going to say. She waited to see if he was coming back, but he hesitated near a white pine shutter console that had been part of her grandmother's trousseau. The shadows couldn't hide his expression. It was somber and filled with portent.

"There's a curse on me, Kerry, and only you can break it."

She just stared at him. Stared and wished she'd bought a gun for her nightstand. Guns didn't need electricity.

"Kerry . . . you're looking at me like I'm crazy."

"Duh," she said softly.

"I'm *not* crazy, believe me."

"Oh, you're not crazy, but you're cursed? Do you know how crazy that sounds?"

"Yes, I guess it does, doesn't it."

He smiled and she released a helpless sound. "Oh, God, please let this be a dream. It has to be a dream because otherwise I *really* do need antipsychotic medication."

"What kind of curse?" She ducked her head. "No, stop, don't tell me. Don't say anything! I can't go there."

Whatever this was, it was totally outside her experience and she had no idea what to do. She just wanted him out of her bedroom and out of her head. She could hear his voice, reverberating in the lower registers, even when he wasn't talking. It always made her think of water—of rivers and deep canyons. That was a sure sign of insanity, wasn't it? When you started hearing phantom music or instructions from above?

Maybe if she shut her eyes he would vanish in a puff of smoke. All she wanted was to wake from this terrible dream that had taken over her life. She didn't understand what was happening to her. Suddenly, everything was out of control. Her entire world was a flipping TV test pattern. Fear was her constant companion, her only companion, and she was trapped in her own home.

Why was she trapped? What was she afraid of, really?

When she looked up, he was still there, still observing her in that somber, stoic way that Jean Valjean did.

"Oh, all right," she snapped. "What kind of curse?"

He shrugged. "The kind that gets you imprisoned in a video game?"

He didn't sound any better at this hocus pocus than she was. "Yes, but who put the curse on you? And why, what did you do?"

"Good questions, but I'm short on the salient details. Given my track record, I'm guessing it has something to do with pride and power, with lack of humility. There are experiences I've never had and emotions I can't feel, and I won't be free until I've felt them."

"What experiences?" She gave him a wary look as he returned to the foot of her bed. "You're not here to deliver my fantasy, are you? Because I don't really want you all over me like a blanket. I have a perfectly good blanket right here. And there are no strawberries in the fridge. It's the wrong time of year, and as far as belts go, I don't really find them that fascinating."

What else had she said? Quick, what else?

Was he smiling? Always a bad sign.

"I was just kidding about all that stuff, okay? Even if it sounded like I meant it, I *didn't*. It was probably stress or the amino acid I've been taking. Brain chemicals, you know. They can make you do and say things—"

His nod was understanding. "You certainly did that. You said things *and* did things."

"What did I say? What did I do? What?"

"It's okay. You were fine."

"No, really, what did I do? It couldn't have been *that* bad. I remember everything, except . . . oh, dear . . . when I was under hypnosis?"

"Except then," he said.

She didn't like the dark glint in his eyes. "What? Did I do something terrible?" What could be worse than undressing in front of the computer screen?

So many things.

"Did it involve one of the five senses?" she asked. "Touch, taste?"

"I'm not saying anything. You were fine, Kerry. Now, do you think we could finish our conversation about the curse?"

"Not until you tell me what I did."

"Not until we finish with the curse."

Obviously they'd reached an impasse. He said he was short on time. Maybe she could wait him out.

Unexpectedly he laughed, and it was a rich, rugged sound. "You have a gift, Kerry. I've never heard noises like that before."

She frowned.

He nodded.

"All right, all right." A sigh. "Tell me about this curse."

He sat on the end of the bed, positioning himself in the way that guys sometimes did, with one leg pulled up. Doctors were famous for that pose, news anchors, even cowboys, men of some authority, men with a problem to fix.

"Bottom line?" he said. "There's an emotion I've never experienced."

"Which one?"

"The one that makes you shudder."

"Fear? Is that the one you mean?" No wonder he'd been sent to her. Kerry Houston was an expert on shuddering.

"Not necessarily, although fear could be part of it. It's an emotion that can never be mastered by the human will. I can't explain it beyond that, but I'll know it when I feel it."

Now she was curious. Maybe this was one of those lucid dreams, the kind that were so vivid and real you couldn't tell them from everyday life. Was that even remotely possible? And if it was, then maybe the dream had something to tell her. It might be her own subconscious, trying to communicate.

"But you do know who put the curse on you, right? Someone had to—a practicing witch, the computer gods, your ex-wife?"

Irony tempered his smile. "I've come to believe that you can curse yourself. In fact, maybe that's the way it always happens with curses. They're self-imposed and self-fulfilling. But even if that's the case, I'm ready to change. I want to be free."

So did she. Oh, yes, so did she.

"Kerry, there was a moment when I thought I saw you peering back at me through the screen, and it was like waking from a deep sleep. There's a reason that happened to me. There's a reason it was you and there's a reason I'm here. I don't have much time."

"But why was it me?"

"Because you woke me up, because you wished for me to be here? Maybe you even needed me to be here."

Because she needed him to be here. How strange that her grandfather had always said that life had a way of bringing you whatever you needed, but you had to ask, and most people never did.

"Kerry . . . I may be trapped for all time."

Okay, she thought, *so maybe this is a dream and maybe it does have something to tell me.* She could certainly use the feedback. Her life wasn't exactly a picnic in Lover's Park lately. And it probably wouldn't hurt to go along with it—with him—for a while.

"I could be stating the obvious," she said, "but you are

here. You are free. Why don't you just walk out that door and go merrily on your way?"

"It doesn't work like that. There are things a man has to learn, things that maybe only a woman can teach."

Her stomach was doing that handspring thing again, and Kerry could hardly contain a sigh. He had her at *things a man has to learn.*

"You know, Jean, I'm not exactly a poster girl for mental health."

"You're perfect."

His voice resonated softly through the dark, tapping at the stubborn barriers that protected her heart. She drew the comforter around her, warding off a shiver.

"What do I have to do?" she asked him.

"Teach me how to shudder, the crash course?"

She laughed at that. "We could put it on video, the companion piece to 'Discover the Secret, Sensual You!'"

"You'll do it then?"

"Honestly, Jean, I don't think that can be taught."

There was pride in the lift of his head, pride and sadness. "Then show me the way back to my soul. Isn't that where shuddering comes from?"

She tugged on the comforter, trying to cover herself, but there was nothing she could do. He was sitting on the other end.

"The crash course sounds easier," she admitted.

"What makes you shudder, Kerry? How does it happen?"

You, she thought. *Don't you know? Can't you see?*

"It's cold in here," she told him. "I should probably get some clothes on."

"Can I help with that?"

Again, Kerry found herself staring at him. *I gave him the wrong name,* she thought. *He isn't Jean Valjean from* Les Mi. *He's Starman from the movie.* She had her own personal starman. He thought it was just fine offering to help a crazy naked lady get dressed. He was from another planet.

"I'll stick with the comforter," she said, "but it would be nice if we had some light in here."

She half-expected him to point a finger at her table lamp and zap it on. Instead, he walked over and began to tinker with it while she gathered up the comforter and created her own igloo. She watched him expectantly, waiting for the moment when light flooded him and she could finally see the details of his face. She was dying to know what he looked like in the flesh, how he dressed and carried himself.

The shadows gave him a graceful, fluid presence, but she was very aware of his height. He was a good-sized man, and as darkly gorgeous as the winter night. She had an instinctive feel for the dimensions of her bedroom, and she could just make out the substantial contours of his hand as it worked the switch of her antique table lamp. She could also remember how it felt on her arm, how much area it took up, how commanding it was.

A slave bracelet encircling pink satin skin . . . a slave bracelet, his hand.

Warmth rushed up Kerry's throat. She loosened the comforter, and had a momentary flash of him reaching for her, lifting her out of her igloo and into his arms. He could do it easily, she realized. He was tall enough that her feet would never touch the floor. Tall enough to curl your bare legs around and ride like a wave to its crest. *Tall enough to bounce your head in the clouds with every rip and swell.*

Wooooooo . . . where was she going with that one?

She lifted her head and felt the dizzy weight of her own eyelids. The warmth had flooded her face and gone straight to her brain.

"I think you've blown a fuse," he said.

She didn't dare laugh. "I have candles somewhere." They wouldn't need light the way she was glowing. She was steamy enough to throw off the comforter and start fanning herself. It was an odd thing having a strange man this close to her in a darkened bedroom. She wondered if he knew how intimate it was, or the effect he was having on her.

If she could find a way to have that effect on him, she could free him from any old curse in a matter of minutes.

The candles were in her closet. She rose from the bed to get them and wondered what he would do. The answer might have frightened her if she hadn't sensed from the first that his purpose was not to do her harm. When she turned, he was there, standing behind her, close enough to feel his heat and breathe in his male scent. It startled her, but he seemed to anticipate her concern.

"Shhhhh," he whispered as he took an armful of votive candles from her. "It's okay."

He began to arrange them in small circles around the room and light them.

For some reason it pleased her to watch him do that, but she wondered about the matches in his pocket. Where did a cursed man who lived in a computer get those? You're having a dream, Kerry, she reminded herself. A revelatory dream. That's why you're going along with it, and that's the *only* reason. Your unconscious is trying to tell you something, and you're going to listen, even if it makes you want to squeal and hide under the bed.

Her questions vanished as she realized he was gone. She looked around the room, bewildered, and saw him returning from the living room, absent the blue aura. He'd turned the TV off, but he was carrying the one remaining candle, and she was finally able to see him. The sinuous flame played its tricks, but she was certain this was the same man she'd seen on her screen.

She wondered if the sexy dark curls on his head had been cropped short to tame them. His lashes were equally dark and feathery. His mouth was even moodier and more sensual than she remembered, given its width, the curvature of his upper lip, the tilted corners. He was better looking than on the screen.

"You bring a word to mind," he said.

"I do?"

"Beauty. You have so much of it."

"I was thinking that about you," she said.

"How difficult is it?"

"Shuddering? It's not hard at all. There are so many ways. Your voice," she said. "Your voice makes me shudder."

He took in her flushed features, obviously pleased. God, how he made her heart beat and the blood hum through her veins. It felt like her body was making music, trying to sing.

A circle of candles flickered from the mirrored dresser, setting fire to the glass.

"Can you tell me how it works?" he asked.

"Your voice touches nerves. I can't explain it, but if I could touch you in the same way, you'd shudder too."

He was wearing a black sweater shirt that buttoned up the front. She slipped a hand through an opening in the comforter and touched the material. What was she doing? The room was so quiet you could hear her fingernails click against the bone buttons as she began to undo them. Her heart was beating unnaturally hard, but it seemed the right thing to do, the only thing. Moments later, the silky material fell away from his torso, letting the firelight reveal him. His abdomen was hard and smooth. Above it, sienna-colored nipples peeked through glossy dark hair.

He caught a breath as she touched his midriff.

Rippling muscles tightened torturously.

"There," she said. "See? See how easy it is? You're a free man."

He laughed and threw back his head. "God," he whispered.

"It worked, right?"

"Oh, no, Kerry," he said, nearly as breathless as she was, "no, I'm still cursed. I'm more cursed than ever."

Kerry was crushed. "That wasn't a shudder? It was a quiver maybe?"

"I don't know what it was, but it was unbelievable."

"Then what's wrong?"

He pressed a hand to the fluttering muscles. "It's an amazing feeling, but I don't think it's the one I'm missing."

"Really, are you sure? I guess we should try something else then. How do you like to be touched? Lightly? Firmly?"

His lips melted into a smile. "Are you my guide now?"

It was impossible not to smile back. "I could be. Would you like to go on a tour of Jean?"

"Lead on," he said.

"This is just a dream, isn't it?"

"It feels pretty real to me."

Well, of course, she thought, what else would she expect a dream character to say? He wasn't the one under stress and popping amino acids. This was her learning experience. Who cared what he thought?

She solved the problem of her comforter by tucking it in like a bath towel and wearing it like a cape. After that she eased open his shirt to allow more access. The silky material slid off one shoulder and dropped down his arm. It was an incredibly sexy accident. She didn't want to think about how sexy.

A river of muscle, sinew and bone, that's what she was dealing with. His belly button was the only reasonably soft thing she could see. She could start there, but like the apex of a wheel, it would only lead to things that were hard, no matter which way she went. She drew a little circle, keenly aware of the taut heat beneath her fingers, of the sensitive puckers and tucks, and the bull's-eye at its center.

"How's this?" she asked.

He shook his head as if to say "Nice, yes, but still not the right one."

But she had seen the way his muscles sucked in and his shoulders lifted.

She tried those same shoulders and his neck next. There were some irresistibly tawny cords and tendons that actually quivered when she touched them. Now *that* could make a woman want to die, it was so thrilling. What must be going on inside him, she wondered. The same exquisite sensations that were stirring in her? He had such a marvelously responsive body.

"I don't think so," he said.

An idea came to her, but was it too reckless?

"This is only in the interests of helping your cause," she told him. "It's nothing personal."

She tilted up and pressed a breathless kiss to his mouth.

Air jetted from his nostrils, but his expression barely registered the impact.

"Anything?" she asked.

He shook his head.

"No? Really? Are you sure?"

She brushed her mouth over his again, only this time she let her fingers glide down his body, over his hardened abs and across his crotch. Just so very lightly, she brushed him and felt him turn into a girder beneath her fingers. He was certainly built like a human.

A groan shot through him and his whole body quaked.

She stepped back with a secret rush of pleasure. "Congratulations," she said.

"Whoa," he breathed, "I'm still vibrating. What did you do to me?"

She wasn't sure herself. "It was just a touch, and barely one at that. Maybe it was what I *didn't* do."

It seemed as if he needed to sit down to get his bearings. He stepped back and ended up on her bed, but when he looked up at her, he was shaking his head.

"You're not going to believe this," he said with the huskiest of voices, "but I don't think that was it. No, I don't think so."

"What? How could it not be? Your stomach muscles were practically in spasm." She really was at a loss—and then lightning struck again. God, the creative process. She loved it.

"Do you think it could be that you need to touch *me*?" she asked.

She was still bundled inside her igloo, and he looked her

over as if to say that he couldn't see how much touching was going to get accomplished with only her face showing.

"Here," she said, "I'll just move the comforter off my shoulder. See, like this." She touched her fingertips to bare skin and quivered. "Oh! Try that."

His fingers brushed her flesh and her igloo fell away. It dropped to the floor, revealing her tank top and bikini panties. She stood there, staring at him, wanting to gasp, gasping deep in her soul where shudders start. That was the moment she knew that something momentous was going to happen to her tonight. He was going to touch her in ways she'd never been touched before, redefine the very word, touch. And not only that, she wanted him to. Let the journey begin. It was only a dream, after all.

And she hadn't shuddered this way in such a very long time.

Chapter Five

Whatever you secretly desire in life has already imprinted itself on you. All you have to do is recognize its existence . . .

Kerry heard his voice as if he'd just whispered the words, but he couldn't have. He was doing something much more thrilling and terrifying with his mouth than whispering. He was showing her what she secretly desired. It was the only part of him that touched her body, his hot, whispering mouth.

"Oh!" she cried as he rolled her nipple between his teeth. She felt the sharp edges against her aching flesh, and nearly swooned with pleasure. It was sweet relief. She was stretched so taut that even a nip would have felt good. Anything that released the pressure. How she wanted his hands on her! How she wanted to be touched and squeezed and fondled until she did swoon. She would fall into unconsciousness, aroused only by each nip, by each sharp, unbearably sweet thing he did to her.

It's a dream . . . it has to be . . . I couldn't do this if it weren't.

She had fleeting thoughts of turning away from him, of trying to cover herself, but that was impossible . . . and this was perfect. In some way, it was perfect.

She was naked and wantonly displayed for her dream lover. . . . The comforter had fallen away at his touch, as had her tank top, and she couldn't remember how it had happened. She didn't know when her breasts had come to be bared. How her whole body had come to this wild flash point of desire.

She had to turn away.

This was her last chance.

That thought took hold of her, but when she tried, he spun her back into his arms. Her head dropped back with a gasp and weakness flooded her. Shock burned her face and her jaw fell slack. *What was happening? The more powerful he became, the weaker she got, and that made her utterly breathless.*

"You can't win this game by bluffing, Kerry. You have to show your hand."

"I'm naked," she whispered. "Look at me. What more can I show you?"

"Yourself, show me that."

Show him that.

"The entire rainbow, Kerry . . . it's all yours to feel."

"It's too much feeling."

"Breathe . . . let go of everything else . . . breathe and float . . ."

Her eyelids fluttered, and she became aware of her breathing. It was deep and regular. She was succumbing again, falling more deeply under his spell, and soon there would be no hope for her. Maybe there never had been. A sensation lived in the pit of her stomach. It was as crystal clear as a violin's song. Her body was making music again. She could hear the clarion tones that rang from within, and they were even more compelling than his voice.

A moan slipped out. "Mmmmmmmmm . . ."

He gripped her arms, and she was glad. If she made him crazy with her sounds, then yes, she was glad. She wanted power over him, any little bit of power she could get.

They were standing by the console, his legs braced wide and hers between them. He had brought her here to make love to her, female intuition told her that. He had laced his hands through her hair and searched for the secrets in her

gaze and said her name. *Said it with hunger.* Passion burned
off him like radiant energy—rough and tender passion—
and it was all she could do to stay on her feet.

"A highwayman," he whispered near the lobe of her ear,
"who sees a woman running through the fields in a transparent gown . . ."

*Who rides her down on his horse and takes her against a
tree.*

Kerry's toes curled into the carpet beneath her feet. The
edge of the console dug into her back, but she was grateful
it was there to steady her. She couldn't move against him,
but he could move against her. And he did.

"A male slave so aroused by a woman he can't hide it . . ."

His erection burned her belly, and she melted against it
like candy in the heat. It was beautiful the way he wrapped
her in his arms, protecting her nakedness, and at the same
time whispering forbidden things in her ear. *Terrible, terrible things and she wanted every one of them to happen to
her.*

"The handsome stranger behind you in line, who mur-
murs that he has been fantasizing about you in a dress with
no panties underneath . . ."

A sound vibrated in his throat. It ran all through Kerry.

He startled her by holding her at arm's length and looking down at her body, admiring her in the way that hungry
males do succulent females. She had never thought of herself as edible, but his expression forced her to. His eyes
were hot and his mouth was just slack enough to make her
imagination run wild. Those moody lips and white, glistening teeth.

What those teeth could do. *Had done.* She felt another
bolt of electricity at the thought. Such excruciating pleasure.

"Come with me," he said. "Come with me on a tour
of *us.*"

He lifted her onto the console and moved between her
legs. The inside of her thighs ached with anticipation, and

the ache deepened as he moved closer, spreading her legs wider. Pressure built within her, and it was wildly irresistible, one of the more glorious feelings she'd ever experienced.

She hadn't paid any attention to the fact that he was still dressed. She barely knew what she had on. But when he trailed his knuckles up her thigh and toyed with the leg of her bikini panties, it released a shower of thrills. She was down to one skimpy article of clothing, which wasn't doing her much good at all.

His fingers had become her sun, the center of everything. She could think about nothing else. Every move they made riveted her, especially as they delved inside the elastic of her panties and touched the nest of curls there. She was hit by bolt after bolt, and moisture gushed.

He continued his exploration, delving farther.

Kerry's head snapped up, and her breath caught fire.

Lord, how she wanted him to touch her there, deeply, taste her there. But to her surprise, he didn't do either of those things. He shocked her breathless by asking her to pleasure herself.

"What?"

"Touch yourself the way you want to be touched. Show me, Kerry. Show your hand."

She was self-conscious, but with his encouragement, she caressed the curve of her own throat, including the sensitive little pocket just beneath her chin—and decided it must be the softest part of her body. Of course, that was before she got to the insides of her elbows and wrists. Hundreds of receptors? She had thousands. Her thighs were like water and her fingertips, sunlight. They left diamonds everywhere they traced.

God, how she ached, how wonderfully she ached for him.

There wasn't anywhere she *didn't* want to be touched.

He guided her hand to where his had been, and she had

barely brushed the silky curls before the voltage started. A shaking breath slipped from her throat. Her whole body throbbed. For a moment she was swept by the intensity, and all she could do was rock forward. When she opened her eyes, he was picking her up in his arms.

He laid her on the bed, and then he began to undress. Candlelight flickered over him as he pulled off his shirt, and Kerry was dazed by how powerful he looked. His shoulders were wide and muscular, his arms dark with hair. He unbuttoned his pants, but left them on as he moved over her.

His weight pressed her deeply into the mattress, and she gave out a little cry. They really were going to make love, and she was stunned by that possibility. She had to stop him.

"Can you feel that, Jean? Are you shuddering like I am?"

"God, yes, I can feel it." He pulled her into his arms. "It's beautiful, even my breath is shaking."

"Then you're free? You must be free."

Something compelled her to search his face, even though her body ached for his attention. She was quivering for completion, for the journey she'd never taken. But she had to know if he felt the way she did.

"Is this it? Is this the shuddering you were talking about?"

He touched her face, her mouth, but he didn't answer her right away. He looked a little shell-shocked too.

"Kerry, I'm not sure," he said. "It has to come from the soul. This is incredible. I've never felt anything like it, but I just don't know."

Kerry was hurt and bewildered. She couldn't hide it. "How can you not know? You said that you *would* know. I remember."

He studied her searchingly. "This isn't about me. It's about you, your feelings. It's about the rainbow. Let me give you that—"

Her shuddering did come from the soul. He didn't feel that way?

"No," she insisted, "this has never been about me. It's about freeing you from the curse. Why else are we doing this?"

"Because we want to. I can't imagine any greater pleasure than making you happy, than making *you* shudder."

He didn't feel the tremors she felt, this ecstasy? She had failed utterly in her attempts to reach him? That destroyed her. It simply did.

"I can't do this," she said. "I can't go on with it."

"Kerry, don't—"

"I'm sorry, I can't."

She covered herself with her arms and refused to look at him.

"Kerry, for God's sake, don't," he whispered. "There is no curse on me except you. If I can't have you, I don't want anything else. To live like a normal man would be hell."

His rough voice sent a thrill through her. It didn't sound like Jean at all. He sounded desperate, and Kerry was torn. She didn't know what to do. She couldn't let him do these things to her. The feelings were too intimate. They had to be mutual. She couldn't be the only one falling in love.

She looked up to tell him that . . . but he was gone.

This time Kerry got traction on the doorknob the first time she tried. It was even more amazing that she'd been able to walk to her front door, turn the knob, and open it without an internal earthquake. The floor didn't ripple and warp, the lights didn't dance, but her pulse was kicking painfully. And now that she had the door open, she couldn't seem to move.

He was gone, and she had to find out if he'd ever existed. Could she have dreamed him? Was she crazy? Someone had aroused her to the point of delirium last night, but this morning she awoke to burned down candles and her own discarded clothing. He was gone. Parts of her body were still throbbing, and her heart was an aching knot. What had happened? Was she so desperate that she had to dream a man into existence to make love to her?

It didn't seem possible to feel things so intensely in a dream. But if he really did exist, the implications were staggering. It meant that a virtual stranger had come into her bedroom last night and rendered her naked and utterly helpless with desire. Despite all the stories her grandfather had told her, Kerry no longer believed in curses and fairy tales. The man was real, and therefore he must have broken into her house.

He wasn't a stranger either. He looked exactly like Jean, and he knew about the game. He talked about it. Malcolm's paranoia seemed less scary to her in comparison to this. Maybe her tenant was right. Someone was spying on them through their computers and Palm Pilots. Everyone was under surveillance and it was a government plot.

But why did the government care whether or not she had an orgasm?

She was going crazy. She was.

Icy air gusted through the open doorway. She hadn't thought to put on her parka or flap hat. Talk about shuddering. Her legs began to shake, but her hands were clammy, despite the frigid weather.

She should have called the police immediately. Why hadn't she done that?

She rubbed her arms for warmth. No, it was too soon to bring the police in on something like this. And it was too strange a story. She had to find out for herself what was going on before someone had her carted off to an asylum.

Go outside and check the door, Kerry.

It was early, and the world was still hushed under a fresh layer of white, but someone had shoveled her walk, she saw. The concrete steps were wet with a film of melted snow. It was probably her neighbor, the retired grocery store manager who'd pretended not to see while she was being mugged. The gangs had made everyone afraid of reprisals, but Kerry would never understand why someone who'd lived next door long enough to know her grandparents hadn't tried to help. She would have taken on the thugs herself if he'd been attacked.

She checked the knob on the outside of the door, but there weren't any visible scratches or marks. That didn't mean there wasn't a break-in, however. A real professional wouldn't have left any evidence. Kerry had no idea what she was dealing with, but this was beginning to feel more bizarre every moment, if that was possible.

"Kerry? What's wrong?"

The whispered question came from behind her.

Kerry nearly slipped on a patch of ice, trying to get turned around. It was Malcolm, standing alongside the house. He'd scared her half to death, but she didn't have time to be upset with him.

"Malcolm, did you see anything odd going on around here last night? Anyone strange lurking around?"

He crept toward the porch, peeking out at her from under a baseball hat. He was bundled up in the pea jacket and a heavy turtleneck that was mostly hidden by his beard. His breath was as steamy as a horse's.

"Why?" he asked, flipping up the collar of his coat. "Has someone been lurking around?"

"I just asked *you* that question, Malcolm."

A smile glimmered. "Oh, yeah, you did. No, I haven't seen anybody. Are you missing something?"

"Not really." *Just my sanity, my dignity, and possibly my faith in mankind.* "I thought I heard noises, but you know how that is. Maybe it was a dream. Thanks anyway."

She gave him a halfhearted wave and started inside. The plan was to beat a hasty retreat, but something stopped her midstride. Her other hand was frozen on the railing, and she couldn't move. It felt as if she were being zapped with electric current. She could not move. Could not. Move.

Dear God, she thought. She was outside, and she couldn't get back. This was her worst fear realized. She was as paralyzed as the statue across the street. She hadn't been out of the house in weeks. What had made her think that she could do this?

At some point she realized Malcolm was on the porch with her. He was trying to help her, but she was so rigid with fear, he couldn't get her unfrozen, either. With some prying he got her fingers unlocked. And then, to her horror, he picked her up in his arms, carried her into the house and dropped her on the sofa.

"Are you all right?" he asked, kneeling next to her. His blue eyes were dark with concern. "Are you sick or something?"

"No—Yes, maybe. I didn't get much sleep last night."

"Should I call the doctor? I could take you to a clinic."

She pulled a woolen throw over her and huddled inside it. "Just c-c-cold," she said. "I'll be fine in a minute."

"How about something to drink? Wine? Whiskey? Something stronger?"

"*Is* there anything stronger?" She managed a little smile. Malcolm obviously thought she needed sedation, and he was right. "Some hot tea would probably help, but I can get it myself."

He crammed his hands in his jacket pockets and shuffled his feet. "Well, if there's nothing I can do, maybe I should be going. *Is* there anything I can do?"

Kerry didn't want him to go. It hit her all at once that she didn't want her odd duck of a tenant to leave. Boy, that was scary. But even scarier was the prospect of being alone with her bizarre fantasies and suspicions. At least Malcolm was someone to talk to, another human being, not an assortment of pixels like Jean. Okay, a gorgeous assortment, but pixels nonetheless.

"Heard any good conspiracy theories?" she asked him.

He gave her a look that said she was scaring *him*.

She tucked the blanket under her chin, brought herself to a sitting position and began to mutter. "Think maybe you could get up, Kerry?" she said. "Think maybe you could

make you and your guest a cup of tea? Something herbal?
Something calming? And no more L-tyrosine?"

"Kerry, who are you talking to? Are you all right?"

Poor Malcolm. Now he had one more thing to worry
about. Her.

"No, I'm not all right," she said impulsively. "I'm lonely,
Malcolm. I'm lonely, and I think maybe what I need is a
roommate. Would you like to live with me?"

Malcolm was already up on his feet and inching toward
the door. "I really have to be going," he said. "I hope you
feel better soon."

Kerry shrugged. "Me, too, Malcolm. Me, too."

"Kerry?" Something seemed to have halted Malcolm's
progress. He acted as if he wanted to tell her something, but
he was rocking back and forth like a self-conscious teen-
ager. "You will overcome your fear," he said, "when there's
something more important to you than your fear."

Kerry sat up. "Malcolm? What does that mean?"

"I—uh—" He shook his head, seeming as bewildered as
she was.

As the front door closed on her tenant's fleeing form,
Kerry gave out a resigned sigh, followed by a bittersweet
sigh, which seemed to bring on a huge, wistful sigh. Now
she knew how to get rid of Malcolm. That should have
made her happy. But it was true, she was lonely. Lonely,
confused and afraid.

It was her grandfather who'd always told her if you
wanted something badly enough, you should wish for it.
"With an open heart," he'd said, "because only open hearts
can receive." There were times when she could feel her grandparents' presence so strongly it felt as if they were still
about, keeping an eye on her. They knew she hadn't had
good luck with men, and it had occurred to her that if some
wonderful guy ever did come her way, they might have had
something to do with it.

Silly child, she thought.

Her computer sat forlornly on the secretary, silenced by a poof of smoke. Kerry tried to ignore it. She made her tea, drank it and tidied the kitchen, but finally she couldn't postpone the day any longer. She had work to do. There were other games to test and she had to make a living. No more wandering around in a daze. She'd done that all night. She told herself sternly that she could get the computer working again without being tempted to revisit the scene of the crime. She was never going near Jean Valjean or his criminally seductive video game again.

She wasn't.

Well, she wasn't, damnit.

"Jean, are you in there?"

Kerry peered into the depths of her computer screen with a feeling of despair. She could feel the sequence of sighs starting again, but she'd been sighing all day, and she wasn't going there again. She'd been wrestling with what to do all day too. It had taken her entire supply of tea bags, but finally she'd realized that no mattered how frightened—or crazy—she was, she couldn't pretend that nothing had happened.

"Knock knock? Anyone there? Jean?"

"I don't seem to be programmed to answer that," the game guide said.

How like a man, she thought. They weren't programmed to answer the really important stuff. And how like her life. She tried to have a relationship with a computer simulation, and even he turned out to be a jerk.

"Perhaps you would like to start by giving me a name?" the guide suggested.

"You have a name. It's Jean. My name is Kerry and I've played this game before. You must have a record of me somewhere in your memory. Dammit, Jean! look again!"

"You're not in my memory banks, Kerry. I'm sorry."

"Not as sorry as I am."

Kerry sprang from her chair and walked away from the

computer. It had become the source of all her frustration and pain, and she couldn't sit there any longer. She had to escape it, or she would go crazy, but how was she to do that? It was also the source of her income. She was trapped in her house and had no other way to make money.

She had to let go of this obsession with Jean and get on with things. Her survival depended on it. Even if there was a slight possibility that he'd ever existed, he didn't now. She lost him the first time when the keyboard shorted out, and she lost him the second time last night when she wasn't able to free him. Whatever the missing emotion was, she had not touched it. She hadn't been able to give him what he lacked, and that had made her feel like a failure. That was why she'd told him to go. She was afraid of the feelings he touched in her and devastated that she couldn't touch him the same way.

Out her window Kerry could see Lover's Park and the defiantly graceful statue. Neighborhood folklore had it that the two young lovers were caught together against the wishes of their families. They were betrothed to others, and their punishment for falling in love was imprisonment. They were kept in separate towers, chained and naked, until they came to their senses and did as their families wished. It was believed that to venture out into the icy winter without clothing would freeze them solid and they would die the moment they touched.

Kerry had wholly accepted the story as a child, probably because the existence of the statue seemed to prove it. Her favorite part was the ending, which her grandfather swore was true. He told her the young lovers missed each other so grievously they felt as if they were dying anyway, and one night, with the help of servants, they both escaped their prisons. A terrible blizzard had blown in, but the passion flowing in their veins kept them warm until they found each other. The moment they touched, they froze, forever inseparable and locked in a lover's embrace.

Decades passed but the exquisite ice sculpture did not

melt as much as one drop, even in the hottest summers. The lovers had preferred death to separation, and the statue Kerry saw out her window was said to represent the way they were found by their families, entwined in naked splendor.

The statue was called *Winter Lovers,* and Kerry had often wondered if a love like that was possible. She wanted to believe it was true. She wanted to *believe.* But there was little in her romantic past that would allow her to. She'd had so few good experiences with men . . . until now, she realized.

"Kerry, are you there? Do you want to play the game? If you don't, just say 'Go to sleep' and I'll turn myself off."

Kerry whirled. It was the game guide. "No, wait! Don't go to sleep, don't!"

She dashed back to her chair and sat down. The *Winter Lovers* had given her an idea. *Please let this work,* she thought. *Please please, please.*

The man staring back at her from the screen had Jean's features—the same dark eyes and hair and mouth—but he wasn't anyone she knew. Certainly he wasn't the man who'd materialized in her house last night. He had the blank stare of a computer simulation. He didn't look like he ever had been or could be human.

She began to speak to the monitor, but she wasn't talking to him.

"Jean, I know what it is now! I know how to make you shudder. You have to come back. Please, Jean, come back. I can free you this time, I'm sure of it."

Chapter Six

Kerry lay in bed, frowning at the fire ring of burning candles and wondering what kind of stupid you had to be to believe in fairy tales. She'd even arranged the candles in threes as he had. But he wasn't coming back. She had to stop waiting, wishing, hurting so badly she could die with every second that passed, every second he didn't show up. She had to stop.

She rolled over and buried her face in the pillow. *Jean, please. If you exist, don't let it end like this. Find a way to come back. Find a way.*

"Stop this, Kerry," she told herself, "just stop."

She didn't understand why she couldn't let go of this fantasy and put it out of her mind. She wasn't in love with him. You couldn't be in love with someone who existed only in video games and dreams, no matter how lonely you were. But she knew what it was like to be held prisoner against your will, and maybe that was why it had seemed imperative to help him. There had to be some reason she and Jean had been brought together, something for her to learn from the way he'd come into her life . . . even if it was all a dream.

If she could free him, then perhaps she could find a way to free herself.

She closed her eyes and envisioned the cloudlike images that had hypnotized her, hoping they might help put her to sleep. Still, it seemed like hours before she finally did drift off . . . and only moments before a vaguely familiar noise woke her. The beeping was soft and intermittent, but she'd heard it before. She lay there, dozing, her mind searching for connections, and suddenly she was awake, aware. It was the video game. She'd heard the same sound the first time she played the game. There was a feedback loop keyed into the player's responses. If your heart rate went up, it beeped.

Her heart rate had just gone up.

She sat up and scanned the dark room, wondering what was going on. Her eyes were slow to adjust, but as far as she could tell the whole house was dark. The computer couldn't be on, but she could still hear the noise.

She slipped out of bed and put on her heavy chenille robe. She wasn't wearing her usual layers of flannel. She'd hoped the panties and tank top she wore last might somehow magically encourage him to come back. What kind of stupid? *That* kind of stupid. Sadly, there wasn't anything she hadn't tried, including bargaining with the angels for their help.

Her phone! If it wasn't the computer, then it had to be her cordless phone, she realized. It made a beeping sound when it ran out of batteries. She'd probably left it off its cradle.

The moonlight was so bright she didn't need her flashlight to get around. Silvery rays lit her way into the living room, where she began to search for the phone. She usually left it on the catalogs by the rocking chair, but the beep didn't sound as if it were coming from that direction. Where the heck—

"Is this what you're looking for?"

Kerry let out a scream that could have brought her grandparents out of their graves. There was a man standing in the shadows of the front hallway, and she had no weapon, nothing to protect herself. For a second, she thought it was Malcolm, but the intruder was so well-concealed she couldn't tell.

Her voice quaked. "Who are you, and what are you doing in my house?"

"I was under the impression that you wanted me to be here. Was I wrong?"

No one talked that way, except— *"Jean?"*

"Kerry, I came back."

The floor tilted and the lights danced, even though they weren't on. Kerry took that as a sign that she was going to faint, and when she sat down, it was in the old rocking chair. The creaks and groans drowned out her soft exclamation as he walked into the room, and she saw his face.

"My God, Jean, why didn't you say something? You scared me to death."

"I did. Didn't you just hear me? I said, 'I came back.'"

And she wanted him back, but did it always have to be unannounced?

"Oh, never mind." She was dealing with Starman. She had to remember that. "What is it you're holding?" It looked like a gun in his hand.

"Your phone. It's making funny noises."

I would be too if you were holding onto me like that.

Forlorn little beeps echoed through the darkness. It was a sound that had always made Kerry acutely aware of her own loneliness, and she rose from the chair to put the phone out of its misery.

"I'll do it," he said. "I know where it goes."

He knew where it went.

He seemed to know where everything went, including her. This was the man who picked her up and set her on the console last night, the man who sent wild delight tumbling through her. Was that magic or madness?

There was no time to stop and ask him if any of this was really happening. No time for that or any of the other nonsensical questions that were piling up in her mind, like what he'd done before he was cursed and why he'd ended up in a video game, of all places. That must have been symbolic.

There were other things that had to be taken care of first, before he disappeared again.

"Do you remember when you hypnotized me?" she asked him.

"You're an excellent subject."

"Well, let's hope you are, too, because I think that's the way to free you."

He looked skeptical. "You're going to hypnotize me?"

"Yes, with the help of a Web site that specializes in trances and hypnotic suggestion. Of course, the key suggestions will come from me."

"And what will those key suggestions be?"

"Jean, when you hypnotized me you asked me to entrust myself to you. Now I'm going to ask the same of you. If I told you what I'm going to do, I might create conscious resistance, but I can promise that you will enjoy your journey as much as I did mine."

"You're serious about this, aren't you?"

"Absolutely," she said, hoping she appeared more confident than she must look in her pink chenille robe. "Do you have a better offer?"

"Okay, now that you put it that way." He gave the room a questioning once-over. "Where do you want me?"

A short time later she had him stretched out in the rocker. She was grateful it could handle a man his size, although the chair was tilted so far back it could have been a recliner. She also arranged the computer monitor on the catalog tower so he could easily see the screen. The patterns oscillating on the screen were much like the ones that had mesmerized her.

"All I want you to do is breathe and relax," she said softly. "Listen to my voice and relax. Feel yourself breathing, feel how deep it goes with every breath, and go with it, deeper . . . deeper . . ."

"One condition," he said, his eyelids beginning to droop. "You can put me under but you have to wake me with a kiss."

She tried not to smile. "You drive a hard bargain."

Within moments his eyes were closed and his facial muscles had surrendered their tension. He appeared to be deeply relaxed and, hopefully, deeply suggestible, because her next step was to coach him on being open and receptive to everything she said. When she'd done that she would attempt the feat that she hoped would free him.

She studied his face in repose, admiring the sharp contrasts. Eyelashes as black as soot threw lyrical shadows over features set at dramatic right angles. She was especially drawn to the mouth she was going to kiss awake. He looked almost vulnerable, and she wasn't too comfortable with the idea of taking advantage of him in this way, but it was for a good cause. How else was she going to save him? There was no other option, and if her plan worked, she would explain it to him when this was over—and he was grateful, she hoped.

"As you listen to my voice," she said, "your mind is opening and expanding, and you are experiencing an emotion you've never felt before—a longing that is both deep and beautiful. Relax and let yourself feel it, Jean. Feel it awakening within you, this longing, rising like a flame. Something vital is missing, and you ache for it in every part of your being. It's the hunger in your heart and the fiery urgency in your loins. It runs like a flood through your soul, this need. Feel it, Jean. Let yourself feel it. You ache for the most essential element of life—a mate, a lover, someone to complete you, to fulfill you in every way possible . . . someone to thrill you . . ."

Kerry's mind flicked back to the way he'd aroused her the night before. Pleasure rippled through her, awakening a sensation in the deep reaches of her own belly. Her thighs tightened with that strange humming sensation. Her voice grew breathless.

"Someone who can make your heart leap painfully and send the blood searching through your veins," she whispered. "A woman who can bring you to your knees with a sigh and bring you awake with a kiss. To love her is the sweetest kind of madness, and yet you have no choice. You need this woman, this siren of your soul, and you need her now."

Kerry stopped herself, wondering what she was doing. The way her heart was pounding, she could have been spinning out her own fantasies. Was she programming him to want what she wanted? She cautioned herself not to say anything else, but the suggestions just kept tumbling out of her mouth . . . about how inflamed he was with longing, and how nothing would satisfy him except to make her his own.

"You must possess her, Jean, possess her or die of the longing . . ."

The rocker groaned, or was it him?

Kerry searched his features, aware of their sudden sensuality. His lips were parted and the heat rushing through them was steamy. Even his skin looked a little flushed.

What she had already done was nothing compared to what she had to do next. *Had to.* How could she suggest that he was falling in love and that love could save him, and not follow through with the rest of it? And anyway, she had a backup plan. If the hypnosis worked, and she freed him, she could put him back under later and erase the suggestions.

She traced her fingers over his lips, another irresistible impulse, and felt them quiver. Lord, what that did to her. She was humming everywhere.

"When you wake up, Jean," she said, "you will see the woman you've always loved, the woman you were born to be with . . . and the only one who can save you."

The hand that had touched him was shaking. This was the moment when she had to bring him back, but she was frightened.

Her heart ran riot as she bent to kiss him.

She brushed her lips over his, and a sound she couldn't control slipped out.

His lids flickered and came open. Maybe it was the

lashes, but Kerry didn't have a chance. She was instantly immersed in the dark pools that gazed up at her. He was supposed to be the one in a trance.

"Kerry?" He said her name as if he'd just discovered how softly it could be mouthed.

She didn't dare answer. Her voice would give her away.

"You're beautiful," he said, visually searching out every aspect. "I know I've said that before, but this is different, this I can't define."

"It's all right." She tried to stop him, but he caught a handful of her hair and drew her down for another kiss. His mouth touched hers with a force that was magically soft, yet frenzied. It was breathtaking. She was as dizzy as a child on a merry-go-round, and before she knew it, he'd pulled her right into the chair with him.

"Wait, Jean."

"Wait for what? My God, Kerry," he whispered, "can you feel what's happening? Can you feel what you do to me?"

She could feel plenty. She'd landed on top of him, and her chenille robe had come open. He was generously endowed in more places than just his mouth . . . and getting more generous all the time.

"Jean, I don't think—"

"That's right, Kerry, *don't think*. Don't think, just feel. Feel what's happening to me, feel what's happening to you."

She was vibrating. That's what was happening to her. It was no longer a pleasant humming sensation in the pit of her stomach. It was a powerful current, and she could feel it all the way to her fingertips. She was sprawled on top of him and half naked under the chenille robe, which had fallen open and was no protection at all. Neither were the skimpy tank top and French-cut panties.

What had she done? Created a monster, that's what she'd done.

He gazed at her through beautifully drugged lids, and his

hands closed around her waist to position her atop him. The way he moved her, willfully nestling her soft curves against his hard ones, sent a sharp thrill through her nether parts.

"Jean, do you think maybe we could talk first? Just for a minute?"

"No, Kerry, I must have you. It's not an option."

His features were dangerously dark. "I need to possess you in every way a man can possess a woman. Every way and everywhere."

"*Every*where?" Her thoughts went spinning to the hardness she'd landed on. His entire body was rock-solid, but the bulge between his legs could only be described as formidable. If what was happening there was any indication, then she was probably too small to be possessed *any*where, much less everywhere.

"Here," he said, caressing her mouth with his fingertips. He tickled her pensive expression into a sensitive smile. "These beautiful lips must be conquered and made soft and slack."

Next he traced a vibrant line down the length of her body to her hipbone, where he curved his thumb deeply into the hollow of her pelvis. "And *here*. This must be made wet and wanting."

There was no question what part he was referring to now. He meant the tender throb between her legs, but he didn't stop there. Kerry was stunned as he smiled and reached around to trace the delicate cleft.

No, not there! She would have tumbled off him if he hadn't caught her and held her firmly with his hands. His dark river of a voice nearly drowned her.

"Yes, Kerry, there and everywhere. This drive is too powerful to fight. Can't you feel it? Tell me that your tender body isn't aching to be penetrated in all the places I touched you. Tell me you don't ache."

She did. God, she did.

She closed her eyes and felt herself swaying with the

chair. He brought her back with those persuasive, possessive hands. *What was happening?* If this was the perfect fantasy he promised, then was he the perpetually erect male slave or the plundering highwayman? *Maybe a little of both.*

The rocking chair crooned softly with each movement.

"Come to me," he said.

She'd given him no choice when she hypnotized him. Now it felt as if *she* had none. Her needs were too raw. This ache was too great.

He clasped her by the thighs and guided her to a kneeling position. As her knees came forward and her body came up, she found herself straddling him at the juncture of his thighs. Now she was even more intimately pressed against the molten steel in his pants. Her legs were spread wide, her sex parts shyly kissing his.

The gentle sway of the chair created a steady, glorious friction. It hit her all at once that he was going to make love to her that way, rocking her deeply into orgasm after orgasm. She would straddle him, fully penetrated by his hardness, and rock until she dropped.

Even more shocking, she wanted it that way. She wanted it as urgently as he did. But when she tried to take off her robe, he wouldn't let her, and it became clear that he had something else in mind.

"Wrap your legs around my waist," he told her.

He lifted her into his lap, and once she was settled there, he rose from the chair and took her with him, robe and all. His hands were cupping her bottom, and Kerry thought she would die, it was so erotic. The steam heat of his palms, the placement of his fingers near her most intimate parts. If he moved a hair's breadth, he would be molesting her.

Her thighs clenched tightly against him as she wondered where this reckless act of possession would take place. On the coffee table? Against the wall?

Where would he take her?

But he turned, and she found herself back in the rocking

chair, arranged in the most exotic way imaginable. Her robe was hanging open, her arm was flung above her head and long, pale legs were draped over the arms of the chair. The fact that she was wearing panties made little difference now. She was completely exposed to his view, to his whim. He set the chair rocking, then sank to his knees and savored her from that angle, as if he were imagining every forbidden delight known to man.

Her poor mind was riveted on a single thought. *Just look what she'd done with her hypnotic suggestions . . . just look!*

As the chair rocked up, he blew a kiss to the soft pink crotch of her panties. A strange little sound caught in her throat. She tightened with anticipation. He let the chair swing freely for a moment, then caught it and held her there, held her in thrall as he bent over her and aroused her through her panties with feathery touches of his lips and tongue.

If she had a secret garden, then this was a dragonfly, touching down. She could barely feel him and it was the most erotic sensation imaginable. If he stopped, she would die. If he didn't, she would die.

"It's too light," she whispered, "too light, I can't bear it."

But she couldn't be heard over the moaning of the chair, and apparently Jean wasn't inclined to stop anyway. Certainly not in the way that she meant. He actually caught the crotch of her panties between his teeth and pulled the material out, letting air rush into the heat between her legs.

Kerry arched in surprise. Her legs were suspended in the air for a second, and it felt as if the dragonfly were inside her now, gossamer wings beating.

"I don't know what will happen if you don't stop . . ."

"I do."

The chair groaned as he released it, letting it rock gently back and forth.

Kerry groaned too as his tongue slid up and down the most sensitive part of her anatomy. The way it languidly swirled, she could have been an ice-cream cone or a cloud of cotton candy. What an exquisite thrill that was, like the point of a baton lightly riding the sole of the foot. His mouth was an instrument of sweet torture. Deep muscles fluttered tightly, and she could feel dampness seeping through her panties.

"Can't bear—" was all she got out. The rest of it died in her throat as he gathered her up in his arms. He kissed her lips lightly, and when she made a sound of distress, he kissed her deeply. Kissed her to her very soul.

"Now I want you on *your* knees," he told her under his breath.

She assumed they would exchange places, and that he would be the cotton candy, but if she was learning anything in this adventure with him, it was not to assume. There was a lovely old Aubusson carpet on the living room floor by the window, and they ended up there, with Jean lying on his back and Kerry on her knees at his head. Her panties and robe were gone now, draped over the rocker, but she was still wearing her tank top, and her breasts were hotly excited. It was sheer nervous anticipation. He hadn't even touched her there, and yet her nipples were flushed and taut. Every shiver rustled the silky tank top against her skin. Every shiver set her more on edge.

He spread her open above him with his fingers, and then he inched her legs wider and wider, bringing her down to his mouth. The tension was fierce and wonderful. Her thighs shook as he tongued her softly and with the eloquence of a maestro. She raised her arms above her and cried out softly, barely aware of how she must look, like a penitent, begging for mercy.

The first orgasm that shook her brought her to her hands and knees. By the second, she couldn't control the tremors anymore. She crumpled to her elbows and then fell onto her side, next to him. He gathered her close with his arm, and she drifted off, into some kind of ecstasy, floating . . . floating. Some time later she felt him easing from beneath her. She drifted again, and when she awoke next, she was aware that he had rolled her onto her stomach, and that he was above her, possibly even astride her, whispering into her hair.

"Stay just as you are," he said, "I'm going to take you this way."

Somewhere inside Kerry was a barely discernible bleat of alarm. It was a frantic little sound that brought Jean close, whispering and touching her soothingly. Apparently he thought he'd frightened her. And he had. But she was also stirred to the depths of her being.

Kerry wondered if she was still breathing.

He moved over her, and his weight awakened something primitive within her, a mating response. His hands were in the hair at her nape, lifting, sifting. It was glorious. She felt his hardness pressing into her thigh and she responded helplessly, lifting her hips in enticement. It was an involuntary response. She wanted him in the most ancient, urgent way a female can want a male. She wanted him there, now, deeply and fast.

She heard the soft whine of a zipper being opened, and her whole body contracted. The familiar feel of denim against her bare legs told her that he hadn't removed his clothes—and that he wasn't going to. This was more than an act of possession, it was ravishment, and he was neither a highwayman nor a slave. He was a phantom lover who would steal his way into her heart, as well as her body. He would hold her in thrall until he'd stolen everything . . . even her naked, quaking soul. Especially that.

"Stay just as you are," he whispered again. "Utterly still."

She tried, but it was nearly impossible not to quiver as he brushed his lips over her uptilted derriere. A hand slipped through the seam of her thighs and lightly caressed her where she was hot and tingling. Wetness gushed at his touch, and nothing more was needed. She was wild to be entered.

"Rock back as if you were still in the chair," he told her.

He guided her with his hands, and she did exactly as he said. She swung her hips and tasted ecstasy. Tasted him.

He took her there, now, deeply . . . and slow.

It was the sweetest pressure in life, a sensation of being possessed and released all at once. Kerry surrendered herself with barely a whimper, shuddering helplessly at the lush thrill of penetration. He thrust into her reaches as smoothly as a hand into a snug velvet glove, and she tightened immediately. Tightened and quivered at the same time. *Possessed and released at the same time.* From the moment he entered her, she was floating in a sea of sensation, a shimmering world of light and sound.

It was delirious. She made pleading noises, unable to help herself. He was weight and darkness and the source of all pleasure. He was everything at that moment. She would be nothing without him. He couldn't leave her. This couldn't end. Even as the floodtide hit her and she knew that she was in the last throes, that this pleasure could not go on forever, she also knew that she had changed. Her body had changed, simply from this one act of possession. Her mind, her spirit, everything had been changed in some way, and she could never go back.

"Our journey isn't over, Kerry."

It will never be, she thought. And when he turned her on her back, she reached for him. They rushed to reconnect in the most intimate way possible, clinging mouths and yearning limbs, all pining for unity and oneness, and she told herself then that he would never leave her. If he felt anything like she did, he never could.

The first time she woke up, she realized they were still on the floor, and he was holding her. "We can't stay this way," he said. "Let me take you to bed."

"No, not the bed, the rocker."

"You want to be in the chair?"

"Yes, with you. We can cover ourselves with blankets and rock until we fall asleep. Please."

He gathered her up and gently settled her in the soft leather cradle, then got a comforter from the bedroom and joined her. When they were all bundled up and she was blissfully pressed next to him, her leg draped over his thighs, she wondered if this was what it was supposed to be like between men and women. She'd never had anything like this. She felt whole for the first time in her life.

He'd said he was missing something. It had to be this.

She couldn't ask the question that meant everything— Are you free, Jean? Did it work? But fortunately, there was another one.

Her mouth was so dry it was hard to speak. "You said there were things that men could only learn from women. What things, Jean?"

He shivered as she lightly raked her fingers through his chest hair.

"How to touch like this?" she asked. "How to be tender?"

He rested his chin against her forehead, and she could hear him breathing. She could almost hear him thinking.

"It's not about giving as much as it is about receiving," he said. "Women teach men how to *receive* tenderness— and other things, like love."

His mouth must be dry too. His voice was grainy and thrilling.

"You taught me something important tonight, Kerry."

"I did?" She looked up at him, aware that she couldn't swallow. It was virtually impossible to swallow. Could you die from that? she wondered.

"It's not about success or personal power or even courage," he said. "Those things keep a man enslaved. It's about love. That's what sets his soul free."

It's about love.

Now she didn't need to ask the other question. It must have worked. He must be free of the curse, and she had been a part of it. She'd given him the key to unlock the cage. Now, for the first time in her life, she could sleep through the night in a man's sheltering embrace, dream in his arms, and believe that he would be there.

The journey was over. Her life had only begun.

Chapter Seven

Several moments passed before Kerry knew where she was. The gentle rocking motion conjured thoughts of a boat, anchored in a harbor . . . and then she opened her eyes. Her living room was cast in a bluish haze, but it was light coming from the window, not a TV or computer screen.

Dawn, she realized. The sun was coming up, not going down.

And she was alone.

She pushed off the comforter, wondering if Jean had gone to the kitchen for something to eat. The unsteadiness she felt as her feet hit the floor brought a vivid reminder of the surreal experiences of the night before. She was still shaking; it was that intense. She could hardly believe it had happened. Certainly nothing like that had ever happened to her before.

Her pink robe was in a heap on the floor, but she didn't bother with it. She was too anxious about where he was. Too anxious even to call his name. *Please don't let him be gone again,* she thought. *Don't do that to me. It would be too cruel, like tormenting an animal at the zoo.*

Her kitchen was hazed with blue, too, and a pinprick of fear touched her when she realized he wasn't there, either. The breakfast nook looked out on her snowed-covered backyard, as well as the garage apartment, where Malcolm lived. There was no sign of her tenant or anyone else, although she wouldn't have expected to see Malcolm. He worked at an assembly plant during the day, and whether he was at home or not, his blinds were always tightly closed.

Kerry's mouth had gone dry with excitement the night before. Now it was coppery, bitter. She already knew what she was going to find when she went to the bedroom, but she had to go anyway. A desperate feeling came over her as she scurried through the living room, knowing it was hopeless. *He was gone.*

The entire house looked alien to her. The place that had given her comfort and refuge now gave her nothing but torment because he wasn't there.

"Oh, God," she whispered, "this can't be happening. It is *too* cruel."

Her bedroom was the proof she dreaded. It was exactly as she'd left it, the sheets thrown back the way they were when she'd crept out of bed to investigate the noise. Her bathroom looked untouched, too. There was no trace of him anywhere. Other than her robe on the floor, she couldn't find evidence that he'd ever been there.

Under her breath, she said, "No one has dreams like that."

She stared at the Aubusson carpet with a growing sense of horror. Was she delusional now? She couldn't tell this story to anyone. It would have sounded like the ramblings of a madwoman. But Jean was as real to her as her own heartbeat. Either she hadn't freed him with her ridiculous plan, or she had, and he had better things to do than hang around with a housebound crazy.

She turned in the room, searching for answers that were becoming more incredible than the questions. Maybe his curse required that he pass more than one test, and this was only the first. Now that he'd conquered the maiden, he had to go out and fight a dragon or something. And maybe Kerry Houston really *was* in need of antipsychotic medication.

"Our journey isn't over, Kerry."

She spun around, thinking it was Jean behind her. Someone had spoken, hadn't they? But there was no one there. The sensation that ran up her spine was like an icy breath of air. She clutched her arms and held herself, fighting the pain that flared every time she tried to breathe. What was it he couldn't feel? He had shuddered in her arms and told her that love could free him. What deeper emotion was there than that? She didn't believe the feeling he spoke of existed. It couldn't.

Her body quailed with another chill.

"Damn, drafty old house." She was freezing, but that wasn't causing her to quake from head to toe. It was despair. Despair and a burning sadness. She had to sell this place. She couldn't live here any longer. The neighborhood had gone to pot and taken her along with it. Even her grandparents wouldn't want her to be here now, not like this. How she would get through the ordeal of packing up and moving out when she couldn't even get through her door was beyond her. But if she didn't do something, they would soon be coming for her with a net.

Gooseflesh needled her bare arms and legs.

That was when she realized she was standing in her living room half naked He'd left her in nothing but a tank top, and she was *still* in nothing but a tank top. The awareness nearly made her ill. It was symbolic of her downfall, of the whole mess. It shouted at her that she wasn't just an emotional wreck, she was guilty of frighteningly bad judgment and worse. She'd given in to dangerous urges with a man she didn't even know, possibly at the risk of her life, certainly at the risk of her sanity. Who knew what he might have done to her? Or who he might have been? On a sliding scale of moral character, you couldn't slide much lower than that.

Real or not, he's gone, Kerry, and you're a fool for believing . . . in anything. She rushed back into the bedroom, vowing to put on her three layers of clothing and never take them off. That was when the tears started.

*   *   *

Kerry was sorting through her kitchen cabinets and tossing out old pots and pans when she heard the commotion out front. It sounded like shouting. Probably another fight breaking out, she decided, and went right on sorting. Did she take her grandmother's old cast-iron skillet or not? It was heavier than lead weights, but the sentimental value was great. She put the skillet in the pile to be packed, wondering when she'd become one of those people who turned a deaf ear to the chaos on the streets.

The shouting got louder, and something about the voices caught her attention. One of them was familiar.

Empty packing boxes tumbled over as she dodged through them and headed for the living room's bay window. Outside, the neighborhood thugs had circled an elderly man like a pack of dogs and they were harassing him. Kerry rushed to call 911, even though she was afraid it wouldn't do any good. By the time the police got there, the victim would be mugged and beaten or possibly dead. It had happened to her, and no one had come to her aid.

She hit the Talk button, but couldn't get a dial tone. Either the lines were out or her batteries were dead again. The phone had never worked right, and there was no time to investigate the problem. The harassing had turned into a full-fledged attack and the old man had been overpowered.

"Malcolm?" Kerry saw him fall to the ground and realized who he was. It was her tenant being bludgeoned. "Malcolm!"

She ran back to the kitchen and grandma's skillet. The baseball bat would probably do more damage, but there was no time. There were four or five of them. If she could back a couple of them off, Malcolm might be able to get to his feet.

She shrieked "Fire!" as she ran out the door, and kept shrieking it. When the thugs turned to look, Malcolm struggled to get up, and Kerry began to swing for all she was worth. She didn't hit anyone, but she cut a swath through them, and she was coming back around when she heard Malcolm shouting at his attackers.

"Back off!" he bellowed.

Kerry turned just as he pulled a deadly looking revolver from his coat.

Two of the thugs lunged at the exact moment that the gun's hammer clicked. It was an explosive sound, and they did back off. Immediately. Within moments the entire pack had begun to retreat.

Kerry waited until they were out of earshot before she turned to her tenant. "Malcolm? You have a gun?"

"It's a cap pistol," he said, "but keep it to yourself."

Kerry's grin died on her lips when she saw the real reason the thugs were leaving the scene. It wasn't because of Malcolm's cap pistol. A second gang was approaching, and these were the hoodlums who'd assaulted her. Fear slammed into her like a fist as she remembered the way they'd terrorized her. She even recognized the ringleader, a vicious punk called Axe.

Axe confronted Malcolm with an insolent smirk. "You could hurt yourself with a gun that big, bozo."

"Or I could hurt you," Malcolm declared quietly.

Kerry was surprised at her tenant's soft menace.

Axe's laughter incited the gang to catcalls, but Malcolm seemed unfazed. He was outnumbered and out-armed, but if he was frightened, he didn't let on. This wasn't the Malcolm who assailed her daily with dire news of the world outside her door.

Suddenly the thug nearest Kerry pulled a knife.

"Drop the gun or she's dead!" he shouted.

He dragged Kerry into a choke hold that nearly cut off her breathing. She could feel the knife blade at her stomach, and she went deathly still. She had the skillet, but apparently her assailant didn't consider it—or her—a threat. She was a convenient means to his end, whatever that might be.

A siren began to wail, and the thugs looked around for a

police car. That was all the advantage Malcolm needed. He grabbed the skillet from Kerry's hand and waylaid two of them before they knew what hit them. The arm clamped to Kerry's neck released, and she was free. Her attacker ducked as the skillet whistled passed his shaved skull.

Malcolm was a demon possessed. Within moments he had cleared out every gang member but Axe. The ringleader reached into his boot for a knife, and Malcolm clipped him with an uppercut. On the way down, Axe grabbed Malcolm's ankle and they both dropped.

Kerry picked up the skillet, but they were rolling and thrashing to get the knife, and she couldn't tell where to strike. Fists flew and they grappled like wrestlers. She winced as Malcolm's head hit the pavement, but finally it was Axe who slumped to the ground, out cold.

"You're hurt!" Kerry knelt next to Malcolm's sprawled form. He seemed to be conscious, but blood gushed from a deep cut above his brow.

"A scalp wound," he got out. "It's superficial."

Kerry hoped it was as she tugged on the sleeve of her sweater and used it to blot his face. She wanted to tell him how incredible he was, and how grateful she was for what he'd done. He'd saved her life. But she knew it would embarrass him. He was such an unpredictable man. She would never have expected this of him, not an act of outright heroism.

She was still cleaning him up when Axe began to regain consciousness. Instantly another siren went off. It whooped and wailed so loudly that Axe labored to his feet and fled.

Malcolm pulled a tiny battery-operated case from his coat pocket. He pressed a button and the siren stopped.

"You were the police car?" The noise vaguely reminded Kerry of the sirens that had gone off when she was wearing the finger glove.

A light snow had started to fall and Kerry had no coat. Malcolm heaved himself up and struggled out of his. He draped it over her shoulders. Again, Kerry was surprised and touched. There was something fundamentally different about her neighbor, but she couldn't figure out what it was.

"Are you okay?" she asked.

"Kerry, there's something I have to tell you."

"What's wrong?"

"Wait—" He was trying to pull off his knit cap, but his hands were shaking. Kerry wanted to help him, but he wouldn't let her. He seemed bound and determined to handle it himself, and when he had the cap off, he began to yank at his beard.

He ripped off the bushy patch right in front of her eyes. His moustache went next.

They weren't real, she realized. The beard and moustache were fakes.

Kerry stared at him, totally stunned. Without the props, Malcolm looked a little like— No, that was impossible.

"*Jean?*" she whispered. "Is that you? What are you doing dressed up like Malcolm?"

"Kerry, listen to me," he said. "Before you say anything or do anything, give me a chance to explain. Promise you'll do that much."

Kerry didn't know whether to nod or shake her head. It took him a minute to get to his feet, but that wasn't nearly enough time to collect her thoughts.

"My name is Joe Gamble," he said.

"What?" She staggered backward and lost her balance. A slippery patch sent her feet out from under her and she landed on the bottom step of her stoop, which, fortunately, was cushioned by a thin layer of snow. Now she *couldn't* say or do anything, but it had nothing to do with the fall she'd taken.

The man she was staring at wasn't Malcolm, her tenant. He wasn't Jean Valjean, her fantasy. He wasn't even Starman. He was the CEO of Genesis Software, and her former boss. He was the straw who'd broken Kerry Houston's back!

* * *

"Jean, Joe—whatever your name is—how could you do this? How could you take advantage of another human being like this?"

Kerry was up and pacing. She turned in the street and faced him. The snow was still falling, and her breath was a lacy white mist. But she wasn't cold. For the first time in ages, she wasn't cold.

"You deceived me," she told him. "You've done nothing *but* deceive me."

Joe Gamble was holding a handful of snow to the cut on his forehead. He looked like someone had been using him for a punching bag, which they had. Still, he was roguishly handsome in a brainy sort of way. A thinking woman's roughneck, she decided. She could see a faint resemblance to the bearded adventurer she'd met at the picnic, but she wouldn't have been able to pick him out in a lineup.

"I wanted to help," he said.

"You wanted to help? Who? *Me?* Dear God, what if you'd been trying to harm me?"

He winced, but Kerry couldn't tell if it was his head or his conscience that hurt him.

"I messed up," he said. "I admit it, I messed up badly. But don't I get a little credit for trying?"

"What was it you were trying to do? Traumatize me for life?"

He looked up carefully, one eye squeezed shut. "I was trying to set you free, Kerry. Not unlike the way you, well—deceived me, trying to set me free."

There were several things she wanted to contradict in that statement. She went for the last and most obvious.

"I didn't deceive you," she declared. "No way."

His slitty, one-eyed stare said otherwise.

"You're saying I did? When?" She was shaking her head when it hit her. "You mean when I hypnotized you and suggested that you were in love with me? You mean like that?"

"I mean like that. You said that loving you was the *only*

way to save me, and among other things, you whispered in my ear that my loins were aflame and my heart was hungry. 'Possess her or die of the longing.' Remember that one, Kerry? You had a field day with my poor, unsuspecting, unconscious mind."

"Yes, but I was only . . . trying to help."

"My point exactly. So was I."

He took the snow away and she could see his eyes—beautiful eyes, Jean's eyes, fire stirring in them like embers in dark ashes. The fluttering sensation was back, only it was her stomach this time, and it felt more like little white moths than dragonflies. There were millions of them. Moths in a frenzy. Moths in search of a naked porch light. Silly, silly moths.

"As it turns out, you were right," he said. "There *was* no other way to save me."

The moths went nuts at that one. It seemed they'd found their naked bulb. Him. Could she possibly have heard him right? Was he saying that he loved her? Love, the L word? No, she couldn't have heard him right. She was always hearing voices and this was another one—confusing her, tormenting her, saying everything she'd ever wanted to hear.

Kerry refused to let herself react in any obvious way. She'd exposed far too much to this man who'd said he was cursed. How could he have done that?

"How could you do that?" she whispered.

He started to answer, but she shook her head. He didn't even sound like Jean anymore. He sounded like Phil, the Human Resources guy from Genesis, and that was because he *was* Phil. And Malcolm. And George, the video game's creator. And probably Starman. He'd admitted taking on all those personas to try and get through to her. He was desperate to "break through The Great Wall of Kerry" was how he'd put it. He'd even admitted to altering his voice via some high-tech device so that she wouldn't recognize him as the different men.

But why? Why would anybody want to get to Kerry Houston that badly?

The thought that this might be some kind of prank, and that she could be fodder for the office gossips again, was devastating. Too devastating to bear.

"I won't be the butt of another one of your jokes," she blurted, turning away from him.

"Kerry, this isn't a joke. Whatever made you think that?"

"That humiliating E-mail I sent you before I left Genesis. You didn't even have the courage to come and tell me yourself what you thought of me. You sent your assistant to do your dirty work."

"I never got the E-mail," he said. "Apparently my assistant intercepted it and took it upon herself to deal with you. 'For the good of the company' was the way she put it. When I found out what she'd done, I fired her on the spot."

"You fired her?" Kerry's voice was faint. "And you didn't tell me?"

"How could I tell you when you wouldn't talk to me? The first time I called, you hung up on me. The second time you said if I wanted to sue you I should call your attorney, and then you hung up on me. After that, you wouldn't take my calls at all, so I became Phil."

"Phil, with the simmering pot of a voice," she murmured.

"Excuse me?"

"Nothing."

"You made it clear that you didn't want anything to do with me or Genesis, except as a game tester. Maybe I should have let it go at that, but I couldn't. I'd seen you on the videotapes, and I was smitten."

"Smitten by what? My beauty, my wit or my social graces?" Okay, so she didn't *quite* believe him.

The closer he got, the more Kerry backed up.

"Listen," he said heatedly, "you were dynamite in those sessions, and I wanted you back. I thought it was for the company, but after Jean came to life the first time, I knew it was for me."

Pain stabbed her. Jean. He was Jean, and she had cared about him.

"Congratulations, man of many voices," she said. "You really suckered me good. You actually had me convinced that Jean was cursed and needed me to set him free. How stupid, huh?"

"It wasn't Jean who needed you, it was me. I'd lost my passion for anything but work, and believe me, that's its own kind of curse."

"You were never cursed," she protested hotly. "Your life is blessed. You have everything."

"When there's no feeling attached to what you have, it's meaningless. Everything is *nothing*.

"What I did was wrong," he admitted. "I concocted this whole elaborate fairy tale to get close to you, and obviously I got carried away with the poetry of my plan. I've been known to do that."

The breath he took sounded like a sigh, a weary one. "The truth is, I was worried about you. This neighborhood isn't safe, and you were all by yourself in the house. I wanted to be around in case you got into trouble, so I invented Malcolm. That's when I realized what was really going on, that you were trapped."

Recognition dawned. "So you pretended to be trapped yourself, as Jean?"

He nodded. "I thought if it became your goal to free Jean, you might be able to get past your own fears. But I didn't realize what it was going to take until Malcolm spoke up in your living room that day. He surprised me as much as he did you."

Kerry remembered it word for word. "'You'll let go of your fear when something is more important to you than your fear.'"

"That's when I knew something was going to happen to

Malcolm, something bad. It had to be more important to you than your fear, and I figured if you thought Malcolm was in trouble, you'd stop at nothing."

She stared at him, confused. "But he *was* in trouble."

"Well . . . no, not at first. Those were some kids I bribed to make it look like they were roughing me up. What I didn't count on was the second gang. They were the real thing, and when I saw that punk grab you and pull a knife. . . . God—"

The words balled up in his throat. Muscles locked powerfully, struggling with some unexpected emotion, some savage emotion. "The thought that I'd endangered you when all I wanted to do was protect you—"

Kerry didn't know what to say, but she couldn't let him go on.

He looked away and roughly cleared his throat. "Last night I told you that you'd taught me something important, but I didn't really know what that meant until now. I had to almost lose someone I loved to understand."

"Joe, don't—"

"I felt it to my soul, Kerry. When I thought I'd lost you, I . . ."

He didn't finish, but Kerry knew what he was going to say. And she knew what he was feeling for the first time. There was an emotion welling inside her, too, a new emotion. It was piercingly sweet.

A snowflake landed on her lashes and melted away like a tear.

"I told you I was cursed," he said. "I don't expect you to forgive me for invading your life like this." He looked up, apparently resigned to his fate, whatever that might be. "I'm not asking that, but whatever happens, it's almost worth it to see you this way. Outside like this."

"Oh, my God," Kerry whispered, realizing where she was for the first time. "I'm outside."

Her heart began to race, and she reached out involuntarily. His hand caught hers, and she squeezed it hard enough to cut off his circulation. Any minute now she would fall to her knees because she couldn't walk. She could almost see herself crawling to the stoop. She would never make it back into the house. *What was she doing out here?*

"Let me help you," he said.

He tried to lead her to the steps, but she held him off. She had to do this herself, and she wasn't running back inside. She had fought off thugs in the street without giving it a thought, and she would fight her way out of this.

"Breathe."

He said the very word that she was thinking, and his voice was as hushed as the falling snow. It cut through her rising panic and spoke to the urgency inside her. Instead of struggling with the sensations, Kerry stopped and drew in a breath, and even that first draught of air had a calming effect. The second restored her thought processes, the third her voice.

He was good. Maybe he was even good for her. The way she figured it she was probably going to have to take a chance on that.

"Did you mean it about me being dynamite in those sessions?" she asked him accusingly.

He nodded. "I meant it, Kerry. You are a force of nature."

"And did you mean it about not wanting to live like a normal man if you couldn't have me?"

"I did."

She still wasn't at all sure she ought to forgive him. He had gone to elaborate lengths to deceive her, and yet when she tried to imagine life without Joe Gamble, it made her want to shudder . . . to her soul.

Make your wish with an open heart, because only open hearts can receive.

Kerry's lips curved into a smile as bittersweet as Joe's. *Grandpa*, she thought, *if you had anything to do with this, it worked.*

She reached for Joe, and he pulled her into his arms.

They kissed under a veil of new snow, and the last thing Kerry saw before she closed her eyes was the couple in Lover's Park. She had always wondered how it would feel to be that much in love, and now she would have her chance to find out. This was the beginning of a new journey, and Kerry Houston, perhaps the most unlikely of winter lovers, would not be making it alone.

No Mercy

Thea Devine

Chapter One

Deep in the night, when plans and schemes and desires and dreams seem within the realm of possibility, what is the one thing a woman wants above everything else?

A pair of Mascolo five-inch stiletto heels digging into the prostrate body of the one man who got away.

And Regan Torrance was not immune to the allure and the attraction of a Mascolo fantasy, real or imagined, especially when the two collided in the form of The Shoes flung carelessly in the window of the exclusive east side Mascolo shop with the words On Sale in seductive gold letters across the bottom of the display.

"Ang . . ." she called to her former sister-in-law who was already several yards ahead of her and utterly unaware that she wasn't following. "*Ang—*"

Angie stopped, turned, groaned, and started back toward Regan. "Oh, Regan, we don't have time for—" She stopped short as she saw Regan's expression and where she was standing. "Don't tell me—"

"I'm telling you." Regan shook herself. "C'mon." She pushed open the door and stepped down into the elegant, minimally decorated shop, with its burnished mahogany wall that showcased the most outrageous and expensive shoes on elegant ledges.

"Don't you have a Mascolo fantasy?" Regan asked, picking up the shoe in question, a black satin sandal with a sky-scraper heel and crisscrossed straps studded with crystals, and handing it to the discreet saleswoman. "Size seven please."

"Yeah," Angie said. "It's called a bank account. I add to it every time I *don't* buy a pair of Mascolos. You're not planning to wear those things in public, are you?"

"Maybe tonight," Regan said, sounding slightly distracted as she browsed through the several other styles that were on sale.

"Jesus. Tony'll go nuts."

"You think so?" The saleswoman returned with the shoes and Regan sat down, kicked off her own inch-heeled pumps, and reverently slipped them on.

"I think I don't know how you're going to walk in those things."

"Oh, it's easy," Regan said airily, levering herself to her feet, a little unsteadily. "You just . . . Just do the model walk thing." God, she felt like she was walking on stilts. The "things" lifted her as high in the air as a crane, and putting one foot in front of the other instantly became a logistical nightmare of trying to look good while balancing on the head of a needle.

"See—?" She wobbled a little. But, Lord, they were the epitome of *fuck me* shoes, the kind you wore barefoot with deep red nail polish.

"Sure, I'll just get your bustier and whip."

"Just what I planned to wear tonight," Regan murmured.

"Oh, yeah, Ms. All Business All The Time who never walks out of the house in anything but a suit and practical shoes?"

Regan wasn't responding. Angie paused in her tirade and slanted her a look. "You're serious, aren't you?"

"Sure am. I've coveted these little babies for months. And now that Tony's finally promoted me, I'm going to celebrate for all I'm worth and dress like I'm worth it."

"Wait till you see the bill for those things. It'll take all you're worth," Angie muttered as Regan slipped off the shoes and indicated she wanted them.

"Anyone who walks in here knows the price they have to pay," she said gently. And stumbling onto a sale was just icing on the cake, pure synchronistic luck, when she'd been considering paying full price for them. Which didn't mitigate the fact she was still signing a charge slip for just over three hundred dollars, but what was the point of being successful if the money didn't buy you the things you wanted?

And she was successful. Tonight was a celebration of just how far she'd come: Regan Torrance, the girl from the wrong side of town, the young ex-wife of Bobby Torrance, the now well-known media mogul and her ex-husband of seven years; and she herself, a top real estate agent, who, along with Tony Mackey, and his real estate agency, had been instrumental in developing Riverside Heights, the sleepy enclave just north of Manhattan, into the hip and happening place to live.

It didn't take long, once the prices for a Manhattan apartment soared into the stratosphere. The Heights had apartments to spare, and undervalued and roomy homes built in the twenties. And low taxes. And an underutilized waterfront. Not to mention proximity to highways for that East Hampton weekend or that skiing vacation in Vermont. The same highways on which Bobby Torrance rode out of town seven years before, after their divorce.

A lot had changed in seven years. The Heights had become a suburb of elegant homes, roomy apartments with priceless vistas over the Hudson River, trendy restaurants, name-brand shopping, and seasonal waterfront events to take advantage of the new park and facilities that had been built under the auspices and sponsorship of the Mackey brokerage firm.

And now it was time to bring in big business, to offer them what they were finding on the other side of the Hudson—low-cost space and lower taxes—and that was to be Regan's purview. That was what she was celebrating: increased responsibility, more money, and the excitement of the chase.

Especially more money. And the chase. She just loved the chase. There was something about getting there first and closing the deal that was as satisfying as good sex. And thank heaven for that, because there hadn't been any good sex for a long time.

Not that there hadn't been offers. Not that she wasn't looking.

She shook off the thought. Not to think about that now. She took the elegant Mascolo bag from the salesperson. "Ang..."

"I'm there."

And that was the eloquent punctuation that defined her relationship to her former sister-in-law: Angie was there, always there, never ever talking about Bobby, never taking sides, somehow keeping her brother separate from her friendship with his ex-wife, and how she'd done it all these years, Regan didn't know. But they never talked about Bobby, and she had to assume that Angie didn't talk to Bobby about her, either.

If Bobby ever came for a visit, Regan never knew about it. He had been discreet and invisible since the divorce. The stormy year she'd spent with him seemed, in retrospect, like a bad novel she'd read, and she'd had no contact with his family, barring Angie, in all that time.

"You have a dress to wear with those stilts?" Angie asked as they walked briskly toward the subway.

"What time am I supposed to be at Mary's?"

"Six o'clock for drinks and hors d'oeuvres. Buffet dinner at seven-fifteenish. I think there's a cake. You know Mary. If she can go over the top, she'll jump the barricade."

"She's Tony's sister."

"She'd like to be your *other* sister-in-law," Angie said trenchantly.

Regan knew it. It was nothing they hadn't discussed

many times before. Nothing Angie hadn't said before, either. But tonight was tonight: the crest of a rolling wave of new money and increased interest in the Heights, and a time when they were all euphoric over annual sales, and the possibility of major expansion into the commercial market.

So Tony was thinking about other possibilities, too.

Again.

She could be certain it would come up again: the partnership, monetary and personal, the thing that rumbled through and underpinned her whole working life at the Mackey agency.

"That won't come up tonight," Regan said firmly, as if saying it would make it so.

"It doesn't have to. It's in the air all the time. The way Tony looks at you. The things he says. The way he treats you. Why don't you just say yes?"

"I don't know what the question is."

"Sure you do. That's what those shoes are about. You're sending him a signal as clearly as if you'd issued an invitation."

Was she? She'd made such a point about being businesslike all these years. Only on off hours or when they were entertaining clients did she *dress*. Only in her dreams did she wear sexy, strappy Mascolo stilettos. And not much else.

She kept her buttoned-down business life separate from her unbuttoned home life, and her fantasies were nobody's business, not even Angie's. And never Tony's. Not ever. Not even in gratitude for how much she owed him. And his father. For taking in the notorious Regan Torrance and making her respectable.

Hell, this was a celebration, the dawn of a new chapter in the history of the firm. Angie was making too much of it. One impulsive pair of five-inch heels. It *wasn't* unlike her. Angie didn't have a clue what was unlike her. In fact, Mascolo shoes were *exactly* like her—the *her* that she bound up in pinstriped suits and silk blouses. The *her* of the slender body covered over by long jackets and knee-length skirts, and skin-toned panty hose—or black, if she were wearing black—and sensible shoes. Low key makeup and pulled back hair.

That *her*—the caged lioness. The one who reined in her impulses and controlled her libido, and only let it hang out in private and on rare occasions late at night.

She'd learned her lesson all those years ago, married to the possessive Bobby Torrance who wasn't nearly as sexually mature at age twenty-four as she was at twenty. Gorgeous Bobby Torrance, in jeans and leather, big-time bad boy, born to wealth and privilege, who always got what he wanted.

And he'd wanted *her*—with her smoky blue eyes and tumble of midnight-black hair, her long, long legs and voluptuous body, and high-voltage sexuality that burned everyone in its orbit.

Bobby was going to teach her everything.

But she discovered too soon that Bobby was not nearly as experienced as she thought. Not nearly as knowledgeable. Not nearly enough.

Greedy Regan. Old man Torrance, deceased now, willing to buy her off to get her out of Bobby's life. Whatever she wanted—Money? Cars? Clothes? All of that and more? A new life for her parents, still living in poverty on the wrong side of town?

Oh, he had been ruthless, the old man, and she'd gotten no end of enjoyment out of defying him.

How could she have known then that Bobby wasn't perfect, that his jealousy was like a piston, pumping him, pushing him, driving him, and ultimately driving her away, and that their life together would nearly destroy them both?

Not the time to think about Bobby. He was long gone, off to conquer the world, and he had done it too; and the only thing she'd asked for in the divorce settlement was enough money to go to school.

"That's not what this is about," Regan added emphatically, shaking off the memories. This wasn't the time to *dwell*.

But if Angie thought it was about Tony's long-suppressed desire, then likely so would Tony, and it meant that she would have to put the Mascolos in the back of her closet with the rest of her fantasies, and once again rein herself in, and come more *appropriately* dressed to Mary's party.

Her party, damn it.

"I think you should go for it," Angie said. "Put the guy out of his misery. He's been in love with you ever since you walked in the front door seven years ago. You put him through hell during *that* year, and you've kept him dangling since, and he deserves to be rewarded."

"What are you, his PR person or something?"

"No," Angie said. "Just someone who wants to see you happy."

"I'm happy. Couldn't be happier." Maybe a little happier? Maybe some love in her life? No. Not love. Love hurt too much. Love sapped you and drained you and left you in pain.

Only she had never found the right partner.

Bobby could have been the right partner.

No. No. She hated that she was still thinking that way. She had to wipe that thought from her mind—this instant.

"Oh, yeah, you're dancing for joy."

"Tonight I will be," Regan said firmly. "Tonight is the first night of the rest of my life. Big move up, big money. Big chance to make a name for myself. There's nothing to *not* be happy about. So why are you so negged out?"

Angie shrugged. She hadn't really tried to push Tony's cause, but every once in a while, she just couldn't help pointing out the obvious. Not that Regan didn't know it. Regan ignored it, and sloughed it off. As usual.

That was it as far as Regan was concerned. For today. So Angie regrouped and found a reason. "Three hundred bucks for a pair of shoes is why. You know me, I still come from New England thrift in spite of all our money. My accountant would have a fit if he had to pay a charge like that."

"As opposed to the charges you run up at Nordstrom? Come on, Angie."

"You're having a brainstorm. This is *not* like you."

"Sure it is," Regan murmured. Angie didn't know everything about her life, after all, nor did she know everything about Angie's. And she didn't even know if she was all that curious either. "It's like enough, in any event. Maybe I'll surprise you."

Maybe I'll surprise myself.

Oh, God—I don't want to surprise myself. I just want to enjoy this. That's all I want to do, and I don't want to think about how it looks to Tony or to Angie or any prospective clients.

I just want to deal with how it looks to me.

Some things you couldn't plan. Sometimes fate just stepped in and handed you the means and motive to go after what you wanted. And sometimes fate just tripped you up.

Bobby Torrance couldn't decide which scenario was in play the day he heard that the Heights *Herald* was on the auction block, and that Regan had jumped feet first into the big leagues. It just shot a man's plans all to hell, these unexpected events, didn't give him time to react and strategize. Gave him five minutes to make choices that would immediately upend and impact his life.

But because of those two events, he'd dropped everything, taken the first plane out of Chicago, and was standing on the doorstep of the family residence in the Heights, girding himself to defend his actions about decisions that were both visceral and no-damned-body-else's business but his own.

Nevertheless, he was here, and he thrust open the door with all the authority of the head of the house just as he heard Angie's excited shriek behind him.

She barreled into him and wrapped her arms around him from behind. "You—you—oh, my God, what are you doing here?"

Bobby tossed his two carry-ons into the vestibule and pulled her around to envelop her in a bear hug. "Business. Where've you been?" He put his arm around her shoulders and guided her into the house.

"Manhattan. Shopping. What else does a Torrance heiress do?"

"Work. Contribute her talents and insights to the bottom line."

"Yeah, you really need my crack forehand on your team."

"Maybe I do," Bobby said.

"Meaning what?"

"Meaning you wouldn't have to move to Chicago. Ah, here's Mother." He relinquished Angie to take his mother's hands. "The fatted son is back, Mother, so tell the chef to cook the prodigal calf in my honor."

"And that means just what, Bobby?"

No fulsome welcomes here. His mother was suspicious of everything, bitter as poison since his father died and Bobby had taken over Torrance Media. And it wasn't that he'd run the company to the ground: rather, he'd made more of it than his father ever had, and reversed losses and increased profits, and his mother couldn't, for some reason, forgive him for that.

"I'm home for the moment." Less was more where his mother was concerned.

"How many moments?"

"As long as it takes to do business, Mother."

His mother pulled her hands from his and turned away. "I know *what* business, Bobby. I know just what you're up to, and all those years you spent away from here—you never fooled me."

"Don't know what you're talking about, Mother." But he was damned certain he did. She knew. *She knew.*

"Don't do it, Bobby. Just don't do it. We went through enough with it. Time won't have made it better. She is what she is. Breeding shows. You can put her in pinstripe suits, and you can give her a corporate gold card, and all the money in the world, and at the end of the day, she's still a slut. And she'll make your life miserable, just like before."

And you'll make my life miserable, Mother—just like before.

"Appreciate the advice, Mother, but I'm just here on business." Not a lie. He supposed Regan could be called business—*unfinished* business. He knew how to do spin. "I can just as soon stay at a hotel if my presence here bothers you."

"You pay the bills," his mother said, waving her hand listlessly. "You'll do what you want." She drifted off toward the library, looking fragile, ethereal, miserable.

"Bobby!"

He shook himself. There was no rescuing his mother. And at that, he'd never exerted the effort to try. He turned to Angie. "What?"

"Regan?"

He shook his head. He could deny that she was his first order of business, at least—or rather, he could, and would, lie to Angie until he had some sense of how things were. "Nope. The Heights *Herald.*"

Her eyes widened. "That low-rent rag? You're kidding."

"Not kidding. Got the lawyers making an offer right now. You're not thinking, Ang. We're talking about a small, weekly shopper newspaper that covers some local events, which already has a subscription list and a viable advertising base, nipping at the border of Manhattan. You don't think there's some value to the company there?"

"I'm not sure, what're you thinking?"

"Oh, features editor? Office manager? What do you think you'd like to do?"

"Oh, Mother's gonna die, Bobby. She didn't want you within a thousand miles of New York until Regan was safely out of the way; she never forgave her for staying in town after the divorce. She hates her with all her heart."

"Okay," Bobby said. "And you're her friend, and I'd bet the store you haven't told mother a thing about that. That's a bigger betrayal than anything I could ever do, Ang. But that's your business. The buy is a go, and I expect to find a nice niche with distribution into Manhattan and to make big inroads into other turf. So get used to it, and think about how you're going to help me."

"I have been helping you," Angie said stiffly.

There was no doubt about it: guilt worked. And he had labored under it for seven years, and the burden of knowing that his mother wanted him as close as the next room, and as far away as he could get. China wouldn't have been too far, had there been a reason for him to have gone there.

And Angie had been the buffer, the rock, her mother's companion, shielding her against everything unpleasant.

But old grudges died hard.

"You're right," he acknowledged, "you're here with Mother when you should be having a life of your own. I owe you for that. But the fact is, I'm here to get this thing up and running and pointed south. So Mother is just going to have to deal with it."

"And it has nothing to do with Regan?"

"It's business and the rest is none of your business."

"That's what I thought. Mother's right, isn't she?"

"You know I haven't seen her in years," Bobby said softly.

"Right." But she didn't know anything, actually. She felt as if she didn't know *him,* and that was the worst thing of all. "What does that have to do with anything?" she asked.

"Probably nothing," Bobby said. "The topic is off the table, Ang. And I have to unpack."

And that was that. Regan had come between them again. All these years, she'd kept them niched in separate places. It'd been easy, too, because Bobby lived in the middle of the country, and flying trips home left him no time to do anything but hold meetings and make sure Mother was comfortable.

Her association with Regan was barely ever mentioned—a passing question now and again, which made her think sometimes that Bobby had his own sources to provide him with information about Regan. But, then, the divorce had been so acrimonious, she thought most times she was wrong, and he was just as happy to know nothing about her at all ever again.

Bobby had made his own life, deliberately headquartered far and away from his youthful mistakes. It had worked out well, only Mother hadn't wanted to move cross country. Mother wanted to stay, but Regan hadn't left and nothing their father offered in settlement could move her, so Mother had suffered all these years with Regan flaunting herself around town.

And Bobby was right: Angie *had* snuck behind Mother's back to maintain the relationship with Regan. Regan had been her best friend, before, during and after the marriage. You didn't throw that away when a marriage didn't work, or if a mother was mired in hate. That was Mother's problem, and Bobby's, and Angie had tried so hard to remain neutral for the benefit of both parties.

Which had been so easy when he was far away, but now Bobby was here for the foreseeable future. And he was no callow twenty-four-year-old, and Regan wasn't the exotic and romantic twenty-year-old she had been.

Trouble. It could only mean trouble. Regan hadn't changed in one respect over the years. She was still a man magnet, still attracting attention like a heat-seeking missile. All flash and fizzle, that was Regan. With loyal Tony invariably downrange, waiting for the right time, the right place, the right weather.

Regan wouldn't want her past dogging her just as she was stepping up and out. She'd want to keep out of Bobby's way. She'd run as far as those wiggly wobbly Mascolos would carry her, if she knew Bobby was back in town.

Angie was sure of it. She'd tell Tony, she thought, and Tony would tell Regan, and then he'd protect her, just as he always did.

So maybe this wasn't such a disaster, Bobby's return. Maybe it would be the impetus for Regan to begin valuing Tony's unswerving friendship, and to see finally that Tony really was the man for her.

Tony wasn't going to tell Regan anything. He put down the phone slowly, thinking about everything it meant to have Bobby Torrance back in town.

It meant everything was gone to hell. It meant a continual looming presence at a time when the last thing Regan needed was that kind of distraction. And it would be a distraction; their past would underscore everything she did, and she'd be looking for ways and means to avoid him. She'd always be conscious he was somewhere around and that would take her focus off business, and that alone could shoot everything to kingdom come.

Shit.

God, that man had the timing of a master clock maker. Of all the times for him to stage a return.

Damnit to hell.

The less Regan knew, the better. She'd find out soon enough, anyway. Which was what he told Angie. He wasn't going to tell her. And especially not on the eve of the party celebrating her success.

Tomorrow was soon enough, he told Angie. Although he didn't want to bet that someone wouldn't tell her at the party tonight.

No matter: this was Regan's night. And his. And maybe, in some small way, his father's. His father who had taken a gorgeous out-of-her-depth twenty-one-year-old and molded her with kindness and care, and made her into the spectacular businesswoman she was.

Oh, yes, all the memories. They flooded out at the thought of Bobby Torrance. All the fights. All the jealousies.

Bobby banging at the agency door, demanding his wife back. Bobby threatening him. Bobby demanding that Regan give up her job. Bobby, Bobby, Bobby—spoiled bad boy the-world-was-his-because-he-was-rich Bobby. . . . Possessive, entitled Bobby. . . . who'd just swept into town after graduating from that high-powered, high toned university in Chicago, took one look at Regan, and had to have her. Had to, *had* to, and stopped at nothing until he'd married her.

And for several dazzling months, she'd been deliriously happy. And then it all deteriorated, first in bed, and then in their day-to-day life. First, it turned out that Regan's needs and capabilities didn't mesh with Bobby's in bed. And the mother didn't want her working. And Bobby was insanely jealous of every man she came in contact with because their private life was in such a shambles.

And then Alex came along.

Alex—mature, sexy, sympathetic, knowing, manipulative Alex. . . . Whatever it was that was between them, it broke up the marriage like a time bomb, imploding from the inside and radiating out.

The papers were filed, the settlement was made, and Bobby tore out of town like a tornado.

And now he was back like a storm cloud, dark, ominous, hovering, ready to unleash a torrent of trouble when conditions were right.

Still rich. Still on the hunt. Still thinking he was entitled.

Men like Bobby never gave up what they thought belonged to them.

Well, Bobby had to learn what they all had learned over the years: Regan belonged to no one, and Tony had reason to know that better than anyone else.

Chapter Two

She wore the Mascolos. And black. A column of long, slinky, shimmery black that grazed her curves, showed off her legs, and fastened with a jet-black choker collar around her neck. Crystal and jet earrings dusting her bare shoulders, framed by her tumbling curls, her only jewelry. A black sequined bag. Restrained makeup. A long glittery sweater coat to ward off the chill.

Nothing out of line here. Perfectly fit, formal and worthy of a celebratory party. Even Angie couldn't quibble. There wasn't a hint of anything blatant. No cleavage. Nothing tight. No messages here that could be misinterpreted by anyone.

But she was disabused of the comfort of that notion the moment she walked in the door of Mary Mackey Lee's spacious Tudor home.

Everything stopped dead as she paused in the archway to the sunken living room. She felt a wave of heat suffuse her whole body as she realized how many people were there, and that they all were staring at her.

"Come on, Regan." Tony came forward, and took her hand to help her down the step. "You look fabulous." But *fabulous* didn't begin to express how she looked. She looked different: sensual, elusive, exclusive.

Not his.

No. His, while the world outside could be held at bay.

His, while she was on Mackey turf, surrounded by Mackey friends, family and colleagues. His, as she always was, one minute at a time.

His, for tonight.

He led her to the open bar. "Here we go. What would you like?"

"White wine—Riesling if you have it."

"Sure. Anything you want, Regan."

Oh, God—did that mean something other than casual conversation?

She took the goblet and lifted it to him. This was *not* the time to say she owed everything to him. "Thanks, Tony."

"Hey"—he grabbed his beer and clinked his glass against her wineglass—"you earned it."

She sipped and savored the fruity taste of the wine while she surveyed the crowd. "God, everyone's here."

"Everyone we've ever sold to. All your neighbors and friends, everyone you grew up with and everyone you never wanted to see again," Tony said with a trace of irony. "That about covers it. And my sister, of course," he added as Mary came up to them.

"You look *stunning* tonight," Mary murmured, signaling for a refill. "And it's about time Tony promoted you—shame on you, Tony."

"Hey, you, too, can earn those kinds of commissions, and you don't need a title to do it," Tony retorted, putting his hand on Regan's shoulder and squeezing lightly. "And the best is yet to come." He slid his hand down her arm.

"I think so too," Regan said. "We've got the right strategy at the right time." She sipped again so that she could move her arm out of Tony's reach. "It's brilliant, actually. No one else has thought of it—yet."

"*Yet* is the operative word," Tony said. "But that's business, that's for tomorrow. Tonight—is pure pleasure—and we should enjoy it while we can."

"Thank God he has a sister who can wave a magic wand and set it all up with one day's notice," Mary put in. "It's my pleasure, too, Regan. You deserve it. You're like family, but you know that, and frankly, I don't know what Tony would do without you."

Regan ignored the warning bells. "Thanks, Mary. It's not an exaggeration to say that your family has been like a second family to me too."

Mary hugged her. "I wish you even greater success then, and I leave you to it."

Regan lifted her wineglass to her as Mary withdrew. "You don't know how lucky you are, Tony."

"Sure I do." He took her elbow. "Let's mingle."

But she couldn't take a step without someone stopping her to comment on her dress, or to congratulate her on her promotion. It was so lovely to have all these people, some she'd known all her life, some of them new friends she'd made in the course of selling them a house or an apartment, so undeniably pleased for her.

She felt full, suddenly, in a way that she hadn't in a long time. What Mary had said was true: Mackey's *was* her family, and they were pushing her out of the nest and letting her fly.

And, in a way, it made up for all the barren years.

"Well, look at you. . . ." Angie murmured, as she joined her and Tony in a little knot of friends near the door. "Oh, my, Mascolos and everything."

"Yep. I've got nothing to hide. What about you?"

Angie cringed. "That's for sure, in that dress." Oh, that was snappish. There was nothing wrong with the dress and everything wrong with her. She was still disturbed by Bobby's unexpected return, still unsure of how to handle it.

She caught Tony's eye and he shook his head imperceptibly.

Right. Pretend it didn't exist. Pretend *Bobby* didn't exist.

She needed a drink, said so, and Regan offered to come with her. "I need five minutes away from Tony; he's absolutely smothering me."

Angie ordered a martini. "Told you. You should've deep-sixed the shoes."

"You're completely overboard today," Regan muttered, taking a refill on her wine. "What is it with you?"

Angie shook her head as she sipped at her drink. "It's nothing. I guess I'm a little unsettled by the way things are changing—for you, I mean. Sometimes you think things are going to go on the same way forever."

"Well, nothing much is going to change, either, except I'll be in Manhattan more, pitching the project. And the money. I *love* the change in the money."

Oh, yes, the money. Hadn't that always been the corner-stone of everything Regan had ever done, including marry-ing Bobby?

It was absolutely nerve-wracking to have Bobby back in town and have to act like nothing was different.

Everything was different, everything was going to change.

Tony cornered her when Regan went off to the powder room. "So where are we at?"

"You probably know as much as I do at this point. Bobby's bidding on the *Herald,* and he's staying on site to manage and relaunch it. That means, he'll be in our house, in our town, and in our lives."

"Shit."

"Exactly."

"So how did you manage to get out of the house without him asking questions?"

"I waited till he went into the library with an armful of papers."

"Good thinking."

"Well, I can't keep sneaking around, and he's going to see Regan by the simple expediency of going to the office. And then what?"

"We'll sell him some commercial space," Tony said mor-dantly. "Actually, that's not a bad idea. The *Herald*'s office is this cramped little storefront on the avenue. . . ."

"Tony—"

"Right. Tonight is mine, tomorrow, the deluge."

"Always assuming my feelings have been on target all along," Angie murmured.

"On target? Hell, bull's-eye. She hasn't had a serious relationship in seven years, she hardly plays around, she lets off steam at the local spa—and she goddamned doesn't want me," Tony growled. "She's been on a girls-just-want-to-have-fun kick for years, but I haven't seen any evidence of it, and when you ask her, she makes up the most outrageous stories, and everything just rolls off her like teflon. You're abso-damn-lutely on target. And now he's back . . . God . . ."

"We'll lose her," Angie interpolated.

"Or get burned in the conflagration," Tony said moodily as he watched Regan make her way back into the room. She was so magnetic; people just stared at her, drawn to her, to her unfeigned interest and the way she listened. To her beauty, although that really was the least of it, because in any setting where business was a priorty, Regan was as proper as the most Victorian matron.

Even in that dress, which was eye-catching and subtle at the same time, she showed completely how well she understood the complexities of appearance.

"My father always said—"

"He hated her."

"He did," Angie agreed. "Mother still does. She never forgave Regan for making everything so complicated."

"Your mother always had other plans for Bobby."

"She still does."

"Good luck," Tony muttered in an undertone as Regan joined them.

"What are you guys talking about?"

"Luck. Money. Possibilites," Tony said lightly. "Yours, mainly."

"You're making too much of this, and it's getting me nervous."

"Okay. We'll talk about something else."

"Like what?" Regan asked, saluting an acquaintance who had just come into the room.

"Well, there you go—what about your friend Jay Cargill over there? I hope you're taking note of all the prospects in the room."

"Tony—I'm not *doing* business tonight."

"That's all right. I made sure they were all aware of your new responsibilities."

"Isn't that just the kind of thing you *would* do. That's the reason for this party, isn't it? You're lining up the pigeons—"

"Now, Regan—" He broke off suddenly, staring at something over her shoulder, and then he went on, "When have you ever known me not to mix business with pleasure? And what an opportunity—with every executive who's ever bought a house in the Heights all in the same room—and possibly a CFO or two looking for reasonable office space in commuting distance of midtown."

It was just the usual party conversation, but she suddenly felt uneasy. He was a little bit too party-hearty tonight. A little bit too aggressive.

And Angie was a little too wary.

"You are a piece of work, Tony." She sensed everyone's attention turning elsewhere, saw Angie's eyes flash, Tony's mouth tighten. "*I* thought it was all about . . ."

All about . . . Every muscle in her body tightened. Every nerve ending crackled. *All . . . about*—

She turned slowly as Tony vainly sought to grasp her arm, her hand, just as Mary Lee rang a little dinner bell to get everyone's attention, and just as Bobby Torrance stepped over the threshold.

The moment she'd dreaded for years was here. Regan mentally pulled herself up straight and tall, knowing—absolutely knowing—that she was the first person Bobby had seen the moment he stepped into the hallway adjacent to the living room.

And feeling like she wanted to run and hide.

But there was no hiding from Bobby. He was too charismatic, too *there*. Too tremendously changed and too much the same.

She felt her chest tighten, her breathing constrict. She felt ambushed, vulnerable, as if everyone had known he was back in town but her.

But that wasn't possible. Angie would have said, wouldn't she?

There was music somewhere in the distance, and she thought perhaps she was imagining it, and that it was just like Bobby to carry his music with him, surrounding him, punctuating his every move.

He carried himself differently. He *was* different: he'd grown into his body, his face, his destiny. There was power there now, so much more than before, surrounding him like an aura. And there was a surety, a confidence that came from experience instead of arrogance.

But the arrogance was there, too. It was in his stance and the way his dark, unfathomable gaze roamed the room as Mary Lee sang out, " Everyone, everyone—look who's here! This is Bobby Torrance, everyone."

He stepped into the room to a chorus of greetings, and Mary's pointer, "The bar is over that way."

But he wasn't interested in wine: Regan knew it to her toes.

"Angie—" she hissed over her shoulder as he veered toward them while seeming to stop and speak to every one of the several old friends scattered throughout the room.

Angie choked. "I . . ." but, then, Regan didn't really seem to require a response. Rather, she was staring at Bobby as if she'd never seen him before. And nothing could be worse.

Tony moved closer to Regan.

"You don't have to protect me," she whispered. But she couldn't take her eyes off of Bobby. God, he was formidable. What must he be like in the boardroom?

Or the bedroom?

No! *She couldn't possibly be thinking that way after all their past history.*

She felt numb as a statue. Or maybe she was impervious. And nothing mattered. Finally.

"Regan." His voice was like a depth charge inside her, calling up a hundred emotions, all explosive. "Angie . . . Tony." He held out his hand and Tony took it warily.

"Bobby. Back in town for a visit, are you?"

"Back in town, period. Surprised Mother, to say the least. Angie was gone by then," he added meaningfully, and Angie threw him a grateful glance. "So, I called the one person who knows everything that goes on in town—your sister."

"Ah, yes—my sister, the queen bee," Tony murmured. So no one could mention his putative purchase of the *Herald.* Damn. And why would he cover Angie's behind, knowing that? What a guy. Read the situation like a football play. And faked out the opposition at the one yard line.

Hell, Ang had been walking that tightrope for years. It was none of his business anyway. Regan was his business, and he couldn't tell what she was feeling or even what she wanted him to do.

He knew what he wanted to do. He wanted to throw Bobby out of the house. He felt a primitve urge to conquer him, totally unrealistic and out of line. But that was how he felt about Regan: as possessive as Bobby ever was.

And Bobby knew it. And Bobby wouldn't hesitate to use it, either.

He turned to Regan. "Regan?"

"Bobby?" Her voice was as soft as her body was ramrod with tension.

"Let me buy you a drink."

What could she do in a roomful of people? "Do I have to?"

His lips quirked. "I think you have to."

"Tony—?" She threw him a helpless look.

"We'll circle the wagons. If he makes a move, he won't get far."

"Nice reputation I have. What *has* Angie been telling you?"

"Nothing, actually," Tony said. Well, not nothing. Just not much, but Bobby was probably very well aware of that.

"Come on, Regan. We can do *civilized.*"

"I suppose we must, given how many people have known us forever."

"I promise it won't hurt."

"The scab dried up and fell off years ago, Bobby."

"That doesn't mean old wounds don't throb occasionally."

"I take a Motrin and make it go away."

"Not possible tonight, Regan."

"I haven't taken one yet."

"Let's just do the right thing, shall we?"

"This is the absolute wrong thing to do," Tony whispered in her ear.

She shrugged, feeling trapped between the two of them. "All right, Bobby. If we must—if *you* must." She shot a warning look at Tony, and then let Bobby take her elbow and guide her away.

"And there they go," Tony muttered. "And don't they look perfect together?"

"Oh, God," Angie moaned. "It's starting all over again. Didn't you feel it, Tony? I knew it. I just knew it. He was looking for a reason to come back, but the real reason he came back was for *her.*"

It was the oddest thing, walking through the crowd with Bobby, a step ahead of him, and miles and miles behind him figuratively. This was her worst nightmare and most cherished dream. Or it would have been, a month, six months, a year after they broke up and divorced.

This was a parody; this was the fates laughing at her, telling her point blank how far she'd run only to come back to the same place.

She took her refilled wineglass, tipped it to Bobby's and sipped.

"This is it? You wanted everyone to see us together?"

"You really think that's what I want?" Bobby murmured. "I don't think you're quite that disingenuous, Regan."

"Hell, no. This is a room full of prospective customers, Bobby. I'll play by the rules—here. And tonight only."

"Good you said that. That's just how I feel."

"I was afraid of that."

Well, that gauntlet was down, and he wondered what the next gambit should be. This was a whole new game, now, this night, with this woman, who was everything he'd dreamed she'd be, and nothing like he'd imagined all these years he'd been away.

Standing here in Mary Lee's living room, they had no past, they had no present except insofar as it was as if they had just been introduced.

He didn't know *this* Regan, and she sure as hell didn't know him.

It was a level playing field suddenly, and that left him a little off balance.

She left him a little off balance. She was cool and elusive, cordial and distant. Beautiful and serene. And she'd been none of those things the last time he saw her.

Rather, she'd been wild and a little desperate. Beautiful and needy. Sensual and in an unstoppable fury. And unable to handle herself—or him.

And he—he'd been unbearably possessive, aggressive, and jealous. He'd been callow, inexperienced, and righteous. And he hadn't listened. And he hadn't done things, and he'd spent seven long years and three thousand nights repenting his stupidity.

Or maybe the dissolution of that marriage had been inevitable: they were both too young, but she'd been way more mature in ways that counted, and he never had a prayer of catching up.

Not that year, anyway.

And she got tired of waiting.

And Tony Mackey was there to cushion the fall.

Their whole lives inextricably entwined with the Mackeys'. It felt like a betrayal to be drinking the man's wine when he was going to take away the woman Tony had always loved.

But—they weren't engaged, they weren't dating, they weren't anything except employer and employee as far as he could find out.

And that suited him just fine. And Angie's tiptoeing around things all these years was meaningless. She couldn't have prevented him coming back for Regan any more than she could have prevented a tornado from sweeping up everything in its path.

"There are rules and there are rules," he murmured in response to her comment. "Depends on the situation, don't you think?"

"I don't see a situation, Bobby. What are you talking about?"

"Rules for business. Rules for social occasions. Rules for ex-husbands and ex-wives. . . ."

"Rules for them too, huh? What are those rules, Bobby?"

"Oh, civility, communication, second chances. . . ."

She thought her heart would stop. He couldn't mean that. She didn't want him to mean it—or did she?

She slanted a look at Tony. He was still where she'd left him, with Angie, and the two of them were watching her and Bobby like Bobby was about to steal the silver.

No, Tony was watching Bobby like he was about to steal *her*.

Oh, Lord. . . .

"Bobby—"

He held up his hand. "Don't."

"Well, you don't, either."

"Don't be naive, Regan."

"Me? I'm far from naive, Bobby. But you can't just waltz back in here and turn everyone's life inside out."

"I don't care about anybody else's life."

"This is a guy thing, right? One of those divide and conquer moves because you just can't leave well enough alone. Should I be flattered? Or annoyed?"

"Civility, Regan. Communication."

"You haven't communicated in years, Bobby, but, all right, I'll bite. Communicate."

What? "This isn't a flying visit. I'm buying the *Herald,* and I'm staying on as managing editor."

Oh. What?? She felt breathless suddenly, as if what they were talking about had nothing to do with business. "Oh." It took a moment for her to focus. To understand he meant it: he wasn't going anywhere. "The *Herald.* Right. It was up for auction. Well. Good."

"So glad you think that way."

She swallowed and forced herself to regroup. "It's your money, and your life, Bobby. If you want to throw it away on a small-town neighborhood advertising supplement that was losing money in tidal waves, it's fine with me. Call me when you need to expand your office space."

She turned away, and he grasped her hand and pulled her back gently. And she allowed him to do it rather than call anymore attention to them, even though his hand was dry and hot and melting her skin at his very touch. "I'll call you because I came back for you, Regan."

No! No. Really? No, no, no! You're not going to get to me that easily, Bobby Torrance. Oh, no. No. Damn. . . .

You're not going to have everything your own way all the time even now, damn it.

"Did you?" she murmured, reaching for a cool response and composure she didn't feel. And her hand. She disengaged her hand from his with one subtle movement. And rubbed it against her dress.

"Yeah. I did."

He meant it. That was the scariest thing of all. Seven years, no contact, no concern, no care, and he just barged in and expected she would fall into his arms because he still wanted her.

And was certain she would still want him? Oh, no, oh, no. Even if she did, she'd die before she'd admit it, and even then . . . and it was too public a place to take the discussion any farther.

"God, you're arrogant."

"Yeah. I am."

"So what you're saying is, you still want to fuck me."

His eyes narrowed. "Yeah. I do."

"You must think I fall into bed with just about anybody."

"No. I think you will fall into bed with me."

"Right. What—do I have a sign on my back that says, *I'm easy?* I don't think so, Bobby, but it's an intriguing thing to think about. The sign, I mean."

Hell. Trust the defiant Regan, the street fighter Regan, to take things to that level just to aggravate the situation. He felt like he was twenty-four again. He felt possessive, jealous, like the hunter circling his prey.

"Oh, I think you'll think about it, Regan. Going to bed with me, I mean. I think you'll think about it a lot because I'm older, wiser and a lot more experienced. And, as I have good cause to remember, you just love experienced older men."

Going lower still, warrior that he was. Why had he stooped to that?

Her body stiffened, taking the hit. "You bet. Nothing beats an older, experienced man," she said coldly. "So I'll tell you what—I'll think long and hard about sleeping with you"—and she turned away from him in a slow, deliberate move—"and you try just as hard to catch me—if you can."

Chapter Three

The nerve of him! The goddamned outsized, overblown, ego-driven balls of him! Just take her off the shelf, try her on for size and put her back until the next time he wanted to play. Damn him, damn him, damn him. . . .

It took every bit of wit and control she possessed to just coolly and calmly walk away from him.

"What did he say?" Tony demanded, coming to meet her.

She was furious enough to tell him, without thinking how it would sound. "He wants to sleep with me."

"Jesus effing—"

"Yeah." *Oh, yeah—oh, hell, imagine how that sounded to Tony. Poor long-suffering Tony.*

Maybe it was the Mascolos.

Oh, the hell with all men.

"I'm going home."

Tony put out a restraining hand. "Can't. It's your party, remember?"

"Did Mary hire a guy to jump out of the cake?"

Tony snapped his fingers. "You know, I knew I forgot something."

She forced herself to smile, and to look at Tony as if he were the only man in the room. *Are you watching, you bastard?* "Okay. I'm calm now. Calmer. That son of a bitch. After all these years."

"Oh, yeah? And are you thinking about it?"

Tony knew her too well. "Are you *nuts?*"

"You're thinking about it."

"Tony . . ." He didn't deserve that, not even as a joke. He'd been so devoted, so patient. And he knew it was hopeless and he never gave up.

An admirable trait, that.

"You sparked like firecrackers," Tony said.

I'm not interested—she started to say, and it came out, "He'll have to find me first."

"You're planning to leave town?"

"I'm planning to go on with my life." But she didn't know what she meant by that.

Yes, she did.

What *did* she mean?

She was so furious, she didn't know what she meant. No, she meant that *that man* deserved no mercy. None. And that she wasn't flattered, and she didn't care—she'd stopped caring well before the divorce, when he hadn't even tried to get her back or make things better, and then after that, when he'd skipped town, leaving her to clean up the mess altogether.

Big deal, he knew how to fuck now. Big fucking deal. It was years too late.

"Okay," Tony said carefully. "What life is that, as opposed to the one you have now?"

"A life full of good times and no responsibility," Regan muttered.

"Oh. I thought you'd been living *that* life," Tony said.

"Guess I am. Guess I'm still angry."

"Guess you do want to sleep with him."

"Tony." She put her hand on his arm, knowing—since she was always so careful not to touch him—what the gesture meant. "Honestly, I'm just not thinking clearly right now. This is the last person anyone expected to show up tonight."

Not anyone, Tony thought, *but a man must keep his se-*

crets. Especially from Regan. "Sell him some office space," he suggested, keeping his tone light and the edge out of his voice. "Make him pay."

"You bet I will. Right through the nose I'll make him pay."

"I'll tell you how, too," Tony said, taking her arm as he saw Mary Lee appear and gesture to him that dinner was served. "Ignore him, Regan. It's the worst thing you can do to a man who wants to fuck you. Just goddamn ignore him, and then watch him squirm."

Bobby watched through hooded eyes as Regan conversed with Tony. He knew that body language, he knew that look. He'd seen it a hundred times before, and it boded trouble. But, then, Regan had always been trouble, had always been a handful. Always had been more than one youthful badass, knowitall babe-in-the-woods could handle.

But there wasn't anything Regan could throw at him that he couldn't handle now. Including Tony Mackey. Including a roomful of older, *experienced* men who were all half in love with her.

Hell, they probably all had hard-ons just looking at her.

Speak for yourself.

Right. He could be fifteen again, the way his body reacted to just the sight of Regan.

Jesus. All those nights. All that regret.

No more. Penance had been paid. Seven long hard years working, establishing himself, finding his footing, finding the man he really was.

Finding out that no woman could replace or compare with his deep down unseverable connection with Regan. With his *memories* of Regan. And that had nothing to do with the reality, and everything to do with his gut, and his heart.

It was a stunning realization. A turning point, even. When he'd stormed out of the Heights seven years before, he'd gone on a sex bender of epic proportions. And none of the women, none of the sex, none of the wild, wicked kinky nights of unbridled, unfettered lust could quench his desire for Regan.

It was Regan he needed, yearned for, desired.

And he'd thought it was an annoying itch and that any-damned-body could scratch it. A year had been long enough to comprehend that wouldn't happen. Three years to establish a base in the midwest after his father died. Two more to expand the company to profitability. And another year to find the thing that would legitimately bring him back to stay.

And so now, watching Regan sashay down the buffet line with Tony, he felt that telltale tension in his body, in his manhood, in his soul. His whole body tightened, length-ened, went electric with a need that was so powerful, he felt like he would crack in two.

And it didn't profit him to keep watching her with Tony. Tony was part of the cause and effect of what had been wrong with their marriage, and Tony was still living on hope and adrenaline, and taking himself in his hand every night.

He'd spilled enough seed himself to know what that was like.

"Angie." He pulled her out of the corner where she was tucked away with a small plate of food—hiding, it looked like, and she'd damned well better, given her lying little heart.

"Yeah, Bobby, what's up?" she asked warily, not liking the look in his eye, or the way he was looking at Regan for that matter.

Things couldn't be worse, she thought miserably, and her feeble attempt to protect them both had backfired big time.

"You snuck out on me." He plucked a piece of chicken off her plate and bit into it. "Didn't tell Regan, huh?"

"You know I don't talk about you."

"I thought it was big news I was back in town."

"Yeah, headline news. I told you, I never talk about you

to Regan." There was an admission fraught with misplaced intentions.

"Tell me about that."

His tone was dangerous, silky as a cat stalking its prey.

"She didn't want to know. I respected that."

"Even to the point of not telling her I'm back home? You really thought she wouldn't want to know that?"

Of course, he didn't believe it, and even Angie didn't expect him to. "There wasn't much time to bring the subject up," she hedged. "Your appearance kind of undercut the need to say anything. How did you find out about the party anway?"

He shrugged and took another chicken piece. "Just as I said: I called Mary."

"So what are you going to do?"

"The worst of all possible things, my darling sister. I'm going to do my damnedest to get her back—and you're going to tell me everything I need to know."

And the next day, it was as if nothing had happened. No one stormed the Mackey Agency doors. No one rode up on a white charger to kidnap her. No one *happened* to bump into her on the street.

Nothing untoward happened at all.

It was business as usual, which left her feeling a little off balance. Regan went to meetings, looked at property that owners wanted to sell, had lunch with Tony, showed a handful of houses to a couple of prospective buyers, talked to several financial officers on the phone and pitched the idea of relocation.

And before she knew it, the day was done, and the sky didn't fall, and nowhere did she see Bobby Torrance; and he could've been in Antarctica for all anyone knew.

Angie called her at seven o'clock, just as she walked in the door and kicked off her shoes.

"Yeah, hey, so are you two still civil—and communicative?"

"Civil, anyway," Regan said. "It's easy when the party in question is nowhere around. Just how I like it, actually." She hadn't told Angie much of what the conversation had been about the night before. It was bad enough she'd said anything to Tony, and she was having major regrets today.

Bobby, to his credit, left her alone after that fraught interchange, although she was intensely aware of his presence for all the time he remained at the party. But to his credit, he had the tact to leave early, well before the excellent congratulatory cake, which in fact did not have a male stripper poised inside.

That was a good thing. Regan wasn't sure she could've taken it in the spirit it was meant after the shock of seeing Bobby.

"So what else is happening?"

"Same old thing," Regan said. "How about you?"

Angie sloughed off the implications of that question. "You wouldn't think anything had changed at our house. It's like he never left." Which was more than she meant to say, and she changed the subject quickly. "What's up for tonight?"

"You feel like going out?"

Angie felt a twinge of unease. "I knew it. You're upset."

"Don't be silly. Why should I be upset? I'm just feeling a little frisky," Regan said lightly. *Like another-lonely-night kind of frisky for a woman who didn't dare live out her own fantasies.*

But she liked pulling Angie's chain. Angie thought she led the life of a wild woman. But that went with the territory: she looked the part, her name made everyone think she acted the part—*oh, that Regan Torrance, they would say, her name sounds just like her—lush, torrid, erotic. . . .*

When you came from the waterfront side of town, everything you did was suspect, and everything counted against you, even your name. . . .

"I was afraid of that," Angie said, worry lacing her voice. "Bobby's coming back sent you off the deep end."

"I've been there before." Oh, yes, that end-of-the-marriage, crawl-into-a-hole-and-wallow-in-a-pity-party deep end. Damned right, deep end. Bobby's appearance set off every nerve ending, every memory. Every feeling of loss, regret, despair and abandonment.

The kind of feelings people drowned—in drink or in sex.

Or in talking about drink and sex and forbidden things they never in a lifetime would do.

"Where, off the deep end?" Angie said. "You don't have to tell me."

Yes, she'd shared some of it with Angie. Not all. Not nearly. Not ever.

"You shouldn't be alone tonight," Angie added suddenly. "Stay home. I'll come over."

Regan flinched. She didn't want that. For some reason, she really didn't want that, nor did she want to examine why.

"I'm okay. I won't do anything stupid. Besides, I've been protecting your innocence all this time, Ang. And I think that tradition should continue."

"Regan—"

"I'm just going to get a beer or something at Gus's. That's about as much hell as I plan to raise tonight. So you're still on the side of the angels, Miss Angel-a."

"You think?" Angie asked uncertainly.

She hated to turn Angie off like that; Angie was such a good friend.

"Oh, I know," Regan murmured, comforted, as she hung up the phone.

Even more comforting was the atmosphere at Gus's, the local hangout: warm, cheerful, noisy, welcoming. The restaurant and menu hadn't changed since the nineteen forties, and you could always order a burger and beer, soup and a sandwich, wine and cheese. And the real Gus still owned and ran the place.

Gus knew everyone. Gus knew her. "Hey, Regan," he

called to her from behind the turn-of-the-century walnut bar. "How's it going?"

"It already went," she said trenchantly, seating herself and ordering a glass of wine.

Gus grunted. "That bad, huh?"

Regan sipped. "Ummm." *That bad.*

Really? Well, she wanted it to be that bad. She knew where to come for sympathy.

But in the glow of the dimly lit bar, with jazz playing on the old jukebox, the sibilant murmur of conversation underscoring the music, delicious smells wafting from the kitchen, and the heightened sense of intimacy, things suddenly didn't look that bad at all.

Really, what was so bad? she thought idly, tipping her glass of wine so the soft light warmed the golden liquid. In fact, everything was golden—if you counted your blessings piece by piece: she had a good job, had just been promoted, made good money. Had a great boss. Good friends. Nice town. Good place to live, to work. Super apartment.

She had, for a once-destitute girl, achieved everything she'd ever dreamed about.

Almost everything.

She didn't have a husband, or a family.

She'd failed dismally at marriage. Had fallen flat on her face and into the morass of married too young, divorced too soon.

That was her most incriminating secret, that *she* had failed, too. It had been so easy to put it all on Bobby, but she bore some of the burden as well. Maybe more than *some*. Something she'd never ever admitted to anyone, even herself, in those tumultuous days when there was barely anything left to save of their relationship.

It wasn't all Bobby.

It wasn't all Bobby.

Oh, God, all that pain, all those years of regrets ... everything she'd pushed into that deep well of longing and covered over so it wouldn't bubble over ever again. ...

And now he was back.

And that just shook her up from top to toe.

And he *said* he'd come back for her.

Easy for him to say. That had jolted her more than anything.

Tony said to ignore him.

But Bobby was a man who couldn't be ignored.

Maybe you shouldn't ignore him.

Oh, God—where did that thought come from?

She checked the time. Midnight. The clubs were just revving up. The bar was crowded, the restaurant full. This was the hour people made connections, corrections, raised hell, or just went home.

Well, she was the original homing pigeon—

Someone sat down beside her. "Buy you a drink?"

Tony.

She sank back onto the bar stool. "You and Angie do not have to play baby sitter."

"Oh, sure, you're the tough, together Regan Torrance," Tony said, motioning for a beer on tap. "And you're so tender and raw on the inside, it's a wonder your heart isn't bleeding all over the sidewalk. Thanks, Gus," as Gus flipped his beer expertly down the long counter.

"Um-hmm." Regan sipped her wine. Better that than give Tony an opening to play father confessor yet again.

Tony slanted her a look, noted the stubborn set of her chin, took a long, deep swallow and banged the stein down on the counter.

She jumped, and she looked at him, as he intended, because he was not a man of extreme gestures. But it was damned hard to hold it in. For years, he had dreaded this moment, and today it had hit him with the full force of a hurricane.

And it wasn't Bobby's return. That was the least of it. It was watching Regan last night and the whole of today, and finally, fully comprehending what was what, and why Regan held everything and everyone at arm's length.

"You are still goddamned in love with him," he said savagely.

"No." No hesitation. Absolute certainty. But she looked as if he'd slapped her, she looked stunned, and then she prickled up. "Are you out of your mind?"

"Are you?" he retorted, and took another long swig. "You should've seen yourself today."

"You're crazy." She didn't sound convincing.

Oh, God—more secrets. . . .

"You're lying to yourself."

She felt upended all over again. Tony, of all people, to unleash this on her tonight. But, then, Tony had so much more than she to lose. "I'm not. And don't you play the martyr with me."

"Hell, I'm the one who's been holding you together all these years, Regan. And it's clear as glass after last night and today, that all you ever wanted was that smug bastard. And don't think he doesn't know it."

Regan got up abruptly. *No. NO. Oh, God, No . . .*

"I think we're done for tonight, my knight erroneous. You're wrong. And I'm not up for a scene right now. I'll see you in the morning."

"I'll take you home."

"I think I can manage that much by myself. Obviously, I haven't been able to manage anything else. According to you."

"Regan . . ."

"Don't bother."

"Fine." Tony eyed her over the rim of his beer. "It was time for some plain speaking anyway."

"Good night, Tony," she said stiffly.

"Sure." He watched her leave, every line of her body inflexible with fury.

Plain speaking. Plain crazy. He shouldn't have said it, shouldn't have voiced the thing they both most feared. It changed everything, bringing it out in the open, and that he feared most of all.

* * *

Ignore him.
Who?
She didn't want to even think about it. She was too tired, and he was a man who could not be ignored.

She stepped into the elevator of her apartment building.
Maybe you shouldn't ignore him.

She shucked her coat, as she entered her foyer, and flopped down on the couch.
Who?

Who was she trying to fool? she thought, draping an arm over her aching head. The last seven years had been a marathon of trying to ignore the thing she most wanted to forget, and it had all been for nothing: she was transparent as glass and she was the only one who saw her life through a frosted lens.

It sure blurred the outlines. Prettied things up. Made everything softer, fuzzier. Bearable.

And now—?
Maybe you should fight fire with fire. . . .
What? She bolted upright.
What was that thought?
Don't let them bulldoze you, either of them. Why not just . . . ?
Just—what?
Lord, she *was* tired. Or else she was having a nightmare.
. . . just let Bobby catch you . . . ?
Yep—sound asleep, not in her right mind.
Or maybe you're not as upset as you're pretending to be?
Maybe Tony was right and that's why you're so upset?
No, it was the headache talking—she was delirious. Not thinking straight. Thinking . . . what?
Thinking she would just hand herself over to Bobby on a silver platter?
Wearing a little paper frill around her neck. . . .
And nothing else. . . .
Cute thought. She eased back down on the sofa. *I need*

some aspirin. My head feels like a basketball. Needy but beautiful girls who are too full of themselves should never fall in love with young, rich, bad boys who are too full of themselves.

It had been a recipe for disaster. . . .

And yet—and yet . . . *he came back—for her. . . .*

How? Why?

Why her? Why now?

They were different people now. They didn't know each other. Whatever Bobby thought he came back for didn't exist. She wasn't malleable anymore; she was too strong, too headstrong, less emotional, absolutely in control except when people turned up where they shouldn't be.

So . . . why not just—go with it?

Oh, something hadn't changed. That insidious little thread of hope knotted around her heart . . .

Just go with it—and turn it all around. . . .

Chapter Four

So—he'd set his plan in motion, and Regan was already running as fast as she could. Or had Tony made sure she was nowhere around when he arrived for his appointment this morning?

Catch me if you can. . . .

Regan Torrance, broker on the go, who, being a modern kind of woman, had never relinquished her divorced husband's name.

It was enough to give a man hope.

Business. First.

The storefront where the paper was housed was small, too small for the plans he had for it. The title closed this afternoon. His walk-through was scheduled for this morning. And it was definitely part of his plan to have Regan find him the right commercial space.

So where was Regan at ten in the morning?

"Out with a client," Tony said blandly, pushing agency papers in front of him with all the disclosures and percentages spelled out.

Bobby signed the papers. "When can we start?"

"After your closing, if you like."

Bobby took his copies and folded them away. A couple of hours now, he thought, he'd own the building, the assets, everything.

Everything except Regan.

And that was on the docket, the next item to be attended to.

Tony escorted him to the door.

"Well, talk about timing," Bobby said, keeping his tone neutral. "Here comes Regan."

And there she was, her dark hair whipping in the morning wind, long and lean in a severe pantsuit, a classic polo coat and big round sunglasses out of a nineteen sixties issue of *Vogue*.

And Angie.

A client. Now what did that mean, Tony's deliberate lie?

"Ang." He nodded at her curtly as they came close enough to speak. "Tony. I'll call this afternoon. I'll assume Regan will have time to show me something then."

"Sure," Tony said, sending a warning look to Regan, who was about to protest. "We'll set up a couple interesting things that are available. Whenever you're ready."

Angie looked at Tony. "I have to go."

"Bye, Ang." Tony held open the door for Regan as Angie and Bobby went off together. "Back to work, hotshot. We've got megabucks on the line here."

"Maybe I need a vacation," Regan muttered as she followed Tony into the office. "Maybe I should get out of town for a couple of weeks until this brainstorm passes, and Bobby leaves town to pursue more profitable ventures."

"Hey, I wouldn't have thought the *Herald* would qualify as a profit center for Torrance Media, but obviously Bobby's pinpointed something there that's worth his time and energy," Tony said. "So, you'll sell the man some space."

"No sacrifice is too great," Regan murmured, "to fill the company coffers." For sure, she thought grimly. Bobby's money was as good as anybody else's, and nothing personal would ever get in the way of that, even for Tony.

The deal was done by noon, the deed signed and in his pocket, and the doors of the Herald open for business as usual. And Regan was waiting.

Or rather, Regan was at her desk, not at all looking like she was waiting. But when he hovered at the door, she put aside her papers and grabbed her coat.

"Okay, Bobby. Let's go. We could cab if you want."

"I have my car." Business as usual. But what did he expect?

She shrugged. "All right. We want the building at Endicott and Metro."

It took ten minutes through village traffic at the noon hour.

"Here we go," Bobby said, expertly drawing into a parking space in which he had perhaps an inch between the fenders, front and back.

Good at everything, Bobby was.

Regan launched into the sell. "This is the Endicott Building. They'll subdivide, build to suit. Price per square foot is unequaled anywhere in Manhattan right now. Not the best neighborhood, not the worst. Up and coming, and after the right tenant moves in and leads the way, there'll be no stopping development here. This is super space for your purposes."

However, it was the top floor of a five-story elevator building right near the el, which would need a gut renovation to bring it up to code for his operation.

Regan was striding around the huge floor, pointing out places where he could install things, partition things off and possibly set up the plant.

Striding was the word for it. Like she didn't want anything remotely sensual between them. Like she didn't look sensationally sexy in that pantsuit and camel hair coat.

Don't think about it. It's not about sex.

Hell, everything was about sex.

Back to business. "Is the building for sale?"

She consulted her notes. "Nope. I could put out the suggestion, if you're really interested."

"I'm probably going to have my architect look at each of the properties before I make an offer. So . . ." He was at the opposite side of the room, which was big and lofty as a warehouse. *If he took a flying leap across the room . . . ?*

"Okay, I've seen enough."

"It's a good opportunity," Regan said. "It's great space."

Too much space, he thought, between them. Still.

"You think? A printing plant on the top floor? I think we'd have a lot of shoring up to do every which way."

She looked up at him. Big mistake. Even in as vast a space as this, she felt his power. He was formidable. Maybe even more than someone like her could handle, given the spheres he traveled in these days.

Fire with fire? Maybe she was the one who had had a brainstorm. Up close and personal, it just wasn't realistic. She'd get burned to a crisp. It was way too late. *It was.*

"Maybe so," she said finally, tearing her gaze away, and moving restlessly across the room. "But at this price, it's doable."

"Anything is doable—for a price," Bobby said. "The only questions you have to answer are, is it worth the price, and do you want to pay the price. . . ."

She stopped in her tracks. "You're giving up an awful lot to come back and take on a business that to the outside world looks like small potatoes."

"I'm giving up nothing," he said softly, "in comparison to what I'm going to gain."

What? What were they talking about—really?

"Are we finished here?"

"Finished *here*," Bobby said. "Only just beginning elsewhere."

She made a sound in the back of her throat. *Ignore him.*

Down the service elevator they went. Into the car, and out from between the cars with three flicks of his wrist, and . . ."Have lunch with me."

"I don't think so, Bobby."

"Business lunch."

Backed her right into a corner. She didn't like this line where her past intersected with her present. *Go with it—?*

Easier to fantasize than to do . . . even though he was bent on making it easy. Painless. Close your eyes and let it rip. But how did you mend the tears and make the fabric whole after so many years?

He clearly didn't care what he had to use to get what he wanted.

Maybe she should take her cues from him.

"Whatever the client wants," she murmured. God, she sounded like a paid escort. Anything for the client, whether it was for a flat rate commission or a flat out fee.

He couldn't help the faint smile playing around his mouth.

Whatever the client wants? It wasn't printable what the client wanted. Just the thought of Regan wreaked havoc with his body. Having her beside him in the car was pure torture.

And he'd better stop thinking about her as if she were a fantasy. He'd lived with that Regan for far too long. The reality was so much better.

And prickly as hell. Without so many words, she was making it perfectly plain that business was business, and personal things were not allowed on the table.

He could get around that. Even that obstinate expression. That intent stare at the road ahead as he maneuvered his Mercedes into another tight parking space in front of Gus's. "Gus's okay?"

"Just fine."

The place was nearly empty, anyway. Gus was not at the bar. A hostess took them to a booth in the back, and they settled in there, Regan shrugging out of her coat with a sexy shimmy of her shoulders. And totally unaware of it, too.

"Regan?"

She lifted her gaze to his. This was too civilized, she thought. This is dangerous. Bobby had a look on his face that was pure predator.

"Yes, Bobby?" Tony hadn't exaggerated. Firecrackers. Boom, boom, boom. Flash and burn—she had to remember that. And sputtering down to nothing. She had to decide—now. Go with the fantasy or forever hold her peace. . . .

And he saw it, just a shadow of past pain and shared memory.

"We're not the same people."

"Of course we're not."

"It's not the same."

"Not in the least," she agreed, picking up the menu the hostess had left on the table. Don't make it easy.

"So let's just proceed as if we'd just met and felt this attraction."

"Or, we can choose not to proceed," she countered. "Much cleaner that way, Bobby."

"You're not denying what's going on."

"What do you think is going on, Bobby?" Hard to get was good, she thought, make him earn it. Or was it just a ploy for her to get some distance before she took the unthinkable leap?

. . . *Tony was right, you know* . . .

Fire with fire . . . go with it, and let him catch you—

But not quite yet. . . .

"You have some fantastic notion that because you want to rekindle something that burned to a crisp seven years ago, that I'd be willing to scrape and saw to get the flame going again. I'm not going to go through that again. It's too late for anything like that."

"It's not too late, damnit. And our past has nothing to do with what's going on now."

"What's going on now is lunch. I'm perfectly willing to talk about anything—except this."

"And I'm not willing to talk about anything else."

Stand-off. Now what? He was too close, she felt too vulnerable. Things she didn't want on the table were spread out like a buffet for him to chew on.

He was about to devour her.

"I'll have a salad," she said abruptly.

"I'll have you," he said in kind.

She flushed. That was as overt as he had been since their conversation at Mary Lee's party. Boy, it was one thing to decide not to ignore him, quite another to deal with him *mano a mano*.

"Pretend we're strangers," he said. "We have no history. We have no past. We just have two high-powered people lighting each other up."

"And sparking and fizzling out."

"You're a regular romantic."

"I'm a regular pragmatist."

Her stubbornness made him impatient. "Regan—"

"You said it yourself. It's all about sex."

"Isn't it?" he murmured. "All right . . . It's all about sex."

Oh, yes, the sex. Sex with an older, wiser, more experienced Bobby. She shuddered; she saw him, the boy, the body she'd idolized, saw him naked and young and bursting in her mind's eye. That Bobby . . . that . . . *part* of Bobby . . . she'd wanted to hold it and fold it deep inside her where she could keep it safe.

He didn't miss the slight movement of her body.

"It's about you," he added softly.

There was a statement that could melt glass. Could melt a woman. Bobby Torrance, at his high-powered, high-handed, most arrogant best, in spite of all that vaunted new maturity.

Ignoring him right now was not a bad strategy.

They ate in silence, Bobby having ordered a hamburger and a beer. Her salad was tasteless, with all that sizzled between them, and she couldn't wait to get away from the intimacy of the booth. "Are you ready?" she asked briskly, gathering up her notebook and bag.

"Are you?" Bobby murmured, signaling for the bill.

"For the next showing," Regan said, keeping her tone neutral, and clamping down on the creamy feeling that assaulted her vitals. He was stalking her with words and that look in his eye. Very effective, too.

Next time, she thought, she'd bring a chair and whip.

"I can't wait to see what you've got to show me," Bobby said, tossing a five dollar bill down on the table for the waitress.

"Nothing that can't be seen in public," she retorted.

A ground-floor property this time. Ground zero. Quick in and out.

Oh, God—it was getting worse the longer she was in his company.

Same area, but this lower floor came with access to the full basement, which put this property way on the plus side.

Plus Regan prowling the perimeter to keep as far away as possible from him because she was feeling everything he was feeling. And more.

It was amusing, and it was irritating.

And she was not distinterested.

And he didn't give a shit about the dynamics of space and cost per square foot at that moment.

Regan—?"

She turned to look at him.

God . . . that mouth, those eyes—

That body, even clothed to the neck in Ralph Lauren . . .

A ton of bricks all over again. It was the only way to describe it. Knocked sidewise, on his ass, all over again.

His whole body surged.

She was feeling it too. Shaken. Uncertain.

He could walk over there, take her in his arms and . . . he was moving, it was almost as if everything were in slow motion. Moving, going to her, to where she was waiting, she'd always been waiting—this moment seemed right, inevitable, here, now . . .

Too easy—

So close . . . don't move . . . not too late—

His mouth found hers, soft, testing, pliant, and then suddenly, explosively deep, probing, wet, intense.

She hadn't expected this—this instant connection, this hunger that came roaring up from deep in her core and pulled her into the undertow. She wanted to surrender everything to that mouth, and that was wholly unexpected—devastating, even.

She had no defenses. He pressed deeper and deeper, demanding more and more. She remembered this, remembered how she always wanted to imprint herself on him, how she couldn't get close enough to him. She wanted to open herself to him; she shuddered as the familiar excitement gushed through her like a waterfall.

Oh, Lord, she'd missed this. Needed it. Rejected it. Suppressed it deep inside her like some dirty little secret.

. . . Bobby . . . known and unknown . . . so familiar, so different, so much more in every way . . .

This . . . as his hand slid down toward her buttocks . . .

. . . this . . .

. . . as he slipped between her legs . . .

. . . this—her body jolting as his fingers pressed against her fully clothed vulva . . .

. . . and this—as she canted her hips to feel it, feel him, harder, tighter—her body creaming, yearning, reaching—

What????

Oh, God, what was she doing?

. . . come and get me—

He had. So easily, too quickly—

NO! NO! She wrenched away, out of his kiss, out of his reach, her body heaving with the force of her arousal.

"We're finished for today."

"We're not finished," Bobby said, his eyes glittering. He was breathing hard, too, and he didn't feel equal to taking no for answer. He was too hot, too hard, too fired up and too long without Regan except in his dreams.

Regan froze. There it was, that certainty, that presumption. You kiss your ex-wife, and she's yours, and seven barren years and everything bad just vanished into the ether somehow, and nothing else needed to be said.

"You can take me back to the office."

"I'm taking you home."

"I'm not going anyplace with you but back to the office. Or I'll walk."

He knew that expression on her face. She would walk. Some things hadn't changed despite the differences. His gut knew it, he had to accept it—she was in strict control where her emotions were concerned.

Except just now. Just now had nothing to do with her strength and her firewalls, and everything to do with the things she wouldn't admit she was feeling.

"We're not finished," he said.

"We haven't begun."

"Oh, what just happened says we've begun, Regan. I think we're miles beyond *begun*. I think we're exactly where we left off seven years ago."

"Right—with you leaving, and me picking up the pieces."

"You're scared."

"Nothing scares me," Regan said. "Not even you."

But that was a lie. The torrent of need he'd aroused scared her to death, and the only way to cope was to run. *Catch me if you can. . . .*

. . . And he had . . .

"Regan?"

"Umm?" She looked up from a contract she was scanning, but her eyes weren't focused, and Tony didn't like that one bit. She hadn't been back an hour, and she was thinking about Bobby instead of business, damn it, why else would there be that unfocused look in her eyes?

Shit. Taking Bobby on as a client was the worst mistake he'd made in all his years in business.

Still in love with him. He knew it in his bones. . . .

It just drove him to the wall, imagining them together again. Imagining Regan, soft, open, wanting. Wanting Bobby. It just jacked him off that Regan was still in love with the bastard, knowing Tony wanted her too.

There hadn't been a day in all the years he'd known her,

that he didn't make it clear one way or another that he wanted to get in and get off with her.

That look in her eyes . . . soft, heated . . . suppressing her feelings, her needs—knowing *he* could fill them, and never ever offering him the opportunity. He could have taken her on the desk, against the wall, on the chair—how long did a man have to endure before the woman he wanted even noticed his hard-on?

She never did. Or she pretended not to. After all these years, he couldn't tell. The only thing he knew was that she was the most carnal woman he'd ever met, that she was utterly unaware of it, and she was tearing herself up when he was right there for her, all the time.

"Regan . . ."

She stared at him. There it was again: the pitch of his voice, the way he said her name, the bulge between his legs.

"Yeah, listen." She rattled the paper to get his attention off of her. "Cargill's office faxed me: they're interested in setting up his offices here. So clever of you to invite him to my party. That's why he thought of it."

Tony knew when he was licked. And it was not the way he would have preferred to be licked either. "Did you set up a meeting?"

"I'm about to."

"Good. This is the beginning. Especially"—and now he was torturing himself—"especially if Bobby bites."

Her eyes flashed.

He knew it—something had happened this afternoon. Damn, damn, damn.

"Bobby doesn't bite; Bobby gnaws," Regan said. "Bobby nips. Bobby sucks. We can't wait for Bobby to make a decision about anything. I'll just tell Cargill he's impressed by the numbers and is seriously considering space under the el."

"Nice strategy."

She picked up the phone. Was that a strategy? She couldn't devise a strategy to save her life right now. God, speaking to

Cargill was the last thing she wanted to do at the moment. She hated Tony for bringing her back to reality. His reality. His need that she never could see a way to handle. It was easier keeping him at arm's length, because he would never have been satisfied with crumbs.

He would have been worse than Bobby, come to that, even more possessive and more demanding. And Bobby's return had only made it worse. The fact she was sitting and fantasizing about Bobby, and that kiss, was proof enough her whole carefully constructed life was going to hell.

Tony knew her too well.

She spoke to Cargill's secretary. They could meet tomorrow morning—at the Inn, if she'd prefer. That was fine. That was the way you did business in the Heights.

And business was business. And fantasy was . . .

Fantasy was the stuff that made you crazy.

"Going out," she called out to Tony.

"Hey, wait—I'll go with you. We'll get a drink." And he didn't give her a chance to say no.

It was the only way he knew to make sure she wasn't going to be with Bobby.

Chapter Five

She had calmed down, finally. And all it had taken was an hour with Tony over a glass of wine at Gus's. Tony knew just when to pull back and be a friend. He always had. And now that she could look at the situation with an objective eye, she decided she had overreacted to everything, including what had happened this afternoon.

She could handle Bobby.

She shouldn't have bought those damned sandals, she thought with a trace of humor. All this had started because she'd let out that one little piece of herself that she normally hid away. It was true: there was nothing like a pair of Mascolos to drive everyone nuts, including the person wearing them.

Even Angie had gone off the deep end over them.

And then—that kiss. She should never have given in to that heat between them. Never should have let him within ten feet of her. Never should have agreed to be his sales rep altogether.

It just wasn't good business.

And she shouldn't have to change her life just because of that kiss and that sensual grope.

Oh, yeah? Define your life.

Good job, good friends, good money, good times.

An occasional fucking.

More secrets.

It was laughable. Angie thought she was a wanton; Tony thought she was a nun. Not hardly. And to preserve everyone's illusions, she went out of town to spend a rare night with a date, where neither of her best friends could find out about it.

Catch me if you can. . . .

She felt heat swamping her body. She should have known better than to challenge Bobby like that.

Catch me. . . . Drive him crazy, drive him away.

Drive into me . . . it had been so long—

No. Yes.

Why not?

The intercom buzzed. Angie, probably, when she wasn't up for girl gossip tonight. She pressed the callback button. "Ang?"

The phone rang. "Regan?"

The intercom: "I'm coming up."

Bobby. And you didn't argue with that tone, either.

Damn. "Ang? Hey, can I call you back?"

"What's up?"

Angie was checking up on her again. The lie came straight and fast. "Just got out of the shower. Give me twenty minutes."

"Okay." Angie hung up the phone just as the doorbell rang.

Thank heaven. Angie would have wanted to know who that was. Angie had sonar when it came to ferreting out things Regan didn't want to tell her, especially anything about Bobby.

She flung open the door. And there was Bobby at his bad boy best. The worn jeans, the chambray shirt, the beaten-up leather jacket.

"Oh, you're good," she murmured. "You're really good."

"*We're* good," Bobby corrected her. "Really, really good."

"Really nice to see you too, Bobby. Just why did you barge in here?"

He wasn't exactly sure himself. And ascending to the twentieth floor of the newest condo apartment building in the Heights, the one with *two residences* per floor, hadn't cemented his resolve either.

Rather, it had made him feel just a little disoriented.

This was a far cry from the docks where Regan grew up. Light years from the Regan of seven years ago. And a million miles from anything they'd shared together in their Roman rocket of a marriage.

Yet she looked exactly the way she had all that time ago. She looked twenty again, in jeans, tee shirt clinging to her full breasts, no makeup, hair in a ponytail.

And she was even more beautiful like that.

"You could really invite me in."

"Guess I could. But maybe it works like vampires—you can't come in unless you're invited."

"Not too civilized, Regan."

"I'm not feeling too civil right now, Bobby. And I think you're here for your pound of flesh, so the vampire analogy seems pretty apt to me."

"Let me in, Regan."

He meant it, on so many levels.

She threw up her hands. He would suck her dry with words, if nothing else. She motioned him in, and he strode into the entrance hallway with its soft lights and length that led every guest straight toward the bank of floor to ceiling windows in the living room that framed the view across the river.

The palette was neutral against jewel tones, in the oriental rugs, in the sofas and chairs, in the rich wood of antique furniture played against ivory-colored walls and curtainless windows, and the glow of uplights everywhere.

She watched him prowl the living room, picking up objects and looking at them, making his way around the room until he came back to where she stood with her hands on her hips in the entry hall.

He felt a little off balance, as if he couldn't assimilate that the Regan in jeans and tee was the same woman who inhabited this sophisticated apartment.

"Want some coffee?"

"I want you."

"No, you don't. You want sex."

He flinched. "Right. You're every man's damned wet dream. Or at least those men you know. *My* purpose hasn't changed, Regan."

"What was that again? No. I don't want you to say anything. Or do anything."

"Yes, you do. We both know you do."

"This afternoon didn't change anything."

"No, not a thing. Just showed how obvious it is you're running away."

"Nonsense. What from?"

"Me."

"Oh, yeah, I've just been running my life around your timetable, Bobby, you know, the one where you leave for seven years."

"How about, you've been running in place for seven years?"

Regan turned away. This was a conflagration, already out of control. She couldn't put out this fire, not with words, or deeds, or even a cold shower.

He had cornered her well and truly. It would be easier to surrender than to fight. "What do *you* want?" she asked finally.

"Nothing's changed. I want you back."

She made a sound. What did "back" mean exactly? Oh, she knew; he'd said it already in twenty different ways.

It was all about sex.

"Tell me what you want," Bobby said.

She stared at him. In her most flagrantly wishful dreams, she had never imagined Bobby standing in her living room, handing the power over to her. Never imagined she would still feel anything for him after all this time. Or that she wouldn't have all the answers when this longed-for moment finally came, and he was saying things any woman would want to hear.

. . . Be careful what you wish for . . .

What did she want, really?

She wanted not to follow the first impulse and dive into bed, not to succumb to her hormones—or his.

No mercy. She wanted to make it not *easy for him.*

"No sex," she said finally.

"No . . . sex . . . ?"

"No. None."

"Do you think that's even remotely possible for more than thirty seconds?"

She didn't actually; she was already feeling those magnetic waves. And his tight jeans hid nothing. But that was nothing new, either.

"That's what I want."

"And that's it?"

She swallowed. Not one minute of mercy for Bobby after all these years.

"Courting," she added, through a dry throat. After all, patience was not Bobby's strong suit. And that ought to keep him at arm's length. He wouldn't agree to that. Wouldn't have, in the past. Bobby had always wanted everything yesterday, including her.

Bobby raised his head. "Courting? Like—"

"Like people used to do back in the Dark Ages."

"Which people are those?" Bobby muttered. "Fine." This was a sweet five minutes of nineteen-fifties sensibility.

Or was it a way for Regan to deal with him without getting to the main issue? But that would come soon enough. "Fine. We're still going to be looking at property, so we'll take it from there."

"Take it where?" Regan asked suspicious.

"Movies, dinner. Bowling." *Bowling*! "Theater. Parties." *Fucking.* "Whatever."

"No sex."

"Your call. But you're done hiding. And I don't care what Tony thinks."

Oh, God. Tony. Tony wanted that megabucks commission and then he wanted to put Bobby out of commission.

Bobby watched the emotions chase all over Regan's face. "I'm not going anywhere, Regan. You can't scare me off."

"Well, you scare the hell out of me," Regan muttered.

"And no sex on top of that. Nice ploy. When do we start?"

"What?"

"When do we embark on this odyssey of *no sex?*" Crazy. He was nuts to agree to this, nuts to think he could keep his hands off of her for more than—well, it had been an hour now, and that was only because he was still trying to maneuver through the minefield that was *this* Regan.

He thought he was handling her well. Not that he expected her to fall into his arms. Not yet, anyway. He could deal with *no sex* for about—oh, an hour. But in his fantasies, he handled her until she was so spent, so exhausted, she could only collapse.

He couldn't look at her without wanting to plow her. It was a pure, ongoing never-ending ache deep within him. One kiss had been hardly enough to assuage it. A lifetime with her might just begin to satisfy it.

No sex.

Whatever she wanted, whatever it took, he'd do.

She was oh, so prim and proper when, the next day, she arranged for him to see the next property. She wore a creamy silk blouse, open at the throat in an innocently provocative way, tucked into a long skirt of swingy black crepe, a short matching jacket, and strappy sandals; her hair in a topknot, understated makeup. A big mock croc tote bag. Those Jackie O sunglasses.

That Regan aura, of innocence and knowlege, even as she was scrabbling through the bag looking for information on the listing.

It was the damned sandals. That touch of eroticism that made men salivate.

"You could renovate your own building, you know," Regan pointed out as they drove past the next location on Main Street. *Forget about yesterday, forget Angie. This was business. It* was.

"But think of the rents I could get if the *Herald* relocated. Want to be my building manager?" *Want to manage me?*

No sex . . . God, he felt twenty-four again.

The property was a single level full-block storefront that had been a Laundromat.

"Maybe a little too close to Main Street?" Bobby said, as he prowled the premises. The good thing—the work was done. One floor and basement, location near-prime. And that was reflected in the price.

"Maybe. Or maybe you want to be that accessible."

I am as accessible as a man can be right now.

"But that probably depends on what your plans are for the *Herald*."

Oh, those plans.

No sex. That's what those plans are.

"Okay. I've seen enough."

"Okay." She switched off the lights and locked the door behind them.

"How about some pizza," he said. "In line with courting and bowling and all that." And watching her bite into that thick doughy crust . . .

Lord help him. . . .

She slanted a flashing look at him. "Sure, I'm game." Playing games altogether, being seen with Bobby? What was she thinking?

And when they were seated in the booth and had ordered: "Civility works," he said.

"No sex works, you mean."

"No, I don't think *no sex* works at all," Bobby said.

"And yet here we are," Regan murmured, "having no sex and being civil."

"I like being primitive better."

"What are you going to do with the *Herald*?" she asked to distract him.

"Turn it into a porn publication."

"Obviously *no sex* is too hard for you."

"No. *No sex* makes me too hard for you."

"You asked what I wanted you to do—"

"And I'm doing it. I'm just not liking it."

No pity, no mercy. "Well, here's the pizza," she said, as the waitress set it down.

They ate in silence, or rather, he watched her biting and chewing, getting harder and more restless by the moment.

"Regan . . ."

She looked up at him, mid-bite.

God, that mouth—he never could get over that mouth . . .

"*No sex* is getting us nowhere."

"Where do you want to get, Bobby, except back in my bed?"

"That'll do, for starters."

She was silent for a moment. There was no denying this was a test, testing his endurance, his mettle, his patience.

Testing herself, and what she wanted after all this time, at a distance where she could feel as if she had some control. But that was an illusion at best. It really came down to sex: he wanted what was between her legs. That was a certainty. Everything else was heartbreak.

Catch me . . .

She'd thrown down the challenge.

No sex.

"Yeah, well—" she temporized. "That would be too easy."

"Oh, stop it, Regan. Just—just let me back in."

"You *were* in, all that time ago." She bit into another slice, hard, and he felt that telltale spurt between his legs.

"Let me in again." His voice was husky, urgent, arousing things in her she didn't want to remember, to feel, things that were heightened by the way he looked at her all the time, and were underpinned by her unrequited feelings about him, and his undeniable sexual magnetism.

She didn't know this new Bobby—or what he was capable of, in bed or out of it.

He grasped her hand suddenly, explosively. "Caught you, Regan."

Her throat tightened, her body liquefied. "You can't come up tonight."

"I don't have to *come* up—I am up. I've been up for days. I could push out walls, I'm so hard for you. Try me, Regan."

"You're not the house specialty, Bobby."

"Maybe I am."

"Not on this menu, and not tonight."

"Right. The menu: Dinner. Bowling. Whatever. Twelve ninety-five with soup and salad."

"Exactly."

"So, then, what's for dessert?"

She had an instant vision of *creamy* things. She *felt* creamy, all soft, pliant, her body unfurling like a flower. He was a magician to make her feel like that when she was resisting him so hard. "Don't go there."

"Oh, I'm already there, Regan."

A recipe for disaster, this was. There was too much against it—not least, their past. And they were sideswiping everything about that in his tearing need to quickly reestablish a connection.

And everyone was opposed to it. *Everyone?*

All good reasons to forge full steam ahead.

Which was exactly what the old Regan, pre-divorce, would have done.

Hell, Bobby had a head of steam on him already that was damned hard to resist, even with all her resolve. Her every instinct was to touch him, melt into him, take his heat, his hardness, for her own. The urge was so tempting, so much folly.

. . . so what? . . .

Who would know? Who would care?
Sweet little lie.

"Regan?"

And then that softness in his voice, that emotional break. His warm, hard hand still grasping her own. Those dark eyes with worlds more experience, full of promise. When Bobby Torrance was hot, hard and ready to go, there was no getting in his way. He was mesmerizing.

I came back for you . . .

Irresistible.

I want you . . .

Indomitable.

The night was young, and she'd punished herself—and him—enough, she thought.

She pushed out of the booth. "You win. Yes, sex. Let's go."

In the elevator. She lifted her skirt before the door even closed. She was naked underneath. His possession was swift, hard, the prelude to a night of hot, unrelenting fucking.

There was hardly time as the elevator shot up to her floor, to do anything but feel the pleasure of him cramming into her before they had to pull apart.

She'd forgotten how hot he was, how hard, how *there*. Like granite between her legs. Her hand shook as she opened the door.

She stripped in thirty seconds and pulled him onto the couch, her legs spread, her pubic hair glistening with his ejaculate.

He mounted her without preliminaries; she was slick, hot, tight, endless.

Home.

He rocked against her hips, working himself deeper, tighter, harder, his head buried against her shoulder, listening to the erotic sounds of her accommodation, her pleasure.

"I may never move again," he whispered. "This is where I belong."

And the minute he had made that admission, his body seized and spewed, and he reared back and drove his point home.

Chapter Six

This was fine. On her back on the sofa, with him mounted on her, his penis swimming in his cream deep inside her, oh, that was so fine. So luscious.

So necessary. How did she live without it—without him—so long?

She felt a swamping greed. She wanted more. She felt his penis flexing inside her, still rock hard.

He wanted more.

"I want your nipples," he murmured.

"You just don't stop."

"We haven't even started."

"I didn't think so."

He shifted his body and maneuvered her onto his lap, his penis still embedded in her, and her breasts now at mouth level.

Gorgeous, responsive breasts, the nipples pebble hard and pointed. Inviting. Just waiting to be fucked by a mouth and tongue that knew just what to do with them.

"I need that nipple now."

She braced her hands against his shoulders as he settled his lips around her left nipple.

Just his lips, soft and moist. Just the nipple, tight and hard. Just the faintest of pulling sensation. Faint, faint, growing more definitive, more precise, just the tight, hard tip of the nipple compressed in his lips.

No tongue. Not yet. Just the pull, the sucking, pressing pull on her nipple, growing harder now, and harder. His other hand cupping her right breast, his fingers seeking that nipple, so that she felt two sensations centered at each hard tip: a sucking, pulling wetness and a soft caressing compression between his fingers.

And all the while, the hot upright penetration of his penis, the root, the root on which her body writhed and skirled as he sucked and squeezed. Sucked and squeezed. Hot, hard, his lips now squeezing her left tit in erotic tandem with his fingers playing with the other, with the grinding of her hips as she rocked and rolled her body against his penis.

And then his hot, wet tongue flicked it, curled around it and he began to pull on that nipple while he held the other compressed between his fingers and the pleasure, the pressure, his control of her body by his owning her nipples, the hardness of him intimate and naked within—it was more than she could bear.

So much more.

But she couldn't get away. She didn't want to. The pleasure skeined through her, primitive and profound. She wanted only to keep watching his possession of her nipples with his mouth, his tongue, his fingers, until she shattered into a thousand pieces.

And it was coming. He was eating her nipple, compressing it between his lips, and holding onto the other nipple as he fed at her.

Oh, God, he knew just how to do it. *Just* . . . her body heaved . . . *like* . . . and bucked on him . . . *that*—as lightning struck. Down she went, down, down, down on his hardness and into that gorgeous oblivion where the only thing that existed was the pouring pleasure centered on her nipples.

And he never let her go.

Down. Hard. Tight. Reverberating all over her body. Silence. Raw. Swirling away. And gone.

Tension in him, as he relinquished her, taut as a bow.

She lowered her mouth onto his, the first kiss since that previous day—could that be so?—and his orgasm rolled out of him like a storm.

And then he gathered her in his arms, shifted to his side, which caused him to withdraw, and pulled her on top of him as he lay down.

Feeling so right, so sated, her body languid and drenched with semen. She swiped a finger full and rubbed it into her swollen breasts.

Perfect. She'd never again deny herself this. If this was all there was to being with him, for whatever time it was— then, yes . . .

Yes, sex.

And no regrets.

That was the first hour. Regan awoke a short time later to the awareness of his hands all over her, stroking her, feeling her, caressing her slit, her buttocks, thumbing her nipples.

Instantly, she was erect and aroused, and groping for his penis.

He was huge, tender, thrusting. His mouth took hers as he inserted his fingers between her legs. She grasped him tighter as his tongue plunged against hers.

Kisses, naked in the dark—that was what was missing. These incredibly hot, voluptuous kisses, sweet and insistent, swirling down to her toes.

His fingers, probing her, spreading her, exploring all that she was.

She had never felt so naked, so excited, so out of control. He knew just how to hold her down there, just how to manipulate the delicate folds. Just how to make her wanton with need and lusting for his penis, his possession.

But no penis this time. This time his expert fingers playing with her nakedness, delving into her wet, finding the nub. And his mouth distracting her. And her hands frantically stroking the hard part that should be between her legs.

Just there. Oh, God. He splayed her legs wider apart with his leg. He spread the folds of her cleft further outward to reveal her pleasure point.

And there he played, exposing her nakedness to his expert manipulations.

She could do nothing more than bear her heaving hips down on his writhing fingers, nothing more but succumb to the pressure of his nestling fingers rubbing and sliding all over her naked clit.

There was nothing like this, ever—her whole world focused down on the rhythmic movement of his fingers on her point of pleasure. And it was coming. Her fingers convulsed on his shaft as she felt it coming, like a thundercloud rolling in, it came, rolling, rolling, dark, dark, swirling, catching her up as lightning bolted through her body, crackling through her bones, and flashing away.

"Don't move," she whispered.

"I couldn't . . . I'll explode."

But he still held her between her legs, her folds still spread, and she loved the way her nakedness was wholly open to him.

She made a restive movement toward, and his fingers inexorably moved with her, and she loved the feeling of that, too.

They spoke in whispers. "Kiss me."

"I am kissing you. Where it counts."

"I love the feel of your fingers doing that."

"Good. I love doing it."

"What else do you love doing?"

"Everything you can imagine."

"Let's start."

"We have." He pushed against her cleft to widen it farther and she writhed her hips against the pressure of his fingers. He flicked her clit gently. "Nice. You're all aroused again."

She made a helpless erotic sound, but he wouldn't release her.

"I want to hold you like this all night."

"Anything . . ." She felt wild, primitive, aggressive. It was feeling his fingers, the way he kept spreading her. She felt as naked as a cavewoman and just as primeval. He owned her pleasure point. There were no more secrets from him, and now he owed her his penis.

"I want you to feel my fingers there every minute of every day." His voice was low and fierce. "I want you to know where you live and you'd better remember who knows it more intimately than you do, and who owns it, and who fucks it."

"I know," she whispered.

"Now you do." He caressed her clit and she shuddered. "All ready all over again."

"Then give me your penis."

"Not yet. I love holding you all wide-open like this." Her hips churned against his fingers. "Bobby . . ."

He silenced her with a kiss, deep, wet, swamping as he kept pushing at her labia. She pulled away, breathless, panting. "I need . . ."

"Not yet." He took her mouth again, pushing and pushing, battling her writhing, demanding body. Winning because the feel of his fingers pushing at her like that was so erotic, she didn't want him to stop. Yet. Soon. Maybe.

And, then, one well-placed touch of his fingers and her body exploded. The only word—just *boom*—and a thousand pinpoints of light sparked all over her body and flicked out in the darkness.

He had relinquished his relentless hold, and she nestled up against him, half asleep. If this wasn't his best wet dream, he didn't know what was. Regan wholly his in every way possible—except . . . that one.

And they needed to talk about that. Maybe not now.

Maybe the thing was just to get her to say yes while she was all soft and sated and cuddly.

Cuddly—Regan? In the aftermath of hot raunchy sex, she was as pliant as a sponge, everything absorbed into her and utterly wrung out.

For this five minutes. This was how to deal with Regan: all the sex she could handle—and . . .

Love her. Only differently, this time. Without jealousies and fights and recriminations and withdrawals and withholding anything. Just love her.

He loved her. Always had. Now he knew how.

His penis flexed, reminding him that he'd foregone his own release in the fury and spontaneity of hers.

. . . No, actually, he didn't think so. He wanted something else first.

He brushed a stray strand of hair away from her face and she stirred.

He slipped his fingers between her legs. Oh, yes—she was still wet. Just where he wanted her to be. He moved her slowly and cautiously so that he could reposition himself just there.

It didn't take long for her to awaken. She felt his tongue, flicking in and out of her nether lips, felt him going deeper as he spread them outward, slipping, sliding his tongue all in and out of her, reaching for the elusive point of her pleasure.

She canted her hips upward as he ate her. It was nothing more than full bore possession by his tongue, and she was naked and open to him even more. She wanted to fight it, she wanted desperately to run away from it, the sucking and kissing, and his tongue swirling with intimate knowledge in her very core.

Instead, she let him take her. Let him have all of her that he could get at, all of her he could take in that voluptuous and carnal way.

And when his tongue and lips finally pulled on her clit,

there was nowhere to hide; she convulsed and convulsed with each rhythmic pull until she thought her body could take no more. And then she convulsed again, giving herself up wholly to that tongue, that mouth, that man.

He buried his face in her muff, inhaling her scent, her sex. God, she was something. Endless.

And he wasn't done yet. He still had a penis to satisfy, and he so tender, so bursting, he thought he didn't have a chance to get father inside her than his head before he detonated.

But he'd wait. He'd learned a lot of hard lessons about waiting.

"Bobby?" Her voice was the merest breath, as if speaking out loud would break the spell, the sensual bubble in which she floated.

"What?"

"I love everything you're doing. Everything. But I need to feel something hot and hard between my legs."

"And what would that be?"

"*You*, Bobby. I really need *you*."

"Me too," he muttered, mounting her, taking her, taking her, taking her . . . straight on till morning.

You played chess with men like Bobby, with your boss and even with your friends.

It was a matter of degree. And a matter of the lies, scattered like seed to root and spawn.

"What happened last night?" Angie demanded as she came bustling into the Riverside Inn. "Why didn't you call me back?"

"I forgot." She wasn't going to talk about Bobby. She hadn't quite assessed what had happened last night with Bobby. And it was too private, too personal, anyway. And that was a lie, too. "So don't read me the riot act over one little phone call. Besides, I'm tired and you know I can't talk coherently before I have coffee."

Angie backed off and slid into the booth. Something

happened last night after her phone call, she could tell just by that little slip. She felt a tingle of foreboding. And she wondered why she instantly thought it had to do with Bobby.

She clamped down on her first impulse to ask questions. If she were patient, Regan would spill everything in her own good time.

She picked up the menu. "I never could understand how you could stand it day after day, all those clients, all that juggling, all those moves and countermoves. Doesn't it wear you out?"

Thank God, Angie wasn't going to question the abortive phone call. Smart Angie. So much easier to talk about business.

"It's a lot of money, and some deals come with incentives." *Like sex.* "And the minute we find some momentum, the sky's the limit. So—we play chess."

"I know you're good at it."

"You bet." And before today, it had mercifully kept her too engrossed to think about anything else. But maybe that was the reassurance that Angie wanted.

Needed.

Or maybe *she* needed it.

Angie looked a little tentative this morning, a little unhappy.

"You need a job," Regan said. "Have some coffee."

"I have a job. I take care of Mother."

"Who is perfectly capable of taking care of herself."

"You haven't seen her recently: she looks older, more frail. Bobby's coming home hasn't made her happy."

Damn—mistake to share that. Regan was certain to want to know why.

But Regan didn't comment, and Angie went on, trying to backpedal, "She's kind of isolated herself, doesn't go out hardly at all, or do much of anything."

"She's an iron butterfly," Regan said. "She's punishing someone for something. Bobby, maybe?"

Well, who wouldn't have honed in on that? Angie thought. "Probably. She thought everything was all set up in Chicago. I bet if she'd known Bobby was planning something like this homecoming, she'd have finally consented to move there."

"But then what would she have done? There's no Regan to hate in Chicago."

Angie looked up at her sharply. "No, there isn't. She'd have died of boredom. Now she'll die of resentment. And Bobby came home really late last night, by the way. Really, *really* late." The worst thing. Her worst fears. She hadn't meant to emphasize it quite that way, but that flicker in Regan's eyes was all she needed: Bobby *had* been with Regan last night. And that was why Regan hadn't returned her call.

She wanted to kill Regan just because of that, if nothing else. Because Bobby was in her thrall, ever a man, and couldn't keep his hands off her or his penis in his damned pants.

"None of that is my fault, Angie. None of that—or Bobby's coming back."

"Maybe Bobby's coming back," Angie said tightly.

Regan poured some coffee to warm up her cold cup. Another mistake, getting onto this track. She didn't want to hear that Angie knew about last night.

"We're talking too much about him."

"Mother knows."

"Knows what?"

"He's back because of you."

Well, she wasn't a plague, for God's sake. She wasn't a leper. "Well, she'll just have to deal with it."

Angie set down her cup. One cup of coffee, and she'd already said too much when all she wanted to know was what happened last night.

Maybe.

No, all she wanted to know was whether Bobby had finally screwed Regan last night. And maybe she didn't want to know, because if she did, she might do something drastic. "Forget I said that."

"Why? What do you—what does *she* expect me to do about it?"

Typical Regan. Just mess up everyone else's life with her thoughtlessness and selfishness, and bulldoze right through it without considering the consequences.

And now she *had* to know. And she didn't care how it came out: blunt was best with Regan. "He was there last night, wasn't he? That's why you didn't call back. Did you sleep with him?"

Regan didn't answer.

"After all you've been through, after his rejection of every possible overture, after the spectacle you made with him at your party, and after the sheer stupidity of taking him on as a client? You just fell into his arms after all you put him through and *fucked* him?"

Oh, God, this was worse than she ever could have imagined. Angie's fury, the mother's alienation, Bobby's folly and determination . . . her own inescapable need—of course they were on a collision course . . . it was the only possible end to seven years' repression and isolation.

"Why don't we call it a morning, Ang, before anything else gets said that shouldn't." And, heaven knew, already there had been enough.

Angie reached for her bag. "I think everything's been said. I think there's nothing more to be said except stay away from my brother."

Stay away . . .

She threw down five dollars and stalked out of the restaurant.

No sex . . . ever again—

Regan buried her head in her arms.

Of course it had turned into a disaster.

. . . maybe you should just go away . . .

Chapter Seven

She felt so distraught she didn't know what to do. It just wasn't possible that Angie had harbored such feelings all these years and she hadn't known it.

But maybe it was. Or maybe Bobby was the catalyst. But why, she couldn't conceive for the life of her unless Angie wanted for Bobby what his mother had always wanted: good blood, good bones, good breeding.

And no liaisons with the likes of *her*.

She called Tony on her cell.

"Angie hates me."

"Angie doesn't hate you. Tell me what happened. No, on second thought, let me guess. Bobby." God, there hadn't been a moment that wasn't fraught with Bobby since the party. Since he, looking at the bigger picture, had taken Bobby on as a client. Since Regan had been five minutes in his company.

He was tired to hell of Bobby. And his foreboding about what Regan was going to tell him that he didn't want to know.

"Bobby."

Tony closed his eyes. Enough. "I don't want to know about it."

"But Angie—"

"She'll get over it, whatever it is. She always does. And I guess I will too."

"Tony . . . ? She was so angry—"

"Well, that's the thing with Bobby. You either love him or hate him. And everyone knows what side of that fence you're on, Regan. So . . . spare me the soap opera details. You know what you're doing. And now you know how Angie feels about it—and, now—I guess—me. So, take your meetings this morning, and let me know how they went. I'll see you later at the office."

And what had she expected? Regan thought as she tucked the phone away. That Tony would be thrilled? That he'd say Angie was wrong? That he'd say everything was going to be just fine?

Tony had said that for years, but now that Bobby was a reality in their lives, things weren't going to be fine at all. And she didn't know what had ever made her think they would be.

And all she'd done was traded a night of incandescent pleasure for a whole new menu of lies.

It didn't work, it didn't work, it didn't work . . .

She didn't know where to run, what to do. *Bobby and Regan, Bobby and Regan . . .* for seven years she'd managed to keep them apart, managed to keep Bobby in Chicago, managed to keep her mother mollified, and managed to maintain a friendship with Regan so she'd always know where Regan was, and what she was up to.

And now this. Not even her just falling into his arms after all these years was enough to deter Bobby. God, he needed help, he needed therapy, if that slut was what his dreams were made of. If he thought he would bring that tramp back into the family.

Never. Ever.

"Tony . . . !" She slammed into the office. Regan would be along soon, too soon for her to really talk to Tony.

He was at the front desk, and on his feet the moment he saw her face.

176 / *Thea Devine*

"He didn't come home. They fucked last night. Oh, god-damnit—they *fucked* last night."

He held out his arms and she walked straight into them. "How do you stand it," she demanded. "How?"

Tony stroked her hair. "I don't know how I stand it, year after year, picking up the pieces. Maybe the fact she's never wanted to screw me makes her all that much more desirable. I don't know. I never knew. But this is one humpty-dumpty I don't want to put back together again."

"I just left her at the diner."

"I know. She called. And there you go: who's the first one she thinks of when she's upset? Well, she'd better get un-upset real fast: she's got a second meeting with Cargill, and a new client who's interested in the el area. She won't be back for hours. Which is a good thing."

"Thank God," Angie murmured. "I said things. I'm glad I said them. But it's ruined everything. *She* ruined everything. Oh, Tony . . ." She burrowed her face into his shoulder. "Why couldn't she just leave Bobby alone?"

Wasn't that the question? Or further still, why couldn't Bobby just leave her alone?

"Let's go into my office before the rest of the staff gets here, and we'll talk some more."

She drew in a shuddering breath. "I don't know what to do, I just don't know what to do."

"Coffee?"

She shook her head, and he left a note on his secretary's desk, and herded her into his office. "Take off your coat. Sit down. Take it slow."

She slipped out of her coat, hung it on the door and turned to face him.

She didn't have to say it. It was in her eyes, and her need reflected his own. They both needed comfort—they needed each other.

And he wondered why they'd never thought of doing this as he closed the door and eased her to the floor.

* * *

She shouldn't have called Tony. The thing between her and Bobby was just that, between them, and it was no one's business.

No one's business that she went back to the apartment to reassure herself he was still there, still hers. No one's business how they might spend the ensuing hour that she was scheduled for a business meeting.

Bobby was her business, but it really was time to get back to the office, she thought, eyeing the clock on the kitchen wall.

"I like nipples for breakfast," Bobby said, nuzzling her breasts. "I want you for breakfast, every day." He sat up abruptly. "I want you, Regan."

"I think I know that."

"I mean, I want you back. I want a life, love, marriage, all the stuff that comes with it—with you."

She sat very still for a moment, stunned. Somehow, she didn't expect this. Not on top of Angie's diatribe this morning. And not while what was between them now was so new and fragile.

And breakable.

Somehow she thought he was just getting his rocks off, scratching that seven year itch, fucking her for as long as she didn't bore him, and going on from there.

And she'd been willing to accept that the moment she'd agreed to *yes, sex.*

Or had she?

"I think you're still dreaming," she said finally.

"I think a man wants to marry any woman who has the talent to keep those damned shoes on even when she's fucking. Regan—"

"What?"

"I'm serious."

"You think you are. But you don't bring girls like me home to Mother. You've seen the results."

"For Christ's sake. That wasn't a fairy tale, Regan. I came back for you, plain and simple. I earned you. That's how I thought of it. I was working my way back to you. Putting in time, growing up, working to deserve you."

"Don't—don't . . ."

"I gave Angie dozens of messages for you after I left . . ."

Angie? Her friend. Her confidante—all those years—?

No, Bobby didn't ask for you. He doesn't want, doesn't need, doesn't care . . .

Ohmigod, Angie. No wonder, no wonder . . .

She made a sound that was almost heartbreaking as the ramifications of that admission sunk in.

He got the picture, instantly. "Shit." Every goddamned body conspiring against him, were they? Not anymore, damnit. "Regan? Don't cry."

"I'm not."

"Good. We've got work to do."

"What work?" she asked suspiciously through her tears.

"Marketing. And spin. I'm taking control of this mess and I'm putting an end to it."

Tony. Of all the unexpected things.

Tony . . .

Was it mutual need or mutual vengeance?

In the aftermath of their furious coupling, Angie didn't know quite what to do, or even what to think.

"Hell, don't think," Tony encouraged her. "Just feel. We've both sat on our feelings for too long. Sat on possibilities, and almost murdered our own desire to be loved."

"But you've wanted *her* for so long . . ."

"Maybe I thought I did," Tony said. "Maybe it's habit. Maybe it's territorial. I was completely content until you told me Bobby was back in town. It didn't matter if she didn't sleep with me as long as she wasn't sleeping with anyone else. And she wasn't, Ang."

"You don't know what she was doing."

"And you do?"

"She'd have what she called a *cat's night out*. She'd just go on the prowl in the clubs, and maybe just get off on it."

"Or she said she did, to make us all crazy," Tony suggested. "And you know what, I'm tired to death of talking about Regan. I want to talk about us."

But could there be an *us* when there was a Regan? She poisoned everything, and Angie wanted revenge somehow for everything Regan had ruined.

But revenge for what? Bobby didn't need it. He'd walked into her web with his eyes wide open and he didn't care. Tony didn't need it: he knew exactly what she was, and he hadn't cared either. At least until now. And she wasn't at all sure it was over: but it was pretty clear he finally was ready to have it be.

Her mother? Too late for Mother. Mother would live with her unrequited hatred forever. And when Bobby walked in the door with the marriage license, Mother would divorce him.

Herself? But hers was the biggest betrayal of all, pretending to be Regan's friend all these years, and secretly working to keep her from ever seeing Bobby again.

Hers was the worst sin, the most egregious corruption. She'd coopted Regan's life because she had none of her own—was scared to make one of her own, and then she'd done everything she could to subvert it.

She felt the air go out of her like a helium balloon. There was nothing to fight, and nothing left to fight for.

There was only Tony, watching her closely, sympathetically.

"The thing is," he said finally, "nobody else can be Regan."

She froze in terror. *Oh, God. No. No. I never wanted that, never.*

"And there's only one Bobby . . ."

He knew—he knew . . . She felt a soaring relief that she was not alone. Tony *understood.* Tony had felt it too—that never-to-be-admitted moment of wanting to be someone or something that you weren't.

"And they were bound to come together again," Tony

went on inexorably. "Whatever Regan did—or didn't do—she was always saving herself for him. And that's the end of that story."

"I tried . . ." she said brokenly.

"Fruitless, Ang. For all those years. You couldn't have stopped them. That's the one thing we have to learn from this mess. No one could have stopped them. Bobby was going to come back sometime. There were too many ends left untied. Too many questions. Too many things left unsaid."

"I did that."

Tony held up his hand. He didn't want to know. Angie would have to live with her deceits. And so would he, and maybe those were the things better left in the ether.

"It doesn't matter now, Angie, because the other thing, the best thing is, we found each other."

She smiled tremulously. "Right in plain sight."

"Think of it this way: *they* brought us together and we just have to go on from here."

She groaned.

"So let's not talk about them anymore. In fact," he took her in his arms, "let's not talk at all anymore. . . ."

"No matter what you're planning, Bobby Torrance, *I* have work to do."

"Your work today is me. But we'll go to the office anyway. I have things to say to Tony."

"You have nothing to say to Tony. He was never anything to me but a good friend."

"He was and is a guy who wants to screw you and waited around until he could have his turn. Don't be naive, Regan. That much hasn't changed."

"You're saying every man wants to fuck me? That sensibility hasn't changed, either."

"Yeah, I'm saying that. But I can live with it." He slanted a simmering look at her as he held the door open for them to exit the Inn where they'd just had breakfast.

Immediately she felt his fingers on her, in her, owning her. That was the difference. This time he knew it. And she knew it, too.

She glanced at her watch. "I'm late." Even though it was just a five-minute walk to the office.

"Tony won't care. You're about to give the agency a whopping commission."

"I am?"

"Yep. I made some executive decisions in between ... well, there's nothing like a good fucking to clear the mind."

"Decisions are fine, but we've cleared nothing up."

"Don't worry. Everything will be clear by the end of this day."

She sent him a skeptical look as she pushed open the agency door. "Hey, Kelly—is Tony in his office?"

"Yes ... but—" the receptionist put out a detaining hand—and too late. Regan knocked and opened the door ... and there was Angie, breasts bared, hanging over Tony's chair and offering herself to him.

"Oh. *Oh.*" Regan slammed the door and whirled to face Bobby. "Did you see ..."

"Love it," Bobby said. "There's something so deliciously symmetrical about it. I couldn't have ended it better myself."

"*Bobby ... !*"

"REGAN!" Tony bellowed. "Get the hell in here."

"You, too," Regan said, grabbing Bobby's hand. "She's your sister."

"Does she have to be?"

She pulled him reluctantly into Tony's office where Angie sat in the far corner, all to rights again, except for the pink stain on her cheeks and the fact she couldn't look either of them in the eyes.

"Sit the hell down," Tony said.

Regan sat. "I'll stand," Bobby said. "I have a lot to say."

Angie's head snapped up at that. "Bobby—I ..."

"In fact," Bobby said, ignoring her, "I think I'll just take the command position here. Tony—go away." He eased himself behind Tony's desk and looked at them with a benign expression.

"Okay, first. Ang—I know everything. And you know what I mean. But you know what—I'm not going to hold it against you. Maybe it was the right thing to do, I don't know, and I don't care at this point.

"Here's the thing. I'm still in love with Regan. That's the reality and that's what you still have to deal with. But smart you: you found a way, and I am very happy for you, even if you didn't announce it quite the way you intended to.

"So this is what's going to happen. I will be leasing the first floor in the Metro mall and moving the paper's operation over there. Mother will be moving to Florida. No, she doesn't know it yet, but she'll do it. You'll persuade her, Ang. Tell her she'll be happier when she reacquaints herself with some old friends, and finds some new ones.

"And you, Ang, get the house, because I sure as hell don't want it.

"And the rest—well, that's for me and Regan to decide. Okay? Got it? Big commission, Tony. And Cargill will follow the minute I sign the papers, so you're on your way making inroads under the el."

"Regan's on her way," Tony said, his voice a little hoarse. "That's damned generous, Bobby."

"Well, it's time to reclaim the past. We've all wasted too much of it already. Regan? Work or play today?"

"Oh, I think I deserve a day off after snagging that big client."

"Go for it," Tony said.

"Bobby—?" Angie's voice, tremulous and low.

"Ummm?"

"I'm so, so sorry."

He felt a stab of compassion. "I know."

He loved the shoes. He couldn't think of anything more arousing than watching Regan strut around naked in her stilettos. Anything more provocative than her standing before him, naked in those heels, her legs splayed, her breasts thrust forward, the insolent expression of a well-fucked woman on her face.

"Well, aren't you the juicy one today," she murmured, reaching for his penis. "Marry me," he said suddenly.

"*What?*" Now? This soon?

"Marry me. Why not?"

"Because . . . because—"

"Good reason."

"There's still stuff—" Regan said, emphatically sitting down beside him.

"What stuff?"

"Stuff we never talked about."

"I don't want to talk about it. We both know what happened. I thought our half hour with Tony cleared the air."

She looked at him mutinously. "I hate this guy thing about not talking about it."

"Okay, talk about it."

"I can't talk about it."

"Jesus, Regan, isn't this enough? Isn't my coming back for you, isn't our coming together, enough? What else do I have to do? And don't say *no damned sex,* either."

She eyed him speculatively and then looked at her shoes. Remembered the first fantasy, the thing she'd thought of the day she'd bought the Mascolos.

And when did a woman ever get a chance to exact such a revenge?

"Maybe not."

He threw up his hands. There was nothing like a man in thrall to an aching penis. He'd walk over damned coals just to get this settled and get himself crammed up into her cunt. "Okay. Tell me what do."

"Down on the floor."

"What?"

"On your knees. On your face, actually. Mind your

penis. It's precious to me. Good. Now you're where I want you."

She lifted her leg and planted her foot on his butt.

"Jesus, Regan . . ."

"Oh, this is good, Bobby. I believe now you can figure out something to say."

"Jesus—I'm sorry . . ."

She pressed her heel harder into his naked butt.

"How sorry?"

"Sorry for every damned thing. Sorry it didn't work, sorry I left you, sorry I ran away, sorry I never called, or came back, or seemed not to care about you. Sorry I didn't fight for you, Regan. Sorry beyond belief we lost all these years."

"Go on."

"Sorry I didn't have faith. Sorry I was so jealous. Sorry I didn't give it a chance, didn't give you a second chance. Sorry I didn't stand up to Mother after my father died. God, what a litany of my sins. And I paid for every damned one of them, too."

He rolled over into a sitting position as he felt her remove her foot. "I deserve you, Regan. I love you, and we deserve another chance."

She towered over him, an Amazon, a goddess. The stuff of men's fantasies, the bedrock of his.

"We do and I will," she whispered, she promised. What more did she need than the knowledge he had always wanted her, he'd never given up hope, and he was the man of every one of her forbidden dreams?

And he'd given her everything she'd asked for, besides.

She braced her hands on his shoulders, and slowly, purposefully she lowered herself down, down, down until she sheathed his erection, until she enveloped it, enfolded it, and made it hers.

Satisfy Me

Lori Foster

Chapter One

"Do you believe the audacity?" Asia Michaels asked, staring through the dirty window of the company lounge to the newly painted building across the street. Soft pink neon lights flashed *Wild Honey* with bold provocation, competing with the twinkle of Christmas lights around the door and windows. A porn shop, she thought with awe, right in the middle of their small town. Cuther, Indiana, wasn't known for porn. Nope, it was known for pigs and toiletries, which meant most everyone either farmed or worked in one of the three factories.

Asia worked in a factory as an executive secretary in the marketing department. She liked it, the routine, the security. She'd found independence in Cuther, and peace of mind. Not in a million years had she thought to see a sex shop called *Wild Honey* erected among the main businesses.

Seated next to Asia at the round table, Becky Harte gaped. She blinked big blue innocent eyes and asked in a scandalized whisper, "You're sure they sell porn?"

Erica Lee, the third in their long-established group and a faithful friend, laughed out loud as she set her coffee and a candy bar on the table. "Well they're sure not raising bees."

Asia shook her head. Erica was probably the most sophisticated of the three, and the least inhibited. Every guy in the factory had asked Erica out at one time or another. Occasionally, Erica said yes.

Now, Becky, she didn't even look at men, even when the men were staring as hard as they could. Becky's fresh-faced appearance and dark blonde curls were beyond cute. Not that Becky seemed to care. If anything, she did her best not to draw male attention. Her best pretty much worked. If Asia had to guess, she'd swear Becky was still a virgin.

Asia took a bite of her doughnut. "We should go check it out," she teased, hoping to get a rise out of her friends.

"Get out of here," Becky rasped, horrified by the mere prospect. "I could *never* go in that place!"

"Why not?" Erica asked. "You refuse to date, so maybe you'd find something that would make your time alone more . . . interesting." She bobbed her eyebrows, making Becky turn three shades of red and sputter.

Laughing, Asia pointed out, "None of us dates, at least not much."

"I date." Erica shook back her shoulder-length black hair. It hung bone-straight, looked like silk, and made every woman who saw it envious. Because her own hair was plain brown and too curly, Asia counted herself among the envious group.

"I just don't meet many guys worth dating twice," Erica explained. "That's all. And it's not like Cuther is a hotbed of eligible males, anyway."

Asia accepted that excuse with silence. Her own reasons for not dating weren't something she cared to discuss. Cuther was a new life, and her old life was well behind her.

Try as they might, none of them could stop looking at the sex shop. "It's rather tastefully decorated, isn't it?"

Becky and Erica stared at her.

"Well, it is." Asia shrugged. "I would have thought the curtains would be red velvet and there'd be lewd signs in the windows. But there aren't." The curtains were actually gauzy, sheer and delicate, in a snowy white, with beige shutters against the red brick. Other than the bright neon sign with the name of the shop, the place looked as subdued as a nail salon or a boardinghouse. And being that it was close to the holidays, there was even a large festive wreath on the door to go with the holiday lights, lending the building a domestic affectation.

Becky leaned forward, motioning for the others to do the same. "When I parked today," she whispered, "I could see inside, and you'll never guess who was in there!"

Erica and Asia looked at each other. "Who?"

"Ian Conrad."

Erica dropped back in her seat. "The new electrician the company hired?"

Becky nodded, making her curls bounce. "He was speaking to the man at the counter."

Erica snorted. "Well, I'll be. And here he acts so quiet."

"Still waters run deep?" Asia speculated aloud.

"I'd like to know what he bought," Erica admitted in a faraway voice.

"Nothing," Becky told her. "That is, he came out empty-handed. Maybe he was just greeting a new proprietor?"

"More like he went window shopping." Erica made a face, her voice rising. "Men are all alike. One woman isn't enough for them. They need outside stimulation, like a vitamin supplement or something."

"We should be more like them," Asia said, without really thinking. "Can you imagine how a guy would act if a woman started buying up porn?"

Erica looked dumbstruck, then leaned forward in excitement. "Let's do it!"

Becky tried to pull away but Erica caught her arm and held on, keeping her within the conspiratorial circle. "I'm serious! None of us is getting any younger. I'm probably the oldest at twenty-eight, but Becky, aren't you twenty-five now?"

Looking distinctly miserable, Becky nodded.

"I'm twenty-six," Asia volunteered, proud because each year took her one more step away from her past and her insecurities, her lack of confidence in all things.

"You see," Erica said. "We're mature women with mature needs, not silly little girls." She rubbed her hands together and her slanted green eyes lit up with anticipation. "Oh, I'd just love to witness Ian Conrad's expression if he went out on a date with a woman, and afterward, when they were alone, she pulled out the props. Ha! Let him deal with not being enough on his own."

Asia sat back and blinked at Erica. "Whatever are you talking about?" And then with insight, "You've got a thing for Ian, don't you?"

"Absolutely not," Erica sniffed. "I'm just talking about guys in general who think they need all that other"—she waved her hand—"*stuff* to be satisfied. As if a woman and her body and her imagination aren't enough."

Becky looked embarrassed, but concerned. "Did a guy, you know, pull out the props on you?"

"Nah, at least not in the middle of things. But I came home once to find him rather occupied."

Becky's eyes widened in titillated fascination. "Ohmigosh."

"You didn't," Asia said, enthralled despite herself.

"Yep. I'd been gone all of four hours and we'd had sex that morning." She muttered under her breath, "The pig."

Asia frowned. "You know, I don't really think there's anything wrong with a mature, consenting couple making use of toys."

Becky looked ready to faint—or die of curiosity—but Erica just shrugged. "Well, me, either, but he sure wasn't a couple. He was there all by his lonesome, just him and a video and some strange . . . hand contraption thing."

Becky puckered up like she'd swallowed a lemon. "*Hand contraption thing?*"

Asia tried to hold it in, but Erica looked so indignant and Becky looked so dazed, she couldn't. She burst out laughing to the point where half the people in the lounge were staring. When she could finally catch a breath, she managed to say, "I wish I could have seen his face!"

"His face?" Erica raised one brow mockingly. "It wasn't his face that drew my attention. No, ladies. It was the place where that contraption connected."

Becky choked, and they all fell into gales of laughter again.

"So what," Asia finally asked, wiping her eyes, "do you think the three of us should do? Buy our own . . ."

She started giggling again and Becky finished for her, "hand contraptions!"

"Honey, please." Erica affected an exaggerated haughtiness. "That gizmo wouldn't do us any good at all."

Becky had tears rolling down her cheeks, she laughed so hard. "You're so bad, Erica."

"Which is why you love me."

"Yep, I guess that's part of it."

"Okay, so what do we do?" Asia really wanted to know. Not that she intended to go into that porn shop and buy anything. Just the idea made her hot with embarrassment.

Then she realized her own thoughts and frowned. Part of her liberation, her new life, was doing as *she* pleased, without concern for what others thought. Why should she be embarrassed? The men from the factory had been moseying over there all day! They could appease their curiosity, so why couldn't she?

"First, we'll share our fantasies."

Fantasies! Good grief, maybe *that* was why she couldn't. Asia wasn't sure she had any fantasies.

Not anymore.

Erica had leaned forward to whisper her comment, but still Asia looked around nervously. By necessity, the lounge was large, able to accommodate shifts for the two hundred plus people who worked there. Employees tended to sit in clusters. The managers with the managers, maintenance with maintenance, and so forth.

Asia and her friends always chose the same table in the corner by the window, separated by a half-wall planter filled with artificial plants. Since *Wild Honey* had gone in, they often found their favorite table unavailable because everyone wanted to look out that row of windows. Erica had taken to leaving her desk early so she could lay claim to it.

Asia didn't see anyone paying them any mind, although there was someone on the other side of the planter, alone at a table. He wore jeans and a flannel, so she assumed he was one of the workmen, not part of management. But whoever he was, he wasn't listening. He sat alone, a newspaper open in front of his face, his booted foot swinging to music that played only in his head. A half-empty cup of steaming coffee was at his elbow. Even as Asia watched, he rustled the paper, turned the page, and sipped at his drink.

Satisfied, Asia turned back to Erica. "We share fantasies and then what?"

"Then we wait until some guy buys a prop—a movie, a book, a toy, whatever—that relates to our particular fantasy."

"And?" Becky asked, both breathless and bright red.

Erica shrugged. "We approach him. See if he's interested."

Snatching up her foam cup, Asia gulped down a fortifying drink.

Since her first relationship had turned so sour, so . . . *bad,* she'd never gotten to find out what the fireworks were about. She wasn't stupid; she believed awesome sex existed, it just hadn't existed for her. Not in her marriage.

How would it be to have phenomenal sex with a guy who wanted the same things she did? A man who wanted to please her, not the other way around?

She realized both Becky and Erica were staring at her and she asked warily, "What?"

Becky cleared her throat. " Erica asked if you'd want to go first?"

"Me! Why me?"

Becky lifted one narrow shoulder. "I'm too chicken, though I promise to try to work up my nerve."

"You will work up the nerve," Erica promised, and squeezed Becky's hand.

Becky looked skeptical, but nodded. "And Erica says if she goes first, she knows neither of us will."

Asia nearly crumbled her cup, she got so tense. But she wanted to do this. It would be one more step toward total freedom. Not that she believed anything would come of it. And thinking that, she said, "We have to set a time limit. I don't intend to visit that stupid place more than . . . say, three times."

"It's Tuesday," Erica pointed out. "You can start tomorrow right after work, and stop on Friday. If no one turns up, it'll be Becky's turn. But we all have to keep rotating turns until we find someone, agreed?"

Asia thought about it, then nodded. "Agreed. But if in those first three times I don't see a guy buying what he'd need to buy to interest me, then it moves on to Becky's turn."

Becky closed her eyes. "Oh, dear."

"Promise me, Becky."

Becky bit her lip, but finally agreed. "Okay," she whispered, and then with more force, as if a streak of determination existed beneath her innocence, "Okay."

Erica laughed. "There you go, hon. So, Asia, what's a fella have to buy to get your motor running?"

This was the embarrassing part. But she'd explain, and they'd understand her reasoning. Asia looked at each woman in turn, then stiffened her backbone. "Something to do with . . ."

Erica and Becky leaned forward, saying in unison, "Yes?"

Asia squeezed her eyes shut, took a deep breath, and blurted, "Spanking."

Cameron O'Reilly choked, then nearly swallowed his tongue. He sputtered, spewing coffee across the front of the flannel he wore today before finally gasping in enough air. A good portion of his steaming coffee went into his lap, but it wasn't nearly as hot as he was.

Spanking! Asia Michaels was into spanking!

As the coffee soaked into his jeans, he leaped from his seat, but at the last second remembered himself and turned his back. He could feel all three of the ladies looking at him, especially *her*. Luckily, he wasn't dressed in his usual suit today. The casual clothes, necessary for the job he did that morning, would help disguise him.

The voice he recognized as Erica Lee muttered, "Klutz."

"Who is he?" he heard Asia whisper and there was a lot of nervousness in her tone.

"Who cares?" Erica said. "Ignore him."

Becky said, "I hope he didn't burn himself." Then they went back to chatting.

Cameron didn't give them a chance to recognize him. He quickly stalked from the lounge. Still poleaxed, he damn near barreled into a wall in his hurry to leave undetected. Asia and spanking! He'd never have guessed it. He groaned, just thinking of Asia with her soft brown curls and big, sexy brown eyes. He'd wanted her for two long months.

But she'd refused to move beyond the platonic acquaintance stage, no matter how many times he tried. She was friendly to him, and ignored any hints for more.

One of the other employees had warned him that Asia was a cold fish, totally uninterested in men. Ha!

He ducked into the men's room and hurried to the sink. In his mind, he pictured Asia stretched out over his lap, her beautiful naked bottom turned up, his large hand on her . . .

And the image ended there.

He just couldn't see himself striking a woman. Not for any reason. But, oh, the other things he'd like to do to that sweet behind.

He grabbed several paper towels and mopped at his soaked jeans. She hadn't known he was listening, of course, or he still wouldn't know her secret. The problem now was how to use it.

He wasn't a kinky man.

He enjoyed sex just like any other guy, but he'd never been a hound dog, never been a womanizer. He'd never done much experimenting beyond what he and his partner found enjoyable, which had stayed pretty much in the bounds of routine stuff, like different positions, different places, different times of the day.

He liked relationships, and he liked Asia.

He wanted her. Soon, and for a long while. He did not want to . . . spank her.

Cameron stared down at his jeans, tautly tented by a raging erection, and knew himself for a liar. He snorted. The idea was exciting as hell, no doubt about that. But mostly because it was sexual in nature. If Asia had said she wanted to roll naked in the snow, *that* would have turned him on too, and he absolutely detested the damn snow. Give him Florida, with hot sandy beaches and bright sunshine over frigid Indiana weather any day.

Of course, if he'd stayed in Florida instead of taking the new supervisor's job, he'd never have met Asia, and he most definitely wouldn't have overheard such an intriguing confession.

He shook his head. What to do?

First, he had to change into his regular clothes. At least the dousing had helped to bring him back under control, otherwise he might have blown it by rushing things. He'd been sitting there listening to her, daydreaming, imagining all types of lewd things while staring blankly at the newspaper, and he'd nearly worked himself into a lather. Her confession had all but pushed him over the edge. At thirty-two, he was too damn old for unexpected boners.

Yet he'd had one. For Asia.

Which meant the next thing he had to do was be in that shop tomorrow when Asia visited. She wouldn't need three days to find him. Hell, he'd never live that long, not with the way he wanted her.

And no way would he let her go off with some other guy. He'd been fantasizing about her since moving to Indiana two months ago, and here was his chance.

The spanking part . . . well, he'd do what he had to do. And if she enjoyed it, great.

After he warmed her bottom, it'd be his turn.

Chapter Two

Becky looked faint. "Spanking," she said in a strangled, barely there whisper, clutching her throat.

"I have a theory," Asia hurried to explain. "If a guy gets his kinkier jollies taken care of with props, then he won't expect to fulfill them with a woman."

Erica dropped back in her seat with a guffaw. "You big faker! You really had me going there."

Becky asked, still a bit confused, "So you figure if he buys movies about spanking, he'll have it out of his system and won't try anything like that with you?"

"Bingo."

Erica shook her head. "And here I thought you had a wild side."

"Not even close." Asia thought about it for a moment, then decided it was time for some truths. She could trust Erica and Becky, she knew that. They'd understand. "Actually, I had a wild first husband."

"Get out! You were married?"

"Yes. To a complete and total jerk."

Erica's smile faded. "And he hit you?"

"Not exactly. But he liked to . . . experiment. Everything was geared toward what *he'd* like, whether I liked it or not. And I never did. But he'd claim it was my duty as his wife to try to please him, and I was confused enough then to feel some guilt, because I couldn't please him on my own."

Becky surprised them both by growling, "That bastard."

After giving Becky a long approving look, Erica asked, "How long were you with him?"

"We married right out of college when I was twenty-two. The divorce became final just before my twenty-fifth birthday."

"He did a number on you, didn't he? That's why you don't date."

"Let's just say I like being independent now, thinking my own thoughts and doing my own things. I'm not looking for a relationship, and I don't want—*didn't want*—any part of a quick affair." She tapped her fingers on the tabletop. "But you're right, Erica. I might be missing out on a lot, and to my mind, I've missed enough already. I deserve some satisfaction."

Erica thrust a small fist into the air and said, "Here's to satisfaction," making Becky chuckle.

"So," Asia said, feeling equal parts triumphant for being decisive, anticipation for what might be, and hesitant about the unknown. "That's settled. I'll head over there tomorrow."

"We'll watch from here," Becky told her, and Erica nodded.

Knowing they'd be close would make it easier, Asia decided. "Your turn, Becky."

Becky blanched. "My turn for what?"

"To share a fantasy."

She winced. "I need time to think about it."

As the unofficial moderator, Erica sighed. "All right. You can have until Friday."

Slumping in relief, Becky said, "Friday." She smiled. "I'll be ready."

Cameron stood in the aisle of tapes, surreptitiously watching the door. Unwilling to take a chance on missing Asia, he'd been there for half an hour. Already he'd studied every cover and description of all the more erotic discipline tapes. Some of them were downright disgusting. Pain and pleasure . . . he wasn't at all sure they really mixed. Not that he intended to judge others.

Not that he'd judge Asia.

He had his eye on one in particular, but he waited, wanting Asia to see him buy the damn thing so there'd be no misunderstandings. The cover sported an older English-looking fellow in a straight-backed chair. He had a schoolgirl, of all dumb things, draped over his knees with her pleated skirt flipped up and her frilly panties showing.

Cameron had chosen it because even though the guy appeared stern, the girl wore a vacuous, anxious smile. She seemed to be enjoying herself and that's what he hoped Asia would do. No way in hell could he make her cry—even if she preferred it—which some of the tapes indicated by their covers.

He was engrossed in fantasies too vivid to bear when the tinkling of the front door sounded like a gun blast in his ears. He looked up—and made eye contact with Asia.

Even from the distance separating them, he felt her shock and consternation at seeing him there. She immediately averted her face, her cheeks scalded with color.

The blood surged in his veins. Every muscle in his body tensed, including the one most interested in this little escapade. His cock was suddenly hard enough to break granite.

Cameron couldn't look away as she ducked to the back aisle. He'd already discovered they kept a variety of velvet whips and handcuffs there.

She ducked right back out, her face now pale. Damn. He started toward her, not certain what he'd say but knowing he had to say something. He had the wretched tape in his hand.

"Asia?"

She froze, her back to him, her body strangely still. Several seconds ticked by, the silence strained, and then she turned. A false, too-bright smile was pinned to her face.

"Yes?" And as if she hadn't seen him the second she walked in, she said, "Cameron! What are you doing here?"

As usual, she reached out for a business handshake, keeping their relationship confined.

With no other option coming to mind, he started to accept her hand, realized he held the damn tape, and switched hands. "I'm just . . . ah, looking around."

In horrified fascination, she stared at the movie now held at his side before finally giving him a brisk, quick shake. "It's an interesting place, isn't it?"

"Yes." They stood in the center aisle with display tables loaded down with paperback books of the lustful variety on either side of them. He propped his hip against a table, trying to relax while his testosterone level shot through the roof. "I'm surprised at the diversity. And how upscale it all is." He glanced around, feeling too self-conscious. "I'm not sure what I expected."

"I know what you mean." She relaxed the tiniest bit. "I admit, I never expected a shop like this in conservative Cuther."

The tape in his hand felt like a burning brand. He wanted to set the idiotic thing aside, but that would be defeating the whole purpose of being in the shop in the first place. "Cuther is different," he admitted. "More rural than I'm used to."

"And colder?" she teased, because she knew he'd come from Florida.

Idle conversation in a porn shop, Cameron thought. It was a first for him. "I guess my blood has thinned. I'm almost always cold."

"With the wind chill, it's fifteen below. Everyone is cold."

"True enough."

She tilted her head and her long brown hair flowed over her coat sleeve. It looked like dark honey and burnished gold, natural shades for a natural woman.

"What about your family?" she asked, taking him by surprise with the somewhat more personal question.

"What about them?"

She smiled, a real smile this time. "You've never said much about them."

"No." Any time he'd talked to her, he'd been trying to get past her walls. Discussing his family had been the farthest thing from his mind.

"It's almost Christmas. Will you be heading home for the holidays?"

"Uh, no." He wouldn't go anywhere until he'd had her. "My family is . . . scattered. We keep in touch by phone, but we don't do the big family get-togethers. We never have."

Her brown eyes warmed, looked a little sad. Thick lashes lowered, hiding her gaze from him. "I thought everyone wanted to be with family this time of year."

He shrugged, wishing she'd change the damn subject, wishing she'd look at him again.

Wishing he had her naked and in his bed.

"I guess not." Then he thought to ask, "What about you?"

She turned partially away, giving him her profile. Even beneath the thick coat, he could see the swells of her breasts, the plumpness of her bottom.

A bottom she wanted him to swat.

Cameron swallowed hard, willing himself to stay in control. "Asia?"

"I'm not sure what I'm doing yet. Mother is . . . well, she remarried and she gets together with her husband's family. I have one sister, but I think she's making it an intimate occasion. Just her husband and two children."

"So you're an aunt?" He liked learning more about her, but she'd picked a hell of a place to open up.

"Yes. I have two adorable nephews, four and six."

He took a step closer. "If you find out you're not doing anything, maybe we could get together?"

"I . . ." Her smile faded. "I don't know."

He could feel her shutting down, closing herself off from

him. He hated it. "I'm free," he said, watching for her reaction, "whatever you decide."

She nodded, but didn't say a thing.

Having all but killed that conversational gambit, Cameron looked around for inspiration. "This your first time in here?"

"Yes." Her face colored once again.

Drawn to her, Cameron rubbed the back of his neck and tried to keep his wits. "You looking for anything in particular?"

She gave him such an appalled look, he wanted to kick his own ass. Any idiot would know you didn't ask a lady something like that.

But she surprised him. She cleared her throat, lifted her chin, and pointed down at the video in his hand. "I see you made a selection."

It was stupid, but he felt heat crawling up the back of his neck and prayed she wouldn't notice.

Determined on his course, he held the tape in front of him so she'd get a good look at it and see exactly what it was. "That's right. I suppose I should be paying." He took a small step away.

Asia looked after him.

He edged into another step, willing her to say something, anything. He waited.

Nothing.

"It was, ah, nice speaking with you."

Eyes wide and watchful, she nodded. "You, too."

Damn, damn, damn. Had the tape not been risqué enough? "All right, then." He forced a smile, but it felt more like a grimace. "Take care."

He started to turn away, teeth clenched in disappointment, body on fire.

"Cameron?"

He whipped around. "Yes?"

She didn't look at him, but that was okay, because she

asked, "Would you like to . . . maybe do something Friday after work? If you're not busy, that is."

His knees went weak with relief. He didn't know if he'd last till Friday, but he said, "Yeah. Sure. That'd be great."

A tremulous smile brightened her expression. "I could cook you dinner."

"No." He shook his head and walked back to her. "I'll take you out to dinner. Someplace nice. All right?" He didn't want their first date to be only about sex.

She teased, "What? You don't trust my cooking?"

"I imagine you're a terrific cook." It was difficult not to touch her, not to grin like a lecherous moron. But, damn, he was hard and there wasn't a thing he could do about it. He wanted her too much. "This week is my treat, though, okay?"

She studied him closely, then nodded. "All right."

"Do you want to go straight from work?" *Do you want to go now, to my place,* he thought, *where I can get you naked and sate myself on your . . .*

"I'd like to go home and change first. If that's okay."

This smile came easier. At least he had a confirmed date, even if he had a two-day wait. "I'll pick you up at six? Will that give you enough time?"

"Perfect." She wrote her address down for him, then accompanied him to the checkout. Time and again, her gaze went to his movie. Was she excited? He wished like hell she didn't have the thick coat on. He wanted to see her breasts, to see if maybe her nipples were peaked with anticipation.

God, many more thoughts like that and he'd be in real trouble. Luckily, he'd worn his long coat today, which concealed his lower body and straining erection. His jacket wouldn't have hidden a thing.

They stepped outside together, his purchase safely concealed in a plain brown paper bag. He felt like a pervert, even though his logical adult mind told him a grown man could purchase whatever he pleased. But he knew what was in that bag, even if no one else did.

The wind kicked up, blowing Asia's hair. It licked against his chin, scented with female warmth and sweet shampoo. He caught a lock and brought it to his nose, wondering if she'd smell so sweet all over, or would her natural fragrance be spicy, like hot musk? He couldn't wait to find out, to nuzzle her throat and her breasts and her belly . . . between her thighs.

His muscles pulled tight with that thought. "You have beautiful hair," he all but growled.

Her lips parted at his husky tone, and her big eyes stared up at him. "I do?"

He wrapped that silky tendril around his finger and rubbed it with his thumb. "Hmmm. It's almost the exact same shade as your eyes."

Her laugh got carried off on the wind. "You mean plain old brown?"

"There's nothing plain about you, Asia, especially your coloring." They had reached her car, and he opened her door for her. He saw her surprise at the gentlemanly gesture, and it pleased him. "I'll see you at work tomorrow?"

"I'll be there."

Pretending to be much struck, Cameron said, "I just realized. You didn't buy anything. I hope my presence didn't inhibit you?"

Her small nose went into the air. "Not at all. I only wanted to see what they had."

He couldn't resist teasing her. "You didn't find anything you liked, huh?"

Those dark mysterious eyes of hers stared at him, and she said, "I found you, now didn't I?"

Cameron stepped back, stunned and so horny his stomach cramped.

She smiled with triumph. "Tomorrow, Cameron."

He watched her drive away. The next two days would be torture, waiting to get her in his bed, open to him, willing. He shook with need, then glanced down at the bag in his hand.

He'd use the time until then to study up on this kinky preference of hers, just to make sure he got it right.

That thought had him grinning. Were there rules to spanking? A time frame to follow? Did you jump right into it, or ease the way? Did the spanking follow the sex, or was it a form of foreplay?

He didn't know, but he'd sure as hell find out.

He shivered from a particularly harsh blast of icy wind, and realized he'd barely noticed the cold while Asia was close to him. Now that she'd left, he felt frozen. He hurried to his own car.

He had some studying to do.

Asia crawled into bed that night and pulled the thick covers to her chin. The sheets were icy cold, making her shiver, and she curled into a tight ball. It had been so very long since she'd felt a large male body in bed beside her, sharing warmth and comfort.

Sharing pleasure.

During her marriage, she'd learned to dread the nights her husband reached for her. Lovemaking had been tedious at best, uncomfortable and embarrassing at worst. His preferences at trying anything and everything—including discipline—whether she enjoyed it or not, had worn her down. He'd told her it was necessary, that she wasn't exciting enough, her body not sexy enough, to get him aroused without the added elements. After a while she'd begun to believe him, and it had taken a lot for her to finally realize he was the one with the problems, not her.

In the process, she'd gotten completely turned off sex. But she wasn't an idiot. She knew it wasn't always like that.

She didn't think it'd be like that with Cameron.

Thinking his name brought an image of him to mind. She rolled to her back and closed her eyes. Cameron, with his straight black hair. Not as straight or as black as Erica's, but in many ways more appealing, at least to her.

His hair had a chestnut cast to it in the light. And though

she knew he was only in his early thirties, a bit of silver showed in his sideburns. His hair was a little too long at the nape, as if regular haircuts weren't high on his list of priorities. And judging by how often it was tousled, he didn't bother much with combs, either. She imagined him showering, shaving, combing his hair—and ending his personal grooming right there. She smiled.

The mental picture of him in the shower lingered, but his suits were so concealing, she could only guess at his physique. He was tall, lean in the middle, and his feet and hands were large. Beyond that, she didn't know.

She liked his eyes best. The many times when they'd spoken, his vivid blue eyes had been very direct. He tended to focus on her with a lot of intensity.

She shivered, but it wasn't from cold.

So many times her mind had wandered while chatting with him. Her heart would race, her skin would flush. She'd thought him dangerous to her, a threat to her independence, and she'd deliberately kept their association as casual, as businesslike, as possible.

But now she'd sought him out.

Would his eyes look that intense, hot from within, when he made love with her? That alone would be nice, she decided, remembering how her husband had always looked . . . distant from her. He'd treated her like nothing more than a convenient body, using her to gain his own pleasure.

Cameron would be aware of her, she was sure.

Was he at home right now, watching that risqué movie? Was he excited? Hard?

Her own soft groan sounded in the silence of her empty bedroom. Rolling to her side, she looked out the window. Snowflakes fell steadily, making patterns on the dark window. She could just make out the faint glow of colored Christmas lights on the house across the street.

Cameron would be alone for Christmas, just like her.

Her heart gave a funny little thump, sort of a poignant

pain. The holidays were so lonely, so sad. If she and Cameron were together . . .

No! She wanted this one night of sex, but that was all. She didn't want or need another relationship, and sharing a holiday, especially one as emotional as Christmas, would definitely be a commitment of sorts. Wouldn't it?

She shook her head. Her independence was important to her, and she did just fine on her own. A steady relationship would intrude on that.

Was Cameron watching the movie? Was he thinking of her?

Disturbed by her own conflicting, changing thoughts, she sat up abruptly and turned on the light. Curiosity swamped her, made her body hot and tingly. She reached for the phone and dialed the operator. Cameron was too new to the area to be in the phone book, but the operator had a listing for him.

Asia clutched the phone, daring herself to call him, to ask him . . . what? If he was pleasuring himself? She imagined what that would entail and sensation exploded, like a tide of moist warmth, making her breath catch. She could easily visualize his large strong hand wrapped around his erection. She could see his beautiful blue eyes vague with lust, his hard jaw clenched, thighs and abdomen tensed as he stroked faster and faster . . .

She gasped with the image, feeling her own measure of burning excitement. Shaking, breathing too hard and fast, she bit her lip and dialed the number.

Cameron's sleep-rough voice answered on the third ring. "Hello?"

Asia froze. Oh, God, he'd been *sleeping,* not indulging in erotic daydreams or self-pleasure! Talk about missing the mark.

Her mouth opened but nothing came out. She'd awakened him when she didn't have a legitimate reason for calling.

"Hello?" he said again, this time with some impatience.

Asia slammed down the phone. Her heart galloped hard enough to hurt her ribs, and her stomach felt funny, kind of tight and sweet. In a rush she turned the light back off and slid under the covers, even pulling them over her head.

Cameron O'Reilly.

He turned her on, no doubt about it. Now if she could just not make a fool of herself, everything might go smoothly.

Cameron stared at the phone. Moving to one elbow he switched on the lamp at his bedside and checked the Caller I.D. *Asia Michaels.* A small curious smile tipped his mouth. There surely weren't two women in all of Cuther with that particular unique name.

She'd called him—then chickened out.

What had she wanted?

Naked, he eased back against the pillows, plenty warm now, thank you very much.

Very slowly, the smile turned into a toothy grin. Oh, he knew what she wanted, he reminded himself. She wanted sex. She wanted kink.

She wanted him.

Arms crossed behind his head, Cameron glanced at the tape sitting on his dresser across the room. He hadn't watched it yet. Because of what he'd overheard in the lounge, he hadn't gotten much work done the rest of the day. He'd been too distracted with thoughts of Asia and how he'd make love to her.

His preoccupation on the job meant he'd had to bring several files home to finish on his personal computer. By the time he was done, his eyes were gritty and he'd wanted only a few hours' sleep.

Now he only wanted Asia.

He wasn't at all sure he'd be able to wait until Friday. He needed to taste her before that, just to tide him over.

Soon, he promised himself. Very soon.

Chapter Three

"Cameron O'Reilly?" Erica repeated in disbelief, and fanned her face dramatically. "What a hunk!"

"You think?" Asia chewed her bottom lip. *She* thought him sexy as sin, especially now, but did other women think it too? "I mean, I admit I was surprised. He's just such a . . . suit."

Erica snorted. "Honey, all men are the same, white collar and blue collar alike. They're all sex addicts."

"I agree," Becky said. "O'Reilly is hot."

"You been checking him out?" Erica asked in some surprise.

"I'm not blind"—Becky sniffed with mock indignation—"if that's what you mean."

They all chuckled. "I wouldn't mind getting to know him better myself," Erica teased. "But he's never really noticed me. When I talk to him, he's polite, but always businesslike."

Asia fiddled with her coffee stirrer, then admitted, "We've spoken several times." She glanced up, then away. "At length."

"Ah." Erica grinned. "Do tell."

She shrugged. "He sort of . . . sought me out. He comes to my office, hangs around a bit, or catches me in the halls, or right after meetings. I . . . I like him, but I got the feeling he wanted to get more personal, so I . . . brushed him off."

"Are you nuts?"

Asia was sort of wondering that same thing herself, but for different reasons. "I just couldn't see starting something that likely wouldn't go anywhere."

Becky touched her hand. "You were afraid he wouldn't follow up?"

That nettled her new independent streak. "Ha! I wouldn't want him to. It's more likely that *I* wouldn't follow up."

Erica grinned. "That right?"

"Yes." And then, "Why is it always the woman who's supposed to sit around and wait for a damn phone call?"

Erica said, "Amen, sister. You'll get no argument from me. That's why even on dates, I buy my own meals, and I refuse flowers or gifts. If I want something, I can get it for myself. I don't *need* a guy. But sometimes I want one. So I go on *my* schedule, not his."

"Sounds to me," Becky said, "that you both like playing hard to get."

"No playing to it," Erica corrected. "I *am* hard to get."

Asia chuckled. She wasn't playing, either, though her motivation differed from Erica's. "Most of the guys here understand that I'm not interested, that it's a waste of time to want more from me than casual conversation."

Erica nodded knowingly. "But Cameron was new, so he didn't know, and he's been after you?"

"I figured he'd find out soon enough and leave me alone."

"But he didn't?"

She shook her head. "Whenever we're in the same room together, he watches me, and he smiles if our gazes meet." *And what a smile,* she thought privately, *enough to melt a woman's bones,* so, of course it was hell on her reserve.

"And now you know he has kinky sexual preferences," Erica pointed out with a sinner's grin.

"Now I know," Asia corrected, "that he has a healthy outlet. Honest, all the documentation I read said that what one fantasizes isn't generally what one wants in a real-life situation, which is why it's strictly a fantasy. Fantasies are safe. They are not, however, something we'd ever really try or even want to try."

"I used to think about getting stranded on a desert island with three hunks," Erica mused aloud. "None of us had clothes."

Asia and Becky snickered.

"But granted, I like modern luxuries too much to want to rough it just for male attention. Besides, I imagine one day on an island is all it'd take for me to start looking pretty haggard. No lotion, no scented shampoo, no blow dryer . . ."

"No birth control," Becky pointed out.

"And three men fighting for my body? That could get ugly."

"Maybe they'd just share," Asia suggested.

Erica shivered. "To tell you the truth, it's fine as a fantasy, but the idea of three naked sweaty guys bumping up against one another with me in the middle just sort of ruins the fantasy of them being there for *me*."

They were all still chuckling when suddenly Cameron approached. He had his hands in his pants pockets, a crooked smile on his handsome face.

He looked at each woman in turn. "Afternoon, ladies."

Agog, Becky wiggled her fingertips in a halfhearted wave.

Erica lounged back in her seat and grinned. "Mr. O'Reilly."

"Cameron, please." Then to Asia, "I'm sorry to interrupt your break, but could I speak to you for just a moment?"

Asia felt dumbstruck. She glanced at her friends, who made very differing faces at her, then nodded. "Uh, sure."

"In private." He gently took her arm and headed to the back of the lounge, to the large storage closet. Asia almost stalled. *A closet?* She felt workers looking up in casual interest; she felt Erica and Becky staring hard enough to burn a hole into her back.

She felt excitement roil inside her.

As if inviting her into a formal parlor instead of a closet, Cameron gallantly opened the door and gestured her inside.

She only hesitated a moment. He closed the door, leaving them in near darkness. One narrow window over the door let in the lounge's faded fluorescent light. Shadows were everywhere, from boxes and brooms and supplies. Asia backed up to a wall, a little apprehensive, a lot eager, and waited.

He tipped his head at her, frowning slightly. "I wanted to ask you something."

Oh no. No, no, no! He knew she'd called last night! He'd ask her about it, want to know why, and what the heck could she possibly tell him—

"Would you mind too much if I jumped the gun a little here and . . . kissed you?"

Asia froze, her thoughts suspended, her panic redirected, her heart skipping a beat.

"I know, I know." He rubbed the back of his neck, agitated. "The thing is, I can't stop thinking about it—or you—and I doubt I'll get any work done today if I don't." He looked at her, and his voice lowered. "You see, I'm going nuts wanting to taste you."

Taste her? It was like a dream, Asia thought, far removed from reality. Never had she expected any guy to say such a thing to her.

Asia collected her wayward thoughts and replied stupidly, "You are?"

He gave a slow, considering nod, took a step closer. "Would you mind?"

"Uh . . ." She looked around. They had privacy here in the dim closet, never mind that a crowd of people was right outside the door, oblivious to his request.

Even in the shadows, she could see his beautiful blue eyes watching her, hot and expectant. So very aware of her.

Her pulse tripped. She sucked in an unsteady breath and

caught his scent—subtle aftershave and heated male flesh. Delicious scents that made her head swim.

He stepped closer still until he nearly touched her, his gaze now on her mouth, hungry and waiting. She licked her lips and started to whisper, "All right—"

And with a soft groan, his mouth was there, covering hers, gentle and warm and firm. His hands flattened on the wall on either side of her head and his chest almost touched hers. Not quite, but she felt the body heat radiating off him in waves, carrying more of that delicious scent for her to breathe in, letting her fill herself up with it until she shook.

"Open your mouth," he murmured against her lips, and like a zombie—a very aroused zombie—she did.

He didn't thrust his tongue into her mouth. No, he licked her lips with a warm, velvet tongue, gentle, easy. Then just inside her mouth, slowly, over the edges of her teeth, her own tongue.

Asia moaned and opened more in blatant invitation, wanting his tongue. Wanting all of him.

He slid in, deep and slow, then out again.

"Jesus." He dropped his head forward and she felt his uneven breaths pelting her cheek. He gave a short, low laugh, roughened by his arousal. "You make me feel like a schoolboy again."

Her heart in her throat, panting and trembling, Asia managed to say, "Made out in a lot of closets, did you?"

"Hmm?" His head lifted, his eyes burning on her face, still eager, still intent.

She swallowed back a groan. "In school."

"Oh." He smiled, looked at her mouth and kissed her again, a brief, teasing kiss to her bottom lip. "No. No, I didn't. But I did walk around with a perpetual hard-on, and damn if that isn't what you do to me."

Was there a proper reply a lady made to such a comment? If so, Asia had no idea what it might be.

His big rough hands settled on her face, cupping her

cheeks, his thumbs smoothing over her temples. He looked concerned. Horny and concerned. "I'm sorry if I'm rushing you."

She almost laughed at that. The way he made her feel, she wanted to be rushed. "Do you hear me complaining?"

"No," he said slowly. "No, you're not." His expression turned thoughtful. "Can I take that to mean you want me too?"

He was so blunt! She hadn't expected it of him. In her experience—admittedly limited—well-dressed corporate types were more reserved. She heard lewd jests from the factory workers all the time. And she heard the maintenance guys make ribald jokes throughout the day. But the suits . . . they generally feared sexual harassment charges and any kidding they did remained very private.

Erica claimed all men were the same when it came to sex, but Asia knew that wasn't true. Some men approached sex as a free-for-all. Her ex-husband had been that way. He wanted it whenever he could get it, whoever he could get it from.

Some saw sex as a commitment, others as a challenge.

And some, she hoped, saw it as a mutual exchange of pleasure, best experienced with respect and consideration.

So far, Cameron struck her as that type of man. Finally, she answered, "Yes."

He let out a breath. "You took so long to answer, I wasn't sure." He rubbed her bottom lip with the edge of his thumb, smiling. "You've got a masochistic streak in you, don't you?"

"No, I just wasn't . . . sure how to answer."

This time he laughed. "That'll teach my ego to get excited."

She covered her face with her hands. "I'm making a mess of this aren't I?"

"Not at all. You gave me my kiss, and that was more than I had a right to ask for." Stepping back, he said, "I should let you get back to your friends."

But she didn't want him going through the day thinking she *didn't* want him. Because she did. More so with every blasted second.

Forcing herself to be bold, Asia lifted her chin and looked him right in his sexy blue eyes. "Will you give me another kiss first?"

He stared down at her, that charming crooked smile in place. He leaned back against the wall and said, "Why don't you kiss me this time? Just to be fair?"

He kept taking her by surprise! She'd been under the impression all men liked to be in control, at all times. She realized this proved her theory about the sexually explicit movie he'd purchased. Even though he bought a tape that showed a man dominating in the most elemental way, he'd just offered to let her take the lead. She braced herself.

In for a penny . . . Asia put her hands on his shoulders, then stalled. He was so hard.

His suit coat hid some broad shoulders and a lot of solid muscle. She hadn't realized before, but now the proof was in her hands and it was unbearably enticing. *Would he be that hard all over?*

She shivered. What a thought.

Trailing her fingers downward, she found his biceps and inhaled in triumph. Solid, strong. No underexercised executive here! Cameron O'Reilly was all rugged male.

Eyes closed, Asia flexed her fingers, relishing the feel of hard muscle, strong bones and obvious strength. Her stomach did a little flip of excitement and she stepped into him while going on tiptoe. When he'd kissed her, only their mouths had touched.

But Asia wanted more and she saw no reason to deny herself. She fitted her body to his, soft breasts to broad chest, curving belly to hard abdomen . . . pelvis to pelvis. He groaned low and rough, and then his hands were on the small of her back, pressing her closer, and she felt his solid erection, long and hot, pulsing through the layers of clothes.

"Oh my," she whispered, going well beyond impressed to the realm of awed.

"Give me your mouth, Asia."

No sooner did she comply, kissing him with all the pent-up desire she suffered, than he turned them both so she was the one pressed to the wall. One of his hands slid down her back to her behind, and he gripped her, lifting, bringing her into startling contact with his erection.

He pressed into her rhythmically, rubbing himself against her, setting her on fire, all the while kissing her, soft eating kisses, deep-driving kisses, wet and hot and consuming.

A rap at the door made them both jump.

Erica called in, "Sorry kiddies, but playtime is over. Time to come in from recess."

Asia slumped against the wall and groaned. She'd totally forgotten her surroundings!

Watching her closely, Cameron cleared his throat. "We'll be right there."

With laughter in her voice, Erica said, "If you wait just two little minutes, the room will be clear and you can escape without notice." They both heard the sound of her retreating footsteps.

"I'm sorry."

Asia looked up. "For what?"

Stroking her cheek gently, he said, "I meant only a simple kiss—well okay, not so simple—but I didn't mean to embarrass you."

She sighed even as her heart softened. What an incredible man. "Cameron, you called a halt," she felt compelled to point out, "and I insisted on one more kiss. I'm the one who should be apologizing."

"Are you sorry?" he asked, and he wore that absorbed expression again, which now looked endearing.

"The truth? Nope." He grinned at her and she added, "I've never done anything like this before. It feels good to be a bit naughty."

"Yeah?" He tilted his head, studying her. "Any time you wanna get naughty, lady, you just let me know."

He was full of surprises. "You're not worried about how it might look to others?"

"You're worth the risk."

The things he said played havoc with her restraint. "I'll keep your offer in mind," she whispered as she opened the door, and they were both relieved to see the room was, indeed, empty.

Tomorrow, she decided, couldn't get here soon enough.

Cameron threw his suit coat over the arm of a chair, kicked his dress shoes into the closet and loosened his tie. All day long, his thoughts had centered on Asia. Damn, but she tasted better, felt better, than he'd imagined. He'd wanted to make love to her there in the closet with the two of them standing, a crowd in the outer room.

He closed his eyes a moment and imagined lifting her long skirt, feeling her grip his shoulders and hook her long slender legs around his waist. He pictured her head back, her eyes closed, her lips parted on a raw cry as he pushed into her.

She would be open, unable to meter the depth of his strokes, and he'd take her so long, so deeply, she'd scream with the pleasure of it. His stomach cramped with lust.

Better *not* to use the closet, he decided with a rueful grin. He didn't want her stifled in any way, not after the two months he'd spent fantasizing about her. At first, it had been simple lust—she looked exactly as he thought a woman should look. Soft, sexy, capable, and her brown eyes were always bright with intelligence. She was friendly, but not flirtatious. Subtly sensual, with only her natural femininity on display. She didn't flaunt, didn't go out of her way to enhance her looks.

The more he'd gotten to know her, the more he'd wanted her. But she gave him only casual conversation, allowing him to view her generous spirit, her quick smiles and easy nature from an emotional distance. In the two months he'd known her, he'd absorbed all the small glimpses of her character, which had acted as more enticement. He not only wanted her sexually, he just plain wanted her.

Tomorrow night he'd have her.

He didn't know if he'd survive that long.

He tossed his tie onto the chair with his coat and reached into his pants pocket for the gift he'd bought her. He hadn't meant to go shopping, but on the drive home he'd stopped for a red light, and his eye had caught the festive Christmas display in a jewelry store window. Once he saw the bracelet, he wanted it for her.

For a first date, it was a bit extravagant, he thought, but what the hell. He'd known her two months now, necked with her in a closet, fantasized about her endlessly, and besides, he liked to think positive; he had a gut feeling that this would be the first date of many.

He could call it a Christmas gift. After all, he still had hopes of convincing her to spend the day with him.

The exotic burnished gold and topaz-studded bracelet reminded him of Asia's coloring. As he'd told her, she was far from plain. He put the bracelet back in the velvet-lined box and set it on his dresser, then put the spanking tape into the VCR. He picked up the remote and stretched out in his bed on top of the covers, two fat pillows behind his back, one arm folded behind his head.

He hit play, and settled in to be educated.

As the story—*ha! what story?*—started, he thought of Asia and knew there wasn't much he wouldn't do to win her over. Including indulging in a little kinky sex.

Chapter Four

Cameron sat behind his desk, a spreadsheet on his computer screen, early the next morning. Steaming coffee filled the cold morning with delicious scents. The windows overlooking the parking lot were decorated with lacy frost, while more snowflakes, fat as cotton balls, drifted down to the sill. The quiet strains of Christmas music from the outer office drifted in.

The knock on the door jarred him and he looked up. "Come in."

Asia peered around the door, smiled at him and asked, "Are you busy?"

Without a single hesitation, he closed out the computer screen. "Not at all."

She inched in, looking furtive and so sexy, his abdomen clenched. Both hands behind her still holding the doorknob, she rested against the closed door. "I hoped you were in."

A glance at the clock showed him she'd come to work almost a half hour early. He'd been there for an hour himself. After watching the tape, he'd found it impossible to relax. He kept seeing Asia in every position depicted by the actors, and when he'd finally drifted off to sleep, he'd dreamed of her. Not since his teens had he awoken in a sweat, but last night he had.

Heart thumping and cock at full attention, Cameron eased out from behind his desk. "Is anything wrong?"

He searched her face, looking for clues to her thoughts. If she planned to break their date for that night, he'd need to find a way to change her mind.

Her cheeks flushed and her beautiful eyes, locked on his, darkened to mahogany. "Do you mind if I lock this?" she asked, indicating the door.

Cameron stepped closer. "Please do."

The lock clicked like a thunderclap, echoing the sounds of his heartbeat. When she turned to face him again, Cameron murmured, "I'm glad to see you, Asia."

She folded her hands together at her waist. Her long brown hair hung loose, like a rich velvet curtain. The ends curled the tiniest bit, barely reaching the tips of her breasts, which were enticingly molded beneath a beige cashmere sweater. Her neutral-toned patterned skirt ended a mere inch below her knees and was trim enough to outline the shape of her thighs. Wearing flats, she just reached his chin, and she looked up at him.

"I thought maybe we could . . ." She stalled, shifted uncertainly.

His testicles drew tight and his cock flexed at the thought of touching and kissing her again. "Yes?"

She lifted one shoulder in a self-conscious shrug. "I liked kissing you yesterday."

"Liked? I'm surprised I didn't catch on fire." He smiled, trying to take some of the heavy desire from his words. He didn't want to scare her off. There were few people in the building yet. Most wouldn't show up for another twenty-five minutes. He had her all to himself. "I dreamed about you last night."

Her lips parted. "You did?"

Cameron couldn't stop himself from touching her. Using the backs of his knuckles, he smoothed a long tendril of hair—right over her breast. Her nipple puckered, and deliberately he rasped it, teasing her, teasing himself more. He heard the catch of her breath. Her eyes were closed, her chest rising and falling.

"Are you wearing a bra, Asia?" he asked, unable to detect one with his easy touch.

She shook her head. "A . . . a demi bra."

"Meaning your nipples," he murmured, lifting both hands to her, "are uncovered?"

Ah, yes, he could tell now as he caught each tip between his fingers and thumbs and pinched lightly. The cashmere sweater was incredibly soft and did nothing to conceal his touch. Her nipples were tight, pushed up by the bra, but not covered. He gently plucked and rolled and she suddenly grasped his wrists.

"I don't believe this," she moaned.

Cameron didn't remove his hands. She wasn't restraining him so much as holding onto him. He leaned close and nuzzled her temple. "This?" he asked, unsure of her meaning.

"I don't . . . I'm not usually . . ."

He had no idea what she wanted to tell him. "You like this?" He tugged at her nipples, making her sway toward him. Her breasts were very sensitive, he discovered, as heat throbbed beneath his skin.

"I do," she rasped, then dropped her head forward to his shoulder, panting. "I'm not usually so . . . so easy."

Cameron pressed his mouth to the delicate skin of her temple, then her cheekbone. "Easy? I've wanted you for two months." He drew the tender skin of her throat against his teeth, careful not to mark her. "I don't call that easy."

"No, but . . ." She sucked in a breath, then cried out. Her fingers clenched on his wrists and her hips pressed inward, trying to find him. "Cameron, I feel like I'm going to—"

Realization dawned, and he stared at her in wonder. "You want to climax, Asia?"

She didn't answer for the longest time while he continued to toy with her breasts, and she continued to writhe against him. "Oh, please," she finally gasped, nearly beside herself.

Cameron released her, ignoring her soft moan of disappointment, and put an arm around her waist. "C'mere," he said, almost blind with lust.

He led her to his desk. She looked at him with darkened eyes, a little unfocused, a lot hungry. "Just a second," he said and reached for her narrow skirt.

She made a slight sound of surprise when he worked the snug material up to her hips, then lifted her to sit on the edge of the desk. She looked up, a question in her eyes, but he stepped between her thighs and took her mouth, devouring her, his tongue licking, his teeth nipping.

She wrapped both arms around his neck and held on.

He hated panty hose, he thought, as he trailed his fingers up her nylon-clad thighs. Stockings that left her vulnerable to him would have been better, but he'd make do.

He teased her, kissing her while stroking the insides of her thighs until she was nearly frantic. Then he pressed his palm against her mound and they both went still.

"Mmmm," he whispered, his fingers pressing gently, exploring. "You're wet."

She ducked her face into his throat.

Blood roared in his ears, but he made himself move slow and easy. "I can even feel you through your panties and your hose."

"Oh, God." She lurched a little when he stroked over her with his middle finger. "This is awful."

He smiled. "You want me to quit?" he teased.

"Please don't!"

With her legs parted, the panties and panty hose couldn't hide her state of desire. He could feel every sweet inch of her, the curly pubic hair, the swollen lips. Her distended clitoris.

He groaned. With one arm around her holding her tight,

he used the other hand to pet and finger and tease. Her hips shifted, rolled against him. "Is this good, Asia?" he asked, wanting, needing to know if it was enough.

Her head tipped back, lips parted on her panting breaths, her body arched—and then she broke.

Her eyes squeezed shut, her teeth sank into her bottom lip to hold back the moans coming from deep in her throat.

Cameron felt like a world conqueror, watching her beautiful, carnal expressions, feeling the harsh trembling in her body.

"*Yes,*" he murmured, keeping his touch steady, even, despite her frantic movements and the mad dashing of his heart. "That's it, sweetheart. That's it."

By slow degrees, she stilled, her body going boneless. Cameron gathered her close into his arms and held her. His own desire was keen, but at the same time, he felt a heady satisfaction. She smelled warm, a little sweaty despite the frigid winter storm outside and the nip of the air in his office. And she smelled female, the scent guaranteed to fire his blood.

He rocked her gently and smoothed his big hands up and down her narrow back.

Against his throat, she whispered, "I think I'm embarrassed."

"You think?" He couldn't help but chuckle, he felt so damn good. Sexually frustrated, but emotionally sated. "Please don't be. I'm not."

"This was . . . unfair of me."

"This was very generous of you."

That left her speechless. Cameron tangled one hand in her silky hair and tipped her head up to him so he could see her face. "Thank you."

She laughed, groaned and dropped her forehead to his sternum. "I can't wait until tonight, Cameron. I didn't believe it at first, but I know it's going to be so good."

What did she mean, she hadn't believed it at first? Then

the rest of what she said hit him and he stilled. "You intend to make love with me tonight?" He had hoped and planned, but he hadn't expected a confirmation.

She looked up in surprise. "You want to, don't you?"

Bemused, he said, "More than I want my next breath."

Her smile was a beautiful thing. "I'm sorry about doing this now. I'd only meant a few more kisses—more of that naughtiness we'd joked about. But then you . . . you touched me and I lost it."

"I'm not sorry, so don't you be either. I'm glad you're so sensitive, so hot."

She looked down at his tie. "I didn't know I was." Then, "I never was before." She met his gaze with a look of confusion. "I think it's just you."

Cameron didn't bother denying that. He couldn't think of a woman hotter than Asia Michaels. But he'd be damned if he'd explain it wasn't him, taking a chance that she'd find another guy. No way.

"Tonight will be even better," she said, then peeked up at him as if waiting for his reply.

Was this his cue that tonight he was supposed to do something different? Something more . . . forceful? He said, his tone filled with caution, "I want you to be satisfied with me, Asia."

Her eyes brightened, and she threw her arms around his throat again, nearly strangling him. "Thank you." Leaning back, she added with sincerity, "I really am sorry to do this, to leave you . . . unsatisfied. But I never suspected it'd go this far."

He kissed the end of her nose and said, "I'll think of it as extended foreplay."

His phone rang just as she pulled away and began straightening her skirt. Her cheeks were rosy, her eyes slumberous and sated. Watching her, regretting the necessity that kept her beautiful legs hidden from him, Cameron hit a button and said absently, "Yes?"

"You asked that I remind you about the meeting first thing this morning, Mr. Cameron."

"Thank you, Marsha."

He disconnected the line. Marsha was a secretary for the entire floor, which included four supervisors. She kept everyone punctual and was observant as hell.

He looked at Asia. "Do you mind if Marsha knows we're seeing each other?"

She shook her head. "Do you?"

His grin turned wolfish as he stepped past her to unlock and open the door. No one was in the hallway to notice, and for that he was grateful. He wouldn't tolerate gossip about Asia.

"I want everyone to know," he told her, and turned to face her again with a smile. "Maybe it'll keep the rest of the men from pursuing you."

"The guys here?" she asked, and scoffed. "They all know I'm not interested."

"But you are," he reminded her, looking at her breasts, her belly and thighs. "You're interested in *me*."

He waited for her to deny it, but all she did was shrug. "It's strange. You affect me differently."

He sauntered toward her, filled with confidence. "I make you hot."

She looked perplexed as hell when she said, "Yeah."

Cameron shook his head. It had taken her two months to notice the sexual chemistry he'd picked up on within two minutes of meeting her. If it hadn't been for the damned porn shop just opening, she still wouldn't have given him the time of day. He couldn't forget that. Asia with her big bedroom eyes and standoffish ways had a sexual predilection, and last night he'd watched the tape and learned how to appease her.

Her preferences were still foreign to him, but less unappealing. Some of the scenes, in fact, had really turned him on. He'd imagined Asia in place of the overblown actress.

He pictured her firm, lush bottom turned up to the warm smacks of a large male hand—*his hand*. The smacking part didn't interest him much, even though the swats had done little more than redden her bottom, and ultimately prepare her for a hard ride.

But the touching afterward, the utter vulnerability and accessibility of the woman's sex to probing fingers and tongue had made him hot as hell. The actress had remained in the submissive position, bent over a footstool, hands flat on the floor, knees spread wide, and in Cameron's mind it had been Asia, waiting for him, ready for him.

He sucked in a deep breath, drawing Asia's notice.

Her eyes were again apologetic when she asked, "Are you okay?"

"Other than being hard as a spike, yes."

She smiled. "That might make your meeting difficult."

Cameron took her arm and led her toward the door. "Once you're gone I'll get myself in order. That is, if I can stop thinking about tonight."

The hallway was still clear, not a soul in sight. Memory of the movie still played in his mind, and when Asia turned away, he gave her rump a sound smack. She jumped, whirled to face him with both hands holding her behind and her eyes enormous.

Cameron forced himself to a neutral smile, though the look on her face was priceless, a mixture of surprise and awareness. "I'll see you tonight," he said.

Frowning, rubbing her backside, she gave an absent nod and hurried away.

His palm stung a little, and his cock throbbed. He could do this, he told himself as he went to his desk to gather the necessary files. And if he did it well enough, he'd be able to reel her in.

He wanted Asia Michaels, and one way or another, he'd have her.

* * *

Asia thought about that rather stinging smack throughout the day. It meant nothing, she told herself, just teasing gone a little overboard. Cameron had been so gentle, so concerned for her and her pleasure, that she trusted him.

But she'd left his office and gone straight to the restroom. After their little rendezvous, she needed to tidy up. And she couldn't stop herself from peeking once she had her panty hose down in the private stall.

Sure enough, Cameron's large hand print, faintly pink and still warm, showed on her white bottom. The sight of that handprint made her heart race with misgivings . . . and something more.

Long after she'd returned to her desk, she'd been aware of the warmth on her cheek, the tingling of that print. It kept Cameron and what they'd done in his office in the forefront of her mind throughout the entire day. She could not stop thinking about him, about the pleasure he'd given her so easily when that type of pleasure had always eluded her. She couldn't put his thoughtfulness or tenderness from her mind.

And she couldn't forget that swat.

As she dressed for the date that night, she again surveyed her bottom. But the mark was long gone, with only the memory remaining. It meant nothing, she told herself yet again, but still her heartbeat sped up whenever she thought of it.

Cameron was right on time. The second she opened her door, he leaned in and kissed her. Snowflakes hung in his dark hair and dusted the shoulders of his black coat. He'd dressed in casual slacks, a dress shirt and sweater.

Asia waited for the verdict as he looked her over from head to toe. Her dress was new, a dark burgundy with gold flecks around the low-scooped neckline and shin-length hem. She wore dark brown leather boots with two-inch heels. Her long hair was in a French braid, hanging down the middle of her back, and gold hoop earrings decorated her ears.

"You look incredible," Cameron murmured, then pulled her close and kissed her again, this time with purpose.

Asia quivered with need. When her mouth was again free, she said, "Maybe . . . maybe we should skip dinner?" She didn't want to eat. She wanted to be alone with Cameron, to find out the extent of these amazing sexual feelings he inspired.

She'd told Erica at break that she owed her big time, because if it hadn't been for her, she'd never have discovered the truth. As she'd always suspected, fireworks did exist. You only needed the right man to set them off.

Cameron was evidently the right man.

He took her hand and kissed her palm. She felt the brief touch of his warm, damp tongue and nearly moaned. "Do you need to be up early tomorrow?" he asked.

"No, my weekends are always free."

He took her cloak from her and helped her slip it on. "I hope they won't be free anymore."

Asia had nothing to say to that. She couldn't deny that she wanted to see him again.

"I'll feed you," Cameron continued, "and then we'll go to my place."

She sniffed and turned away, a little put out that he seemed less anxious than she.

Cameron hugged her from behind, chuckling softly. In her ear, he whispered, "The tension will build and build, sweetheart. Just be patient with me, okay?"

She didn't want to be patient, but she figured he had to know more about this than she did. Her experience with sex was that it wasn't much fun most of the time, and other times it was just plain awful.

"All right."

An hour later, Asia was ready to kill him. The restaurant where they had dinner was elegant, expensive and crowded. Festive Christmas music played softly through the speaker system, and fat gold candles, decorated with holly, lit each table.

People talked and smiled and laughed, and Asia felt conspicuous, as if everyone there knew she was aroused, but was too polite to point at her.

Cameron kept her on that keen edge, touching her constantly, her cheek, her chin, her shoulders—touches that seemed innocent but still made her burn because she knew exactly what he could do with those touches, how he could make her body scream in incredible pleasure.

What would it be like when he pushed deep inside her, when he rode her and the friction was within as well as without? She bit her lip hard to keep from gasping aloud with her thoughts.

And still she couldn't stop thinking them.

Feeling his touch through the barrier of clothes had been indescribable, but when he touched naked flesh, would she be able to stand it? When it was his mouth on her nipples, not just his fingers, how much more would she experience? She shuddered at the thought and felt her body turning liquid.

They danced twice, and the way he moved against her should have been illegal. He *knew* what he did to her, and he enjoyed it.

She was on fire, her breath coming too fast and too deep, and still he lingered at the table, watching her closely, talking idly about inconsequential things. Her heart threatened to burst, and though the wind howled outside, she felt feverish and taut.

"Asia?"

She jumped, nearly panicked by the unfamiliar lust and anticipation. She stared at him blankly.

Cameron just smiled. "I asked you where you got your name."

She squeezed her hands together, trying to concentrate on things other than the way his dark hair fell over his brow, or how his strong jaw moved as he spoke, or the warm male scent of him that made her stomach curl deliciously. His large hands rested on the tabletop, his wrists thick, his fingers long and rough-tipped—fingers that had touched and teased her. Fingers that would be inside her body tonight.

She closed her eyes, remembering.

Cameron smoothed a curl behind her ear, and his voice was rough and low. "Tell me how you got that name, honey."

She swallowed down her growing excitement. "My grandmother's name was Anastasia. My father wanted to name me after her, but my mother thought the name too long."

"So they shortened it to Asia?"

"Yes." Talking required too much concentration.

"It's a beautiful name." His fingertips drifted over her cheek, down her throat, trailed along the neckline of her dress.

She gasped. "Cameron . . ."

"Are you ready to go?" he asked, even as he stood and pulled out her chair.

"More than ready," she muttered. While he tended to the bill, Asia pulled on her wrap and turned to leave. Cameron caught her arm before she'd taken three steps.

They walked in silence to his car. The parking garage was freezing cold and her accelerated breath frosted in the air. Cameron saw her seated, then went around to his side of the car.

They were on the road, only minutes from his apartment, before he asked, "You're not nervous, are you?"

Asia stared at him. She was so beyond nervous, it was all she could do to keep from jumping him. "I'm so excited I can barely stand it."

He kept his profile to her, but that didn't diminish the beauty of his masculine satisfaction. "Good. I want you excited."

Asia thrust her chin into the air. "I want you excited, too."

Without looking her way, he reached across the seat and caught her arm. His hand trailed down to her wrist, then lifted her fingers into his lap. She inhaled sharply at the well-defined, pulsing erection.

"Believe me, I'm excited," he said simply.

Rather than release him when he replaced his hand on the steering wheel, Asia scooted closer. He was a large man, his sex strong and long. She traced him through his trousers, glancing at his face occasionally to see his jaw locking hard, his nostrils flaring. His blue eyes looked very dark, frighteningly intense.

His penis flexed in her grasp, and she tightened her hold. She stroked him with her thumb, forcing the material of his slacks to rub against him. Her thumb moved up and over the head of his penis—and just that quickly, he grabbed her hand and forced it away.

"No," he said harshly, but without anger. "I won't be able to keep us on the road if you do that."

"When we get to your place," she murmured, understanding now why he enjoyed teasing, because she enjoyed it too, "I'll do that to you again. Only you'll be naked."

Cameron gripped the wheel hard, his mouth open as he sucked in air. "I'll hold you to that, sweetheart." And then he turned in toward his apartment complex.

Chapter Five

Cameron kissed her as he opened her car door, kissed her in the parking lot and on the stairs up to his apartment. He couldn't seem to stop kissing her and she didn't try to make him.

Getting his door unlocked was no easy feat with Asia smoothing her soft little hands all over his body, her mouth open on his throat, her fingertips gliding down his abdomen.

He tugged her inside, slammed the door, and fell with her onto the couch. He felt like a caveman, but his control was shot to hell; he'd teased too long.

She shifted around until she laid atop him. "Cameron," she muttered, and then kissed his face, his ear, his jaw.

He caught her, holding her steady so he could devour her sweet mouth. They moved together, hampered by coats and too many clothes and an urgent desire that obliterated reason.

"Damn," he growled, startled as he felt himself sliding off the couch to the floor.

They landed with a thump. He was dumbstruck for a moment, then heard Asia giggle.

"Witch," he groused low, and sat up beside her. He yanked at the fastenings of her cloak and spread it wide. Her breasts heaved, her legs moved restlessly. Cameron lowered himself again, this time with both hands cupping her breasts.

The air filled with their moans and sighs, but again, it became too frustrating. He didn't want to stop kissing her, but he stood up and jerked his coat off, tossing it aside, then pulled his sweater over his head.

Asia stayed on the floor, sprawled wantonly, watching him. When his chest was bare and her eyes were soft and wide, looking at him, he knelt and began removing her boots. "These are sexy," he said low, tugging them off and eyeing her bare legs beneath. His gaze sought hers and he raised one brow. "No panty hose this time?"

She shook her head. Silky fine tendrils of hair had escaped her braid and framed her face. Her lashes hung heavy, her eyes nearly black with lust. "I wanted to make it easier for you to touch me."

Her words were powerfully arousing. In a rush, he plunged his hands up under her skirt and caught the waistband of her minuscule panties. He started to drag them off her, but seeing her face, the anticipation there, he forced himself to slow down.

He had to remember that Asia had special requirements, a refined inclination toward erotic discipline, and if he wanted to keep her for more than a night or two, he had to adjust. Her pleasure meant everything to him, was half of his own pleasure, so he slowed himself. Instead of pulling her panties off, he cupped her through the thin silk.

"Hot, swollen," he said, watching her back arch. "You want me, don't you sweetheart?"

"Yes," she moaned, her eyes now closing.

He petted her, letting one long finger press between her lips, rub gently over her clitoris.

"Oh, God," she whispered brokenly.

Watching her was almost as good as sex, Cameron decided. She was so beautiful to him, so perfect. So open and honest and giving.

He removed his hand and flipped her onto her stomach.

She froze for a heartbeat, her hands flat on the carpet at either side of her breasts. "Cameron?"

"Let me get this dress off you," he explained, and worked the zipper down her back. The bodice opened and he caught the shoulders, pulling them down to her elbows. She freed her right arm, then her left.

Kneeling between her widespread thighs, Cameron eyed her slender back, the graceful line of her spine. In a rush, he pulled the dress the rest of the way off.

Asia half raised herself, but he pressed a hand to the small of her back and took his time looking at her. Her bottom was plump, her cheeks rounded and firm. He stroked her with both hands, feeling the slide of silken panties over her skin.

"Cameron . . ."

"Shhh." He unfastened her bra and let it fall, freeing her breasts. Leaning over her, his cock nestled securely against that delectable ass, he balanced on one arm. With his free hand he reached beneath her and stroked her breasts, paying special attention to her pointed, sensitized nipples. She gave a ragged moan.

Cameron languidly rubbed himself against her, almost blind with need. It would be so easy to enter her this way. She was wet, hot and slippery and he could sink right in.

He groaned and pushed himself away. He had to do this right.

Before he changed his mind, he kicked off his shoes, sat on the edge of the couch, and pulled off his socks.

Asia was near his feet and she turned her head to look at him curiously. Their eyes met and she started to rise.

Cameron caught her under her arms. Her bra fell completely off, and it stunned him, this first glimpse at her bared body. She wore only transparent, insubstantial panties; they offered her no protection at all.

"You are so beautiful," he said with complete inadequacy.

She smiled shyly, reached for him—and he pulled her across his knees.

For a brief moment, she froze. "Cameron?"

When he didn't answer, determined on his course, Asia twisted to look at him. He controlled her easily, his gaze focused solely on that gorgeous behind. He could see the deep cleft, and the dark triangle of feminine curls covering her mound. He traced her with a fingertip, down the line of her buttocks, in between. She stilled, her breathing suspended.

Her panties were damp with her excitement and he pressed into her, feeling her heat, her swollen lips. His eyes closed. He wanted to taste her, wanted to tongue her and hear her soft cries. Her hands, braced on his thigh, tightened, her nails digging into his muscles even through his slacks.

He had to do this right.

Teeth clenched, Cameron opened his eyes, looked at his big dark hand on her very soft feminine bottom, and forced himself to give her a stinging slap.

She yelped.

"How does that feel?" he rasped, lifting his hand for another.

Asia was frozen on his thighs, not moving, not speaking.

He brought his hand down again, doing his best to meter his strength, to let her feel the warmth of the smack without actually hurting her in any way.

His heart thundered and his pulse roared in his ears. He thought he might split his pants he was so turned on, despite the distaste he felt in striking her. After all, they were minutes away from making love and she was a warm, womanly scented weight over his lap, all but naked and so beautiful—

"You bastard!"

Like a wild woman, she launched herself away from him. Stupefied, Cameron looked at her sprawled on the carpet some feet away, her naked breasts heaving, her eyes wet with tears.

Tears!

Her bottom lip trembled and she said with stark accusation, "I thought you were different!"

Very unsure of himself and the situation, Cameron said, "Uh . . ." And then, "I'm . . . trying to be."

"You hit me!"

He had. Cameron looked at his hand, stinging a little from contact with that beautiful behind, and said again, "Uh . . ."

Asia pushed to her feet. Her breasts swayed, full and still flushed from arousal, the nipples tight points. Feet planted apart in a stance guaranteed to make his blood race, she glared at him.

Slowly, very slowly so he didn't spook her or make this bizarre situation worse, Cameron came to his feet. "You wanted me to," he reminded her.

Her eyes widened even more. "What are you talking about?"

He shrugged, gestured toward his bedroom where the damning tape was still in the VCR. He rubbed the back of his neck and felt a sick foreboding close around him. "You, ah, wanted a guy who was into spanking."

She gasped so hard her breasts jiggled, further exacerbating his desire. "You *listened*!" she accused.

"Not on purpose."

It was as if she hadn't heard him. "You were the guy with the newspaper in the lounge. The guy wearing jeans!"

"Yeah. I, ah, had to work outside that day, to oversee work on the compressors, so my clothes were different." He nearly winced as he admitted that, then thought to add, a bit righteous, "The lounge is a public place and I heard you say plain as day that you were into spanking."

"I said no such thing!"

"Yes, you did." Didn't she? Her face was red, but he barely noticed with her standing there, the body he'd been dreaming about for two full months more bare than not.

"You said you would hook up with the guy who bought a spanking tape. Well, I bought the stupid thing."

"Stupid thing?" she growled, and advanced toward him. "You mean you don't watch them?"

"I never had before." He was mightily distracted from the argument by the way she moved, and how her body moved, and how much he wanted her. "But I'd have bought a tape of monkeys mating if that's what it took to get your attention."

She drew up short, a mere foot away from him. "That's sick!"

Cameron leaned forward, his own temper igniting. "No, sweetheart. That's desperation. I wanted you. You barely acknowledged me, except in that too cool, distantly polite voice that kept miles between us. I heard you in the lounge and took advantage. So what?"

She looked slightly confused for a moment, then pugnacious. "You struck me."

"Because I thought you wanted me to. Hell, do you think *I* wanted to?"

"Didn't you?" She gave a pointed stare to this straining erection.

Cameron grunted. "You're almost naked. You're excited and wet and hot, and I've been hard since the day I first saw you."

She blinked uncertainly. "You're saying you didn't want to swat me?"

Hands on his hips, he leaned down, nose to nose with her. "There are a lot of things I'd rather do to your beautiful naked ass than spank it."

She half turned away, then back. Watching him with suspicion, and what appeared to be sensual curiosity, she asked, "Like what?"

Cameron took a small step forward, further closing the gap between them. In a lower, more controlled but gravelly voice, he said, "Like pet you, and kiss you—"

"My behind?"

"Hell, yes." Moving slowly, he reached out and caught her shoulders. "I can't imagine any man alive not wanting to kiss your behind."

She giggled at the wording, but flushed at the meaning. "My husband would have never considered . . ."

He released her so fast, he almost tripped. "Husband?"

"Ex-husband."

Clutching his heart, Cameron said, "Thank God." It took him a second to recover from that panic. He hadn't heard anything about her being married. "So you're divorced?"

"Yes."

"You still care about him?"

She laughed, which was a better answer than a straight out "no," but she gave him that too.

"I stopped caring about him almost as soon as I said, 'I do.' Unfortunately, it took longer than that for me to admit it to everyone else and to get the divorce."

He didn't want to talk about any idiot ex-husband. Holding her shoulders again, he said, "Know what I want to do?"

Her hand lifted to his crotch, cuddled his cock warmly. Her smile was sweet and enticing. "I can maybe guess."

He drew a deep breath. "You're willing?"

"No more hitting?"

Cameron kissed her. "It took all my concentration to get it done the first time. Believe me, it was for you, for what I thought you wanted. Not for me."

She looked touched by his gesture. "Then, yes, I'm willing."

Disinclined to take the chance that she might change her mind, Cameron lifted her in his arms and started for his bedroom. "I promise to make it up to you," he said. And he meant it. Now that he could think clearly, he'd know to concentrate on her responses, not on the dumb conversation he'd overheard. But that made him think of something else.

"Can I ask you a question?"

"That is a question," Asia replied, but she didn't sound put out. She was too engrossed in his chest, caressing his chest hair, finding his nipples and flicking them with her thumbnail until his knees nearly buckled.

Cameron quickly sat on the edge of the bed, Asia braced in his arms. He kissed her, then against her mouth asked, "Why did you require I buy that stupid tape?"

She tucked her face into his throat while she explained her theories—dumb ones, Cameron thought privately—and when she'd finished, she looked up at him.

"My ex-husband was forever trying to force me to do . . . kinky things that turned him on. He said it was the only way I could satisfy him. I didn't like it, and then he'd be angry about it and call me a prude and a cold fish. I used to wish he'd get his jollies that way with a movie or a book." She shrugged. "I wanted us to just make love, like two people who . . ."

Cameron squeezed her, wishing he had her damned ex close at hand so he could offer her retribution. But all he could do was say, "Like two people who loved each other?"

She gave a tiny nod. "Yes." Then she shocked the hell out of him by adding, "I haven't been with anyone since him. I needed to prove to myself first that I was independent, that I didn't believe all his garbage about me not being woman enough. He made me feel so low, and in my head, I knew he was a jerk. I knew he was wrong, too. But no man tempted me."

"Not even me," Cameron admitted, more for himself than her. He'd gained a lot of insight tonight, and most of it broke his heart. He'd handled things all wrong. Asia hadn't wanted him. She hadn't wanted any man.

She'd only needed validation, and instead he'd shot down her beliefs by spanking her. Damn, he was a real idiot.

Asia touched his jaw. "That's not true." She bit her lip, then let out a breath. "I think if it had been anyone other than you in that store, I wouldn't have had the guts to go through with it. But it was you, and I liked you already, and respected you a lot."

"You hid it well," he teased, shaken with relief.

"That's because I wanted you, too, though I was afraid to admit it. It scared me to want someone again."

With a trembling hand, Cameron stroked her throat, her shoulder, her breasts. "Let me show you that there's nothing to be afraid of, sweetheart. Let me show you how it should be." *How it'll always be between us.*

"Yes." Asia closed her eyes on a soft moan. "I think I'd like that."

Like a lick of fire, Cameron's kisses burned her everywhere. With incredible gentleness, he tilted her back on the bed and half covered her. She loved the tingling abrasion of his chest hair over her sensitive nipples. She loved the exciting, not-so-gentle stroke of his hand on her body. He seemed to know exactly how and where to touch her. And he found sensitive places she hadn't known about—the delicate skin beneath her ears, her underarms, below her breasts, the insides of her thighs and backs of her knees.

He kissed her, but not where she wanted his mouth most. Her breasts ached for him, her nipples so tight they throbbed with need, but he kissed around them, his tongue flicking out, leaving damp patches on her heated skin. He kissed her belly, tongued her navel until she squirmed, then put tiny pecks all around her sex, not touching her, but she heard him breathing deeply, inhaling her musky scent with appreciation.

She moaned, then caught her breath as he turned her onto her stomach.

"Easy," he whispered, his mouth brushing over her shoulders, down the length of her spine. He caught her panties and stripped them off. Through dazed eyes, Asia looked over her shoulder and saw him lift them to his face and inhale deeply. He gave a rough, growling groan of appreciation, and when his gaze met hers, his blue eyes burned like the hottest fire.

As promised, he kissed her bottom, especially the pink handprint on her left cheek. He murmured words of apology but she barely heard them because his hand slipped between her thighs. His long fingers just barely touched her, teasing and taunting while his mouth continued, so very gentle, so careful.

She couldn't hold still. She pressed her face into the bedclothes and squirmed. "*Cameron.*"

He turned her over again, and this time when his fingers went between her thighs he parted her and pressed his middle finger deep.

Her hips lifted sharply off the mattress and she cried out.

"Asia," he whispered huskily. "Baby, I want to watch you come again."

Oh, God, she thought, almost frantic with need. How was she supposed to answer that demand?

He didn't give her a chance to worry about it. He lowered his head and sucked her nipple into the moist heat of his mouth. His tongue curled around her and he drew on her, even as his finger began sliding in and out.

She moaned and gasped and clutched at the sheets on his bed. Cameron switched to her other breast, licking, plucking with his lips. She braced herself, but he took her by surprise with his teeth, catching her tender nipple and tugging insistently.

"*Oh, God.*"

"Open up for me, Asia," he whispered, and worked another finger into her. "Damn, you're snug."

He had large hands, she thought wildly, feeling herself stretched taut, but with his tongue licking her nipple she didn't have time to worry about it. He kept moving his hand, deep, harder, and the rough pad of his thumb pressed to her clitoris, giving a friction so sweet she screamed. Her muscles clamped down on the invading, sliding fingers and she shook with an orgasm so powerful she went nearly insensate.

When she was able to breathe again, she realized Cameron had moved and now had his head resting low on her belly, his arm around her upper thighs. With a lot of concentration, she lifted a hand and threaded her fingers through the cool silk of his dark hair. "That was . . ." Words were beyond her. How could she describe such a remarkable thing?

"Very nice," he answered, and she felt his breath on her still-hot vulva. Her legs were obscenely sprawled, she realized, but when she started to close them, he shushed her and petted her back into the position he wanted.

He turned his face inward and kissed her belly, then pressed his cheek to her pubic hair. "I love your scent," he growled, and Asia knew his arousal was razor sharp, that once again he'd skipped his own pleasure for her.

"Cameron," she chided gently, and some insidious emotion too much like love, squeezed at her heart. He kept saying her name, giving to her, pleasing her. He didn't take her for granted. She wasn't just an available woman. He wanted *her*.

"Bend your knees for me, love," he said.

Asia blushed at just the thought, and the pleasure of being called "love." She shifted her legs slightly farther apart.

He pulled them wider, bent her knees for her. He stroked his fingers through her curls, tweaked one, smoothed another. "You're beautiful," he said, looking at her too closely. "All pink and wet and swollen. For me."

She tipped her head back, staring at the ceiling and trying not to groan. But she was fully exposed to him, overly sensitive from her recent release, and it was unbearably erotic even while mortification washed over her.

Cameron repositioned himself directly between her thighs, urging them wider still so that they accommodated his broad shoulders. Using his thumbs, he opened her even more and just when she thought she couldn't bear it another second, he lowered his head and his rough velvet tongue lapped the length of her, up to but not quite touching her clitoris.

Her hips rose sharply off the bed as her back bowed and the breath in her lungs escaped in a rush. *"Cameron."*

He licked again, and again. His mouth was scalding, his tongue rasping against already aroused tissues. Asia gripped the sheets, trying to anchor herself, trying to keep still, but she strained against him, wanting and needing more.

He teased and tasted her everywhere except where she most wanted to feel the tantalizing flick of his tongue. "Please," she barely whispered.

And with a soft groan, he drew her in, suckling at her clitoris, nipping with his teeth. Asia moaned with the unbelievable pleasure of it, her entire body drawing tight and then melting on wave after wave of sensation.

She didn't know she'd cried until she felt Cameron kissing the tears from her cheeks, murmuring softly, reassuringly—and sinking deep into her body with a low, long groan.

"Oh," she said, and got her eyes to open.

"Hi," he whispered, withdrawing inch by inch, and then pressing in again. He filled her up, stretched her already sensitive vulva unbearably, and the friction was incredible.

Dark color slashed his cheekbones and his blue eyes burned with an inner fire, intense and wild and tender.

"You're making love to me," she said, awed and a little overwhelmed because she'd thought her body was spent, as boneless as oatmeal. Yet she couldn't stop herself from countering his every move.

"I'm making love *with* you," he corrected.

"But I'm not doing anything," she said, thinking of all the ways she should have kissed him and touched him in turn.

His beautiful smile made her heart do flip-flops. "You're you— that's all you need to do."

"Cameron." She lifted limp arms to wrap around his neck and squeeze him tight. He kissed her lax mouth, and she felt his smile and kissed him back.

After a minute or two of that, she felt the need to shift and did, only to find the one position that really gratified was wrapping her legs around his waist.

He groaned, then drove a tiny bit harder, farther into her, until it was both an awesome pleasure and a small pain, a joining so complete that she was a part of him, and he of her.

She answered his groan with a gasp, her hips lifting into his, urging him on.

"That's it," he said, and cupped her buttocks in his hands, working her against him, his face a fierce study of concentration.

Incredibly, the feelings began to well again, taking her by surprise with the suddenness of it. "It can't be," she said.

And he said, "Hell, yes," and started driving fast and deep and faster still.

Asia tightened her hold on him, overwhelmed with it all as she experienced yet one more orgasm, this one deeper, slower, longer, not as cataclysmic, but still so sweetly satisfying she wanted to shout aloud with the pleasure of it.

No sooner did she relax than Cameron rubbed his face into her throat and began his own orgasm. She heard his rumbling growl start low in his chest, felt the fierce pounding of his heart, the light sweat on his back and the heat that poured off his naked body.

"*Asia,*" he groaned, and his body shuddered heavily, then collapsed on hers.

Too lethargic to move, Asia managed a pucker to kiss his ear, then dozed off.

Ten minutes later, Cameron levered himself up to look at her. She snored softly, making him grin like the village idiot, and she looked beautiful, melting his heart. *Mine,* he thought with a surge of possessiveness that took him by surprise. Asia Michaels was his, in every sense of the word.

As gently as possible, he disengaged their bodies and removed the condom. He doubted she'd even noticed when he'd rolled it on, she'd been so spent. Smiling, he located the sheet at the foot of the bed. Asia stirred, rolling to her side and curling up tight from the chill of the air.

The lights were still on and he could see the fading imprint of his hand on her soft bottom. He closed his eyes, wanting to groan but not wanting to awaken her. What an ass he'd been.

Tomorrow they'd talk more, he'd tell her how he felt and give her the bracelet, and with any luck at all, she'd understand.

He reached over and flipped off the lights. She turned toward him, snuggled close, and resumed snoring.

Oh, yeah, she was his all right. Now he just had to let her know that.

Chapter Six

Asia stirred, smiling even before her eyes were open, and feeling good—achy but good—all the way down to her toes. Cameron O'Reilly. Wow. The man really knew how to make love.

She rolled to her side and reached for him, but found only cold sheets. Jerking up in an instant, she looked around, but he was gone. Her discarded clothes from the night before were now neatly folded over a chair, waiting, it seemed, for her to get dressed.

The blankets, which had been irreparably tossed during their lovemaking, were now straightened and smoothed over her, keeping her warm.

She looked out the wide window and saw snow and more snow, and a sun so bright it hurt her eyes.

She groaned. It was two days till Christmas Eve. Of course, the man had things to do, yet she'd slept in. In his bed. Inconveniencing him.

Humiliation rolled over her. Some independent broad she turned out to be. She'd spent the night when she hadn't even been invited. What must he think? Was he wondering how to get rid of her?

She'd just shoved the covers aside and slipped one naked leg off of the bed, shivering at the touch of cool air on her bare skin, when Cameron opened the door. He paused, standing there in nothing more than unsnapped jeans and a healthy beard shadow. His blue eyes were sharp and watchful.

As if shaking himself, he continued into the room and said, "Good morning."

Asia didn't want to meet his gaze, but she refused to be a coward. Attempting a smile, she said, "Give me a minute to get dressed and I'll get out of your way."

Strange after the night of incredible, uninhibited sex, but she suddenly felt naked. Cameron didn't help, staring at her with blatant sexual interest. She could use the sheet from the bed, but again, that seemed cowardly. She had no modesty left, not with this man.

"I'm cooking breakfast," he said. "I was hoping you'd stay and eat with me."

She held her dress in her hands. It was tangled, the sleeves inside out, and wrinkled almost beyond repair. She stared at it stupidly, not even sure where to start.

Cameron pushed away from the dresser and took the dress, tossing it aside. He retrieved a flannel robe from his closet and held it out to her.

Not seeing too many options, especially since her brain refused to function in any normal capacity, Asia slipped her arms into the robe. Cameron wrapped it around her, tied the belt and rolled up the sleeves.

"It makes me hot," he said, "to see you in my things."

Asia stared at him. Her mouth opened, but nothing came out.

"Almost as hot," he continued when she stayed mute, "as it made me to wake up this morning with you in my bed, warm and soft." He touched her cheek. "I could wake up like this a lot, Asia."

Thrown for an emotional loop, she started to turn away, but Cameron caught her arm and led her out of the room. "I'm fixing bacon and I don't want it to burn."

His apartment was slightly smaller than hers, with a kitchen-dinette combination. Asia sat at the thick pine table and watched Cameron complete the meal. Barefoot and bare chested, he moved around the small kitchen with domestic ease. Her ex-husband had never cooked. He didn't even know how to boil water.

Cameron's hair was still disheveled, hanging over his brow with a rakish appeal. Muscles flexed in his shoulders and arms and down his back as he bent this way and that, turning bacon, pouring juice, as he turned to wink at her occasionally, or smile, or just gaze.

He asked her if fried eggs were okay, and how she liked her toast.

Asia answered more by rote than anything else. With the memories of the night, and Cameron in the kitchen looking sexy as the original sin, food was the farthest thing from her mind. But when he set her plate in front of her, she dug in.

And he watched her eat, smiling like a contented fool, his big bare feet were on either side of hers.

Finally, she laid her fork aside. Nothing had happened quite as she'd expected and she felt lost. "What," she grouched, "are you staring at?"

His smile widened. "You." He reached out and smoothed her hair, his fingers lingering. "I've never seen a woman with smudged makeup and tangled hair look quite so sexy."

His compliment put her over the edge. She shoved her chair back and stood up.

Cameron came to his feet, too. They stared at each other over the table, facing off.

Asia drew a deep breath. "This is ridiculous."

"I know. There's so much I want to say to you, but I'm not sure where to start."

She blinked, then covered her ears. "Stop it! Just stop . . . taking me by surprise."

Holding her gaze, Cameron rounded the table until he could clasp her wrists and pull her hands down. "I want to see you again, Asia."

"You mean you want to have sex with me again."

"Hell, yes. I want you right now. I wanted you the second I woke up. I'll want you tonight and tomorrow too."

She laughed, a near hysterical sound. "Will you stop?"

"No." Shaking his head, he said, "Not until you tell me how you feel."

"I feel . . ." She wasn't at all sure how she felt, and gestured helplessly. "Frustrated."

Cameron stroked her arms, bending to look her in the eyes. "I didn't satisfy you last night?"

Her laugh this time was genuine. "You did! Ohmigod, did you satisfy me."

"Well, then . . . ?"

"Cameron." She pulled away. She couldn't think, and she sure as hell couldn't talk, when he touched her. "This was all a . . . lark. You overheard my ridiculous pact with Erica and Becky, and because of that, you reacted and we had . . . better sex than I knew existed."

Cameron's jaw locked, but he kept quiet, letting her talk.

She drew another breath to fortify herself. "But that's all it is, all it was meant to be. You didn't intend for me to spend the night and intrude on your life."

"Are you done?"

He sounded angry, confusing her more. "Yes."

He went to the kitchen windowsill and lifted a small package wrapped in silver foil paper and tied with a bright red ribbon. "Everything you just said is bullshit and you know it. I've wanted you since the day I met you. And yes, it started out purely sexual, and it'll always be partly sexual. You turn me on, Asia, no way to deny that when I get a boner just hearing your name. But I like you a lot, too. Hell," he said, rubbing his neck the way he always did when he was annoyed, "I'm damn near obsessed with you."

Asia bit her lip, doing her best to keep her eyes off that gaily wrapped gift.

"I want you. It makes me nuts to think about any other

guy with you." He paced away, then back again. "I want you to spend the weekend with me."

"But . . . it's Christmas."

"That's right. And if you stay with me, it'll be the nicest Christmas I've ever had."

"You don't have any other plans?"

"If I did, I'd change them." He handed her the gift. "I bought you this. Before we slept together, because even if things hadn't gotten intimate so soon, I still wanted you to have it."

She held the gift with fascination. "Why?"

"Because you're special to me. The way you affect me is special, and the way I feel around you is special. I wanted you to know it."

"Oh."

"Well," he said, once again smiling, although now his smile looked a bit strained. "Open it."

Sitting back down in the chair, Asia pulled aside the crisp paper. She felt like a child again, filled with anticipation. When she opened the velvet box and saw the bracelet, tears welled in her eyes. "Oh, Cameron."

"You like it?" he asked anxiously.

"I love it." She looked up at him, seeing him through a sheen of tears. "It's absolutely perfect."

Cameron knelt down in front of her, lifted the bracelet from the box and clasped it around her slender wrist. "You're perfect. The bracelet is just decoration."

"Cameron?"

He lifted his gaze to hers, still holding her hand.

"May I spend Christmas with you?"

He sucked in a breath, then let it out with an enormous grin. "You may. You may even spend the entire week with me."

Giggling with pure happiness, Asia threw her arms around him. "You're so wonderful."

He squeezed her tight. "I know you want to take things slow and easy, honey. So I'm not rushing you." As he spoke, he lifted her in his arms and started back down the hall. "Your ex pulled a number on you, and I'd like to demolish the bastard. But I want you to know I'll be patient. We can do whatever you want, however you want. You just tell me."

Asia felt ready to burst. "I really do care about you, Cameron."

He froze, shuddered, then squeezed her tight and hurried the rest of the way to the bed. "That's a start," he said, lowering them both to the mattress. "Do you think by New Year's you might be telling me you love me? Because Asia, I . . ." He stopped and frowned. "I'm rushing you, aren't I?"

"You think you love me?" she asked in lieu of giving him an answer. "Is that what you were going to say?"

"I know how I feel." He untied the belt of the robe and parted it, looking down at her body. "And yes, I love you." He bent and lazily kissed her breasts. "Hell, I'm crazy nuts about you." He started kissing his way down her belly, and Asia wasn't able to say another thing. All she could do was gasp.

Epilogue

"A Valentine's Day engagement." Becky sighed. "How romantic."

Asia smiled in contentment. "I'm so happy. I didn't know a man like Cameron existed, and now I've not only discovered him, I have him for my own."

Erica gave her a smug grin. "You see how well my plans turn out."

"What I see," Asia said, leaning over the lounge table to wag a finger at her two friends, "is that neither of you have fulfilled your end of the bargain."

Erica laughed. "We were too amused watching things unfold for you. You and Cameron have stolen the show."

"Uh-huh. I think you both just chickened out."

Erica said, "No way," but Becky just looked around, as if seeking escape.

Erica and Asia both caught her hands. "C'mon, Becky," Asia teased, "you know it's well past your turn!"

Looking tortured, Becky said, "I don't know if I can."

"Trust me." Erica patted her shoulder. "You can."

"And you should," Asia added. "I mean, look how it turned out for me."

Becky folded her arms on the table and dropped her head. She gave a small groan.

Asia and Erica shared a look. "'Fess up, Becky," Asia

urged. "You've had two months instead of two days to think about it. So let's hear the big fantasy."

"I know I'm going to regret this," came her muffled voice. "But if you both insist . . ."

"We do!"

She lifted her head, looked around the lounge and leaned forward to whisper into two ears.

"Wow," Asia said when she'd finished.

"All right!" Erica exclaimed, and lifted a fist in the air.

Cameron showed up just then, forcing the women to stifle their humor. He bent down and planted a kiss on Asia's mouth. "You want to leave right after work to pick out the ring?"

Erica shook her head. "In a hurry, big boy?"

"Damn right."

To everyone's relief, Cameron got along fabulously with both Becky's timid personality, and Erica's outrageous boldness.

Asia couldn't imagine being any happier. Now, if only her two friends could find the same happiness. She eyed Becky, who still blushed with her confessed fantasy. Maybe, she thought, doing some silent plotting, she could give Becky a helping hand. She tugged Cameron to his feet and said good-bye to her friends.

Once they were in the hallway, she said, "How well do you know George Westin?"

"Well enough to know he's got a reputation with the ladies. Why?"

"I think he may just be perfect."

Cameron narrowed his eyes. "For what?"

"No, for who."

"Erica?"

"Ha! They're both too cocky. They'd kill each other within a minute." She smoothed her hand over his shoulder, then patted him. "No, I was thinking of Becky."

Cameron shook his head. "I don't know, sweetheart. She's so shy, he'd probably have her for lunch."

Asia just grinned. There was no one else in the hall, so she put her arms around him, loving him so much it hurt, and said, "You, Cameron O'Reilly, haven't heard Becky's fantasy. I'm thinking George might get a big surprise."

Cameron kissed her. "If it's half as nice as the surprise I got, then he's one lucky cuss."

"I love you, Cameron."

He patted her bottom in fond memory. "I love you, too, Asia. Now and forever."

SOMETHING WILD

Shannon McKenna

Chapter One

There he was again. The Motorcycle Man sped past her for the third time in the last half-hour, shooting her a huge, dazzling grin. Annie Simon's heart gave a startled little leap in her chest, and she forced herself not to smile back at him. It took real effort.

He roared down the highway ahead of her like a bullet, drawing her gaze helplessly after him. His dazzling red motorcycle glittered with chrome, his helmet gleamed, his black leather jacket flapped wildly behind him. He was larger than life, bursting with brilliant energy against the leafless winter backdrop of dull browns and grays.

This was the third day in a row that he had followed her. She noticed him for the first time around Charlottesville, Virginia. At first she had figured that he must be going her way by sheer coincidence and was just flirting with her to amuse himself on the road, but she'd been stopping every day for hours to hike in almost every state and national park that she passed, and he never seemed to outdistance her. She didn't really mind. In fact, the few times she thought she'd shaken him off for good, she'd been surprised at how disappointed she felt—almost angry at him for not trying harder. Then poof, up he popped, flashing her a wild grin so full of rollicking good humor that she couldn't help laughing back.

She knew she should be alarmed at his persistence,

young woman traveling alone, yada yada, but the game was actually giving her a tingle of pleased excitement, and it had been so long since she had felt anything remotely like a pleasant tingle. Lately, her feelings had run more along the lines of dread, exhausted anger, or a crushing sense of impending doom. The little buzz that the Motorcycle Man gave her was a refreshing distraction—as long as he stayed strictly in his place.

Annie had whiled away what would have been many long, depressing hours on the road speculating about him, studying the fascinating details of his bike and his wardrobe—not to mention his powerful, gorgeous body. Three years as a fashion buyer had trained her eye to read the silent language of his wardrobe. She had a feeling that the jacket on his back retailed for over $2,000, depending on the season, and how well things were moving on the floor. And her foster brothers had taught her enough about motorcycles to spot the sleek, sensual lines of an exquisitely preserved vintage Indian. The guy was speeding down the highway on a jewel of a collector's item that had to be worth at least fifty grand, if not more. Whoever he was, and whatever he did, her Motorcycle Man didn't spare any expense in outfitting himself. He looked great.

Not that it made any difference what he wore, or what he rode, of course, she reminded herself. From that wild, wicked grin and those broad shoulders right down to the tight, excellent ass and long, muscular legs, the man had trouble written all over him. More trouble Annie did not need. She'd had a lifetime of it. That was why she was running in the first place. But she shouldn't dwell on the past. She stuck her hand into her beautiful black Prada bag, beloved relic of her days in the world of the gainfully employed, and rummaged until she found the velvet sack of silver dollars. She clutched them hard, trying to ward off the sad, sinking feeling in her belly. "Think lucky thoughts," she whispered to herself. That bag represented the future. Another chance.

Five years ago, at the callow age of twenty-two, she'd taken a road trip with her friends to the Black Cat Casino in St. Honore, Louisiana, where she hit the jackpot at a dollar machine and won almost two thousand bucks. She'd seized her chance and bolted from her dreary cashier's job in Payton, Mississippi, straight to New York, the city of adventure. It was scary, in hindsight, to think of how naive she'd been. She should be grateful it hadn't gone any worse.

Maybe it was superstitious and silly, but the Black Cat was as good a place as any she could think of to petition the gods of chance for one more shot. She wasn't beaten yet, in spite of the mess with Philip. That little sack was the last drop of her lucky money. She'd kept it safe and secret, a good luck talisman. It might not have brought her much luck lately, but then again, she'd actually managed to get away from Philip in one piece, although without most of her stuff. And Mildred, her rusty, trusty Toyota pickup, by some miracle of duct tape, spit and baling wire, was still roadworthy, bless her faithful mechanical soul.

New York wasn't the only place in the world to make a life for herself. She would miss the bright lights and the fresh bagels, but on the plus side, she would never have to apologize to anyone for loving country music ever again. She cranked up the volume on her radio and sang lustily along with Pam Tillis, her eyes still helplessly fixed on the sparkling, wind-whipped figure on the road ahead of her.

The Motorcycle Man hung back, letting her pull up alongside him. He gave her a thumbs-up, and made extravagant gestures toward the Food-Gas-Lodging sign ahead of them, just as he'd been doing all day. He was getting bolder. She supposed she should be worried, but her worry supply was all used up. She stared at his bold, laughing grin, savoring the tingling pull of curiosity he gave her; a pull that had nothing to do with his designer clothes or his costly bike. His smile caught her off guard, like a blaze of sunshine piercing unexpectedly through thick clouds. He radiated light and color in all directions. It was incredibly sexy.

Almost tempting enough to make her stop and flirt with him in person, just to see if the gooey, melting feeling that his smile had provoked had any basis in reality.

But going gooey was the last thing she should do, after everything that had happened with Philip. She had to toughen up, fast. She shook her head with a regretful smile, blew him a kiss and mouthed "in your dreams, buddy," as she accelerated smoothly past him.

The wind whipped Jacob's shout of frustration into nothing as he pulled onto the exit ramp. He'd decided that today was the day to make direct contact; enough road tag, but the touseled honey-blonde was not complying with his timetable. It was driving him nuts. He was ravenous. Didn't she ever eat?

He parked his bike and stalked into the restaurant, grumbling as he yanked off the helmet. He was restless and jazzed, and that taunting kiss she'd blown him from the pickup had given him a raging hard-on. Something about the way that luscious pink mouth puckered up just got to him. She seemed to like yanking his chain.

He ordered steak, salad and a baked potato, and pulled the crumpled Kentucky road map out of his pocket to gauge how far out of his way he'd gone in his wild pursuit. Not that he'd really had any destination to begin with. He'd kept his vacation plans deliberately vague, figuring that it would do him good to practice spontaneity. Well, he was practicing it now, with a vengeance.

It had started at a restaurant off I-95, right after Phila-delphia. The sight of her walking out of the ladies' room had hit him like a fist. He found himself staring helplessly at the fit of her jeans, deliciously snug over her round, lush rear. And those cute little nipples, poking out of the tight T-shirt, bouncing and quivering as she moved.

She hadn't seen him. In fact, she'd noticed barely any-thing. She'd walked like a woman in a dream. Something about the way she swept those heavy waves of honey-blonde hair out of her pale face was eloquent in its unspoken weariness. She looked tired, rumpled, her big gray eyes haunted and vulnerable. Like she needed someone to cheer her up, make her laugh. Chase those shadows away from her eyes.

He'd left his uneaten food on the table and followed her like a man under a spell. She hadn't even noticed him until Charlottesville, Virginia. That had been his first victory. Goofing and clowning at sixty miles an hour alongside her truck until a smile budded on that lush, kissable mouth— and then widened to a big, delighted grin. She laughed at him, and he was ecstatic. That was how bad it was.

He knew where she hiked, where she camped, where she stopped to pee, where she got gas. He hadn't approached her yet, sensing that the moment wasn't right, but no one else had gotten close to her without him knowing about it, and he was cheerfully prepared to tear any guy who bothered her to pieces. He'd reflected at great length upon the irony of the situation while keeping her pickup in full view. He was acting like the guy her mother had probably warned her about; the guy who couldn't stop dreaming about how her nipples would taste when he finally peeled off that little shirt and got her settled on his lap. How he would ravenously suckle her lush, perfect breasts while she wrapped her arms around his neck and squirmed with pleasure. How that gorgeous honey hair would cascade all around them, tickling his face. How her smoke-colored eyes would glow with excitement when he tumbled her into the bed of the first motel he could find.

All things considered, he couldn't really blame her for not stopping. But it still drove him nuts.

This compulsion to follow her was unnerving. He stared idly at the list of dessert specials, telling himself to stop worrying, to just go with the flow. Worry was a waste of energy. He was just following his instincts, like he always had. Following his instincts was what had made him a successful man. They'd just never been this strong, that was all. In the past, his instincts had served him dutifully whenever he'd called upon them. He wasn't used to thrashing helplessly in their grip.

He supposed the situation was funny, in a way. Jacob Kerr, successful architect and entrepreneur, accustomed to calling all the shots, driven out of his mind by one beautiful, mysterious girl who wouldn't stop and talk to him. It was wild, irrational, but he wasn't giving up the chase. He just couldn't.

Thunder rolled, and rain started pouring as the waitress set his steak before him. He scowled out the window, hating the thought of his honey-blonde out there in that rattletrap piece of junk. He'd checked out her vehicle at the campground last night while she was taking her shower. All of her tires were bald.

Worry robbed him of his appetite. He got up and paid for the uneaten food, and stared out at the slashing rain, cursing under his breath. His rain gear was stowed inside the hardcase saddlebags on the back of his bike. And it was insanely stupid to go out into that weather in any vehicle, let alone a motorcycle, the cool, rational part of his brain observed. He hadn't gotten this far in life by being insanely stupid.

Oh, to hell with being rational. Being insanely stupid looked like a lot more fun. He pulled on his helmet and headed out the door.

This, too, shall pass, Annie told herself over and over, clutching the steering wheel in a death grip. The rain had been innocuous at first, pattering down gently, but now it was a deafening roar. Violent gusts of wind buffeted the pickup, shoving her around the road, often into the lane of oncoming traffic. Mildred's bald tires slipped and slid, making the truck fishtail madly, and lightning stabbed down in wild, unnerving bursts. Maybe she was racing toward some freak tornado that would pick her and the truck up and deposit them miles away, in twisted, unrecognizable chunks.

Chill out, she reminded herself, swallowing down her fear. Panic is not an option.

But each time she assured herself that this had to be the grand finale, that it couldn't possibly get any worse . . . it did. Maybe there was no end to how bad things could really get. If only she'd pulled off at the last exit. She could've been flirting with the Motorcycle Man right now over pie and coffee. As dangerous forces of nature went, he was definitely the lesser of the two evils, and a hell of a lot more attractive.

The rain was so blinding that she almost didn't see the exit. She had to lunge for it at the last minute, and the rapid swerve sent her into a long, heart-stopping slide. Once she finally got a grip on the road, she drove very, very slowly, hands trembling, toward the nearest diner. She was pathetically grateful for the coffee, chili and saltines the waitress brought her. She hunched over the steaming bowl, listening to sappy Christmas music, but she couldn't seem to stop shivering.

She was just starting to settle down when the string of bells over the door tinkled delicately. She heard the tread of heavy boots, and a fresh surge of adrenaline jolted through her body. She swiveled her head, and her stomach flip-flopped.

It was the Motorcycle Man, his shiny black helmet tucked under his arm, beaming at her.

He was huge. Much bigger than he'd seemed on the bike, now that those long, muscular legs were unfolded. The restaurant seemed small and shabby, dwarfed by his presence.

He was gorgeous. Breathtaking. And drenched. He squelched as he walked toward her. A puddle formed around his boots when he stopped by her table. The waitress was giving him a dirty look, which he ignored.

"Were you out in the rain?" she asked, instantly wanting to kick herself. What a stupid question. The answer was so obvious.

A triumphant grin blazed across his lean face. "Hah! I finally got you to talk to me."

"Don't let it go to your head," Annie snapped. She tried to drag her eyes away from him, but she was riveted by his intense black eyes, sparkling with intelligence. His eyebrows made a bold, slashing line across his broad forehead. His midnight-black hair was long and glossy, pulled into a ponytail. He was clean-shaven, a hint of shadow across his strong jaw. The fascination on his face made a bubble of flattered pleasure pop up to the surface of her consciousness. She actually felt . . . pretty, under his intense scrutiny. Prettier than she'd felt in a long, lonely time. The sensation was like a subtle caress. She began to blush.

"Why didn't you wait for the rain to stop?" she asked.

He shrugged. "I've been out looking for you," he said simply. "I had to make sure you were OK."

She narrowed her eyes in swift suspicion. "Let me get this straight," she said slowly. "You were warm and dry, and eating your lurch, and the storm hit, and you went out in it? To look for me?"

"Yeah, I know. It was crazy," he admitted, wringing water out of his ponytail. His dark eyes danced with silent laughter. "But a guy's gotta do what a guy's gotta do."

It had been so long since anyone had worried about her that it actually took away her breath for a second. Probably it was just a slick line, she reminded herself. My, what big ears you have, Grandmother. Toughen up, little girl. Still, a reluctant smile tugged her mouth. "I'm fine, as you can see," she murmured.

"Can I sit down?"

"No," she said quickly.

He shifted his helmet to the other arm, undaunted. His eyes swept over her appreciatively, and a ticklish, fluttery feeling raced madly across the surface of her skin. "What's your name?" he asked.

She hesitated, as if giving him her name would give him

some obscure power over her, a hook into her private self. She decided to give him a fake name. Jill, or Monica, or Brooke. She looked into his intense dark eyes, opened her mouth and said, "Annie."

"Annie." He said her name tenderly, savoring it. "Just Annie?"

She gulped. "Just Annie."

He nodded. "OK, just Annie, I'm just Jacob. It's a pleasure to meet you at last. You've led me on a merry chase."

"You haven't caught me," she reminded him tartly. She took a sip of her coffee and stared up over the rim of the cup, her mind spinning with confused excitement. Six foot two and over two hundred pounds of lean, rock-solid masculinity standing there, water streaming off his body, taking up all the air in the room. He was almost too much for a girl to take. But then again, she was tougher than she looked.

"Can I please, please sit down?" His voice was warm and coaxing.

"No," she repeated.

The silence between them lengthened and grew heavy, charging itself with sultry, quivering heat. She licked her lips nervously, helpless to look away. She was locked in a clinch of breathless silence with him. The feeling was shockingly intimate.

His broad, sensual mouth curved knowingly, as if he knew just why she was shifting restlessly on the plastic booth. He knew that a hot, secret little ache of yearning was blossoming deep inside her body, and he was doing it to her deliberately, with his dark, laughing eyes, with his magnetic smile, with his raw male energy. God. This guy was more than just trouble. He was sexual dynamite.

Annie's breath stuttered in and out of her lungs. She forced herself to stop wiggling, and gave him a "don't-mess-with-me" stare, perfected on the tough streets of New York. "Look, Jacob. Whatever you want from me, you're not going to get, so don't waste your time."

His eyes gleamed with wry amusement. "Cruel Annie," he murmured. "Go ahead. Dash my hopes. Blow me off. I don't care. I'm still glad you're OK."

Her fingers tightened convulsively on the handle of her cup. It wobbled, and coffee slopped out onto her T-shirt. "I appreciate your concern," she snapped, dabbing at the stain with her napkin.

"I saw your tires," he commented. "You're lucky to be alive."

"My tires are none of your business," Annie said tightly. She tucked the extra saltines into her purse and slid out of the booth. She'd be lucky if she managed to pay for the gas to get her all the way to St. Honore, let alone buy new tires. "Thanks for sharing your opinion."

She shoved past him, and instantly realized that it was a mistake to have touched him, even slightly. Just brushing against his solid frame made her shiver with intimate awareness. He radiated warmth and power as he followed her stubbornly to the cash register.

"It's not an opinion, Annie," he persisted. "It's dangerous."

She ignored him. "A bowl of chili and coffee," she told the cashier.

He handed the cashier a twenty. "The lady's lunch is on me."

"No, it's not," she hissed. She tried to push down his proffered arm, but it was like swatting an oak branch. She held out her ten to the girl behind the register. The girl's pale blue eyes darted from one to the other of them, bewildered.

Jacob pushed down her arm, handed the girl his twenty. "I insist." His voice was gentle but implacable.

Annie fled the restaurant while the cashier was making change. The rain had stopped, and she splashed heedlessly through the puddles in the parking lot, obscurely panicked. He'd gone out in the rain to look for her, he was so glad she was OK, he'd fussed over her tires, he'd paid for her lunch, blah blah blah. The ploy was so transparent, but so damned seductive, it was embarrassing. Even though she didn't need any rescuing. Even though she knew exactly what he wanted from her in exchange. Men were so predictable.

What was unpredictable was her fluttering belly, her hot face, her scattered wits. She was raw, trembling, acutely aware of the quiet power that filled and defined the space around him, of the streamlined grace of his body and his thousand-watt grin. She cursed to herself as she fumbled for her keys. She had to rely on herself, and herself alone. She always had, ever since she was a kid. It was the one thing in her life that never changed, and she only came to grief when she let herself forget it. Fortunately, the world never let her forget it for very long.

Jacob's shadow blocked the window, knocking on the rain-spotted glass. She shoved the key into the ignition, hands shaking. He kept knocking, gentle but insistent. She rolled the window down a bare two inches, and he leaned close, taking everything in with one sweep of his keen dark eyes. She was suddenly embarrassed by her truck's dilapidated state. For her own limp, travel-worn appearance.

"Annie, listen." His voice had a hint of uncertainty for the first time. "If you really, truly want me to stop playing this game with you, I'll leave you be. Just say the word."

She wrenched her eyes away and stared out the windshield. *Tell him,* her sensible self urged. *He'll believe you if you say it now. You've got enough to worry about. Tell him to get lost.*

She looked up, opened her mouth to say it—and the challenge in his eyes robbed her of breath. She could read sensual invitation on his face as clearly as if he'd spoken aloud. It was a disorienting perception, as if the world had suddenly rent itself apart and revealed itself to be a dull, flat backdrop of painted canvas; and behind it, the glowing colors of the real horizon beckoned and allured.

Her heart seemed to stop for a long, breathless instant. She couldn't back down now. She was too intrigued. Besides, maybe she could teach him a thing or two, and wipe that smug, knowing look right off his gorgeous face. She'd never been able to resist a challenge in her life. It was one of her crowning defects.

Besides, all those miles of highway ahead would be such a dreary prospect without the Motorcycle Man's enlivening presence.

Oh, God. She was going to do it. She actually was. Her heart galloped madly in her chest as she turned the key in the ignition. She shot him a sidelong, provocative glance, let it melt into a tempting smile, and softened her voice to a husky contralto. "Figure it out for yourself, Jacob," she said, putting the truck in gear. She lurched forward, peeking into her rearview mirror.

A grin of delight had lit up his face like a torch, and she couldn't help smiling back, even though he was out of range and couldn't see her. She pulled out of the parking lot, beaming at the waterlogged landscape until her out-of-shape smile muscles ached in protest.

Annie had been so wound up all afternoon, she'd exhausted herself to calmness by the time she set up camp that evening. She made use of the campground shower, and then stood in front of the mirror for a long time, toothbrush in hand, studying her face. Trying to imagine how an outsider would see it. How Jacob might have seen it.

It was too pale. In the harsh, fluorescent light, her face seemed tinged with blue. Her eyes were OK, big and gray, with a ring of indigo around the iris. Long lashes, dark at the root, gold at the tip. Thick dark eyebrows that needed some tweezing. Her lower lip was plumper than she would like. It gave her a sulky look, which she usually tried to offset by smiling a lot, though lately she hadn't had the energy. She looked tired. Washed out and wary. Not surprising, for a woman who was on the run from her wrecked life. it was depressing. She squeezed toothpaste onto the brush, telling herself to stop being foolish.

She was *not* hoping he would show up, she told herself as she fixed her dinner—freeze-dried chicken and rice soup—and opened a can of sliced peaches. Probably he'd lost interest. The gritty reality of Annie Simon, close up and personal, had popped the bubble of his road-sex fantasy. She didn't look like much of a prize in her jeans and shrunken T-shirt. Just a normal girl, with circles under her eyes, in need of a laundromat. She hadn't had either the time or the presence of mind to pack many clothes on that crazy morning when she'd seized her chance to finally get away from Philip. Just what she'd been able to shove into her backpack with trembling hands: some jeans, T-shirts, underwear. None of her nice, pretty stuff. And she hadn't worn makeup since the good old days back at Macy's, before Philip ruined that for her, too.

No, she'd seen the last of the sexy, mysterious Motorcycle Man. He was off in search of a perkier, livelier playmate. She visualized her much-loved and forever lost wardrobe with a sharp pang of regret. If she'd had her usual bag of tricks to work with, the story would have gone very differently. For Jacob she would definitely have opted for her scoop-neck pearl pink angora sweater, the cloud-soft kind that made men long to stroke it. She would have paired it with her wine-red silk wrap skirt, and her spike-heel lace-up boots. Beneath it all, her apricot stretch lace teddy, of course. A dab of cover-up under her eyes, a smidge of brown liner and mascara, a slick of pink gloss on her lips. Her sexy calla lily earrings, for luck. A dab of styling gel and a few minutes with a blow dryer, and voilà, she could have made him follow her to the ends of the earth. Men were so fickle. But it was probably just as well. She fished out a peach slice with a wistful sigh.

Suddenly the little hairs on the back of her neck prickled to attention with a long, delicious shiver. She scanned the forest around her, forcing herself not to leap to her feet.

"Hello, Annie," he said softly. He was a long, dense shadow at the edge of the flickering light of her campfire.

She nodded politely. "Hello, Jacob." She managed to sound cool, even though her heart was thudding. "I thought I'd lost you."

His teeth flashed white in the gloom. "Not a chance."

She tugged her short T-shirt down over her belly, wishing it didn't have a coffee stain. "Want some peaches?" She held out the can.

He remained motionless, barely visible under the trees. "No, thanks. I'm fine," he said politely. "I ate earlier."

She gave him a crooked, nervous little smile. "Why are you lurking out there in the dark? Are you trying to freak me out?"

"On the contrary, I'm trying not to. I won't come any closer unless you invite me."

She laughed, surprised at his unexpected gallantry. "You've been following me ever since Charlottesville. I didn't invite you to do that."

"Philadelphia," he said simply.

Her jaw dropped. "Philadelphia?"

"You just didn't notice me until Charlottesville. Besides, I couldn't help myself. Your beauty is an irresistible lure. You're like one of those sirens in the old stories, enticing love-struck mariners to their doom."

A terribly teenaged-sounding giggle burst out of her, and the peach chunk slipped off her fork and plopped into the syrup with a splash. "I've never lured anybody to his doom," she told him, dabbing at the splotch of syrup that had joined forces with the coffee stain on her shirt. "Still, it was a nice thing to say. Go ahead, Jacob, pull up a stump. Make yourself comfortable."

He glided silently closer, and she noticed that his hair was wet, combed smoothly back from his face. "Did you just take a shower?"

"Yeah, I washed up a bit," he said.

"Bet you thought you were going to get lucky, didn't you?"

He shrugged, and sank into a comfortable crouch across the fire from her. "A guy can hope."

She blushed, and stared fixedly into the fire.

"Your hair's wet, too," he observed in a soft voice.

"Yeah, well, don't flatter yourself," she snapped. "Some of us bathe for reasons other than intent to seduce." He laughed, unabashed, and her blush deepened. "Where did you first see me?" she demanded.

"At a restaurant off of I-95, right after Philadelphia," he told her.

"Philadelphia. That's wild," she murmured, trying vainly to subdue the foolish, flattered smile that kept taking control of her face.

"Yeah, I know," he agreed. "I was intrigued. A gorgeous, mysterious woman, traveling all alone, from who knows what to who knows where. I just got on my bike and followed you without thinking. Annie, the honey-blonde road siren. I'm hopelessly caught in your silken net. You've been dragging me in your wake across five states."

She covered her hot cheeks with her hands, loving the way his smile creased his lean face with sensual, deeply carved laugh lines. "I cannot believe I didn't notice you," she murmured.

He shrugged, studying her with intense curiosity. "You looked pretty distracted at the time," he said quietly.

"Yeah. I must have been." She had gone through Philadelphia on the first dazed, delirious day of her journey. She wouldn't have noticed if an eighteen-wheeler had driven over her.

"Where are you headed, if you don't mind me asking?" he asked.

She hesitated. She hadn't told anyone about her destination. She hadn't decided if it would be good luck or bad, but when she looked into his keen, dark eyes, she felt a surge of energy that could only be lucky. "I'm going to the Black Cat Casino in St. Honore, Louisiana," she said.

He looked thoughtful. "May I ask why?"

She put a possessive hand on the purse that sat beside her. "I have a stash of silver dollars. The last of the money I won there five years ago. That money helped me start a new life." Her voice shook, and faltered. "Now I need to start a new life all over again. I hope . . . that they'll help me a second time."

He prodded at the embers. "I wish you luck," he said in a careful, measured voice. "What's plan B?"

"None of your goddamn business," she flared, stung.

They were silent for a moment. "Don't be mad, Annie," he said gently. "Starting a new life is a hell of a lot to ask of a slot machine."

She snagged another peach chunk, but his calm words had robbed her of her appetite, and she let it plop back into the can with a dejected sigh. "There's no plan B." she admitted. "If it doesn't work out, I'll think of something when the time comes, like I always do."

"What are you running away from?"

Annie's jaw clenched. Thinking about Philip did not feel lucky. "I'd rather not talk about it," she said stiffly.

"Whatever."

There was a wealth of controlled curiosity behind the single quiet word. "I'm not on the run from the cops, or anything, if that's what you're wondering," she snapped.

"Relax, Annie," he soothed. "The thought never crossed my mind."

She shot him a derisive look. "How am I supposed to relax with you looking at me like that? You're a complete stranger, Jacob. All I know about you is that you want to have sex with me."

He watched her silently for a long moment, and she tugged her shirt down again, drawing his gaze to her belly. Under the weight of his eyes, that scant inch of exposed flesh seemed outrageously intimate. She covered it instinctively with her hand. His dark gaze dragged slowly up her body, lingering appreciatively at her breasts. She stared back, fascinated by the stark, elegant planes and angles of his face. The flames of the campfire flickered and danced hypnotically in his eyes.

"I want to be closer to you, Annie," he said softly. "Close enough so I can tell what kind of shampoo you used tonight. May I?"

Annie's lips trembled, and she clamped them together. The velvet-soft tone of his voice made her legs feel as if they wouldn't hold her if she stood, and an unfamiliar ache deep in her belly made her restless and anxious. His taut, muscular backside was beautifully showcased by his loose, crouching pose. She dragged her eyes away from it and pulled her mind back to his question. "Um, yes," she said, trying to sound casual. "And thank you for asking."

He rose to his feet with catlike grace, and walked slowly around the fire. He loomed over her for only a second or two, but the time dilated oddly as she stared at him from that odd perspective, her eyes skittering in nervous fascination up his long, muscular legs, over the bulge in front of his jeans, his flat belly and barrel chest. He sank down in front of her, studying her with grave concentration. He closed his eyes and took a deep breath, and a beatific smile spread across his face. "Lavender," he said softly. "Yum."

Annie's ears roared. His nearness affected her like the deep, pervasive thundering of a huge waterfall, filling her senses and blotting out everything else. She stared, rapt, at the dramatic sweep of his black lashes, his sharp cheekbones, the seductive grooves that bracketed his lazy smile. "It's an aromatherapy shampoo," she explained in a small, breathless voice. "It's supposed to be, um, soothing."

He opened his eyes. "That's strange," he murmured in mock puzzlement. "I'm not soothed at all by the thought of steaming lavender-scented suds cascading over your pink, naked body. On the contrary."

An image of Jacob in the shower assailed her—that big, powerful body gleaming and naked, slippery with soap. Her head swam, and she swallowed hard and leaned forward, sniffing his damp hair. "Pert Plus, shampoo and conditioner in one," she guessed. "You're a no-nonsense sort of guy. Always on the move. No conditioning rinse, no styling gel, just wash, comb, and go. Right?"

His dark eyes held hers with quiet intensity. "That's true," he admitted. "I'm very high-energy. But I know how to slow down."

Annie clutched the can of peaches tightly to her chest with both hands, and looked down into the fire. "That's good," she said, almost inaudibly. "Going slow is very important."

They sat silently for a long moment. He put his big hand gently over hers, stilling its fine tremor. The whisper-soft contact sent a sweet, tingling flood of anticipation through every nerve in her body.

"I've changed my mind about the peaches," he said in a husky voice, tugging the can away from her. He speared a chunk, plucked it off the end of the fork and examined it, heedless of the syrup dripping voluptuously over his hand. He took a bite and closed his eyes for a long moment as he chewed and swallowed, then opened his eyes with a blissful smile. "Succulent," he commented softly. "Tender and soft and silky, dripping with sweet juices. Divine perfection in a can."

She stared, fascinated, as he slid the rest of the peach into his mouth with a growl of pleasure. "I've never looked at canned peaches in quite that way," she admitted.

He laughed softly. "You've got to look at things in just the right light before they'll give up their secrets." He snagged another piece between his thumb and forefinger, and admired it from all sides. "Under the enchantment of sweet Annie, these peaches are the manna of the gods. Come closer, Annie. Let me show you."

She gazed at him, flustered and nervous but irresistibly tempted by the burning invitation in his eyes. She leaned forward and opened her mouth to take a bite of the fruit.

His other hand gently seized her shoulder, holding her still.

"Wait," he said in a low, admonishing voice. He leaned closer, surrounding her with his scent: shampoo and soap, crisp denim, damp leather. "First you have to concentrate. Yield to the enchantment. Let it lead you. There's no hurry."

Annie blinked, and gazed at the chunk of peach. She stared at his long fingers, wet and gleaming with sticky syrup, and she squirmed restlessly, her breath jerking in and out of her lungs. "OK, I'm concentrating," she said testily. "Now what?"

"Look at how beautiful it is," he suggested in a whisper, his warm fragrant breath tickling her ear. "How golden, and full of light. How juicy and plump. It's ready to give itself to you, to be absorbed into your body, to become part of you forever. Let your mouth get ready. Salivate. Savor the moment. Wallow in the sweet agony of anticipation."

The peach slid out of focus and became a shining golden glow in the foreground. His lean, dark face shifted into focus behind it, his eyes fixed intently on hers. "OK, I think I'm there," she told him, her voice low and shaky. "I'm pretty sure that I've, ah, yielded to the enchantment of the peach."

His teeth flashed in a swift, brilliant smile. "Good," he murmured. "Now open your mouth and close your eyes."

She closed her eyes and opened her mouth obediently, making a tiny gasping noise as the intensely sweet wedge of syrupy fruit nudged itself between her lips. She took a bite.

He was right. It was delicious, but she wasn't the one who had cast the spell that made it so. That was all Jacob's doing. The sweetness of the fruit shimmered on her tongue like trapped sunshine, and her body was hot, pulsing, dazzled. She opened her eyes, her defenses swept away, and stared into the endless depths of his black eyes.

Jacob's wild, potent magic tugged at her, opening up

wild, verdant places deep inside her mind; places she'd never shared with anyone. A fey, fearless part of her took over, and she leaned forward, taking his wrist in her hand. She drew it toward her lips and took the last morsel of peach gently into her mouth, licking the peach syrup off his thumb and forefinger with delicate little flicks of her tongue. She drew his fingertip into her mouth and swirled her tongue around it.

His eyes dilated, and his breath shuddered through his chest, harsh and audible. His face was suddenly tense, almost grim, the teasing gleam in his eyes gone and the depth of his hunger unmasked.

Annie let go of his hand and shrank back, startled at her own boldness. Jacob looked down at his fingers as if they were not his own. "Does this mean that I can stay with you tonight?" he asked hoarsely.

A final spasm of doubt clutched her, warring with the ache of longing that he'd awakened, and making her uncertain if she could really live up to her silent promise of unbridled sensuality. And it was insane to make herself so vulnerable, all alone in the dark as she was. But if he'd wanted to hurt her or force her, he could have done so ten times over by now. And she'd been alone in the dark for a long time now, if she counted these last, bad months with Philip. What harm could there be in a lighthearted tryst?

"I've never fallen into bed with a stranger before," she whispered.

Jacob picked up a stick and stirred the coals with it, biding his time. "We're not strangers. I've been courting you for days."

She opened her mouth, and was utterly surprised when the simple, naked truth popped out. "I'm running away from my ex-boyfriend," she blurted. "I'm wrecked, Jacob. You're a really cute guy, and it's nothing personal, but I just got out of a bad situation, and chances are I'd disappoint you anyway."

He gave her a thoughtful frown. "I doubt that very much.

Besides, just because your ex-boyfriend is a jerk, is that any reason to deny yourself great sex with a guy who asks nothing more of you but to worship at the shrine of your incredible beauty?"

That cracked her up. She forced herself to choke the giggles down when they threatened to melt into tears. "Mr. Modesty. What makes you so sure it would be great sex?"

A soft, amused smile crinkled up the lines around his eyes. "Listen to your heart, Annie."

The gentle words moved her. Something softened and shifted deep inside her chest, fanning slowly open like a crimson flower.

The fire crackled and popped, the coals glowed with shifting shades of red, like pulsing hearts. Jacob pushed back a lock of hair that was clinging to her cheek. "Let me please you tonight, Annie."

She gave a quick, jerky nod.

"Is that a yes?" His voice was satiny soft. "Let me hear you say it, so I can be sure."

A delicious shiver racked her, though she was far from cold. "Yes," she whispered.

Chapter Two

Jacob stirred the embers with his stick, shooting for an air of idle nonchalance, but the huge, goofy smile spreading across his face probably ruined the effect. The stick smoldered red-hot at the tip—not unlike the current state of his cock. Just in case there was a God, he sent up a prayer begging for enough self-control to not screw this up.

Annie folded her legs up against her chest and hugged them. "So?" she asked belligerently. "What are you going to do now?"

He studied the rigid set of her spine, the tremor in her hands. She was scared to death. The realization sent a rush of tenderness through him. "Nothing sudden," he said gently. "Nothing scary. Nothing rough."

She twisted her hands together. "Would you, um, like a toasted marshmallow?" Her voice was shaking.

Food was the last thing on his mind, but he smiled gently into her wide, anxious eyes. "Sure."

Annie leaped up and rummaged through a cardboard box on the picnic table, her brisk activity confirming the fact that she was not wearing a bra. Her high breasts jiggled and bounced, and his groin throbbed almost painfully at the thought of touching them, suckling them. He carved points onto the ends of two green sticks with his penknife and handed them to her as she settled down onto the ground again, a full two feet away from him. He grinned wickedly and sidled closer. Grinned and sidled again, and again, until she was giggling like a little girl at his foolishness.

She jabbed a marshmallow with a stick and handed it to him. "There you go. Enjoy my lavish hospitality."

He murmured his thanks, scooting the last few inches until his leg was touching hers. She didn't move away this time. She shot him a shy, sidelong look as they held their marshmallows over the coals.

"So, Jacob," she said with a businesslike air. "Where are you from?"

He turned his marshmallow, admiring the puffy golden underside. "Atlanta," he replied.

"And what brings you here?"

"You," he said simply.

"Oh, come on."

"It's true," he insisted. "I have no idea where I am. I've just been blindly following you. Like a lemming."

"Don't you have a life back in Atlanta?" she demanded. "What kind of person can just up and follow a stranger to hell and gone?"

He hesitated. The tedious tale of finally breaking off his tepid long-distance affair with Bridget, his decision to take a month's leave of absence from his architecture firm, none of it belonged in this magic circle of firelight. It was so workaday, so rational, so boring. Looking into Annie's fey, smoky eyes, he was outside the confines of normal life, in a fantasy world where anything could happen. He thought of making up a new past for himself, but that didn't feel right either. He was abruptly excused from replying by grace of the fact that Annie's marshmallow burst into flames. She blew it out and pried the blackened marshmallow off the stick with a sigh.

"They're good that way," he said in a comforting tone. "I used to set them on fire on purpose when I was a kid."

"I like them toasty and golden, not charred," she confessed.

"Take mine," he said, offering it to her gallantly.

She looked at the perfectly browned marshmallow on the end of his stick, and smiled like a naughty little girl as she took it. She bit into it, and foaming white goo poured out like sweet lava. The sight of her little pink tongue eagerly lapping at it made his whole body tighten with excitement. He stuck the blackened marshmallow into his mouth and chewed it without tasting it.

The marshmallows were a stroke of luck, though, because the glistening, sugary strand clinging to her enticingly plump lower lip gave him just the hook he needed to get things started. He leaned over and delicately licked it off, drinking in her little gasp of surprise. His stick fell into the fire as he wound his hand into her damp, silky hair. Her trembling lips opened and he slid his tongue inside. She was delicious; a fresh, unique flavor, with sweet overtones of peaches and burnt sugar. Sexual hunger slammed through him, threatening his self-control. Every luscious detail of her got to him, tossing him off balance, and he needed balance. Something told him that the first time with the skittish, beautiful Annie needed to be just right. And he was shaking with raw lust, in no condition to give a peak sexual performance.

Annie's big gray eyes were wide with wonder. "You're as good at kissing as you are at sweet talk," she said, touching her flushed lower lip delicately with her fingertip. "It gives you an unfair advantage."

"The advantage, sweet Annie, is all yours," he said, kissing her nose. "The kisses, the sweet talk, it's all for your pleasure and delight."

She giggled, delighted. "Oh, you think you're so slick."

He took advantage of the lightness of the moment to grab her waist and lift her smoothly onto his lap. "Aren't I?"

She wiggled away from him, startled, but he held on tight, making gentle shushing sounds. "Relax," he soothed. "I just want to hold you."

She stopped struggling, though a tremor of nervous laughter shook her. "Yeah, right," she murmured. "I've heard that one before."

"I just bet you have," he said, nuzzling her neck. "You're so pretty, Annie. It's been driving me crazy. Eight hundred miles of pure torture."

She gave him a small, shy smile. "Oh, give me a break."

She was so soft, shifting her light, whispery weight back and forth across his instantaneous hard-on. A little too thin, he thought, running his hand over her back. She needed feeding up. Steak and potatoes, eggs and grits. He would see to it at the first opportunity.

He embraced her slender shoulders and pressed little, nuzzling kisses onto the velvety skin that emerged like a lily from the frayed neckline of her T-shirt. He wanted to taste every inch of that rose-tinted softness, the tender spot behind her ears, under her jaw, the shadowy hollow at the base of her throat, everything. She returned his kiss with a timid eagerness, and he drank in her sweetness, forcing himself to disregard the clawing need in his lower body. The trusting way she opened to him was inflaming him to a dangerous pitch. He slowed down, breathed deep. He wanted to give her a timeless, forever sort of kiss, slow and lazy. A kiss that coiled and uncoiled endlessly in the firelight's writhing shadows, no memory of when it began, no desire for it to ever end.

He rearranged Annie's quivering legs until she straddled him, her soft mound pressed against the hard bulge at the front of his crotch. He cupped her breasts with a sigh of pleasure. They were so soft and full, the hard little nipples tickling his palms. Her hands flew up and clutched at his, and he seized one of them and brought it to his lips, covering her knuckles with hot, ardent kisses. Her faded denim jacket smelled sharply of wood smoke in contrast to the perfumed sweetness of her hair. He wanted her naked so badly it frightened him.

A look of awe and discovery dawned in her heavy-lidded

eyes as he gripped her hips and pressed his aching arousal against her. He urged her silently, with his hands, with his mouth, to yield to his pulsing rhythm. They floated together, his senses wide open, in a dreamy, timeless state in which he knew instinctively just how hard he had to press himself against her as his tongue plunged into her mouth, knew just how he needed to trace little designs on the palms of his hands with her nipples. He knew exactly what was necessary to prepare her, slowly and skillfully, for the demands he would make of her later, in her tent. When she was naked and completely open to him.

For now, there was no hurry, he reminded himself, biting back a groan. He'd promised. Admittedly, in the dreamy, half-drugged state he was in, he couldn't remember exactly what it was that he had promised, but ripping off her clothes and falling on her was not in the plan. He cupped her luscious ass lovingly in his hands, seconding the desperate little jerking movements she made. She was rubbing herself against him now, her breathing rapid, almost panicked. Suddenly she stiffened, arching her back like a bow stretched taut, and shuddered violently.

He caught her, keeping her from falling backward, and gathered her close. He cuddled her as she lolled against his chest, and greedily absorbed the delicate little aftershocks of her orgasm into his own body. "I think it's time to take this into the tent," he suggested gently.

Her eyes were languid and luminous. "I'm not sure if I can walk."

"I'll carry you." He shifted her off his lap and got up, sweeping her easily into his arms. She looped her arm around his neck in a trusting gesture that made his heart turn over painfully. She was so soft and vulnerable. It made him feel fiercely protective; a primitive feeling that he deliberately did not allow himself to examine. Tonight was no time for psychological self-analysis. Tonight was all about Annie. Just Annie.

He set her down, allowing himself a fleeting moment of

self-satisfaction for making her come before he even got her clothes off. Good work, that. Hadn't even stuck his hand under her shirt, though the effort might have taken years off his life.

Enough self-congratulation, he told himself. He crouched in front of her tent and unzipped it. He was still acutely aroused, and the night was young; there was plenty that could go wrong. But damned if he wasn't going to make her glad she'd let him stay. He would repay her trust many times over before the night was done.

Annie steadied herself against Jacob's solid shoulder. He gave her a reassuring grin and began to untie her shoes. She stared mutely at his bent head as he lifted her leg, prying off one of her battered high-tops. He cradled her bare, chilly foot in his warm hands and dropped a kiss on her instep, then set to work on the other shoe. He laid them under the rain canopy and held open the tent flap. "In you go," he said.

She crawled into the tent and sat cross-legged on her sleeping bag as Jacob unlaced his boots. He crawled into the tent and zipped the flap shut. He was huge in the tiny space, dominating it completely. Already his warmth was heating up the tent's chilly interior. And this powerful, completely unknown man was going to be on top of her. All over her. Inside of her. She hugged herself, shivering with delicious terror. She felt like a bird about to fling itself into the heart of a storm, a maelstrom of stabbing lightning and lashing rain. She suppressed a twinge of panic. He'd been nothing but gentle with her so far. He'd made her laugh and relax. And come, oh, God, like she'd never come before.

She gathered her nerve and reached out in the dark. Her hand encountered his chest and she explored the dips and ridges of his thick muscles. His breath quickened as she brushed her fingers across his nipples. As a rule, she didn't get overwhelmed easily, but Jacob's sheer physical presence robbed her of words, leaving her shy and tongue-tied.

Usually she was chock-full of smart-mouthed remarks, a trait that had gotten her into trouble all her life. Her favorite foster mother back in Payton had dubbed her "Scrappy." Philip's preferred endearment, toward the end, had been "you mouthy little bitch."

She shoved the memory away. *Don't think about Philip,* she reminded herself. *Don't let him ruin this for you, too.*

Jacob was feeling around, patting the floor of the tent. There was only a tarp, the nylon floor of the tent and a lightweight sleeping bag between them and the cold, hard ground. "Spartan," he commented.

"Sorry," she apologized hastily. "I know, it's awful. I had to leave in such a rush, and all I thought to grab was the sleeping bag. I've been regretting it every night."

"It's OK, Annie," he said, a hint of laughter in his voice. "You'll just have to be on top, that's all."

"I will?" She shifted restlessly at the thought of Jacob's strong body beneath her, bearing her up, warming her inside and out.

He skimmed his hands gently over her back and settled them at her waist, spanning it easily with his fingers. "Yeah," he murmured. "I must outweigh you by ninety pounds, if not more."

He pulled her onto his lap, and the contact of his hot body sent a shock of intense, melting pleasure through her. She snuggled against his chest, and part of her would have been eternally content to just stay there, listening to his deep, strong heartbeat. Another part of her was acutely aware of the bulge in his jeans that pressed insistently against her rear end, and the soft, yearning ache between her own thighs that answered it. She fought down the fluttery nervousness once again. Don't be a baby, don't be a tease, she told herself sternly. You invited the man into your tent, you've gotten him all hot and bothered, and besides, he seems like a really good guy. So get on with it, already.

She took a deep breath and shrugged out of her denim jacket. Her eyes had adjusted completely to the dim light that filtered into the tent, and she could see the hunger on his face as she peeled off her T-shirt. She tucked it into the corner and faced him, naked to the waist, her breasts sticking out in their usual perky, in-your-face sort of way. There. That had to be clear enough, she told herself. She'd bared her boobs. Now it was his move.

Jacob gave a rough sigh, and his big, hot hands circled her bare waist. Sweet, ticklish energy rippled along the surface of her skin as his hands slid up and cupped her breasts, exploring them with reverent tenderness. They felt oddly swollen, plump and acutely sensitive in his hands. He bent his dark head over her chest, and his hot, wet mouth dragged gently across her skin. Her chest heaved and she clutched him, astonished at the melting ripples of delicious sensation he pulled from her. He caught her nipple gently in his teeth, his tongue swirling with tender skill, and then pushed her onto her back and arched over her, his mouth waking up millions of beautiful nerve endings that had been sleeping all her life.

Jacob pushed her breasts tenderly together with his hands and buried his face in them, licking and suckling both in turn until she was a swirling vortex of sensation, out of control, arching and offering herself to him helplessly. Pleasure was shaking her apart, making her whimper and writhe. At some point, he had unbuttoned her jeans and insinuated his hand inside them, and she hadn't even noticed him doing it. He stroked her through her panties and found her damp and quivering. His finger circled her clitoris through the thin cotton cloth with delicate restraint, then slipped inside her panties.

He pushed his finger into her hot cleft and murmured softly in triumph to find her melting and soft, more than ready for anything he wanted from her. She couldn't stop the whimpering sounds she made as he coaxed her further open. She dug her fingers into his shoulders and spread her legs for him without protest.

"Let me taste you, Annie." His voice was raw with excitement.

Her body went rigid. "Jacob, I don't know how to say this, but . . ."

"But what?"

"But I can't do . . . that. It doesn't work for me," she confessed miserably. "It hurts too much."

"You mean oral sex?" His voice was incredulous.

"Yeah, I know it's really weird. It sounds so great in theory, but in practice . . ." Her voice trailed off as she tried to push away the memory of Philip and his hard, stabbing tongue. He always got so angry when she asked him to be gentle. Finally she'd learned to pretend to enjoy it, hoping he would get bored quickly. Which, praise God, he usually had.

"Your ex-boyfriend, did he—" Jacob cut himself off abruptly and shook his head. "It shouldn't hurt, Annie," he said gently.

She swallowed a sob. "I told you I'd probably disappoint you."

"Hush," he said, his voice low and angry. "Don't ever say that again." He leaned down and kissed her fiercely. "Do you trust me?"

She looked up into the shadowy pools of his eyes, and once again, the naked truth just popped right out. "Yes," she said wonderingly. God help her. She actually did.

"Then let me. Let me just try, and if it hurts even a tiny bit, tell me and I'll stop instantly." Jacob's voice was low and coaxing.

Annie ran her hands appreciatively over the ridges and curves of his shoulders. "It's not like you have to do any more foreplay," she said timidly. "The peaches alone did the trick. The rest is just gravy."

He gently tugged her jeans and panties down. "Oh, Annie. That was only the overture," he said softly. "Lie back. Trust me."

"All right," she whispered, letting him push her down

onto the sleeping bag. Jacob quickly stripped off his own clothes and positioned himself over her, a great solid mass of naked heat. She squeezed her eyes shut, bracing herself instinctively.

She was surprised to feel only a tender kiss, nudging her mouth open. He covered her with his body, not crushing her, but only keeping her exquisitely warm and sheltered. He coaxed her legs open, and his long finger penetrated her delicately, dipping into the sultry moisture pooled inside her hot, sensitive sheath. He spread it extravagantly around until her entire vulva was slick and soft, and gave her a soft, reassuring kiss before sliding down her body and settling himself between her trembling thighs. He nuzzled her navel, covering her abdomen with slow, dragging kisses that made her shiver and moan. He licked her thighs, her hipbones, sliding his tongue tenderly into all the valleys and curves of her hips. His hand brushed teasingly over her pubic hair, barely touching it, concentrating his attention on everything but the hot, aching core of sensation between her legs.

He caressed her slowly, tirelessly, with lazy, maddening thoroughness, until she was moving restlessly beneath his hands and mouth, ticklish and hot and frustrated. She began to burn for his touch to focus between her thighs. She lifted her hips, opening to him in silent, mindless pleading. He laughed softly, delighted, and then she felt the whisper of his warm breath on her inner thighs.

He put his mouth to her, hungry and passionate and incredibly gentle, sliding his tongue tenderly along the wet folds of her sex. She went wild, pushing herself against him, wantonly aroused by the sweet, melting sensations, the soft, lapping sound of his tongue. This was nothing like Philip. The unpleasant memory of her ex vanished and she lost herself in dazzled pleasure. And Jacob didn't get bored. He was insatiable; he seemed to want nothing more than to build her tension higher and push her up toward the crest. She sensed his fierce satisfaction as the wave crashed violently over her, pounding her under.

She floated back, boneless and utterly relaxed, and lay against his sheltering warmth for many long minutes. Slowly she became aware of Jacob's growing erection pressed against her belly. He didn't say a word, just stroked her shoulder and nuzzled her hair, but she could feel the rigidly contained hunger radiating from his body. She reached down timidly, and grasped his penis.

His arms tightened around her, her hand tightened around him, and he cried out in a low voice. "Gently," he murmured.

"Sorry, sorry," she said quickly. She petted him and then let her hand slide down the rock-hard length of it. Her hand curled around the hot flesh eagerly, testing his arousal, and she rolled up onto her elbow to inspect him better. "Do you want me to, um, return the favor?" she offered.

He propped his head up onto his arm. "Hmm?"

"You know. To go down on you," she explained bashfully.

He considered it, and then shook his head. "No."

She was utterly taken aback. "No?"

"I said I was going to worship at the altar of your beauty, and I meant what I said," he said. "This night is all about you, Annie."

She stared at him, suspicious. "Jacob, that's not normal."

"Probably not," he said with a short laugh. "The embarrassing truth is, I'm so turned on right now that if you so much as look at my cock cross-eyed, I'll explode all over you."

She started to giggle. "Cross-eyed?"

"For God's sake, leave a guy a shred of dignity," he muttered.

She reached down eagerly, and smoothed the silky drop of fluid on the tip of his penis around the swollen head, loving his harsh gasp of pleasure. "So do you want to make love, then?" she asked timidly.

"Oh, God, yes," he said raggedly, trembling under her hands.

She was moved, realizing how much effort he was expending to hold back and wait for her. She wrapped her arms around him and gave him a fierce hug. "I'm ready," she urged. "I want you, Jacob."

He rummaged through his jeans until he found a condom, and rolled it on swiftly. He lay down on his back, urging her up on top of him with barely controlled impatience. She reached down to caress his thick, rock-hard shaft with a pang of doubt. She hadn't had all that many lovers, and never a man of these dimensions. But there was no time to get nervous about it, because he was spreading her legs, guiding himself until he was lodged just inside her, caressing the moist lips of her vulva. He rubbed the tip of his penis against her cleft, and began to gently slide himself up and down the length of her hot, slick furrow in a slow, voluptuous rhythm. A shudder of startled pleasure unbalanced her, and she braced her hands against his chest.

"Do you like that?" he asked huskily.

"Oh, yes," she whispered.

He caressed her, teasing her with his hands, and her old self watched with mingled wonder and dismay as the new Annie undulated over him like some sort of wanton sex kitten. She closed her eyes and let him nudge her tenderly into another series of soft, shivering orgasms, linked like beads on a string into a glittering blur of pleasure, long and protracted and achingly sweet.

Finally, he gripped her hips tightly. "Now, Annie," he said, his voice pleading. "I can't wait anymore."

"Of course," she said soothingly. He prodded her, positioning himself, and began to push inside her, slowly and relentlessly. She gasped as the delicate muscles inside her resisted the blunt invasion.

He slowed down. "Relax, Annie," he said shakily.

She tried to relax, but he was so big and unyielding. Not even her first time had she felt so vulnerable. Jacob stopped, having shoved about half of his thick length into her. His grim silence and the steely tension vibrating in his arms attested to the effort he was expending to hold still. Enough, she thought. He'd given so much to her. She had to at least try to give this one thing to him.

She breathed deeply, concentrating on relaxing and yielding, and then tried to move, sliding up and down a tiny bit. She was surprised she could move at all, but Jacob's tender ministrations had made her incredibly slick and soft. Excitement rushed through her as the intense sensation began to slip into focus. She moved again, more boldly this time, clinging to him with every little muscle inside herself, and what had been a blunt, uncomfortable intrusion shifted seamlessly and became a stretched, sensual, utterly fulfilled feeling. She pushed herself down upon his heavy shaft with a shuddering sigh, hungry for more of him. He let out a hoarse cry, and that was it. She loved it. She was drunk on her power over him, she wanted to make him gasp and groan and shout. She slid all the way up the solid length of him, bathing him in her slick, sultry juices, and sank down again at the same moment that he gripped her hips and drove himself upward.

The incredibly deep penetration shocked a low cry out of her throat, and Jacob stopped. "Did I hurt you?" he asked urgently.

"No, no," she assured him, clutching his arms with trembling fingers. "Please, Jacob. Please, move, give me . . . let me feel it."

"Oh, yes," he muttered. His grip tightened, and he drew himself out with lingering slowness, savoring the clinging caress of her secret flesh. He surged in again.

Annie's nails dug into the powerful muscles of his shoulders, each heavy thrust jerking a sob of terrified pleasure from her throat. She had never dreamed there was so much sensation deep within herself. The mouth of her womb pulsed with energy, every cell of her awake and luminous. She abandoned herself to the driving hunger of the powerful man beneath her, riding him higher and higher until agonizing pleasure jolted through her in rhythmic, shuddering waves. She collapsed on his chest, her hair flung across their faces. Jacob held her tightly, his hips jerking violently against her as he spent himself.

They lay there, wordless and trembling. Annie brushed her hair out of his face, wound it back behind her neck and kissed him, trying to silently convey her appreciation for his generosity. Jacob thrust his tongue into her mouth, and his penis swelled eagerly to fullness inside her. She wriggled voluptuously, savoring the sensation of his thick shaft embedded within her. A girl could get spoiled with one of those to play with every night. "Aren't you tired?" she asked, laughing softly.

"I've had this erection since Philadelphia," he said lazily. "It's going to take more than one orgasm to tire me out. But I challenge you to try." He dragged her possessively closer, his hips pulsing against her as his tongue greedily explored her mouth.

"I've never been able to resist a challenge in my life," she told him, her breath catching with excitement.

His laughter vibrated through them both, and she sighed and arched herself wider open to him as he slid his big, hard penis slowly in and out of her yielding body, loving the delicious fullness.

"The night's still young, sweet Annie," he said. "Go for it."

Chapter Three

His first thought when he woke was that the floor of the tent was unbelievably cold and hard. The second, as he opened his eyes, was that the sleeping bag had a threadbare flannel lining upon which could still be seen the dim figures of Santa Claus and his team of reindeer. And the third, which quickly became by far the most important, was the fact that the soft, naked woman in his arms was sneakily trying to slither out of the sleeping bag.

"Good morning, Annie," he said.

She twisted around, her eyes wide and frightened. His gaze dropped to her chest, which she unsuccessfully tried to cover with one arm while groping for her T-shirt. Her body was spectacular by daylight, what little, wiggling bits of her he could glimpse. Deep pink nipples poked impertinently over her arm, and his usual morning erection began to throb painfully. Down, boy, he told himself. After last night's marathon, Annie was going to think he was a sex maniac.

Which, come to think of it, was exactly how he felt.

"Hi," she said, in a strangled voice.

He tried to think of a way to make her smile, but his sleep and sex-fogged brain wasn't up to the task at that hour. He plucked at a flannel reindeer, presumably Rudolph, though his outsized bulb of a nose had faded to a pale pink. "Seasonal sleeping bag?"

"It's mine from when I was a kid," she said. "I didn't want to take any stuff that Philip and I—" She stopped, swallowing visibly.

"Is that the asshole's name?" he murmured.

She pulled the T-shirt over her head, affording him a maddeningly brief glimpse of her stunning breasts. They jiggled as she tugged the shirt down over herself. He wanted to throw himself at her feet and beg like a dog for just one more peek. Dignity, he reminded himself. Dignity was key.

Her face emerged from the shirt, eyes narrowed. "Look, Jacob, I don't want to be rude, but I'd appreciate it if you'd get yourself together so I can fold my tent."

He watched calmly as she struggled into her panties and jeans. Her pale face was slowly turning a rosy pink. He grabbed his clothes, admiring her round, enticing ass as she scrambled out of the tent, and followed her out, stark naked. He stretched luxuriously and scratched his chest. Let her take a good long look at him and face reality.

She turned around, and squeaked in alarm. "Holy God, put that thing away!" she hissed.

He gave her a lazy grin and popped his shoulder blades. "You liked it well enough last night, sweetheart."

Just then, a portly matron in a pink jogging suit trotted down the path on her way to the bathroom. She looked over at them, gave a horrified squawk, and bolted back the way she came.

Annie's face was deep crimson. "You're going to get me arrested!"

Jacob gave her a "little ol me?" shrug, and looked down at his hugely erect cock as if noticing it for the first time. "Gee whiz, would you look at that. It's a tribute to your beauty, Annie."

"Put your pants on," Annie said furiously. "And don't you dare try to pull that Mr. Slick routine. That might work at night by the campfire, but not by the cold light of day."

Jacob grimaced as he folded his hard-on to the side and

zipped his jeans over it. Ouch. "What would work, Annie?" he asked plaintively.

She lit up her camp stove, ignoring his question. "Would you like some instant oatmeal?" she asked in a brisk, let's-move-on sort of voice. "I've got maple sugar, country peach spice and regular."

He snorted. "After last night? Like hell. Let's get some real food."

Her back stiffened visibly. "I'm thrifty," she snapped.

"And I'm buying," he countered. "Let's go to that pancake place back on the highway. We'll get ham and eggs and grits. Orange juice and coffee and a big, buttery stack of pancakes. What do you say?"

She shot him an uncertain glance over her shoulder, looking tempted. Then her mouth tightened. "I'll stick to my oatmeal," she said stiffly. "I don't need any man to buy me breakfast."

He grabbed her shoulder, turning her to face him. "Hey, Annie. Hello. I'm not just 'any man.' I'm Jacob. Remember me? We met last night. Naked. In your tent. For hours. Does that ring a fucking bell?"

His voice came out harsher than he'd intended. She flinched away. "I'm sorry," she whispered. "This just . . . isn't what I expected."

He yanked on his sweatshirt. "What the hell were you expecting?"

"I don't know. I didn't even think about the next day. I thought that a one night stand was a . . . a no strings sort of thing."

He squinted. "Strings? What strings?"

She shook her head helplessly.

Comprehension dawned, and outrage followed swiftly in its wake. "You mean, you weren't expecting to have to deal with me in the morning? You thought I would just fuck you and then disappear?"

She looked miserably confused. "I don't know. I didn't think."

He shook his head, incredulous. "I've been chasing you for eight hundred miles. You think I've scratched my itch, and now I'm done?"

"But I thought that's how anonymous trysts with strange men were supposed to go!" she wailed. "According to the script you should've been gone before I even woke up. Just a . . . a bittersweet memory, like Zorro or something. Maybe a rose on my pillow, at most."

Jacob rubbed his aching lower back with a grimace. "You don't have any pillows, Annie," he muttered.

She looked so distressed that he decided it was time to try to make her smile. "Let's have a whole bunch of anonymous trysts, and let them run together into one long, indefinite tryst. What do you say?"

Annie's luscious lower lip trembled. "I just can't take this right now," she whispered. "I can't handle you, too, on top of everything."

Jacob stifled a sigh. Nice going, bonehead, he thought. He was just a barrel of laughs this morning. "Don't look at me like that, Annie," he said wearily. "I swear to God, I'm completely harmless."

That provoked a soggy little chuckle. "Hah. I can think of lots of words to describe you, Jacob, but 'harmless' is not one of them."

"And just exactly what have I harmed so far?" he demanded.

She stuck out her chin. "You're harmful to my peace of mind."

He made a disgusted sound as he shrugged into his jacket. "You didn't strike me as all that peaceful before."

He had a point, Annie conceded silently, but she would rather die than admit it to him. He leaned quietly against his bike, watching her as she bustled around dismantling her campsite. Not offering to help, which was fine with her, because she didn't need any help. None, zip, nada. Not from him, not from anybody. It was time to take charge.

But it was hard to feel in charge with Jacob's dark eyes following her around. God, he was gorgeous. This morning was the first good look she'd gotten of him naked. The lean, harmonious grace of his muscular body was heart-stopping. She started blushing again just thinking of the formidable erection he had just displayed to her. Incredible to think that all of that had been inside of her, over and over, all night long. A rush of liquid heat made her catch her breath and press her thighs together. She was even regretting the fact that she hadn't given him a blow job, which was odd because it had never been her specialty. But she actually wanted to take Jacob in her mouth, to run her tongue around the swollen crimson head of his penis. To rub her hands up and down that rigid shaft, make him groan and dig his fingers into her hair.

God, what was wrong with her? One minute she was giving herself a bracing pep talk, the next, she was staring into space, dreaming of Jacob's thick penis sliding in and out of her mouth. The man had her under a spell. She peeked at him. He was smiling, and the bulge in his jeans proved that he knew exactly what she was thinking. She had to get out of here, quick, before she started to beg him for it.

She packed her stuff haphazardly into Mildred, and turned back to him, digging her keys out of her pocket. What did people say in these situations? She hadn't a clue. She shook her head helplessly.

Jacob gave her a crooked little smile. "See you around, Annie."

"See you," she muttered, leaping into the pickup. She didn't let herself look back.

The ache started right about when she pulled onto the highway. It was nagging and painful, like a bad toothache, but in her belly. How rude, to just leave like that. She could have said something nicer, after that incredible night. Something sweeter. At least something polite.

She looked for him on the road all day. A couple of times

she thought she saw a faraway motorcycle, but she couldn't be sure. She didn't stop for lunch, or to hike, just at a couple of rest stops to pee and stare blankly at the bare trees. She tried eating some saltines, but they wouldn't go into the cast-iron knot of her stomach.

She couldn't blame him for vanishing. In his place, she would have done the same, but now she would never have the chance to tell him how special and healing that night had been to her. All day she composed little speeches of all the things she wished she'd said to him. To hell with her pride. He was a really nice guy, and he deserved to know the truth—that he was sweet, and sexy, and fabulous in bed, and that he'd made her feel better than she'd ever felt in her life.

She found a campground at sunset, and set up her tent. Don't think about him any more, she told herself. Go about your business. Tarp, tent, pegs, poles. Rain canopy, sleeping bag, toiletries bag, camp stove. She rummaged through her supplies with a sigh. She didn't want the Middle Eastern Couscous Cup or Tia Rita's Black Bean Surprise. And she really, really didn't want any more of those goddamn canned peaches. Thank God the day was finished. Almost time to roll herself into a Santa cocoon and forget who she was in the oblivion of sleep.

"Hi, Annie," came a voice from the shadows behind her.

She whirled around. "Jacob?" She was so happy to see him that her heart swelled like a balloon. She smiled at him foolishly.

He stepped out of the shadows and placed the paper bag he was carrying on the picnic table.

"What have you got there?" she asked.

He looked wary. "Dinner," he said belligerently.

"Dinner?" Annie approached the table and sniffed. Mouthwatering smells were coming out of the bag. She pulled out a foam container and popped it open. Barbecued chicken. Oh, God. Her stomach yawned open joyfully.

"Yeah. So?" he said defensively. "Go ahead, Annie. Let me have it. Get it over with. Tell me what an asshole I am for buying you dinner."

Annie forced herself not to laugh at his martyred face. "Thank you," she said quietly. "It looks delicious. Let's eat before it gets cold."

He blinked, and visibly relaxed. "Really?"

"Really." She threw herself at him and hugged him hard. His strong arms circled her, and she hid her face against his chest, willing herself not to start bawling; she would just embarrass the poor guy.

She stepped back, giving him a shaky smile. Jacob grinned back, smoothing over the awkward moment by giving her a gentle kiss on her nose. "Let's eat, then," he suggested. "You hungry?"

"You have no idea," she said fervently.

They feasted on Jacob's bounty. Barbecued chicken, mashed potatoes with gravy, twice-baked cheese grits, collard greens and coleslaw and cornbread, and the crowning touch: two huge pieces of pie, chocolate pecan and pumpkin chiffon, swimming in whipped cream. It was so delicious it almost reduced her to tears again.

They finished the pie, and the process of licking various sticky bits of chocolate and pumpkin from each others' fingers segued into a sweet, clinging kiss. Jacob lifted his head reluctantly, dropping soft kisses on her upturned face like a sweet, hot rain. "Annie," he said in a soft, pleading voice. "I know I'm pushing my luck, but there's a really nice bed and breakfast in town. Four-poster beds, country quilts, private baths. Coffee and scones and orange juice in the morning."

Annie hid her face against him, trying not to show how tempted she was. How marvelous it would be to just creep under Jacob's big, strong wing and huddle there like a shivering, rain-drenched baby bird.

No. She was not a baby bird and she would not permit herself to act like one. She hesitated, choosing her words carefully. She didn't want to sound mouthy or mean. He didn't deserve it.

"Jacob, it's sweet of you, but I have to travel inside my own budget. If you want my company, then you're just going to have to—" She stopped herself abruptly. That was an ultimatum. Ultimatums sounded snotty and uppity. Be nice, Annie, she reminded herself. Think sweet. Make an effort.

She began again, in a halting voice. "You're welcome to stay with me . . . that is, you're more than welcome. I have to make do with my funky old tent, and I'm sorry it's so uncomfortable. But please stay with me." She closed her eyes, and added in a whisper, "I really, really want you to stay."

Jacob wrapped his arms around her fiercely. "You know damn well that I would sleep naked in the snow for a chance to make love to you again," he said roughly. "I just don't understand why we can't do it someplace warm and dry. But, whatever. At least our stomachs are full."

Annie rubbed her face against the velvety skin of his neck, weak with relief. "I'll do my best to distract you from how uncomfortable it is." She got up and tugged on his hand, drawing him toward the tent. "On your feet, Jacob. I've got plans for you tonight."

"Oh, yeah?" His voice was full of cautious speculation.

"Yeah." She kicked off her shoes and unzipped the tent flap. "Remember how you said that last night was all about me?"

She knelt and untied the laces of his boots. He stepped out of them obediently. "Yeah," he said. "Why?"

She looked up at him with a mysterious smile. "Guess who tonight is going to be all about?"

"Oh, God," he muttered as she dragged him into the tent.

She was different tonight, bold and fierce, shoving his jacket roughly off his shoulders.

"What's the rush?" he asked. "Are we late for something?"

"Cut the smart-ass remarks and get your clothes off, buddy," she snapped breathlessly. "I'm trying to make a point, here."

He wasn't about to argue with that. They stripped with feverish haste, desperate for the hot contact of skin and lips and hands. She ran her hands over his shoulders and arms with a murmur of approval, and yanked out the elastic band that held his hair, ruffling it into a wild mane. "I like you like this," she said. "I love your long hair."

"I grew it out just for you," he told her goofily, laughing as she buried her face in his neck and nipped it. She tugged his earlobe with her teeth and whispered, "Yesterday I asked if you wanted a blow job."

God forbid that she should think he didn't like them, he thought, with a flash of alarm. "Hey, just because I declined one yesterday doesn't mean that I don't—"

"Shut up, Jacob," she said in a low, purring voice.

He strained to read her expression in the dark. "Huh?"

"Tonight, I'm not asking you. Tonight, I'm telling you. Got it?"

"Oh," he said inanely.

"Lie down." She shoved him down imperiously until he was flat on his back, and knelt over him, the canopy of her hair brushing like a wide, whisper-soft kiss down the length of his torso. The hair between her legs tickled his navel as she straddled him, and the hot, moist kiss of her sex pressed intimately against his belly.

She leaned down, raining little kisses all over his face. He slid his hand behind her head and pulled her face down to his, but she made a fierce sound of protest, grabbed his wrists, and jerked them up above his head. He writhed luxuriously in her grasp, allowing her strong, slender hands to subdue him without protest. "I'm at your mercy," he said, with just a tiny tremor of laughter in his voice.

"You better believe it," she breathed into his ear. Her

nails dug into his wrists as she thrust her tongue into his mouth.

He opened his mouth eagerly to her fierce, conquering kiss. It felt odd, being passive. It wasn't his usual role, but, hell, he would wear a pink tutu and hang upside down if that was what she wanted. And there was something very fine about having a beautiful, tough woman holding him prisoner, scrambling around on top of him, rubbing her fragrant, silky self against his aroused body.

She kissed him with an innocent aggressiveness that touched him almost as much as it turned him on, and then slid slowly down his body, letting her hair drag across his face and neck. She nibbled on his nipples while brushing her soft, downy bush gently back and forth across his stiff cock until he thought he was going to scream. She laughed, softly and mercilessly. She was doing it on purpose, just to torture him. It took every ounce of willpower he had not to flip her over on her back and ram himself inside her.

He almost wept with relief when she seized his dick, sliding her hands up and down with appreciative slowness. She measured him with a purring sound of delighted approval. "God, I wish there was more light in here," she murmured. "I want to see every detail."

"There's a flashlight in my saddlebags, on the bike," he gasped.

"And do you want to be the one to go get it?" She leaned down and swirled her tongue around the head of his cock, a wet, luscious vortex of sensation that rendered him breathless with delight. He let his head drop back onto the ground with a thud. "Next time," he moaned.

"I agree," she murmured. Then there was no more speech, just the soft, moist, delicious kissing and suckling sounds she made as she drew him into her mouth and out of his mind.

She was voracious and tender at the same time, swirling her tongue around erotically, licking up and down the whole length of him with voluptuous sweeps of her tongue until he was wet and slick. Then she grasped him, moving her slender hands up and down his shaft in a sensual rhythm along with her hot, suckling mouth. She cupped his balls tenderly in her hand. "There's so much of you, I don't know what to do with it all," she whispered seductively.

"You're doing fine," he assured her, his voice shaking. "If you did any better, I'd probably have a stroke."

She laughed and put her mouth to him again with tender eagerness, making his heart swell and throb almost as much as his cock, and then he forgot everything except for this stunning woman and this perfect, erotic moment. The universe was centered on Annie's hot mouth, her clever tongue, her gentle hands. The silky clutch and glide of her mouth against his exquisitely sensitive flesh was pushing him too close to the brink, and she made a soft, questioning murmur when he put his hands on either side of her face, slowing her down. "Don't make me come just yet," he begged. "It's too perfect."

"OK, OK," she whispered. She waited until his hands relaxed, and he stopped trembling, then began to move again with diabolical skill, patiently taking him to the brink and drawing back, again and again until he was thrashing his head from side to side, chest heaving, tangling his fingers into her hair.

She lifted her head. "After last night, it's only fair to make you come in my mouth, but I've got to have you inside me," she said in a soft, ragged voice. "I'm going crazy. I promise, the next time I'll—"

"It's fine, it's great. Whatever you want is fine, Annie, anything. Make me come any damn way you please. Just . . . do it *now.*"

She clambered up over his body. "Do you have another . . . ?"

"Yeah, of course." He rummaged in the dark for his jeans with a hand that shook uncontrollably. Annie took the condom from his hand, ripped it open and smoothed it over him with bold, sensual strokes of her hand that shocked another gasp of agonized pleasure out of him. He struggled into a sitting position, pulling her toward him, arms trembling with urgency. "Sit on me," he urged.

She crouched over him, reaching down and milking him with strong, slow pulls from the base of his cock to the swollen head. The rich sea smell of her arousal made him drunk and dizzy. He slid his hand between her thighs, delving into the drenched, sultry depths of her cunt. Delicate little muscles tightened and fluttered around his bold invasion. She let out a little sob and moved eagerly against his hand. She was ready. More than ready. She was desperate, just like he was.

She wrapped her arms around his neck and lowered herself over him with a shaky moan of anticipation. Jacob held his breath and prayed for self-control as he guided his erection inside her moist opening. He prodded insistently until they found the perfect angle, and they cried out together as he shoved his whole thick, throbbing length inside her.

They clutched each other for a long moment as if they were afraid of falling. The tight, clinging embrace of Annie's shivering body was so exciting, he was about to come too soon. He held her very still, willing the rising tension to ease down once more. Just one more round, that was all he asked of himself, and then he was going to have to let go.

Annie made an impatient sound, and rocked against him, squeezing him with the delicate muscles inside her body. She licked his neck, and he felt the sharp, teasing nip of her teeth at his shoulder, and the last remnant of self-control fell away. He slammed himself upward into her snug, hot sheath. Her arms tightened around his neck, her nipples pressed against his chest, her soft, pleading cries told him that she wanted him, that she needed what he could give her.

Every time he lost himself inside her, the pull got stronger, his need for her keener; but it was too late to pull back. Annie, sweet and searing, tart and prickly and utterly desirable; he was lost to her, a roiling mass of molten lava, and then a cataclysm of volcanic sweetness exploded through him.

He clutched her desperately, almost afraid of what was happening to him.

Jacob knew before he even opened his eyes that morning that it was going to be another bad scene. He'd been half awake, savoring the feel of her in his arms, wondering about his chances for some cuddling; maybe even another round of hot yummy sex to get the day started off right. He'd sensed the exact moment when she woke, figured out where she was, and went as rigid as a steel rail. Shit. He braced himself.

Sure enough, she started her now familiar I-don't-want-to-be-rude-but-get-the-hell-away-from-me morning wiggle. He resigned himself and let go, even though her sweet, rounded ass rubbing against his cock was having its predictable effect. She unzipped the bag with a sharp snap of her wrist. Cold air rushed in, shocking him and his hopeful privates brutally awake.

Annie clambered out and started digging for her underwear. He enjoyed the view, since it was clearly the only satisfaction he was going to get. Annie was definitely not the lazy morning sex type.

She shot him an uncertain glance. "Jacob, do you mind—"

"Getting the hell out of your sleeping bag and your tent?" he asked wearily. "Yes, I do mind. Since you've asked."

She had the grace to blush as she wiggled into her panties. "All I mean is, I really have to get on the road, and—"

"Yeah, you have that incredibly urgent appointment with a slot machine in Louisiana somewhere."

She made a furious little sound in her throat. "I never should have told you that," she hissed.

"Maybe not. What is it with you, Annie?" he demanded. "What's the formula? Every multiple orgasm earns me a snotty remark the next day? The better the sex, the bitchier you are in the morning?"

She whirled on him, her eyes snapping with fury. "Do not ever call me a bitch," she snarled. "*Ever*. Have you got that?"

He recoiled from her vehemence, drawing in a slow breath. "Whoa," he said quietly. "OK. I've got that. The B-word is totally off-limits. Bit by bit, by trial and error, I'm getting it, Annie."

"Sorry," she whispered, groping for her toiletries bag. She glanced up at him, and he leaned back on his elbows, flicking off the sleeping bag and blatantly displaying himself to her.

A tide of crimson swept over her pale face. "I'm going to take a shower," she said tightly. "When I get back, please be decent. I can't think straight when you're—when you're—"

"Stark naked and on fire for your touch? Sporting an enormous erection in your honor?" he offered.

"Smart-ass." She tried not to smile as she crawled out of the tent.

Jacob's eye fell on her purse as he was dressing, and he grabbed it without hesitation. He was sorry to do it behind her back, but there were things he needed to know, and she was too prickly this morning to ask direct questions. He rummaged through it. Sunglasses, Kleenex. Pepper-Gard defense spray. Wintergreen Lifesavers. A pack of saltines, battered to crumbs. A little velvet sack of silver dollars. A wallet.

He put it all back in except for the wallet, and thumbed through it with methodical precision. A New York driver's license, Staten Island address. Annie Simon. Now he had a surname. He dug deeper. A library card. A membership in a Blockbuster video club. No credit cards, no gas card, no bank card. He counted the cash in the billfold and cursed softly. No wonder she was driving on bald tires.

He put the wallet back in its place and poked around the

rest of her stuff. A backpack of clothes. No winter coat, but she was headed for the deep South, so that could be considered superfluous. Food, however, could not. He rummaged through the box. Canned fruit, some freeze-dried instant soups. A bag of marshmallows. That was it.

It was making him angry.

He gathered up the foam containers from last night's feast, and shoved them violently into the dumpster, just as she came trotting back down the path, shivering. "Showers are cold," she said shortly.

"Thanks for the warning," he replied.

She hurried on without another word and began dismantling the tent with clumsy haste. He stared after her, tight-lipped. If he had any pride left, that would be his cue to leave.

He wouldn't let her see him follow her today. It was the only concession to pride he was capable of making after last night. The woman's ability with her tongue had brought him to his knees. She wasn't getting away from him now. No way.

Annie thumbed through the guidebook for Arkansas hot springs, looking for the page she had folded down. Helmslee Hot Springs. The guidebook promised secluded, undeveloped mineral pools in the streambed of a canyon. It had sounded like a soothing, healing sort of place. She had been making a point of finding beautiful places to hike and camp on this trip, so as soon as she set up her tent, she was heading straight for the trailhead. Maybe she could find some peace in a pool of hot mineral water, but at this point she doubted it.

She wouldn't be seeing Jacob again, after this morning's bravura performance as the knife-tongued hag from hell. Last night's lovemaking had blown her practically to bits. She couldn't handle these wild, seesawing emotions. They were scaring her to death.

"Hi, Annie."

She squeaked and spun around, dropping the guidebook. He stood at the edge of her campsite, holding two big plastic bags under his arms. His face was somber and guarded.

"I thought you'd gone for good," she said faintly.

"I'm not that easy to shake," he said calmly. "I lost you when I stopped at the sporting goods store in Carlson, but I picked you up again pretty fast. I've got an instinct for you now."

She gazed at the harsh planes of his handsome, unreadable face, feeling nervous and shy. "What's in the bags?" she asked hesitantly.

"A foam mattress, a lantern, and two down sleeping bags that zip together into one. Top of the line. Perfect for winter camping."

She stared at him, dumbfounded. "They must have cost you hundreds of dollars," she whispered.

He shrugged. "Don't worry about it."

She shook her head, tears welling into her eyes. "Jacob, I can't accept them."

He stared at the ground and let out a long, controlled sigh. His face was so patient and stubborn, she wanted to slap him, or kiss him, or just knock him down and jump on him. "How about an extended loan?" he asked in a long-suffering voice.

She shook her head, not trusting her voice.

"Fuck," he said in a low, vicious voice, flinging the bags to the ground. He stepped toward her, his eyes burning. She stumbled back, alarmed. "Would it kill you to accept just a tiny bit of help from me?"

She straightened up proudly. "I don't need any—"

"Yeah, right. You don't need any help from anybody. That antiquated piece of shit you're driving needs new tires and an oil change and God only knows what else. You've got nothing to eat that would keep more than a hamster alive. You've got next to no cash. No plastic. No bank card.

No gas card. But you don't need any help. Oh, no. Not the indomitable Annie Simon. *Shit,* Annie!"

Her jaw dropped. "How do you know that I—"

"I looked through your goddamn wallet, that's how!" he spat out.

Fury flashed through her. "How dare you go through my stuff?"

"How can you travel like this?" he demanded. "You're walking a fucking tightrope, Annie! Where's your goddamn plastic?"

"Philip canceled all my plastic the last time I tried to leave him!" she yelled. "I'm not stupid, Jacob! Do you think I like this situation?"

Jacob drew in a sharp breath. "Did he hurt you?" he demanded.

She flinched. "None of your business."

He shook his head, his face rigid with frustration. "Christ, Annie. What about your family? Do they know where you are? Can they wire you money? For God's sake, tell me you've got some sort of safety net! Anything at all besides a fucking slot machine!"

His furious concern was reducing her to tears, pushing as it did at her most sensitive point. She had no sheltering family to call on. A series of foster parents in Payton, some better, some worse, and only one of whom she remembered fondly enough to send her a Christmas card. But no one she could ask for help. No one to catch her if she fell.

God, you'd think she would be used to it by now. She bolted past him, but he kept pace behind her. "Damn it, Annie! Listen to me!"

She whirled on him. "I can take care of myself, Jacob! And how dare you look through my stuff?"

He grabbed her arm. She yanked at it, but his grip was like iron. "I did it because I really care about you, Annie. So shoot me."

Her face crumpled, and tears starting oozing down, robbing her next words of any force she might have been able to invest them with. "I don't need to be rescued, Jacob," she choked out.

"Like hell you don't," he muttered.

It was too much. He was so beautiful and tough-looking, radiating protective energy like great waves of heat, and it was so incredibly sweet of him to care. All she wanted was to fling herself into his arms and say oh, yes, please save me, oh, my hero. She hated herself for being so tempted, for feeling so helpless. She wrenched her arm away and stumbled, catching herself on the trunk of a tree. She dashed her tears away roughly with the sleeve of her jacket.

"Listen, Jacob," she said in a low, trembling voice. "This trip is not about Jacob's red-hot affair with that weird chick he rescued on the road. This trip is about Annie Simon, alone and independent and free, finally getting her life back, in whatever way she can. Do you get that?"

He stared at her, his mouth compressed into a hard line. He gave a short, jerky nod.

"I'm going to hike up to the hot springs now. Please don't follow me. I want to be alone."

He nodded, his eyes bleak, and pulled on his helmet. "Whatever, Annie." He climbed onto his bike, fired up the engine and roared away without another word, leaving the bags he had brought behind him.

Her tear-blurred eyes followed his wavering image as he pulled out of the access road and onto the highway. Rain began to fall.

His gut roiled with anger. Calm down, chill out, demanded the cool, calculating part of his brain. If the damn woman doesn't know what's best for her, let her go it alone. She told you to fuck off in ten different ways, so fuck off already and get on with your life.

It was true, but every mile that passed, the pressure inside him mounted until it was almost unbearable. The whole situation was unbearable. He'd never lost it over a woman. He'd always liked them, enjoyed them, had his pick of them. He'd fully enjoyed that privilege, and been well aware of his good luck. And he had always prided himself on his detachment when it came to romance. He kept his head, didn't get swept away, didn't get trampled on. Ever.

It wasn't that he didn't have strong impulses and intense emotions. He did, and he recognized them and sometimes even acted on them, when he had decided that it was appropriate and in his best interests to do so. He, Jacob Kerr, the choice-maker, stood apart from those impulses and calmly ran the show.

Until he'd seen her shove her honey-blonde hair away from those haunted eyes, that sad, sexy mouth. Until his gaze had dropped to those soft, pointed tits that bobbed so enticingly beneath her T-shirt. Until the instant he'd seen that luscious ass, swaying like a round apple begging to be bitten, as she sashayed out of that fateful ladies' room.

And had subsequently gotten a brutal crash course in what it felt like to be dragged around by his cock.

He accelerated, in spite of the dangerous sheen of water on the dark asphalt. At the rate he'd been going, further exposure to Annie Simon would have reduced him to a slavering idiot. She'd done him a favor by sending him on his way, sparing what pathetically few brain cells still functioned in his head; from the feel of it, all his blood had migrated permanently south to his groin.

Discomfort weighed on him like a stone as the miles passed, making him weary and breathless. A bitter certainty began to grow in him as he negotiated the sweeping curves of the mountain road.

He had to go back. He couldn't leave her there by herself in the woods. She could scream and curse and carry on all she wanted; he just didn't have it in him. It was too fucking dangerous, and if she didn't understand that, well, that was just too bad. He was going to have to make her understand it, in whatever way he could think of; and by God, he could think of a few right off the bat.

He slowed to a stop and turned around, furious at her, at himself, at everything. An unfamiliar seething energy began to gather inside him, and he cursed long and hard and viciously into the whipping rain as he sped back toward Annie, spoiling for a fight.

Chapter Four

Annie sank deeper into the caressing warmth of the steaming mineral water, and watched rain patter into it with deepening melancholy. A stream cascaded to the left of her, and bare trees towered over her, their tops wreathed with fog. Billows of fallen leaves softened the bleakness of winter, their rich red and gold tones glowing in the pearly gray light of late afternoon. Tendrils of steam curled slowly up from the pool, giving it an eerie, mystical look.

The pool was deep and clear, lined with colored pebbles and glittering white sand, as hot as the most perfect bathtub. It was ringed by flat boulders of white stone, veined with fleshy, glittering pink streaks of quartz that gleamed in the rain. It was magical. A place to calm down, to ponder her future, to renew her faith in herself.

And all she could think about as she stared at the rain was the bleak, hurt look in Jacob's eyes.

Oh, get over yourself, she thought. She sank deeper into the water until her nose kissed the steaming surface. It was her own fault, and she knew it. Ever since she met the guy she'd been acting like a hysterical harpy. Predictably enough, he'd gotten sick of it and left. End of story. What point was there in beating a dead horse?

There was no point, but her restless mind was determined to torture itself. She couldn't stop imagining how perfect the hot spring would be if Jacob were in the pool with her, the whole lean, solid length and breadth of him pressed against her, the hunger in his beautiful dark eyes making her feel beautiful and cherished, utterly desirable. For the rest of her life she was going to dream of those two nights with him and probably wake up crying. A sob welled up in her throat, and she almost choked in her effort to force it back down.

A twig snapped in the bushes, and a thrill of fear shivered down her spine. She realized with an unpleasant jolt how vulnerable she was. It wasn't something she let herself think about very often; otherwise she would go stark raving paranoid and lose her nerve entirely.

The sound did not repeat, but her travel- and trouble-sharpened instincts sensed that she was being observed. The tiny little hairs behind her neck stirred, and the thought burst in her mind like fireworks. Jacob. He'd changed his mind and come back, in spite of everything. She dipped her face into the pool to conceal a crazy grin. He had disobeyed her dismissal, she thought, with a rush of feminine power. Bad boy. She would punish him for that later. Better yet, she would punish him right now. Let him watch her like a thief in the bushes and burn for her the way she burned for him. Let him beg for it.

She rose slowly, letting hot water cascade over her. Steaming rivulets snaked their sensual way down over the curves and valleys of her body. The water was hip deep, barely kissing the thatch of dark blonde hair between her thighs. She faced toward where she had heard the sound, arched her back and turned her face up to the rain, raising her arms high in a gesture of gratitude and acceptance. She folded them behind her head, thrusting her breasts forward in an aggressively sensual stance, and stretched luxuriously. The water had made her so hot. Too hot. She was burning up.

Let him look his fill at her in the broad daylight, steam rising off her flushed, naked body. The thought of his eyes on her made her nipples tingle, and she cupped her breasts tenderly in her hands, flinging her head back to the pelting rain. She swayed, lifting her arms like a pagan goddess, dancing a sultry dance of sexual abandon. She scooped hot water over herself and watched the droplets beading on her heated skin, rolling down her body. She was a fey, sylvan creature, lost in her own sensual fantasy, wild and wanton and mysterious.

She sank down onto one of the broad, flat boulders at the pool's edge. The chill of the wet stone was a shock of pleasure to her overheated skin. She reclined against it, opening her eyes, her mouth, her arms to the sweet, cool rain, allowing the ravishing beauty and wild energy of nature to surround and embrace her. Sensual images flooded over her, and her hand trailed over her breasts, her belly, then lower.

She caressed her secret flesh with luxurious idleness until the memory of Jacob's passionate, skillful lovemaking seized her in its grip, playing through her mind like a vivid dream. Her breasts tingled and her sex grew flushed, swollen with liquid longing at the thought of his strong, beautiful body, his joyous grin, his infectious laughter. His big, gentle hands and ardent mouth, teaching her, coaxing her, urging her with infinite tenderness to undreamed-of realms of pleasure. The raindrops that struck her body had to be hissing off into pure steam, she thought, as she undulated against the wet stone. Her legs opened, and her fingers delved tenderly into her own sultry flesh, seeking that blissful, shivering sweet spot. Her hips moved in a subtle pulsing motion, her back arched, her breasts jutted out, pink and swollen. She caressed them too as she spread her thighs like a goddess opening herself to the embrace of a deity.

Jacob stared at her from behind the screen of bushes, transfixed. Part of him wanted to burst out of the trees and demand that she cover herself. A much stronger part wanted to fall on her and become the phantom lover that she was welcoming so rapturously into her body. He wondered with a stab of wild, irrational jealousy who she was thinking about as she parted her slender white thighs and caressed the deep pink glistening folds of her cunt, completely open to his sight as it had never been before in the darkness of her tent.

He bit down on his knuckles to keep from groaning, from screaming, and wondered how in the hell she managed not to hear his heart, thudding against his rib cage like a stallion kicking at its stall. She must know he was watching. She had to be putting on this show for his benefit. Otherwise he had to conclude that she was crazy to bare herself like that to the naked sky. Christ, anybody could be watching from the trees, just as he was watching. Anybody.

Possessive anger jolted through him, tugging at his reason. His cock was so hard, it hurt to move. He was primed to explode and make a mess inside his jeans. Wouldn't that be just the perfect final blow to his battered self-esteem, he thought with a flash of grim humor. Annie really knew how to take a man apart, piece by piece, until he didn't even recognize himself in the rubble.

He would wait, he told himself. He would hold back for just a few more moments, watching her lush, slender body glowing like a rose-tinted pearl as she writhed on the rain-washed slab of stone, as wide open as a sacrificial offering. He would let her finish her little pageant, and then he would burst out of these goddamn bushes and show her just exactly what kind of fire she was playing with.

Then he would drive himself inside her, deep and hard, and make her arch and writhe and open herself like that, just for him.

Then he would bathe himself in that glistening dew that drenched the flushed, pouting folds of her cunt, that gleamed on her trembling fingers, tempting him, tantalizing him.

He watched her avidly, his breath sawing harshly in and

out of his chest. Her hips jerked and she let out a shuddering cry, closing her thighs tightly around her hand as her
face convulsed in ecstasy.

Suddenly, a loud crack and a rustling sound came out of
the woods. Annie sprang up and slid swiftly back into the
water with a startled gasp. There was the sound of bushes
snapping back into place.

A bellow of primordial rage burst out of his throat. He
crashed out of the bushes, ready to hunt down whoever had
just seen the wanton display Annie had made of herself.
And when he found the guy, he would convince him to forget every detail. Limb by broken, bloody limb.

Annie stood up in the water. "Jacob, I think it's just a—"

"Get the *hell* back down into that water!" His voice
cracked like a whip. Annie sank instantly into the pool, her
eyes huge and startled.

A doe leaped out of the bushes. She froze, and stared at
him with enormous, fathomless dark eyes before she gathered herself and bounded away, feather-light and graceful.
She disappeared into the trees on the opposite bank. The air
slowly escaped from Jacob's lungs. He walked back to the
pool, his fists still clenched. "What the hell did you think
you were doing?" he demanded.

She looked up at him, her gray eyes mysterious and luminous. "You saw me," she murmured. "Exactly what it
looked like I was doing."

Her cool, offhand tone enraged him still further. "Yeah. I
saw you. So would anyone else who took a notion to hike
up here today," he said, his voice shaking with fury.

Her lips tightened mutinously. "I knew it was you."

"How? How the hell could you be sure? Did you see
me?"

She shrank away from the harshness in his voice. "I just
knew," she repeated, in a small, stubborn voice.

He tried to stop his chest from heaving. "You knew," he
repeated. "First you tell me to fuck off. Then you put on a

sex show for me. What's your game, Annie? Are you trying to drive me out of my mind?"

She looked up sidewise and gave a small decisive nod.

That smug gesture was too much for him. He grabbed her upper arm and hauled her out of the water. She held herself proudly upright, not giving an inch. He stared down at her flushed, exquisite body, his heart thundering and his mind swamped with erotic images. He reached down and cupped her mound in his hand, thrusting his fingers inside her. She jerked and cried out, her chest heaving. Her cunt was slick and wet, silky soft from pleasuring herself. He slid his fingers slowly out of her tight sheath, then drove in again, deeper, rougher. "You play dangerous games, Annie," he muttered.

The seething darkness in his eyes finally registered. She licked her lips, her silky thighs clenching involuntarily around his hand. Her eyes dilated with alarm as she sensed his primitive instinct to subdue her with his body. His hand tightened on her arm, and she gasped.

He let go of her suddenly, in a spasm of self-disgust, and she stumbled back. "Get your clothes on," he rapped out.

"Jacob, I didn't mean to—"

"Not . . . one . . . word. Get your clothes on, or I'm going to fuck you right here. And I don't think you'd like it. I'm not feeling very generous."

The menace in his words finally appeared to sink in, because she scrambled to obey him. He forced himself to look away as she struggled into her damp clothes. He didn't trust himself in this state. He didn't even know himself.

He was on wild, uncharted ground.

Annie scrambled down the muddy path, clutching the towel over her chest to cover the nipples that were poking through her sodden shirt. She was acutely aware of his seething fury as he stalked silently behind her. It rolled off him in waves, it showed in his burning eyes and the grim set of his mouth. What on earth had she unleashed? She'd wanted to tease him, to make him laugh, to make his eyes light up with desire. By no means had she wanted to provoke a black rage.

God, she was sick to death of tiptoeing around men in black rages, she thought, with a burst of temper. She'd done more than her share of it in her lifetime. She whirled around to tell him so. "Jacob—"

He gave a short warning shake of his head. The look in his eyes made her turn tail and scurry on ahead of him, her heart in her mouth.

After an eternity of stumbling on her trembling legs, they finally arrived at the campground. The place was deserted; not another car or tent in sight. Rain streamed off the canopy over the tent. The sealed plastic bags Jacob had brought were beaded with rain. She was soaked to the skin, but too flushed and agitated to feel cold. Jacob's gleaming hair was plastered to his head. Raindrops slid down over the beautifully sculpted planes of his grim face.

Twilight was deepening. Charcoal gray clouds sat heavily on the hills above them, smothering the horizon in a thick, blurry fog that muffled the sound of the cars passing on the nearby highway. There was no other sound but the immense sigh and rustle of rain on the billows of fallen leaves.

Annie turned to face him, feeling very small and alone. "Stop glowering at me, Jacob."

"I can't. I'm fucking furious. You're jerking me around, Annie."

She shivered, feeling the cold for the first time. "I did it to please you," she whispered. "I'm sorry you didn't like it. I wanted—" She stopped. A hard knot was forming in her throat, blocking the words.

"You wanted what?" he prompted.

"To turn you on," she confessed in a tiny voice.

Instantly he was upon her, one hand pinioning her against his chest, the other twining itself deep into her tangled hair. "Yeah, well, it worked," he said roughly. "In case you were wondering." And his mouth covered hers in a hard, plundering kiss.

Always before his kisses had been exquisitely gentle, and she had loved his gentleness; it had set her sensuality free. But the savagery of this kiss unleashed something deeper, something dangerous and wild. She loved his fierce intensity, his controlled strength, his tongue plunging into her mouth, a possessive intrusion meant to subdue her, but it only inflamed her. She wanted to claw him, bite him, provoke him. The towel fell to the ground, and she grabbed a thick handful of his hair and kissed him back like a wild thing.

He pulled his mouth away with a suddenness that left her reeling. "Never play with me like that again, Annie."

She reached for him, dazed and aroused. "Jacob, I—"

His hands clamped painfully onto her shoulders. "Anyone who happened to be up there in that canyon could have seen you with your legs open and your hands on yourself."

She tried to twist out of his iron grip, but it was useless. "There was no one else!" she protested. "It was all for you!"

His hand moved swiftly, and buttons flew as he ripped open her shirt. "All for me," he muttered, staring at her breasts.

She displayed herself to him, feeling bold and reckless. "Did you like it, then, Jacob? Is the image burned into your memory?"

"Yeah, sweetheart," he said in a harsh, grating voice. "When my time comes and my life flashes before my eyes, that scene is going to get extra play time. Does that make you happy? Driving me nuts, messing with my mind, you find that really entertaining?"

"No!" she yelled, frustrated beyond endurance. "Christ, Jacob, I'm sorry, already! I'm sorry for everything! I'm sorry for the hot spring, I'm sorry I was rude, I'm sorry I was ungracious when you tried to help me, I'm sorry six ways from Sunday! OK? Are you satisfied?"

"Not yet." His eyes glittered dangerously. "A lame-ass apology is not going to cut it."

She jerked her torn blouse together over her breasts. "So just what would cut it?" she demanded, her voice defiant.

He was silent. A gleam of speculation entered his eyes, and his gaze dropped, raking her body hungrily.

She took a step away from him, unnerved by the dark purpose in his eyes. "Oh, no," she whispered. "Not like that."

"Yes," he said, advancing on her. "Exactly like that."

"I don't want to," she said, wrapping her arms defensively around herself. "Not if you're angry."

He regarded her coldly for a long moment, and shrugged carelessly. "Whatever. I'm out of here, Annie. Have a nice life."

Rain dripped off the end of her nose as she watched him pull the cover off his bike. He flapped it vigorously to get the rain off and folded it with methodical precision, as if she no longer existed.

She wrestled with herself out of sheer habit, but she knew from the start that the battle was already lost. She couldn't let him go again. Not now. She would dissolve into the rain, evaporate into the mist, sink into the dead leaves as if she had never been. She couldn't face the night alone, no matter how much self-respect it might cost her.

Jacob put on his helmet, and panic clutched at her stomach. She stumbled forward as the engine roared to life. "Jacob," she called.

He cocked a questioning eyebrow, revving the engine. She tried to speak, but her throat was closed. She swallowed hard and tried again. "I'm really sorry," she called, over the sound of the motor.

Jacob cut the motor and waited, silent and impassive.

She took a deep breath, and slowly spread open her wet shirt, offering herself to him. "All right," she said in a tiny voice.

He pulled off his helmet and smoothed his tangled dark hair off his forehead, staring hungrily at her naked breasts. "All right, what?"

She closed her eyes, hoping he wasn't going to make her beg. "Don't leave me alone tonight. I'll . . . do whatever you want."

Jacob got off the bike without a word. He covered it and came toward her, his face implacable. If she'd hoped that her surrender would soften him, she had hoped in vain. A tiny muscle twitched in his jaw as he stared at her body, the only sign of emotion she could detect. Rain beaded on her pale breasts. He cupped them in his big hands, rolling the tight, puckered buds of her nipples between his fingers. He made a harsh, wordless sound deep in his throat and his hands grasped her shoulders, forcing her to her knees. Her face was level with the fierce bulge in his jeans. He wound her hair around his fingers and unbuckled his belt.

She gasped. "Here?"

"Right here."

"But anybody could just walk by—"

"You're just going to have to hope nobody walks by, if that bothers you." He tore open the buttons of his jeans, and his heavy, swollen penis sprang free. It was flushed a deep angry red, veins bulging on the stiff hard shaft.

"Jacob—"

"Suck me, Annie," he demanded, staring down into her eyes.

Hunger radiated from him, as powerful as a blast furnace. She stared up at him, considering the fierce challenge he was throwing out to her and sensing the subtle pleading in his fingers as they tightened in her hair, urging her to take him in her mouth. Her pride recoiled at his brutal power game, but still she craved his vigor and energy, understanding on a deep animal level that his was a heat that would not fizzle out, leaving her chilled and lonesome. At least this was for real. No matter how much he infuriated her, he was for real.

It was that silent understanding that seduced her at last, pulling her into his dark, seductive vortex. She brushed his hot, hard male flesh against her cool, rain-wet cheek and then grasped the pulsing shaft in both hands, savoring the sinuous energy that was uncoiling inside her. He was burning, his hard flesh warming her cold hands instantly. She stroked him, and his fist tightened in her hair.

"Don't tease, Annie," he warned. "I'm not in the mood."

"I know exactly how much you need this, Jacob," she said in a soft, taunting voice. "Don't even try to bully me."

"Oh yeah?" He covered her hands with his own and dragged them hard up and down the length of his penis, forcing her to pleasure him. "You said you were sorry, Annie. Show me how sorry you are. Suck me."

His mocking tone angered her. She twisted away, but her hair was trapped tightly in his powerful hand. She suddenly hated the submissive posture she was in. "You're poison mean, Jacob."

"I learned it from you, sweetheart," he said, as he thrust himself roughly into her mouth.

It wasn't like last night, when he'd lain back and gratefully appreciated the attention of her lips and tongue. This time he gripped her head and set the rhythm himself. She gave a choked cry of protest, and he slowed down. "Take more of me," he urged. "Come on, Annie."

Anger and confusion and a crazy burst of excitement; the volatile mix blazed through her body, making her impervious to the cool rain. Guided by his big hands, she found a way to give him the rhythm he wanted, relaxing instinctively and swallowing him whole. Even in this arrogant, masterful stance, he was desperate for her to lavish the sweet swirl and glide of her tongue on him. She pleasured him, loving the harsh gasps and groans that vibrated through the steely tension of his body. She was barely conscious of putting her hand between her legs and pressing her thighs together tightly, trying in vain to ease the pulsing agony of arousal that was driving her half mad.

She looked up, dazed, when he suddenly pulled her away from himself. He was still hugely erect and vibrating with excitement, but he tilted her head back, staring into her eyes with a look of discovery. "I'll be damned. Who would have thought," he murmured. "This vibe really works for you, Annie."

Annie shrank back at the predatory look on his face. She saw her hand between her thighs and snatched it away with a gasp, as if she'd let an enemy glimpse a secret weakness she hadn't even known she possessed. "Don't," she whispered.

"Don't what?"

"Don't look at me like that!" she cried out wildly. "Don't get any ideas. Tonight is . . . an unusual situation. The rules are different."

"What rules?" he asked softly. "There are no rules. It's just you and me, all alone."

She pulled away from his hand and scrambled to her feet, eyeing him warily and backing away. "You're scaring me, Jacob."

He followed her. "No, I'm not," he retorted, seizing her hand. "And even if I am, you're loving it." He forced it down and curled it around his swollen penis, trapping it inside his own big hand. His velvety skin was wet, from her mouth, from the rain, and her hand slid easily over his rock-hard shaft. He pushed her onto her knees again and grasped his penis, milking it roughly until a drop of gleaming moisture pearled at the tip. He urged her mouth closer to his hungry shaft. "Lick it off," he commanded. "Taste me."

Her body betrayed her even as her mind rebelled at his arrogant presumption. She opened her mouth and obeyed him, licking away the salty, silky drop of fluid. A shudder of unwilling excitement rocked her body. "Don't do this to me, Jacob," she whispered.

"I can't stop," he said in a rasping voice. "Not now that I know how much it turns you on." He pulled her up onto her feet and kissed her, his tongue thrusting into her mouth, his hands greedily cupping her breasts. "Whatever I want, right? Isn't that what you said?"

She stiffened. "Yes, but—"

"This is what I want, Annie. This is how it has to be tonight. *Look* at me, damn it." He jerked her face up to his, letting her glimpse for an instant the seething conflict in his eyes. He grabbed her arm, dragging her over to the picnic table and pushing her in front of him against it, reaching around from behind to deftly unbutton her jeans. He jerked her jeans and panties down over her hips until they were at her knees, baring her from the waist down and hobbling her at the same moment. She reached down to retrieve them, but he caught her hands behind her back and pressed her against the table, fitting himself against her so she could feel the hot brand of his penis against her cool, shivering backside. "Bend over," he ordered, his voice a husky rasp.

Her knees went weak. "Oh, for God's sake, Jacob," she whispered. "Can't we go in the tent?"

"Too dark," he muttered. "I want to see you, all spread out and open to me. Anything I wanted, Annie. You promised. Bend over."

She was frozen for a timeless, agonized instant, and then the dark tide of desire engulfed her and she bent over, arching her back and parting her legs for him as much as the wet jeans wrapped around her knees would allow. She was so aroused she wanted to claw at the rough wooden boards beneath her hands; the soft, sultry ache between her thighs pulsed and throbbed, and still he loomed behind her, a dark, burning presence, making her wait and wait and wait. Rain pelted down, running in little rivulets down the cleft of her bottom, trickling delicately over the moist, tender folds of her sex, now completely exposed to his sight. He made a harsh, incoherent sound. "God, Annie. You are perfect," he said, his voice a ragged groan.

His big hands fastened on her hips. She braced herself, expecting him to thrust himself inside her, but he sank down to his knees behind her, pinning her against the table. His hot breath fanned her thighs as he nuzzled her tenderly from behind. "I love this view of you," he said huskily. "I love all the colors and textures, the way those beautiful blonde ringlets get all dark and wet and glistening. I like how you're so cool and pale, like a pearl, here"—he caressed her trembling buttocks—"and so pink and crimson and hot in here." His tongue slid up and down the surface of her vulva and then dipped teasingly inside, licking and lapping ravenously at the moist, dewy folds and furrows of her sex. "I love it that you can't hide from me," he muttered, his tongue thrusting deeper, harder.

Annie squeezed her eyes shut, her knees rubbery and weak, gasping at the outrageous intimacy. His tongue teased with rapacious skill, thrusting deep and then flicking delicately across her swollen clitoris. She writhed against the rough, wet wood of the table, pushing herself back against his greedy mouth with a helpless, pleading moan.

"No, Annie," he said softly, holding her trembling hips still. "I'm not going to make you come like this. Tonight you'll wait until I'm inside you." He rose to his feet, his hands still cupping her backside, and leaned his scorching hot body against her. His breath heaved, and his erection prodded her buttocks. "You liked that, didn't you?" he asked, his voice husky and breathless. "You loved it."

"You never asked me what I wanted," she snapped. "Don't you project your teenage porno fantasies onto me, you macho jerk."

He laughed softly, and his hand slid between her legs, feathering across her hair and delving boldly inside her soft cleft, testing her silky moisture. "Tell me the truth," he demanded. "Your body already has, so you might as well." He thrust a long finger deep inside her, sliding slowly in and out, and she clenched his finger tightly inside the quivering muscles of her vagina. "You're so wet, Annie," he murmured. "You can't wait. You're aching for me to give it to you. Aren't you?"

She was stubbornly silent, not wanting to give him the satisfaction, but it was a losing battle and they both knew it. He lifted his hands for a moment, and she heard a little ripping sound. He tossed the condom wrapper on the table and his strong, skillful hands swiftly resumed their agonizing teasing. "Tell me how much you want it," he demanded. "Tell me how you want me inside you. I need to hear it."

She gave up the struggle. It was that or lose her mind completely. "I want you," she gasped out.

"How much?" He slid two fingers inside her, and moved his thumb around her clitoris in a slow, pulsing circle.

"Please, Jacob—"

"You're begging me? Is that what you're doing?" He finally touched her with just the tip of his penis, shallow thrusts that barely penetrated her slick, eager flesh. She pushed herself back to take more of him, but he evaded her. "Beg me," he demanded, rubbing himself in small, wet circles around the bud of her clitoris. "Come on, Annie. I need to hear it. I need to know how much you want me."

The harsh, hungry rasp of need in his words was the key she needed to unlock the maddening puzzle of pride and desire. As long as he was vulnerable to her, she could yield to him and endure her own vulnerability. Tears of frustration spilled out onto her cheeks. "OK, I'm begging," she said in a ragged voice. "Are you happy now?"

His strong fingers dug almost painfully into her hips. "Yes," he muttered as he shoved himself inside her.

The rhythm he set was swift and savage. Annie wanted to kick off the clinging jeans that held her knees together, to spread her legs still wider, welcome him even deeper, but stopping was not a possibility, and soon even the vague impulse was swept from her mind. She stuck her hands in front of her face to protect it from being abraded by the rough table. Her body softened in quivering eagerness for him, welcoming his strength, craving the vigorous slide and plunge of his thick shaft. She had thought that their love-making in her tent had been passionate, but now she sensed that he had been leashing in nine-tenths of the passion that was his to give, hers to take. The sheer mass of him ramming into her from behind was violently arousing. Her doubts, fears, her anger and pride, all fragmented in the force of their joining, and the jagged shards spun in her mind, disconnected and brilliant. It was a kaleidoscope that pulsed and shimmered, pulling her toward a climax so intense she cried out loud, and lost consciousness.

When she came to, Jacob was collapsed on top of her, shivering in the aftermath of his own orgasm. He lifted himself off her with a harsh sigh, sliding slowly out of her body. She struggled upright and turned to face him. His face was as shocked and naked as she knew her own must be. She reached down with trembling fingers to pull up her jeans.

"Don't bother," Jacob said, yanking off his shirt. "Take your clothes off and leave them out here. They can't get any wetter. This rain's not going to stop."

The calm, practical observation grounded her a little. She tugged off her muddy shoes and peeled off her jeans and shirt, leaving them in a wet heap on the tarp. They stood there, stark naked in the rain, staring as if they were afraid of each other, both sharply aware of the heat that licked and curled between them, wholly unabated.

"Get into the tent," he said curtly.

She crawled inside. Rain pounded in a soft, constant roar on the plastic rain canopy, and she was grateful that she had set it up earlier. Her sleeping bag felt thin and clammy.

The zipper opened, and Jacob thrust in a dry, folded flannel shirt. "Dry yourself off with this. Your towel is buried in mud."

She was still rubbing herself with it when the zipper

opened again. He shoved two big bundles into the opening and crawled in after them, closing the tent flap. She handed him the shirt. He dried himself briskly and flicked on his new lantern. It glowed a warm, rosy red.

His eyes were unreadable in the shadows. "Scoot over," he said.

She scooted, and watched him spread out the foam mattress.

"Jacob, I'm all muddy," she objected. "And they're brand-new."

"We need them," he said flatly, ripping the plastic on the sleeping bags open. He flung one on top of the other and zipped them closed. "I want to be on top."

She drew her knees up to her chest and hugged them. "You mean . . . you still want to . . ."

"Oh, yes. I still want to." He grabbed her hand and drew it to his lap, closing it around the hard, scorching flesh of his penis. "I'm not done, Annie. It's going to be a long night."

She pulled her hand away, unnerved by the remote tone in his voice. "Are you still mad?"

He regarded her with narrowed eyes. "Yes," he said coolly. "It's better than it was, but we've got a ways to go yet."

She shook her head. "I can't believe you have the energy to be angry after . . . after what just happened," she murmured.

He smiled, but it was not a smile that warmed her. "You'll be surprised what I have the energy for. Lie down on your back."

She hesitated. "Why does it have to be like this, Jacob?"

He shrugged, his shadowed face inscrutable. "I'll leave you alone, if that's what you want. Just say the word. But if you want me to stay, then deal with me."

She looked away from him, and he made a low, impatient sound in his throat. His hand hooked her chin and jerked her face around. "I'm not going to pretend for you," he said curtly. "Understood?"

She pulled away, her eyes locked with his, and nodded silently.

"Good. Lie down on your back," he repeated.

Annie scooted into the middle of the expanse of blue nylon and hesitantly lowered herself onto it. The fabric was cool and slippery against her skin, but the fluffy down was exquisitely soft and yielding. She lay back, looking up at him apprehensively.

Jacob studied her supine body for what seemed like an eternity before he reached out and put his hands on her knees, spreading her legs. He settled himself between them, holding her wide open and sliding his hands over the soft, sensitive skin of her inner thighs, staring hungrily down at her quivering, exposed flesh. She moved restlessly, but his hands tightened on her thighs, pinning her into place. He grabbed a condom from the box by the lantern, opened it and rolled it onto himself with a calm, purposeful air.

"I can't stand it when you're cold," she burst out.

His eyes flicked to her face. He splayed his warm hand on her belly. "I'm not cold," he said. "I've never felt so hot. I'm burning up." He pushed her thighs wide until she was folded back on herself, and slid his fingers inside her, finding her still moist and flushed from his last onslaught. He stared into her eyes as he mounted her, and she flinched as she felt the hard, blunt head of his penis nudging her open.

"That's not what I meant," she whispered, and then gave a sharp cry as he drove himself inside her, hard and deep.

Even though he had been inside her just moments before, it was still a shocking intrusion, and she stiffened in automatic resistance. His steely strength pinned her down, and she realized that always before he had been gentle with her, careful not to overwhelm her with his strength and size and sheer physical presence.

He wasn't bothering to do so any longer. He shoved himself inside her until he was as deep as he could go. She felt breathless, ravaged and vulnerable, like a city that had been sacked. Panic flared inside her. This was all wrong, terribly wrong. She had miscalculated, she'd thought that she could take it, but she couldn't. It was unendurable, the helplessness, the remote, faraway look on his face. Anger exploded inside her, and she struck out at him, getting in a good, openhanded whack on his jaw before he caught her wrists.

"What the hell?" He bore down with even more of his weight, his eyes flashing with anger.

"I'm sick of your power games, you arrogant bastard," she hissed.

He pinned her wrists over her head and kissed her hard. "I'm not playing a game, Annie. This is absolutely for real."

She struggled beneath him. He responded with a heavy thrust that jerked a cry out of her throat, then another, and another. She shut her eyes tightly and trembled, wondering frantically how many more surrenders could she take, how far she could yield to his conquering energy and still be herself. How long it would be before this man looming over her plundered and claimed everything. She bit her lip to push away tears and forced herself to relax her trembling limbs. "Damn you, Jacob," she whispered. "Just don't hurt me."

His body went rigid. "I would *never* hurt you." His voice was sharp with anger. "How long is it going to take you to figure that out?"

"You're hurting me now!" she cried out wildly.

His chest heaved and he stared down at her with fierce concentration, as if trying to read her mind. "You loved what I did to you," he insisted, his voice low and furious. "I felt how much you loved it. I felt you come. You couldn't hide it from me."

"That's not what I meant," she gasped out. Her body tightened around him eagerly as he thrust inside her once again.

"So what the hell do you mean?" His voice broke in frustration. "I feel it now, too. I feel how hot you are, how wet, how your body hugs me. I'm not hurting you, Annie. And you know that I won't. Ever."

He surged into her, and she squeezed her eyes shut as her hips jerked involuntarily.

"Look at me!" he demanded, and her eyes snapped open at the sharp command in his voice. "Say it, Annie. Let me hear you say that you've got nothing to fear from me."

She shook her head, knowing that he was wrong. He could hurt her. Oh, God, could he ever. He could break her heart into a thousand tiny pieces. That was the nameless terror that had been dogging her from the first moment he spoke to her. But with white-hot anger blazing in his eyes, she couldn't tell him that. Incomprehension lay between them, tangled and snarled, and she was frozen mute.

"Say it, Annie!" he demanded, his voice cracking with strain.

She cleared her throat. "I hope you appreciate the irony of trying to intimidate me into saying I'm not scared of you," she said softly.

He scowled. "This is no time for smart-ass remarks. Say it!"

She took as deep a breath as she could with Jacob's body pinning her down. "I know you would never mean to hurt me," she said quietly.

His eyes narrowed. "That's not what I wanted you to say."

"That's the best I can do," she told him.

A shudder went through him. He scooped her wet hair from beneath her neck, fanning it gently above her head. "Do you trust me?" he asked, his voice rough and urgent.

Her heart twisted painfully. "Yes," she said simply. In spite of everything, it was still true.

He hid his face against the wet hair coiled beside her cheek, and slowly let go of her wrists. "Put your arms around me," he ordered.

She did so without hesitation.

"Now your legs."

She wiggled beneath him, and he lifted himself up, letting her shift her hips until she was cradling him in a position of complete acceptance. He thrust himself deeply into her tight sheath until they were completely joined, and she wrapped her legs around him, clenching herself tightly around his solid warmth.

"That's better," he muttered.

She hid her face against his neck. "Yes, it is," she whispered.

He began to move, more gently this time, and groaned softly at the snug, gliding perfection of her welcoming body. He kissed her neck, lifted his head and said suddenly, "It was all a bluff, you know."

Her eyes snapped open. "What was a bluff?"

"All that stuff I said. About how I would just up and leave if you didn't yield to my dark desires."

She was speechless with surprise.

Jacob surged into her with melting tenderness, cradled her face in his hands and stared into her eyes. "I would never have left you alone tonight, Annie. Under any circumstances."

"Oh," she gasped, staring up at him. He was trying to tell her something, something incredibly important, but it was in code, and she was afraid to translate it wrong. "And I fell for it," she whispered.

"Yeah, you fell for it," he agreed, his lips twitching slightly.

The smile pissed her off. She stared up at him, eyes slitted. "You're a manipulative bastard, Jacob," she said in a low voice.

"Yeah, I know," he said in a wondering tone. "It's a whole new me."

Then he covered her mouth with his and there was no more space or air to examine hidden messages. There was nothing but his elemental force, driving her deeper and higher into herself. His anger had made her feel vulnerable, but his tenderness was even more perilous. It melted her barriers effortlessly, blurred her boundaries, left her utterly bare—a creature made of naked energy, pure emotion. Unrecognizable to herself.

There was no end to the layers he could strip off her soul.

Chapter Five

The rain had finally stopped, and dawn was near. Annie listened to the birds twittering, an ache of sweet exhaustion pervading her body, and tried to think of a way to extricate herself from Jacob's arms without waking him. It was a considerable challenge. His muscular arm was clasped around her waist; his hand splayed possessively across her belly and the tips of his long fingers tangled intimately into the hair between her legs. One long, sinewy leg was firmly wedged between her thighs. And he was so warm. It was hard to get up the nerve to break the seal and let cold air rush between them. She wiggled experimentally. Jacob sighed and pulled her tighter against him, fitting her backside against his belly. Nature called, however, so Annie gritted her teeth and flung back the warm, soft sleeping bag.

His arm clamped around her, as rigid as steel. "Where the hell do you think you're going?"

Her muscles jerked, and she schooled her face to calmness before twisting in his arms to look at him. "I have to pee," she said quietly.

He propped himself onto his elbow, frowning. "Don't go far."

"I won't," she promised, grabbing the only garment in the tent—the damp flannel shirt they had dried themselves with the evening before. She draped it over herself and crept out of the tent, teeth chattering.

The bathrooms were on the far side of the deserted campground, and the shirt only reached to mid-thigh, so she fished a pack of Kleenex out of the glove compartment in the pickup and headed straight into the forest. It was shadowy and fragrant, lambent with the subtle, pearly glow that preceded dawn. The world looked different. Everything inside her was shaken up, intensely alive.

She took care of her business behind a bush, and when she straightened up, she found herself looking into the eyes of a young male deer, no more than fifteen feet away. He gazed at her for a moment, apparently unafraid, and then bounded away with a casual grace that left her breathless. His beauty made her think of the doe at the pool the day before, which triggered an avalanche of images and feelings.

When Jacob had finally dozed off, holding her tightly against his chest, she had been unable to sleep. There was a quiet earthquake taking place inside her mind and her heart. Last night's shining seed of awareness had sprouted and grown over the night, and there was no longer any doubt. She was in love with him. It was a disaster, but it was too late for damage control. It had probably been too late from the first moment he kissed her.

"Annie?" Jacob's voice was sharp with impatience.

She jumped, startled out of her reverie. "I'm over here," she called back, hurrying back to the campsite.

It wasn't that she was afraid of him, she told herself stoutly, analyzing the jagged burst of adrenaline his voice had triggered. He was a force to be reckoned with, that was all; and after last night, she could hardly be blamed for taking him very seriously. And as shaken apart and fluttery as she felt, she didn't have the nerve to oppose him.

She found him in front of the tent, buttoning his jeans. His eyes snapped with annoyance. "You took long enough," he muttered.

"I saw another deer," she offered.

His eyes slid down, staring at her naked legs. She quivered as if his gaze were a licking tongue of heat against her skin. "That shirt is damp," he said. "Get into something warm."

Annie rummaged through the backpack in the cab of the truck and dug out the last of her clean clothes. A wrinkled cotton blouse, the faded jeans she had been reluctant to wear because they fit so tightly, her final pair of clean panties. She had to find a laundromat. Her clothes needed a wash, and so did she, after last night. Her thoughts flashed longingly to the hot mineral pool as she pulled on her clothes.

Jacob was wringing out their sodden clothes, draping them across the picnic table. "I need a bath," she said. "Want to go up to the pool?"

He looked thoughtful, then nodded.

The pool was crystal clear, ruffled by an occasional breeze and wreathed with tiny wisps of steam. Annie pulled off her clothes and tied her hair into a loose knot atop her head, careful not to look at Jacob as she climbed in and let the water close around her like a hot, tender caress. She watched Jacob as he stripped, wondering if he would be— yes, he was. Of course he was. Armed and ready, as always. The man was a veritable sex machine. It was ridiculous, after all they had been through together, that something so silly could still make her blush.

Jacob settled himself comfortably next to her. Annie leaned her head back against his arm and relaxed; as much as a girl could with a magnificent hard-on right at her elbow. They watched the clouds scudding across the sky, pushed by some high, faraway wind. Three stars still gleamed like solitary jewels against the deep, glowing blue. Over the rim of the canyon the sky was lightening.

Jacob's arm shifted, and when she looked up, he was staring at her shoulder. He moved to inspect her better, examining the marks of his fingers from when he had pulled her out of the pool the day before. There was a smaller, matching bruise on her other arm, and he made a soft, incoherent noise in his throat and kissed both of them; hot, tender kisses that made her throat swell and her eyes fill with startled tears.

His inspection continued down her arms, finding every little bruise and mark. The scrapes and scratches she'd gotten camping and gathering firewood, the little burn on her knuckle from her camp stove. Various and sundry mosquito bites. He urged her onto her feet and continued his search. There were little bruises on her hips from when he had held her at the picnic table, and she stroked his dark hair with a sigh of pleasure as he kissed and tongued them in sweet, silent apology. He set her on the edge of the pool, drew her legs out of the water one by one and covered them with kisses, finding every little hurt: the nick where she had cut herself shaving, the faded bruise from a briefcase that had banged her shin on the Staten Island Ferry almost two weeks ago, all the tiny, long-forgotten scars from her haphazard, misspent childhood back in Payton. He missed nothing. She would never have dreamed that the hollows of her ankles were an erogenous zone, or that there was so much exquisite sensation in her toes.

He stood up, his penis jutting out eagerly, and splashed steaming hot water from his cupped hands onto the flat rock at the water's edge. He gestured to it. "Lie down on the rock, the way you did yesterday."

Annie watched the water trickle down the lean, muscled contours of his body. "You're giving lots of orders," she said, but the words were robbed of their tartness by the way her breath hitched in her lungs.

Jacob grabbed her by the waist and lifted her easily. Her backside made a little slapping noise as he deposited her on the wet stone. "Pretty please," he said in a steely voice.

He trapped her eyes in his; he trapped the very air in her lungs, and she wondered frantically how he did it. With a touch, a kiss, with the timbre of his voice, he reduced her to quivering mush. He made her want to fling open every door, give him everything she had to give. His power was terrifying, but still she lay back on the tilted rock, breathless with excitement, and spread her legs for him without being asked.

He ran his hands hungrily over her wet, steaming body until they closed over her vulva. She reached down, trapping his hands. "I'm sore from last night," she murmured, with a flash of uncertainty.

"I'll be gentle," he assured her, coaxing her thighs wider.

And he was gentle, exquisitely gentle, but something had changed, and it took many delirious, writhing moments before she could identify it. When he first seduced her, he had coaxed, persuaded, courted her. Now he was claiming her. She felt the arrogant, possessive authority with which he handled her body, but she was in no position to protest as his tongue swirled sensuously, teasing and laving her, flicking tenderly across her clitoris. He held her trembling body still with masterful strength, and she let her head fall back, staring into the sky. The clouds had turned a startling, wild-rose pink, the world was a wild contrast of dark and light, heat and cold, and her body was at the center of it all, moving helplessly against the wild magic of his sensual mouth. She sobbed with the unbearable perfection of it as he pushed her gently over the crest, just as the last, faint burning star in the sky was swallowed up by the pale blue of morning.

He gathered her into his arms and lowered her body gently back down into the water, cradling her in his strong arms until the tremors melted away. She clung to him for a long time, her face hidden against his neck, before venturing to look up.

He shifted her body to face him. "Tell me something, Annie."

"What?" she asked, wrapping her arms around his neck.

"Your ex. Did he hurt you?"

She stiffened. The tone in his voice put her feminine instincts on full alert. "Why do you want to know?"

"Just answer the question."

He stared into her eyes, and the truth tumbled right out, as it always did when he demanded it. "Nothing really too awful," she said, a little too quickly. "Just . . . ugly. He called me names a lot. And he, um, he got me fired from my job."

"I see." He waited patiently for her to continue.

Annie took a deep breath, and pushed on. "Then it started to escalate. Pushing and shoving, wild threats. He slapped me once. That was when I decided not to hang around and see how bad it could get."

He studied her face, as if trying to read between her words.

"It's all over now, Jacob," she insisted in a forceful voice.

Jacob splashed his face and smoothed back his hair. "If he hurt you, I'm ripping him to pieces," he said with appalling calmness.

"No way," she gasped. "Let him be. I don't want anything to do with him. Case closed, page turned, game over. Got it, Jacob?"

He tucked a damp lock of her hair gently behind her ear and smiled mercilessly. "Let's get going," he said in a matter-of-fact voice.

She stared at him in blank dismay. "Jacob, please don't—"

Water sloshed and cascaded down his powerful body as he stood up. "Come on, Annie. Get a move on. I'm hungry."

Annie scurried down the path, so agitated that her legs trembled and her mind spun in helpless, trapped little circles. She couldn't wait to get on the road and have some privacy. She needed distance from Jacob's intense, brooding presence so she could calm down, get the events of the last two days sorted out in her mind.

She packed her stuff at triple speed at the campsite, and

regarded the soggy tent with dismay. "If I pack it now, it'll mildew," she told him. "It has to dry. Go on ahead if you want breakfast."

Jacob snorted in disgust and began dismantling her tent himself. He flung pegs and rods into a careless pile and bundled the sodden fabric carelessly into one of the plastic sacks he had brought the night before. "You won't be using this again," he informed her.

Her jaw dropped. "What the hell are you doing? That's my tent!"

"You want a tent, fine," he said coolly. "We'll stop at the first mall we see and I'll buy you a decent one. But for now, we're staying in motels. I'm sick of the cold and damp." He stalked toward the pickup.

She scrambled after him, panicked. "Jacob, you can't just—"

"And the Santa sack has got to go." He plucked it, one-handed, out of the pickup.

"No way!" she squawked, lunging for it.

He lifted it out of her reach. "Does it have sentimental value?"

"Not particularly, but it's the only—"

"Then it's history." He shoved it into the plastic bag along with her tent, and headed toward the dumpster down the road with long, purposeful strides. He flung the bag inside with a vicious flick of his wrist and gave her a steely, intimidating stare. "And don't even think about fishing them out."

He marched back to the campsite. Annie watched, dumbfounded, as he calmly proceeded to unlatch Mildred's tailgate and tilt the nose of his motorcycle up onto it. He braced himself, lifting the heavy machine into the truck bed without apparent difficulty, and glanced back at her with a "what-are-you-going-to-do-about-it?" look on his face.

She stumbled toward him, her heart fluttering like a trapped bird. "Jacob, I . . . we've had a misunderstanding. I never said that I—"

He slammed the tailgate shut with a resounding clang. "You still don't get it, do you?"

She shook her head mutely.

"We're traveling together," he said curtly.

She stared at him, rooted to the ground. "We are?"

"Like hell am I letting you out of my sight again."

She stared at him, frozen like a statue with her mouth agape. He grabbed her by the shoulders, all the potent force of his will blazing out of his eyes. "Look, Annie. You want to go to this casino and play your lucky dollars, fine. Well go. But we'll go *my* way." He reached down, plucked Mildred's keys neatly out of her jacket pocket and jerked his head toward the passenger side. "Get in. We need breakfast."

Annie climbed numbly into the truck. Jacob started up Mildred's engine, frowning at the rusty cough. "This thing needs help," he said. "I'll take a look at it after breakfast."

His words gave her a flash of wild, irrational panic. If he stuck his hands under Mildred's hood and won her over too, that would be the final blow. Her last ally, seduced away from her. Jacob had seized the upper hand, and she hadn't the slightest clue how to wrest it back from him. She felt like one of Bo-Peep's fluffy little sheep. Baa-a-a. Meek little woman with her big bad Alpha male. Look at her, sitting in the passenger side of her own vehicle, as docile as you please. He had her completely cowed.

It was not to be endured.

Breakfast helped a little, but not as much has he had hoped. Even after a four-egg Western omelet and a double stack of pancakes, Jacob was still in a jagged, dangerous mood. He'd been in its grip for the past twenty-four hours, and it wasn't getting any better.

Worse yet, sex didn't dissipate it. On the contrary. He clenched his jaw and watched the service station guy pour in the second quart of oil. They had a full tank of gas and four new tires, and he'd met Annie's attempts to pay with a glare so menacing she had shrunk back against the door, her eyes huge. Nice going, he told himself. Now she was scared of him, and he didn't blame her. He was scared of himself.

He yanked the Arkansas and Louisiana maps out of the door pocket and buried his face in them, trying to plot out the quickest route to St. Honore, but he couldn't concentrate worth a damn. He'd shocked her speechless when he ditched the tent and Santa sack. And maybe hijacking her pickup had been a little over the top, he thought guiltily. But he was sick of playing games. It was time for her to face reality. Besides, it wasn't like he could choose what he said and did. Jacob the sexually obsessed macho lunatic was acting out, while Jacob the cool, rational choice-maker watched, aghast.

They were grimly silent on the road. He stared at the highway with eyes that burned and stung, examining the strange new shape of the world now that Annie was in it. There were too many doors in his mind flung open all at once, too many crazy, unfamiliar emotions crowding out. For the first time in his life, he didn't know what strings to pull. The world had never seemed so dangerous and wild.

He pulled off the highway onto a strip mall of fast food restaurants, motels and car dealerships. "Lunch," he said shortly.

She gave him a cautious little nod.

He parked in front of a Lone Star Steakhouse and killed the engine. He couldn't stand her guarded silence for another second. He would rather she scream and yell, give him something to grapple with.

"Annie," he said in a rough, hoarse voice. "Come here." He held out his hand, willing her silently to take it. She stared at it, biting her luscious lower lip, and he wondered frantically what was going on behind those smoke-colored eyes. They were veiled from him by the dark sweep of her lashes, by that rich curtain of honey-blonde hair.

Then she reached out, her slender fingers twined with his

and she scooted tentatively closer to him on the seat. Dizzying relief surged through him, and she gasped in surprise as he dragged her across the seat and onto his lap. He slid his fingers into her hair and kissed her ravenously. He couldn't get enough of her sweet taste, the plump, trembling softness of her mouth, the way she blushed when she was excited. She was rosy pink right now, cuddling on his lap. She slid her hand beneath his jacket and splayed it against his chest as she kissed him back with timid eagerness.

He yanked her blouse out of her jeans and thrust his hand inside, cupping her breast. He rolled her taut little nipple between his fingers and kneaded the soft, luscious roundness hungrily in his hand.

She stiffened and tore her mouth away from his. "Not here!"

"Why not?" He was drunk with her flavor, her scent, her silky texture. She was like a drug, and he was strung out, wild for her. He barely noticed her struggles as he unbuttoned her jeans and thrust his hand down inside her panties, sliding his finger unerringly into her hot cleft, down where she was so slick and sweet and marvelous. He would caress her, slowly and patiently, waiting until she was slippery and hot, until he felt the beautiful little pulses of her first orgasm clutching rhythmically around his finger, and then, when she was shivering and desperate, he would peel off those skin-tight fuck-me jeans she was wearing. He would spread her beautiful white thighs wide open and ram himself into her hot, quivering body, give her everything he had—

"No! Jacob, damn it!"

She was clawing at his wrist, wriggling on top of his raging hard-on. He forced himself to focus on her words. "What?"

"Have you gone nuts? We're in the parking lot of a family restaurant!" she said furiously.

He glanced out the window, dazed. "Oh. I forgot," he muttered.

"Forgot! Hah! I do not want the worthy citizens of Bernhard, Arkansas, to actively participate in my sex life, so get your greedy paws off me, you sex-crazed maniac!" She seized his wrist with both hands and yanked it out of her jeans, glaring at him as she buttoned them up.

He deliberately licked the fingers he had thrust into her panties, savoring the sweet, rich flavor that lingered there, and turned the key in the ignition. "We're checking into a motel," he said. "Right now."

She looked bewildered. "I thought you were hungry—"

"Yeah, and you're lunch," he muttered, putting the pickup in gear. He laid his foot on the gas and the pickup leaped eagerly forward, toward the budget motel down the road.

As soon as the door lock flashed green, he propelled her into the room and slammed the door shut. He flung his jacket on the floor and shoved her against the wall. "Those jeans drive me crazy," he growled, sliding his hands hungrily all over her hips.

"They're too small," she said shakily. "They shrank in the wash."

"They're perfect," he insisted. He wrenched open the buttons of her jeans and fell to his knees, dragging them down around her ankles.

She clutched his shoulders for balance, staring down at his dark head, his thick hair straggling wildly out of its elastic band. He pressed his face against her mound, breathing in her fragrance with deep, hungry breaths, and put his hand between her legs, forcing them apart. He leaned forward and thrust his tongue into her cleft, swirling it tenderly around and around the flushed delicate bud of her clitoris, sucking on it with slow, devastating skill until her knees sagged and she started to slide down the wall. He reached up his arms to brace her, and his tongue plunged deeper, lapping up the heated juices that pooled between her legs. "Jacob, you're obsessed," she gasped.

His teeth flashed in a swift, feral grin. "Yeah," he agreed, prying off her shoes. He yanked her jeans off her ankles. She heard the sound of ripping fabric and her panties sailed after them. She backed away, unbuttoning her blouse as he stripped off his clothes; with that wild look in his eyes, it was clearly up to her to salvage what was left of her wardrobe. He seized her and bore her down beneath him onto the bed, his hands everywhere, as if he were trying to learn her by heart.

Her body clenched. He was too heavy and hot and desperate, and she was jittery and wild, her nerves on edge. "No," she protested, pushing at him, but it was like pushing a mountain.

"What?" His chest was heaving, but he froze in place, waiting.

"It's too much," she said shakily. "It's freaking me out. I need you to be—" She searched for words, but they eluded her.

"What?" His voice was a grating rasp of frustration.

"I don't know. Slower. Softer. You're scaring me."

He rolled off her onto his back, still panting, and clapped his hand over his eyes. "Shit. *Shit*," he said, his voice furious.

His long, muscular frame vibrated with tension, his furiously erect crimson penis rose stiffly all the way to his navel. A tangle of conflicting emotions bewildered her: fear at his raw hunger barely held in check, pity for his evident distress, all mixed with a secret female satisfaction at her own power that she could drive him to such a state. She edged closer to him. "I didn't say you had to stop completely," she said. "I just wanted you to calm down a little." She petted the hair that lay flat and silky against his hard belly, leaned down and gently swirled her tongue around the swollen head of his penis.

He jerked up onto his elbows with a muttered curse. "God, Annie," he groaned. "This is supposed to calm me down?"

She cradled his balls tenderly in her hand, licking him from the base to the tip of his shaft with one long, wet, luxurious swipe of her tongue. "Do you like that?"

"Don't ask stupid questions," he said furiously. "I'm not in control of myself. Bear that in mind if you provoke me."

The low tremor in his voice made her want to soothe him. She crawled on top of him impulsively and pressed her mouth to his in a soft, yielding kiss. "That's just a risk I'm going to have to take," she said. "I trust you, remember?"

His eyes never left hers as he groped on the floor for his jeans. He ripped open the condom and smoothed it swiftly over himself. "Maybe you shouldn't," he said. "Roll over."

She stared at him blankly. He made an impatient sound, and flipped her over himself, and she found herself suddenly on her stomach, the mattress bouncing beneath her as he splayed his hands over her backside and pressed her down onto the bed. He kissed and tongued the little twin dimples at the base of her spine, and his strong hands shoved her thighs wide open.

She pressed her face into the rumpled sheets, lifting herself for him in a fevered agony of anticipation, far beyond any teasing or game playing. He thrust his fingers inside her, spreading her silky juices all around until she was slippery and soft and ready. She let out a low moan as his penis slid slowly into her tight sheath, stretching her wide. She was sore and oversensitive from the last night's endless hours of intense lovemaking, but too aroused to care. She arched her backside up to him in eager, silent invitation.

He drove himself all the way inside her with a hoarse shout, crushing her onto the bed with his big, hot body and claiming her completely, and she finally began to understand what his harsh warning had meant.

She clutched handfuls of the sheet, trembling in confusion. Panic was mixing crazily with excitement as he drove his thick shaft in and out of her in a deep, savage rhythm that bordered on violence; but she knew instinctively that he was too skillful a lover to hurt her. It was his very skill that was so dangerous, his intense, seductive power that battered down her defenses, demanding that she yield herself up. She could lose herself to him, and be utterly possessed.

Their struggle took place on a plane of consciousness she had never known existed, with a clashing explosion of energy that shook her mind, scorched her body, turned her inside out. She yelled at him in raw, incoherent anger, thrashing beneath the plunging, rhythmic invasion of his body, but her struggles only inflamed them both further. He would not be denied; she felt it in the way he held her, the way he arched his long, powerful body over hers and drove himself into her. The desperate tension in her muscles sharpened the edge of the climax bearing down on her to an unbearable pitch, wrenching a wailing cry of pleasure from her throat. She felt his triumph in every cell of her body as she convulsed around him.

He began again almost immediately, rolling her onto her side. He folded her leg up, toying mercilessly with her shivering, unresisting body, relishing the sight of her, heavy-eyed and flushed and panting.

Then he mounted her again, his passionate desire unabated. Annie's body responded helplessly, her sheath supple and slick as he took her from every angle, in every position. He moved and lifted and turned her to suit his pleasure as if she were a doll. He made her come again and again, with his hands and his mouth and his insatiable penis, but when he came close to his own orgasm he stopped, his body rigid. He held her crushed and breathless beneath him—and began again.

"Enough," she begged him. "Please."

"Not yet," he said, his voice a harsh gasp. "I warned you, Annie."

For this round, she was flat on her back, spread-eagled and writhing beneath his pumping body. She reached up and grabbed a handful of his hair, yanking down hard. He gasped, startled. "Damn it, Jacob," she said furiously. "Are you doing this to punish me?"

"God, no." He deftly unsnarled his hair from her fingers and pinned her hands behind her head. "I'm doing it because I love watching you come. I love when you clench up and squeeze my cock inside you, when you make those sexy sounds, when your face gets all rosy red. I just cannot . . . get . . . enough of it." He punctuated each word with a sensual thrust. "Come with me now, Annie," he urged. "Together. Right now. Let's fly together."

"No," she whispered, shaking her head, sure that it was part of his sorcerous plan to bind her to him utterly. She thrashed on the rumpled bed as he thrust his tongue into her mouth and ground his hips against hers. He insisted, using the innate skill of his body, changing the angle so that his hard shaft stroked relentlessly against her most sensitive point. He demanded, compelled, dragged her inexorably over the brink with him, and they fell through dark and light together, fused into a single pulsing wave of rapture.

When she came back to herself, she was weeping. Jacob rolled onto his side and gathered her close. At first she just lay there sobbing in his arms, but as consciousness crept back, her anger slowly ignited. How dare he presume to comfort her when he was the arrogant bastard who had reduced her to this ravished, unglued state. He was still inside her, wedged so deeply that she could feel his heartbeat pulsing against her womb. She lashed out at him, but he jerked away from the blow.

He swelled again to full arousal within her as she struggled, and she was suddenly exhausted. She went limp, sobs tearing at her chest. "Don't, Jacob," she whispered. "Leave me be. I can't take any more."

Jacob stared down at her, a tiny muscle pulsing in his jaw. His face convulsed, as if in pain, and he withdrew from her body. He sat on the edge of the bed and hunched over, putting his face in his hands. Annie curled up on the bed until the sobs subsided, and took deep, shuddering breaths, willing herself to calm down. Jacob's muscular back was rigid and trembling. The room was utterly silent.

Jacob removed the condom without looking at her. He disposed of it and pulled on his jeans, his face an impenetrable mask. "Get dressed," he said curtly. "We're getting something to eat."

Annie forced herself to sit up, draping her hair over her breasts, and watched him silently as he laced up his boots. "Would you bring me back a sandwich?" she asked, unable to control the tremor in her voice. "I'd like to take a bath."

He frowned as he shrugged on his shirt, his face dubious.

"I could really use some privacy," she said softly. "Please, Jacob."

He walked slowly to the bed and pushed back the hair that veiled her face from him. He cradled her cheek and tilted her face up. "Do not leave this room," he said slowly.

She shook her head.

He caressed her cheek with his fingertip, and stepped back, obviously reluctant. He plucked his wallet out of his jacket, and left.

And she could finally breathe.

Theoretically. If she breathed too deep, the tears would start again. If she held her breath, she would pass out. She compromised with short, strangled little gasps and stared at the horrendous motel art—some sort of obscenely bright-colored mallard duck. She put her hands over her eyes to block it out, and tried to pull herself together.

She had to grab onto the last, ragged, fluttering shred of her independent will and run, far and fast. She couldn't let herself be taken over, swept away. For God's sake, the man had just fucked her practically senseless, and she still wanted him. She doubled over with a strangled laugh and pressed her face against her knees.

After three short days with Jacob, the whole Philip story, which had seemed so apocalyptic, was blotted practically out of her mind. The memory now had a tinny sense of distance, like a scary but more or less insignificant movie she had seen somewhere, a long time ago.

She dragged herself upright. Minutes were ticking away, and this might be her last chance. She had to haul ass or she would lose her nerve. One more assault on her defenses like the last one, and she would crumble—and become the body-and-soul property of a man about whom she knew practically nothing.

She had read somewhere that one of the quickest ways to make a person feel helpless was to take away their clothes. Conversely, putting them back on ought to give her a shot of instant backbone. She got up and rooted around in search of her underwear. She longed for a shower, but didn't dare take the time. She found her panties, the crotch ripped out and hanging in pathetic shreds. Whatever. Going without underwear never killed a girl yet. She would find a K-Mart. Buy panties.

She yanked on her jeans, starting to shake. Half of her was terrified he would burst into the room, sandwich in hand, and bend her to his will again. The other half was silently begging him to get back quick, before she did something irreversible.

But he didn't come back. And she knew what she had to do.

Her gaze swept the room. Mildred's keys. Crucial detail. She pocketed them. Purse. Likewise. She grabbed it.

Then her eyes lit on Jacob's jacket, and an idea sprang to her mind. She reached gingerly into the pocket and fished out the keys to his bike. She would hide them in the motel safe. Let him think she had taken them. It would give her the edge she needed without grounding him completely, or weighing on her conscience.

It was time to go, but her damned stupid leaden feet wouldn't move. She grabbed the pen on the desk and scrawled on a sheet of motel stationery.

Jacob, I'm so sorry. I have to go because I need to . . .

She wadded it up and threw it into the trash basket, and grabbed another.

Jacob, I can't let my life be taken over again . . .

She stopped, wadded, threw.

On the third sheet of paper, she watched, appalled, as her hand wrote,

I love you.

Tears started flooding down, and she flung the incriminating shred of paper at the trash basket, despising the little hiccupping sounds that were jerking out of her throat. She wrote

Sorry.

in a big childish scrawl, and laid it on the rumpled bed. On impulse, she dug into her purse and pulled out the sack of lucky dollars. She pulled one out and held the chilly coin until it had absorbed the heat of her hand, silently wishing him luck. All the luck and love in the world. She dropped it on top of the note, and fled.

She blew her nose repeatedly, practicing a cheerful expression in the elevator. She dinged the front desk bell until she got the attention of a plump blonde girl whose name tag read "Tammi."

"Tammi, would you do me a favor? My boyfriend left the keys to his motorcycle in the room. He asked me to leave them in the motel safe if I had to go out. Would that be OK?"

Tammi looked doubtful. "Couldn't you just leave 'em in the room? I mean, it's not like they're jewels, right?"

Annie gave her a woman-to-woman smile. "It's his beloved bike," she confided. "You know how men are. He's paranoid. Humor us."

Tammi giggled. "I sure do know what you mean, ma'am.

I'll just call the manager and have him put 'em right in there for ya."

"Thanks so much, Tammi," Annie said, bolting out the door.

With the help of a couple of burly guys who were passing by, she got the motorcycle out of the truck, though it cost the two of them far more effort than it had cost Jacob to lift it by himself. She was wild-eyed, nervous, sure that he would appear at any moment. He didn't.

She pulled onto the road, and all the accumulated tension from the past few days slammed down on her at once. She knew she shouldn't drive while she was sobbing, her eyes constantly filling and refilling with tears, but she didn't dare pull over to cry herself out. She just blinked hard, wiped her nose on her sleeve, and tried not to drive off the road.

Chapter Six

"For God's sake, all I asked for was a turkey club, a burger, fries, a beer and a Coke. I didn't order a six course meal," Jacob barked to the Lone Star Steakhouse hostess. "It's already been more than a half an hour!"

The hostess's cherry-red mouth tightened. "It'll be right out, sir."

"That's what you said the last four times," he grumbled, sinking back down onto the bench. He was as agitated as hell, his boot pounding a staccato rhythm on the floor. He covered his eyes with his hand, horrified at himself. He had never tried to intimidate a woman with his size and strength before. He had never needed to, but the resistance he sensed in Annie goaded him to keep pushing her, to break down her defenses. He couldn't seem to stop. It was like a bad dream. At this rate, he was going to end up in a padded cell.

He would bring back her lunch and throw himself on her mercy. Apologize for being such a controlling asshole. He couldn't handle the stress of wondering if she would still be there every time he turned around. He might try asking nicely if she would please stay with him, instead of pounding his chest like a gorilla. If he knew she wouldn't bolt, maybe he could calm down.

"Here's your order, sir."

He took the bag, muttering a distracted thanks, and burst through the restaurant doors. He started through the parking lot at a brisk walk, which quickly transformed into a lope, then to a dead run. The more excess nervous energy he got rid of now, the better his chances of not fucking up with Annie.

The thought hit him just as he was shoving the key card into the back door of the motel. It froze him into place for a good fifteen seconds.

He shoved open the door and took the stairs. He needed at least four flights of stairs to process this revolutionary concept. Annie, cuddled up with him on his couch, watching videos and eating popcorn. He wondered if she would like how he had rebuilt his condo. Whatever. He could rebuild it to suit her if she didn't. Annie in a beautiful evening gown, looking gorgeous on his arm at the annual New Year's gala charity ball. Annie meeting his parents. That slowed him down for a moment. Dad was no problem; one look at those big gray eyes and the old man would be eating right out of her hand. Mama would be tougher, but Annie could win her over, he thought optimistically. He would just buy Annie a pastel linen suit and some little pearl earrings, and she could take care of the rest.

By the time he got to the top of the last flight of stairs, he was already planning the guest list. It was so simple, so obvious, so perfect. Why the hell hadn't he thought of this before? He could have been in bed right now, cuddling his fascinating, sexy fiancée. He fished the key card out of his pocket, hoping she would still be in the tub.

He felt her absence like a blow when the door swung open. He forced himself to look around and check the bathroom, even though he knew it was too late. He looked out the front window. The motorcycle sat where her pickup had been. The bag of food fell to the floor.

He should have known better than to turn his back on her. Jacob grabbed the silver dollar off the bed and stared down at the single word scrawled across the sheet of motel stationery, clutching the coin so tightly that it bit into his palm. Then he spotted the crumpled sheet of paper on the floor, and lunged for it. He smoothed out the wrinkles and read *"I love you."*

His knees gave way and he landed hard on the bed.

He wanted to howl like a wolf and trash the room, but there was no time to indulge himself. If he didn't catch up with her by the time she reached the Black Cat, he might never find her. He yanked his jacket from the floor and shrugged it on, thanking God for automatic checkout. He dug in the pocket for his keys. His body froze.

He dug in the other pocket. The inside pockets. He turned the pockets inside out. He checked every horizontal surface in the room, sweeping brochures, menus, stationery, cable guides, all onto the floor.

Then he punched the wall so hard that the surreal duck picture slid down the wall behind the TV. The crash and tinkle of breaking glass and the blood on his knuckles did not make him feel any better.

Christmas Eve at the Black Cat Casino was rowdy and crazed, ablaze with colored Christmas lights. Annie felt as drab as a field mouse as she fingered her little sack of silver dollars and stared at what she was almost certain was her lucky slot machine. She had never felt so unlucky in her life. She had a gaping hole inside her and her luck was leaking out of it, swirling like a whirlpool in a bathtub drain. She could feel the miserable little swirling sensation deep in her gut.

Of course, that feeling could be the result of not eating or sleeping. She'd just driven endlessly, stopping to doze now and then at rest stops until a state trooper knocked on her window, reminding her that she wasn't in a campground and it was time to move along.

Buck up, she told herself. You made it. You're here. But still she stared at the machine, a sick, sinking fear in her belly. Not that she might lose her money; that was the least of her worries. Her fear was that she'd made a terrible mistake back in Bernhard, Arkansas. She'd torn her heart out

of her body and left it in a budget-motel room. And she
didn't even know his last name. She'd burned her bridges
utterly.

Well, that was Annie Simon for you. If there was one
thing she was spectacularly good at, it was burning bridges.
In her current luckless state, she'd be smarter to just take
her silver dollars and buy herself a sandwich and a cheap
room for the night.

Stubborn pride stiffened her backbone. She couldn't give
up now. She'd come too far, given up too much. She had to
at least try.

She let out her breath in a long sigh, held her lucky dollars in both hands and closed her eyes. Concentrate, she
told herself. Think lucky thoughts. New beginnings.
Sunrises. The Milky Way. Colored balloons rising into a
clear blue sky. Ice cream.

But Jacob's face was burned into her memory. His huge,
out-of-control grin lighting him up like a Christmas tree. It
was impossible to think of anything else. It hurt her heart to
think of him.

She opened the bag and began to play, sliding in coin
after coin and yanking down the handle. She lost, lost, won
eleven dollars. Lost six times in a row, won three dollars.
Lost, lost, lost, won two. Lost, lost, lost, in a long string.
The dollars drained away with that same miserable,
swirling, bathroom drain feeling.

Finally she was holding the last coin. She slipped it into
the slot with fatalistic calm. Lost.

Well. That was that. She stared at the machine with
blank, numb relief. Now she knew. No more surprises.
Down to ground zero.

It was time to head to the ladies' room, to wash her face
and comb her hair. Eleven o'clock on Christmas Eve in a
casino wasn't the ideal time or place for job hunting, but
she had nothing better to do. She squared her shoulders,
turned.

Her heart skipped a beat, and started to gallop.

Jacob stood there, his hair loose and windblown, his face haggard and unshaven. A silver dollar gleamed in his outstretched hand. "You've got one more coin to play, Annie," he said quietly.

She drank in the sight of his pale, weary, incredibly beautiful face. "I gave that dollar to you," she whispered. For luck."

He shook his head. "I want more than that from you."

"What do you want?" she forced out.

His eyes burned into hers with piercing intensity for a moment, and then a brief, tired smile flashed on his face, softening his harsh expression. "Everything," he admitted.

She tried to laugh, but it came out like a sob. "You think big."

"You better believe it," he said, reaching for her.

She was losing herself in his eyes, and she couldn't fight it anymore. Her eyes filled with tears as his lips met hers with a kiss of reverent, hushed gentleness, as if she were precious, sacred, adored.

"I love you, Annie," he whispered. His arms tightened and he hugged her so tightly that she could barely breathe.

The colored lights began to dip and spin around her. She wound her arms around his big solid frame and hung on. "You do?"

"Yes," he whispered, his voice muffled against her hair. "Don't run away from me again. I need you."

"Oh, God, I need you too," she choked out. "I love you, Jacob."

His arms tightened. "Then you'll marry me?"

She blinked, astonished. "Marry you?"

His voice was urgent. "I only acted like a lunatic because I'm madly in love with you, and you made me chase you all over hell's half acre. Promise to marry me, and I swear to God I'll calm right down."

"Marry you?" she repeated stupidly.

Jacob's face tightened in dismay. "Don't tell me I'm scaring you away again. I'm so tired of chasing you, Annie. You're wearing me out."

She soothed the anxious line in his brow with her fingertip, and slid her hand down to caress his scratchy, beautifully formed jaw. "It would take a lot to wear you out, Jacob," she observed.

He closed his eyes and leaned his forehead against hers. "Maybe so," he said quietly. "But I'd rather save my energy for other things."

Her heart swelled with tenderness at the exhaustion in his voice. She couldn't fight the feeling any longer, and besides, this had to be right because it felt incredibly, marvelously lucky. She rose up on tiptoe and pulled his head down to meet her kiss. "I won't run away."

His eyes flashed. "Promise?"

"I promise."

"So will you marry me, then?"

She laughed, delighted. "Well, maybe you could tell me a bit about yourself. Like, what's your last name?"

"Kerr. I'm an architect. Very respectable. Nice family, no prison record," he said swiftly. "Now will you marry me?"

Her jaw dropped. "Architect?"

A big man with a red nose prodded Annie's shoulder. "Hey, you guys gonna use this machine, or what?" he brayed in a boozy voice.

Jacob grinned and held out the silver dollar. "So? Are you going to play?"

"I've already won," she said, happy tears trembling on her eyelashes. "But I guess I might as well. This won't take long," she assured the red-nosed man with a smile. She inserted the coin into the slot and hauled down on the handle.

Jackpot. Bells dinged and people cheered. Shining silver dollars clattered out in a thick, liquid-looking stream. Annie leaped into Jacob's arms, and wrapped her legs gleefully around his waist.

"Tonight, the motel's on me," she crowed. "And the champagne, too!"

Jacob buried his face against her neck and held her close, his body trembling. "Deal," he said.

Later, cuddled together in the sagging bed in the first roadside motel they found, Annie stretched and rested her head on his broad, warm chest. "I would never have pegged you as an architect," she said in a wondering voice. "That long hair of yours."

He gave her a guilty smile. "I thought it would ruin my bad-ass, biker dude image if I let on that I know how to iron a dress shirt."

She laughed and reached for her glass, taking a lazy sip of champagne. "I thought you were going to ask me to be your biker babe, and ride off into the sunset with you on the back of your hog."

He wrapped one of her curls around his finger and stroked it against his cheek. "Would you have gone for it?"

"I think you could convince me to do just about anything," she said with absolute seriousness.

"I still haven't convinced you to marry me," he grumbled.

She rested her chin on her crossed arms. "Give me more details, Jacob," she teased. "Like, what's the name of the firm where you work?"

He snorted. "Are you going to call and check my references?"

"Spit it out, Kerr," she said in a steely voice.

He rolled his eyes. "It's called Kerr and Associates," he muttered.

Annie's eyes widened. She was silent for a long moment. "As in . . . Jacob Kerr and his associates?" she said hesitantly.

"Yeah," he snapped.

"Ah," she murmured. "And . . . what do you and your associates build?"

He shrugged. "Various things. Stadiums, office buildings, airports."

"Airports?" She disentangled herself and sat up. "Don't tell me you're a young urban professional with a closet full of Armani suits and ties."

His eyes narrowed. "Are you going to hold it against me?"

She scrambled off the bed, flushed with outrage. "You lied to me!"

"Not really," he muttered defensively. "I just never got around to telling you about myself. You weren't all that forthcoming, either."

But Annie was on a roll. "You snake! You stalk me, and pursue me, and seduce me, and mess with my mind, and bend me to your will, and now I find out that you . . . that you build *airports!*"

His face was abjectly contrite. "I'm so sorry. Really."

"And after all that, you have the nerve to ask me to marry you?"

He reached out a long arm and yanked her back down on top of him. "I'm begging you, then." His voice was rough with intensity.

She scrambled off his hard body and slid off the bed. He followed with catlike swiftness.

"That's enough of that strong-arm stuff," she warned him, backing hastily away. "I won't stand for it. You be nice, Jacob."

He stopped dead in his tracks, his eyes wary. "I'm sorry," he said carefully. He waited, naked and beautiful, his arms at his sides and his fists clenched. The silence between them was thick with emotion, with words unsaid and questions unanswered. The air hummed with it.

Oh, enough, already. Her mind was made up, and there was no reason to keep torturing him.

Well, then again . . . maybe just a tiny bit.

She crossed her arms over her breasts and widened her

stance aggressively. "I'm afraid a lame-ass apology is just not going to cut it."

A wary smile played about the corners of his sensual mouth. "Just what would cut it?"

She put her hands up on his muscular shoulders, and shoved down hard. A comprehending grin of delight split his face, and he folded promptly to his knees. "Your wish is my command, Empress Annie," he said softly, nuzzling her belly.

"It damn well better be," she said breathlessly. "Start apologizing, buddy, and you better make it good, because your ass is mine tonight."

He looked up, laughter crinkling up the gorgeous laugh lines around his eyes. "Do you mean that literally?"

Annie smiled down at him, sweetly, cruelly. "That's for me to know and for you to wonder about, loverboy," she purred.

He shook with laughter. He didn't look as scared as he ought to be, she thought, trying not to giggle. A ruthless dominatrix did not giggle. But there was too much emotion bottled up inside them both. It fizzed out like champagne bubbles, and they laughed until their laughter melted into something deeper, more wrenching. Jacob's shoulders shook, and Annie cradled his dark head against her belly. She sank down to her knees and wrapped her arms around his neck. "Of course I'll marry you, you big idiot," she whispered.

His arms encircled her, squeezing her breathless. "You mean it?"

She pried his damp face away from her shoulder. "You still need convincing?"

He nodded, his face somber. "You better believe it."

She cradled his face in her hands and kissed him tenderly. "I never could resist a challenge," she said.

27189074R00206

Made in the USA
San Bernardino, CA
09 December 2015